Rule of the Night

Record of the Sentinel Seer: II

M. H. Woodscourt

This is a work of fiction. Names, characters, and places are products of the author's imagination.

Cover design by Whimsy Book Cover Graphics.

Published by True North Press

www.mhwoodscourt.com

ISBN (Paperback): 9798788582290

ISBN (Hardback): 9798788583488

To the dreamers who conjure
light to combat the darkest shadows.

And to Tawnee, who never doubted.

CONTENT WARNING

Dearest Reader,

Once again, I feel I should warn you that within these pages are scenes of abuse, trauma, death, and other violence, not limited to battle scenes.

In particular, chapters 13 and 15 of this book involve violence against a child. More sensitive souls may balk against the actions of certain characters therein. Please enter those scenes carefully and skip them if necessary (though, please note, they're crucial to the plot, and one character's development in particular).

Proceed with due caution.

—M. H. W.

The World of Erokel

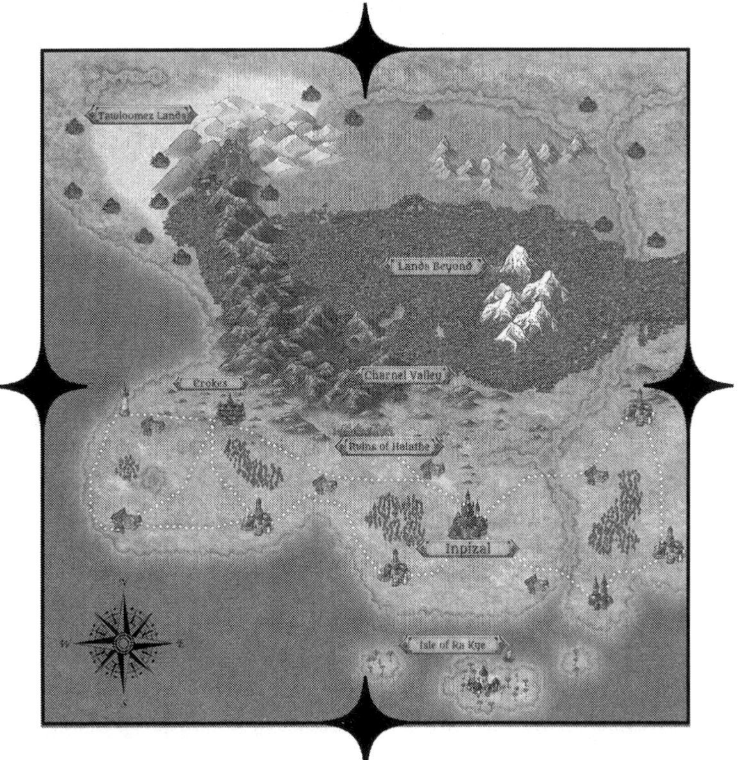

CHAPTER 1

Home.

Every step ushered memories into Lekore's mind as he strode through the palace of the Kel.

A thousand aromas and sounds flooded his frame, overwhelming his senses, beckoning the dreams of eighteen long, lonely years to tumble into conscious thought. He knew this place. Each hallway, sconce, portrait, tapestry. The palace had been his home.

How had he forgotten? How had he thought this place mere fancy?

With the familiar sights, he recalled warm hands scooping him up to squeeze him tight and whisper affection to his soul. Voices, soft and laced with love, cooed in his ear.

Father. Mother. Words with little meaning until now.

He walked with Tora; with the Hakija, Dakeer Vasar; and Nerenoth; with the Lord Lieutenant; and a flock of Kel officials and soldiers who had coalesced to join them. But he stood apart. Remembering. Relishing.

Until Tora strode into a massive chamber. Lekore stopped dead, letting his consciousness settle back into his body. He stared at the vast space spread before him; at a tall, gold-crusted chair on a raised platform, and a solid gold sunburst crest set over that.

"The throne room," whispered Nerenoth. "That is where you will sit to preside over the affairs of your people, my king."

Lekore swallowed down the urge to bolt as his skin bristled. Only yesterday, he'd been an outcast, living in the Vale That Shines Gold with his emockye, Lios; hoping for his Ank to return and bring him home. But Ank was really King Netye, Lekore's uncle—and he'd abandoned Lekore forever in the wilderlands, until Lekore rescued Princess Talanee and became embroiled in Kel politics beyond his understanding.

Now Lekore was supposed to become king like his father before him, and while he was at it, he must protect the Kel from a threat descending from the heavens.

Tora paced ahead, pulling Lekore into the present. The golden-haired Ahvenian placed himself at the center of the chamber, where a sunburst motif spread across the floor. Pillars lined the chamber, embossed with golden suns. More suns decorated pennants hanging in a circle around the vaulted ceiling where a full sun had been gilded.

The Ahvenian tapped a booted foot on a single gilt flagstone. A polished column rose before him, then stopped at waist height. Tora slipped off a glove, then pressed his bare hand over the black surface, and it lit up as a window of light appeared above the column.

Lekore blinked. It was just like the console Tora had activated within the hidden facility in the Wildwood, where Talajin—a rogue Ahvenian scientist—had lived before his demise.

Tora's fingers flew over the buttons of the console, and images flashed across the hovering window of light.

Dakeer smoothed his priestly vestments as he inched toward Tora, red eyes riveted on the display in the air.

"Gods be praised," murmured Rez. "To think I've lived to witness this day."

Nerenoth smiled at his lieutenant. "And this is only a beginning, Rez."

Lekore watched them, holding his tongue. Though he wished to tell them the truth—that Tora and his companions were not Sun Gods—Tora had expressed reluctance, fearing it would fragment the Kel faith. If such faith brought about the murder of innocent children, Lekore ached to shatter it—and yet, Dakeer had uttered a desire to understand, to change the philosophy of the Kel. It was Tora's presence that inspired that change. Lekore couldn't risk shaking Dakeer's newfound resolve.

The flashing images halted on a steady picture of several large spherical splotches and a single red dot. Symbols that might be numbers scrawled across the bottom of the light box.

Tora exhaled through his nose. "I didn't want to doubt your ancestor, Lekore, but I had to be certain. " He pointed at the red dot. "That represents a Kiisuld ship, though it's not a large one. Probably a yacht. I suppose this close to their border, the prince might've been cruising for pleasure before he set a course for your world."

He pressed a few more buttons. "Just as Skye said, at current speed, the yacht is estimated to arrive within four days." Tora's brows pinched together as a pulse of concern rode the air. "He certainly appears eager."

"What about the shield you mentioned?" Lekore twisted the fabric of his tattered black cloak as he tried to block the swelling emotions among the Kel gathered around him.

"I'm running a diagnostic to learn the health of your city. If the solar generators are still operational, they're large enough to encompass the plantations I observed outside of Inpizal. Beyond that, I can't tell anything yet. You said there are more cities like this one?"

Lekore nodded. "Yes, several, though not as large."

"Your Holiness," said Dakeer, "until recently there were six Sun Cities beyond Inpizal. Alas, Erokes fell to the Tawloomez not long ago. Beyond the remaining Sun Cities, we also have a dozen trade cities, and a few farming villages, as well as our plantations."

"Your population is very small, then." Tora punched a few more buttons. "How distant is the farthest city?"

"Ra Kye is three days away," said Dakeer, "though one must sail the last stretch to reach the island. The ocean tides can slow travel. With the recent unseasonable storms..."

Tora didn't look away from the images flashing again before his slitted blue eyes. "Those storms shouldn't be a problem anymore, and I won't need a boat to travel. Have you or anyone here been to Ra Kye before?"

Dakeer inclined his head. "Yes, both the Lord Captain and me. Perhaps Lord Lieutenant Rez as well."

"Yes, Holiness," said Rez, lifting a gauntleted hand. His armor flashed as he shifted his feet. "I visited a cousin there two years ago. Good fishing." The lieutenant flinched. "Not...not that that's relevant. Forgive me." He clamped his lips shut and shook his head.

Tora glanced over with a faint smile. "No need to apologize, Lieutenant." A high note chimed, and he turned back to the image of light in the air. A line appeared between his brows. "As I thought." He tapped more buttons. "I'll need to visit your Sun Cities, including the one destroyed by the Tawloomez. Each city helps to power the shield." He grimaced. "It's an old network. I've not seen anything like this in use before."

Nerenoth stepped near to study the floating window. "How long will you need to be in each city?"

"A few minutes if all is well." Tora pointed as new glowing boxes of different sizes materialized in the air. "This screen tells me the power level of each generator. I can already tell enough power is stored inside every solar generator to light each city independently. The question is, are the generators still linked to the shield system? Especially in Erokes. That's what I need to find out. If the system's damaged, I'll need to bypass it manually. But I'll need to bring someone along who's been to every Sun City."

"I've been to each of them numerous times, Holy One," said Nerenoth, placing a hand on his breastplate. "I volunteer my services."

"I will come as well," Lekore said, chest tightening. He didn't want to be left alone with Dakeer and the other Kel.

Tora smiled. "Then let's be off. I'd like to accomplish this soon and return to catch some rest before the Kiisuld arrive. I've not slept in over twenty-four hours." He tapped a button and the box of light vanished. Another button, and the console slid back into the floor as though it had never existed. "Grab hold, and we'll be off. Captain, please imagine yourself standing within Erokes. Somewhere very familiar."

Nerenoth caught Tora's ornate sleeve. Lekore snagged his other sleeve.

The world tilted, then straightened.

CHAPTER 2

Lekore gagged on the stench clinging to the air.

A stone road stretched before him, heaped with the corpses of Kel and Tawloomez. Cracked townhouses lined the smashed avenue, their dark husks doubling as enormous markers to honor the dead. A merciless sun glowered down on the fallen to quicken their decay, while a few of the Spirits Elemental flitted about, most of them earth spirits intent on aiding nature's work.

Sorrow and wrath rolled across the air, and Lekore found Nerenoth's stoic face. The man held himself together well behind a wall of composure, despite his private grief. Lekore reached out a hand, but let it drop before his fingers could connect with the Lord Captain.

What can I say to ease his suffering?

A wind spirit settled on Lekore's shoulder and chirped as it tilted its birdlike head. He offered a smile that crumbled at once, then turned to track the Lord Captain's gaze to a house at the end of the avenue.

The three men stood on the edge of private grounds similar to Nerenoth's estate in Inpizal. The townhouse rose five stories high, with a dark stone face. A short gravel drive led to wide steps and double doors—but these had been smashed in. As Lekore studied the edifice, a cloud curtained the sun. Shadows painted the building darker hues, and the Lord Captain's emotions dampened further, beating against Lekore's soul like stormy waves.

Tora laid a hand on Nerenoth's shoulder. "I'm sorry I've forced you to return to this city."

Nerenoth sighed. "It cannot be helped, Holy One. We must protect the rest of my people from further devastation such as this. But I thank you for your compassion. Where must we go to accomplish your goals?"

"The center of Erokes." Tora glanced toward the road. "Through the carnage, I'm afraid."

"The mayoral mansion and city offices are situated not far from here," Nerenoth said. "They surround the cathedral of Erokes, which is likely the spot you need."

"Lead the way, please."

Nerenoth strode toward the road, and Tora kept pace. Lekore started after them, but the wind spirit chirped again, and he halted to glance at it.

"What is wrong?" he whispered.

The spirit tugged on his pale hair and fluted an answer. *'This way, Lekki. Come. Hiding.'*

Lekore frowned and let the birdlike spirit pull him toward the house.

"Sire?"

He glanced over his shoulder and found Nerenoth and Tora eyeing him. "The wind wishes me to follow."

Tora's eyebrows arched. "It's always best to heed the spirits if they're in earnest."

"I do not think this one is teasing." Lekore padded toward the house as the spirit pulled his hair again. "It speaks of hiding."

Footfalls crunched behind him until Nerenoth and Tora appeared on either side of his vision.

Nerenoth clutched his sword hilt. "Does it warn of danger?"

Lekore shook his head. "No, not danger. It doesn't mean that *we* should hide." He lifted his hand, and the wind spirit lighted on his finger. "What *do* you mean, my friend?"

'Come. See. It's hiding!'

Lekore glanced up at the Lord Captain. "It says someone is hiding. In the house, I think."

The man tensed, and his eyes darted to the building. "This home belonged to my uncle and his family. I found no survivors."

"Were all accounted for, among the dead?" asked Tora.

Nerenoth shook his head. "The Tawloomez left little to identify their remains. I preferred to think them dead rather than taken into captivity, and I didn't see them among the slaves we freed in the Firelands." He took a step forward. "My men also combed the grounds and found no one."

Lekore stumbled as the wind spirit gave his hair a hard yank. "Nonetheless," he said, "the wind insists we enter."

Tora strode ahead of the Lord Captain. "Lead the way."

Lekore walked fast to keep up with the wind spirit's flight as it led him and his companions through the doorway and into a gloomy passage beyond. A staircase led up into darkness, its banister dislodged and broken in places. Scars marked the steps and wall, where blades had chipped at the stone. The wind spirit passed the stairs by, and Lekore plunged deeper into the mansion until the spirit brought him to a tapestry whose threads had been blackened from some fire long extinguished. Lekore wrinkled his nose as the strong odor of smoke taunted the air.

The wind spirit tugged on the tapestry.

"Is there a hidden room or passage here?" asked Lekore.

The wind spirit nodded as Nerenoth halted at Lekore's side and shoved the singed tapestry aside. A telltale black plate set into the wall confirmed the spirit's disclosure: It was identical to the hidden passageway Lekore had traveled when he and Ademas had escaped from the Temple of the Moon.

The Lord Captain sought the mechanism above the black panel; pressed a flagstone inward; lowered his arm as the wall slid aside to reveal a stairwell. Nerenoth drew his sword and strode down the steps into darkness.

Lekore followed, letting Tora go last. Lifting his palm, Lekore willed his blood to warm until a spark of fire sprang above his hand and a fire spirit danced around it. Nerenoth glanced back as light flickered off the close-hugging walls and offered Lekore a faint smile. Lekore smiled back, then willed the flame to float to the front of their company as they continued downward.

The steps fell away as the walls ended where a wide chamber began. Dust puffed up under Lekore's feet, and the lingering stench of smoke hovered in the air, but it was distant, old. The wind spirit and fire spirit leapt into the darkness, stirring up filth and pitching shadows as they went.

Nerenoth strode forward, then faltered, forcing Lekore to halt again.

The chamber looked empty for two dozen yards—but there, at the back of the room, covered furniture loomed like statuary, and against the lambent light, a shadow shifted among the abandoned décor. The wind spirit fluted as it landed and tucked its translucent wings. The birdlike creature hopped toward the shadow, leading the floating flame closer.

The shadow flinched back and let out a gasp. Nerenoth crept forward again, and Lekore stayed on his heels until they neared a tall, rectangular box covered in fabric.

Nerenoth paused again and turned to search Lekore's eyes, a silent question burning in his countenance. *Who should approach?*

Lekore brushed a hand against Nerenoth's plated arm, took a breath, and inched forward alone. The Lord Captain looked fierce in his full armor, a sword clutched in his fingers, while Tora incited worshipful terror in Kel—and revulsion in Tawloomez.

Fear and crushing grief poured around the shadowy figure...and something else. Something delicate and strange. Something akin to Ank. Lekore frowned as his step stuttered. Ank, who loved Lekore too much to kill him, but not enough to return for him after abandoning Lekore on the plains of Erokel.

Not now. Think on it later.

Lekore peeked around the large, veiled piece of furniture. A young woman hunched in the firelight, knees drawn to her chest, midnight blue hair a matted tangle. The stench of smoke clung to her torn gown, and blood marked her pale, gaunt face. Wide red eyes watched Lekore, as heavy breaths rattled in her lungs.

Lekore crouched where he stood, lifted a hand, and offered a smile. "Do not fear me. I would never harm you."

The Lord Captain's boots scuffed the stone floor as he approached. Tora moved soundlessly beside him. They said nothing, though their gazes bored into Lekore, filled with questions.

The young woman, no older than Talanee, eyed him like a wounded beast caught in one of Lekore's traps.

Lekore inched forward, staying crouched, hand still raised. "I am called Lekore. I am Kel like you. Your enemy has long been gone from this city." He glanced at Nerenoth, then turned back to the young woman. "I am not alone. I am among friends. Perhaps you know one of them. He is Nerenoth Irothé."

The girl sucked in a sharp breath. Something like reason flashed in her eyes.

Lekore beckoned Nerenoth closer.

The Lord Captain sheathed his sword and stepped into view. A wave of relief and wonder flowed off him, and he started forward before he stopped himself. "Mayrilana."

Her eyes jerked up until she found Nerenoth. Fear heightened upon the air like a prolonged note, then tears spilled down her face. She whimpered and crumpled.

Lekore sprang forward and caught her before her head struck the floor. She lay unmoving, a thin, trembling thing in his arms. Lekore glanced at the Lord Captain. "She must have been hiding here for more than a week."

"She needs care," said Tora. He rubbed a finger along his smooth jaw. "We'd best take her to Inpizal, and then return here."

"I will remain there with her," Lekore said, batting down a surge of panic. He must find a way to handle living with the Kel.

Relief rippled over the air as Nerenoth bowed his head. "Thank you, sire."

Lekore lifted the woman in his arms as he rose to his full height. "I am not *sire*, please."

The Lord Captain smiled and said nothing.

"Grab hold," Tora said.

Lekore shifted his grip on the young woman to snatch a bit of Tora's sleeve, smearing dirt on the embroidered cloth. Again, the world tilted. Realigned. He stood in the palace throne room again, surrounded by voices murmuring around him.

"That was much sooner than we expected, Holy One," said Dakeer.

"We're back only for a moment," Tora replied.

Lekore glanced around him. More priests had joined Dakeer and the Lord Lieutenant. All stared, transfixed upon Tora. Teeming awe seasoned the air.

Nerenoth leaned close to Lekore. "Her name is Mayrilana. If you don't feel comfortable tending to her in the palace, feel free to command Rez, and he will escort you to my estate. You might also send word to Jesh and Jeth. They will be pleased to watch over you both."

Lekore pushed a smile to his lips as his heart tightened. "Thank you, good captain. I'm certain we will be fine."

"Ready, Lord Captain?" Tora asked.

"Yes, Holy One."

The two men vanished, and Lekore's heart sank against the weight of his fears. Two dozen red eyes considered him in grim, searching faces.

Dakeer Vasar took a step closer. "Is that Lady Mayrilana?"

Lekore glanced at the young woman's face. "Yes. We found her well hidden in her home."

"Remarkable."

Lekore locked his gaze on Rez. "She needs a place to rest."

The Lord Lieutenant clapped a fist to his armored chest, long blue hair shifting across his shoulders. "Would you like to remain in the palace, Your Majesty?"

Lekore's heart lodged in his throat. He ached to stay here in his childhood home, yet the eyes of so many lingered on him, with so few he could trust...

"Please feel free to stay," Dakeer Vasar said. "This is your palace, and none will molest you in any way. You are protected by the will and favor of the Sun Throne."

No malice laced his tones or churned around his soul; only guilt tinged with confusion. Dakeer stood in an unguarded stance, shoulders relaxed. Lekore searched his face. Strain had drawn lines around his mouth and eyes.

He is not my ally, but nor is he my enemy. Lekore let his spine ease as he released a breath. "I will remain here. It will be easier on her not to move about much."

Dakeer waggled his fingers in the air, and a Kel servant approached, clad in gold livery. "Lead Prince Lekore and Lady Mayrilana to the nearest suite, then have the royal physician brought there, along with food and a bath."

"Yes, Holiness," said the servant, whose eyes flicked to Lekore then back to the floor. "This way, Your Highness."

Lekore frowned as questions collided in his mind. Nerenoth and Rez called him king. Dakeer and others called him prince. The Kel ways were confusing, frightening. How he longed to run, run until he reached a garden, or climbed up high, where fresh air brought the Spirits Elemental and a sense of freedom.

Stay calm. You must keep your impulses under control.

He had always struggled to stay still. The wind tugged at his attention with stories of the sea and sky, while earth whispered of secret caves and distant places underground. Fire always wanted to play and dance. Water laughed at him as it ran away, divulging nothing, teasing his imagination with what-ifs.

The memory of the fifth spirit flitted across his thoughts. It wasn't like the rest, but what might it share with him? Or did the

Spirits of Spirit not flit about as the others? Though he could now see them, as he had always seen the other four, none presently revealed themselves as he glanced around the palace corridors. Meanwhile, fire, wind, water, and earth spirits made themselves known in nearly all places.

The servant opened a door at the end of a wide corridor lined with torches. The large interior beyond contained lavish furniture, with an enormous fireplace taking up half the opposing wall. A circle of fire spirits danced in semi-Kel shapes around the flames within the hearth.

Lord Lieutenant Rez brushed past the servant and stalked around the room. He searched behind curtains pouring down the sides of a window that ran from ceiling to floor; poked around the posh cushions of a settee; disappeared inside the adjacent rooms, one at a time.

He returned with a grim smile. "It's secure."

The servant inclined his head, bowed in Lekore's direction, then slipped past him to move down the corridor. Lekore padded into the chamber and let his eyes flit from the window, to the hearth, to portraits hanging from the walls. Strange, painted faces stared back. Wrenching away from their grim, unblinking gazes, his eyes settled longest on large, elongated containers set into the corners, holding flowers, trees, and some, nothing at all.

He nodded toward the closest container. It shone like a polished green stone. "What is that?"

Rez tracked his eyes. "Oh, that? That's a vase."

"It's beautiful. How is it fashioned?"

The Lord Lieutenant's lip twitched upward. "I'm afraid I can't give you details. You'd have to ask a potter. Usually, they use clay and a kind of wheel and shape it with their hands."

"Ah. I've made clay dishes, but never something like this." Lekore drifted toward the vase, then blinked as he remembered Mayrilana needed treatment. He shifted her weight and turned back to Rez. "Where might I lay her down?"

Rez strode to the nearest door he'd entered earlier, swung it open wide, and gestured. "Right here, sire."

Lekore grimaced at the title but padded into the room just the same. A wide four-post bed crouched against one wall, its gold silk coverlet shining in the ample light of the midday sun streaming into the room. A rug spread across the floor, white with gold sunbursts embroidered in delicate patterns. Lekore circled the rug to rest Mayrilana upon the bed. She moaned as he slipped his hands from under her, but she never woke. Lekore turned to watch Rez grab an emockye fur from a chest at the foot of the bed.

The lieutenant spread it over Mayrilana and nodded. "Best let her sleep until the physician arrives." He strode towards the door.

Lekore nodded and started to follow—

The wind howled a warning. He spun as someone gripping a dagger lunged for his heart.

CHAPTER 3

The fountain's tinkling spray did nothing to comfort Princess Talanee. The mere suggestion of water willed more tears to slip from her eyes, yet she couldn't find the strength to summon anger. Why bother?

She sat on the edge of the fountain and swirled her hand through the rippling water, while mist kissed her burning face. She wiped her nose with a handkerchief and squeezed her eyes shut, while birds trilled in the trees overhead, and the fragrance of blossoms drifted by.

Let the tears fall. How long have you held them in?

"Cousin?"

Talanee sprang to her feet and clutched at her pink skirts as she glared down the young man before her.

Ademas stood on the garden path, a black eye stark against his fair skin. He was clad in a green tunic top and black breeches with boots to match. A pendant hung at his neck; not the starburst he'd flashed in the alleys of Inpizal to buy information, but the Getaal crest. Bold as the sun, he now declared his lineage. And why not? He'd never said he wasn't a Getaal.

He still lied. Omission is still lying.

"I know I'm numbered among those you'd rather not see right now," he said, "but I don't like the idea of you suffering alone."

Talanee tossed her long blue hair over one shoulder. "Oh? You'd rather *witness* my suffering, would you?"

A smile crooked his lips. "You know that's not what I mean."

"I don't know anything you mean. We have nothing to discuss, and I'll thank you to leave. I *want* to be alone."

He sighed, padded to her side, and stared down into the fountain. "I understand why you feel as you do...but none of it could be helped. I certainly didn't foresee a Sun God coming to Erokel, nor the revelation about my older brother, still alive and well. All I knew was—well, your father's betrayal and the church's corruption." He ran a hand through his short ocean blue hair. "In all sincerity, Talanee, I swear I didn't want to hurt you. None of this is your fault, and I feel like you've suffered enough anguish in your life already. If I could spare your father, I would..." He frowned. "Maybe."

Talanee shut her eyes and scrunched up her face. "Stop! Just stop talking." She whirled on him and jabbed a finger at his face. "You wouldn't spare my father if you could. We both know it. The fact is, you *can* spare him. You're a prince. Second in line to the throne. Lekore will listen to you!"

The restored heir had already said he could never hurt the former ruler, yet sometimes feelings could fester and poison a Kel's heart. And what if Ademas tried to sway Lekore to make a different choice?

Ademas's eyes narrowed. "And so? I should pardon a man who murdered his brother, not to mention the rightful king, and then abandoned his nephew—the *crown prince*, mind you—simply because he's your father."

"He's all I have!" She swiped hair from her face and whirled away from Ademas as tears blurred her vision. Her chest tightened and her lungs burned.

He circled to stand before her and seized her shoulders. "Look at me, Talanee."

She stuck her chin out. "*What?*"

"I don't want to be cruel. I really don't. But you need to face two facts: Your father is a selfish madman who never cared a fig for you—"

A shriek shot up her throat, but she choked it down as her frame trembled. "And the second fact?" Her voice came out as a hoarse whisper.

He drew a long breath. "He's not all you've got. You have real family now. Lekore and I will be your family. We'll all get what we've always longed for and never had."

She stared into his eyes, fury nipping at her heart. How could she trust him? How could he think she might? "You're insane. You're completely mad, just like my father. We're not family. We're strangers. And Lekore is the strangest of all. How can he lead our people? He's...he's an urchin. A wild creature! He doesn't even *know* the Kel!"

Ademas tilted his head to one side as his lopsided smile reappeared. "Yet Holy Tora advocates for him. And he's clever enough. He survived living in the Charnel Valley, didn't he? I think he can learn to handle Kel. We're hardly different from emockye."

"You have so little love for your own people?"

Ademas sighed. "I do love Erokel and its people. I just think we've lost our pride, our heritage. I don't think the Sun Gods returned because we're worthy. They came to show us how to be better."

Talanee shook as a dozen rebuttals scurried through her mind. Her mouth opened. She snapped it shut. *What if he's right? My father wasn't worthy...and the Hakija turned a blind eye to the king's crimes. Lekore was always meant to rule.*

The Lord Captain's loyalty had always been to King Adelair and his son, and his so-called heresy had been a quiet, steady faith in the gods in reality, not in how they were perceived by church doctrine. How long had that man suffered in silence, knowing truth, unable to speak, for the gods had commanded him to say nothing?

Ademas released her and dropped his arms, exhaling. "Technically, I'm not sure the gods intended to come in the first place. I'm not sure *how* they crashed to start with, but I suppose that's not important just this minute." He rubbed the back of his neck as he stared into the fountain's bubbling water. "What I'm trying to say is that you're not alone. We can build a family, something better than we had before."

Talanee wrung the handkerchief in her hands. "What about your mother?"

Ademas grimaced. "What about her?"

"You said she's been seeking vengeance all these years. What will she do now? She thought Lekore was dead. She expected you to take the throne. It's all she's cared about. So, what now? What happens to you? And how will she react to me?"

He blew out a breath and shrugged with his hands. "I can only make guesses. She adored her eldest son—but she knew him as a memory, as a toddler, not as a man, and a peculiar one at that. Can she accept him, alive, breathing, after all her years of obsession? Maybe. Maybe she always knew he was alive in her heart of hearts."

He turned to meet Talanee's gaze. "As for us, who's to say? I'm useful as a spare, I suppose, and you're not your father. From what I understand, my mother and your mother were friends. She might come to care for you if she can manage to bury her grief at last."

Talanee's heart lurched as she studied her cousin. She'd known Ademas Getaal a handful of days, though it felt much, much longer. Yet now, as her world crumbled, he offered friendship. Indeed, he offered blood ties. She scowled. "How do I know you're not mocking me? How can I trust you're in earnest?"

He caught her hand in both of his. "Look me straight in the eyes. That's the ground. Look up here."

Her scowl deepened as she hoisted her chin and met his gaze.

Ademas chuckled before his mirth faded. "That's better. Listen to me well, Cousin. I may mock my surroundings, and the stupidity of people, and a hundred other things, but I'll never, *never* mock the heart."

Talanee drew a long breath as a tear tracked down her face. She mopped it up with her handkerchief. "You'd better not be lying."

"If I am, you can stab me with your diadem as much as you please."

Laughter broke from her lips before she could stop it, but she rolled her eyes and stalked away from Ademas. "You're ridiculous." Her step faltered. "I won't have a diadem anymore."

Under the devastating weight of her father's treachery, the fact she was no longer the crown princess had been a fleeting thing. All her life she'd trained to become the queen of Erokel. She'd done all she could to please her father by poring over books on policies, doctrine, tradition...all useless information now.

Ademas rested a hand on her shoulder. "You must feel directionless right now, but your life hasn't been a waste."

Talanee snorted. "Oh? What *has* it been? What am I supposed to do with all the knowledge in my head?"

He shrugged. "Teach Lekore."

She snarled as she gathered a retort—then choked on air. *He has a point. Someone needs to train him.* She shrugged off Ademas's hand. "Well, it's *one* idea. But ultimately, the Sun God gets to decide all that. After all, by the Lord Captain's report, Lekore was raised by the divine. What could I possibly offer—"

Footsteps brought Talanee and Ademas around to spot an armored palace guard sprinting into view beyond the rose bushes, green cape streaming behind him.

He saluted and bowed. "Your Highness."

"What is it?" asked Talanee as her heart quickened.

"It's...it's the king. King Netye, I mean. I wasn't certain to whom I should report—"

Ademas strode forward. "Report to us. I'll see that the appropriate people receive your information. What about King Netye?"

The guard swallowed hard as he straightened his spine. "My

lord, he's escaped from the cathedral dungeons. The guards on duty were found dead."

Talanee threw a hand over her mouth. "But how?"

The guard shook his head. "It must have happened shortly after he was locked up. So High Priest Lithel told me. He's waiting at the palace steps. Lithel, I mean. I couldn't find Lord Captain Nerenoth, and I thought..." He glanced between Talanee and Ademas. "Well, you were closest."

"You did well," said Ademas. "I'll inform the Lord Captain and Hakija. You may let High Priest Lithel know as much."

"Yes, my lord." The guard bowed and retreated.

Talanee caught Ademas's eyes. She drew a shaky breath. "What do we do? How could he possibly...?"

Ademas ran a hand through his hair. "I have theories, and I don't like them." He stalked up the garden path. "We'd best find Nerenoth."

She caught up with him, and together they marched through the garden and into the palace proper. Ademas knew his way through the corridors, though when he'd learned them, Talanee didn't know.

Perhaps his mother drew maps or something. Obsession is terrifying.

A fast trot of ten minutes brought them to the throne room, and Ademas entered without preamble. The Hakija stood with several other gold-and-white robed priests, a few armored soldiers, and servants, conversing in soft tones. Dakeer Vasar looked up as Ademas and Talanee approached, the wrinkle of his brow deepening. Talanee glanced around for the Sun God and Nerenoth, but neither were present.

"Yes, Your Highnesses?" asked Dakeer.

"We have a problem." Ademas halted before the Hakija and folded his arms. "Where's the Lord Captain?"

"He and the Holy One are away, performing a miracle to protect our people from a great evil."

Ademas hesitated. "Ah. Well, my news can't wait. Your high priest sent word that Netye has escaped from your dungeon."

Dakeer stiffened as his fists clenched. His eyes narrowed and he inhaled through his nose. "That sniveling coward."

Talanee flinched like he'd struck her. She'd always known no one respected Father, yet to hear thoughts spoken aloud, to witness the disgust the Kel had for him, stung more than she'd suspected it might.

The Hakija turned to one of his fellow priests. "Send an order to Lithel. Ask him to start a search if he hasn't, and to expand it if he has. Netye mustn't get away. Things are troubling enough without a rogue king on our hands."

"Yes, Your Eminence." The priest sprinted from the room, ceremonial robes flouncing.

Dakeer sighed as he tugged on his vestments. "Word will soon spread of all that's transpired. Luckily, the Sun God's arrival is all-consuming, and I doubt there will be nearly the panic we might otherwise expect from Netye's...malfeasance."

Ademas snorted. "Is that what you're calling it?"

The Hakija grimaced. "That's all I *can* call it until Netye stands trial and is found guilty. What a mess that will be."

Ademas shrugged. "I think Lord Tora can clear everything up without so much hassle. But, as you say, we'll have a problem if we don't catch him. You *know* the most likely way he escaped. Not everyone is happy the Sun Gods have returned."

Talanee's heart sank.

Dakeer's hand found his sun pendant as his eyes drifted to the sunburst above the throne. "Yes, the Star Worshipers will become a more active concern."

"They already were," said Ademas. "They *kidnapped* the rightful king. *Took his blood*. I don't think they've been dormant."

Talanee glowered at him.

Ademas's lips lifted in a half-smile. "All right, so I know they've not been dormant. I infiltrated their ranks on Ra Kye, which enabled me to meet with their leaders here in Inpizal. They've been excited about something for months now. I don't know what."

Dakeer started to pace. "I have an inkling."

"Do you?"

The Hakija nodded. "I suspect it's the same thing that's been stirring up the Tawloomez. From history, we can assume the heathens worship the same dark gods that the Star Worshipers do. Something celestial, something far away, is fueling these recent uprisings. And I suspect that same something is heading for Erokel. It's what the Sun God and Lord Captain are working against.

"But from what the Holy One says, we have only four days to be ready for the Star Gods' return, or else we shall perish."

CHAPTER 4

The afterzen sun dragged beams of light down the back of Nerenoth's head until sweat sequined his brow. Still, he didn't move. He wasn't confident shielding Tora from the direct heat was helpful to the Sun God, yet it was all he could do while the god crouched before a steel box atop the domed roof of Erokes's cathedral.

Tora fidgeted with strange threads he called wires for several minutes, then leaned back on his heels with a sigh. "I think I've repaired it, but it's a patch job. I don't know if it's sustainable." He rose to his full height and wiped his forehead. "Let's move to the next city. If the other terminals are in better repair, this one won't strain as much." He exhaled. "Rarenday is much better at this than I."

Nerenoth blinked. "Ruh-ren-day? Do you mean your wounded companion?"

Tora's shoulders tensed. "Ah. Yes. I suppose it makes little difference to divulge his full name under these circumstances." His blue eyes flicked north, past Nerenoth, as a frown dusted his lips. "He's my protector. Rarenday. A distant cousin of mine."

Nerenoth held up his hand. "Forgive my bluntness, Holy One,

but you needn't explain anything you'd rather not. I shall refrain from awkward questions in future. I apologize."

Tora's eyes widened. "Don't do that, Captain. I value questions as another values art." His lips lifted in a faint smile. "Indeed, I value questions as *I* value art." He wiped grime from his fingers with a pristine handkerchief, then tucked it back into his inner jacket pocket. "I won't guarantee I can answer each one, but I'll do so if it's not too complicated or too dangerous. Now, let's head to the next Sun City."

Nerenoth bowed his head. "As you desire." He pinched a bit of Tora's sleeve and visualized the city of Jadom due south, along the coastline.

The world teetered before it settled into place beneath his feet. The salty air curled around Nerenoth's face, as a warm, beckoning breeze tossed his long hair. Sea birds cried overhead. He stood on the steps of the city cathedral.

"L-Lord Captain?"

Nerenoth glanced up the steps to find two Sun Warriors in golden armor. Both gawked at him—and at the young man beside him. One warrior dropped his spear. The clatter echoed across the grounds, drawing the notice of a sizable crowd milling about the lawn in their festival dress. As heads turned, Tora grabbed Nerenoth's arm and drew him up the stairs, the threaded gold of his clothes flashing in the sun.

"Excuse us," Tora murmured and slipped in through the open doors and into the holy building where the aroma of incense tickled Nerenoth's nose.

The Lord Captain matched the young god's pace as he wrestled with the mixture of sensations churning through his soul. Since seeing a god in person eighteen years ago, Nerenoth hadn't doubted a day would come when the Sun Gods would return, just as King Erokel the Second, Holy Hakija of the Sun, had declared in scripture.

How many times had he ached for such a day as this? To at last feel catharsis after years spent in agonizing silence; called heretic and doubter; regarded with suspicion and disdain by priests of the very church he revered.

Now, he strode beside Tora, a Sun God. Already his presence had ushered in a new era. Lekore would become king, Netye would be tried and executed for his crimes, and the true doctrine of the Sun Throne would be preached again among the Kel. Thrills of awe and relief prickled Nerenoth's flesh, and his heart danced a wild beat.

Yes, things remained complicated. Ademas's position had gone from heir to spare, and while he'd sworn an oath to serve his elder brother, words alone weren't enough to prove one's loyalty. Politics among the Kel would remain. Many would argue against Lekore's birthright, even with a god's sanction, because some Kel were too foolish to accept the will of the Sun Throne without question. And Dakeer's about-face unsettled Nerenoth. The man should be tried alongside Netye.

Worst of all, the Star Worshipers had summoned a darkness which now threatened the world. And the Sun God looked worried. Fear had brightened Tora's strange eyes as he'd spoken of the coming danger. Color had faded from his face. His movements now were fluid yet swift, like every second mattered.

Despite that, he deviated from his goal to aid Mayrilana.

Were Sun Gods supposed to be compassionate? Five hundred years ago, King Erokel had scribed pages painting a portrait of fierce, exacting gods, inclined toward violence. They had declared the Kel to be a superior mortal race, blessed by the Sun Throne.

Yet Lekore told a different tale, and Tora's mild, kind nature supported him. Nerenoth had seen a fallen god for himself; Talajin had betrayed the Sun Throne and become a Star God. *He* had been violent, fierce, exacting. In the end, Nerenoth had slain him to protect his companions.

Nerenoth longed to sit down with Lekore and ask him questions. What had *really* happened in the War of Brothers? Who was Skye Getaal, that he now walked as a ghost across the land of Erokel, and mentored Lekore alongside a Sun God? How could the Kel have all been taken in by Erokel if Skye was indeed an innocent man betrayed? And what of the church could Nerenoth rely on as truth?

"Holy Light be praised!"

The voice shattered Nerenoth's reverie. His eyes refocused, and he spotted a train of priests standing in the hallway before the chapel, red eyes pinned on Tora. They flung themselves to the marble floor.

Tora's mouth pulled down. "I need access to this cathedral's dome, please."

"Whatever you desire, Blessed One." A familiar priest lifted his head. His name was Kalith if Nerenoth's memory held true. Kalith climbed to his feet, smoothed his robes, and motioned toward a sweeping staircase. "This way."

Tora lifted a hand. "We'll find our own way. Thank you." He strode toward the steps, and Nerenoth nodded at Kalith as he followed. Pleasure shot through his frame. Two years before, while Nerenoth had visited Jadom, Kalith had dared to call Nerenoth to repentance within this very building. Few would ever be so bold. At the time, Nerenoth had merely eyed the priest; he'd then strode on to attend an event requiring his official presence. As always, he had stifled any annoyance or anger. Neither feeling served the gods.

But he couldn't suppress his satisfaction now. Nor did he want to. At last, *at last*, justice would have its way. And he hadn't strayed from his course in all this time.

As the two men climbed the steps up several stories, Tora's eyes darted from walls, to windows, to artifacts on display in nooks along the stairs. Once, he paused to finger a sword displayed on the wall. It was wrapped in intricate etchings from its hilt to its shining sheath, bedecked with diamonds and sapphires.

"What went so wrong?" he whispered, then shook his head and moved on.

When they reached a trapdoor leading out onto a platform hidden at the top of the golden dome, Tora hoisted himself up, and Nerenoth followed. The Sun God paused to stare out at the Southern Ocean, while the fragrant air tossed his golden hair. He dragged in a long breath and turned to face the metal box. "Let's pray this works, Captain. If I must repair each of these, it will take days."

Nerenoth's eyebrow lifted. *Pray to whom?* Did even the gods have a hierarchy of worship?

The Sun God crouched before the box and slid aside a panel to stare at the buttons inside. He pressed a large one. The box hummed as lights flickered inside the panel.

Tora laughed. "It still works. Thank heaven. If the rest of these work like this one, we'll have no trouble." He straightened and brushed hair from his face. "Shall we?"

Nerenoth took the god's sleeve again and imagined Ra Kye; this time he pictured himself on the cathedral dome. The world tilted.

He looked down and found the box nestled on the platform, while all around him an ocean stretched out of sight. The small island of Ra Kye lay around the cathedral, quiet, indifferent to the politics of the mainland. Sometimes Nerenoth longed to live here...but he was no man of peace.

Tora dug into the machine and soon declared the box operational.

Nerenoth had drifted to the edge of the platform, his cape wrapping around his legs in the breeze. "Lekore's mother lives here."

Tora walked to his side and stared down at the quiet streets of the city. Most Kel were on the docks, having fished through the night, now hard at work selling their catch. Others guided their boats to the mainland to sell wares made from seashells, fish scales, and other sea treasures.

"We can return for her once we've accomplished our task," Tora said. "If you think that's a good idea."

A smile flitted over Nerenoth's lips. "With Lady Zanah, one can never guess what a good or bad idea is." He turned from the view. "Let's be off, Holy One."

CHAPTER 5

Lekore summoned *Calir*. The clang of metal throbbed through the room as he blocked the lunging dagger with his humming sword.

Mayrilana stumbled backward, and the dagger fell from her fingers to thud against the rug under her feet. She slumped to her knees, shaking like a frightened minkee as she stared at her hands.

Rez slid his sword back into his sheath, stooped, and plucked up the dagger. "That was far too near a thing."

Lekore sheathed *Calir* in the air and knelt before the young woman. "I do not think she meant me harm." He leaned forward until he snared her gaze. "Mayrilana, you are safe here. Were you confused when you awakened?"

She stared at him, a curtain of midnight blue hair clinging to her face, streaks of lavender locks pale in the candle flames. Then she bobbed her head.

"You see, Lord Lieutenant? She meant nothing ill."

Rez grunted. "Even so, if she's too traumatized to comprehend friend from foe, I'd rather you avoided her."

"Nonsense." Lekore offered Mayrilana a smile. "I know the feeling of captivity—and your mind is captive." He took her hand and squeezed it. "I vow to keep you safe. Let us be friends."

Mayrilana lifted her eyes to meet his. She blinked. "Who...?"

"I am called Lekore. We met in Erokes moments ago. You are safe now in the walls of Inpizal. This is the palace. Do you remember seeing Nerenoth Irothé?"

She started to shake her head, then halted. Nodded. "I...think so."

"Good. Very good. He is your cousin, yes?"

She nodded.

"He will be back quite soon. He has gone to secure these lands from invasion." Lekore squeezed her hand a little tighter as she shuddered. "Do not be frightened. None here would harm you."

Rez squatted down beside Lekore. "Hello, Mayrilana. Do you recognize me?"

"Yes..." A shadow crossed her face. "Gone. All gone." Coils of panic wrapped around her, but Lekore drew her into his arms and held her against him.

"Hush. Shhh. You are safe here." He hummed a lullaby he'd always known; a sweet, soft sound.

The panic ebbed. The girl relaxed in his embrace as he hummed the tune over and over again. Soon she slumbered, locked in his arms; a frail, broken thing. Nightmares picked at her unconscious mind and flittered into Lekore's thoughts. He drew a breath and willed himself to block them. Ter had told him so many times how to fight off the feelings and visions...

Be calm. Let the wind aid you. Feel its dance. Imagine the ripple of water. The slow, endless revolution of earth. The merry power of fire.

The memory of the Spirit of Spirit tumbled into his mind. *Accept the grace of mercy and kindness.*

Mayrilana's tumultuous feelings vanished from Lekore's soul. He sighed and started the lullaby over again, as he rocked the girl forth, back, forth.

Noises drifted from the adjacent chamber, and Lekore let the melody and background sounds roll through his mind like ocean waves. The weariness he'd combated since he escaped from Inpizal days before wrapped him up like vines in the Wildwood. His limbs floated faraway. His thoughts rose and fell like the tide. His aches and bruises throbbed like tiny heartbeats.

When had he last slept through the night? Surely not since he first came with Nerenoth to Inpizal, poisoned and ill. *Can I rest now at last?*

"Sire?" Rez's voice brought Lekore's head up. The lieutenant smiled down at him. "There's a bath ready for you, and the physician is here to tend to Lady Mayrilana."

Hands pried the girl from his arms. Lekore dragged himself to his feet. Wobbled. Rez took his arm and murmured words that tumbled as uselessly into Lekore's mind as rocks thrown into a churning waterfall.

The man led Lekore back to the antechamber and a very large basin filled with steaming water. Three smiling servants stood on the far side of the basin, arms loaded with clothes and colored bottles.

Lekore's thoughts rattled into wakefulness. He slipped free of Rez's gloved grip to tiptoe to the edge of the bath and peered down into the water where several water spirits swam in shimmery fish shapes. He stooped to dip his hand into the water. Hot. He glanced over his shoulder to spot Rez. "How is this done?"

The lieutenant's eyebrows knitted. "What done?"

"The water is so hot."

"Ah. We heat it over the fire. See that cauldron—the, uh, the black thing beside the hearth?"

Lekore found the large black pot. "That is brilliantly managed."

The servants eyed each other with open grins. Lekore cast them a questioning look, but no one caught it to explain what they found so amusing.

One servant stepped forward; a long cloth draped over his arm. "If you please, my prince, I will attend you as you bathe. Please remove your..." His eyes flicked over Lekore's tattered outfit, and his lips puckered, "...apparel."

Lekore stripped off the tattered remnants of his borrowed clothes, piece by piece, and a servant accepted them each in turn.

He reached for Lekore's discarded black cloak, but Lekore snatched it from him and set it in a bundle beside the tub. The servant blinked, bowed, then marched from the room with a wrinkled nose and the rest of Lekore's tatters.

"Now, my prince," said the first servant, "please enter the tub."

Lekore dipped his foot in the water and flinched. Fire spirits leaned out of the burning sconces and candles around the room to watch him ease into the water inch by inch. At last, skin tingling, he sat in the water as it lapped against his chest.

Like scavenger birds, the servants descended upon him. Unstoppered bottles wafted fragrances Lekore had never smelled in the grasslands of Erokel. Hands scrubbed at his limbs with soft cloths. Fingers raked through his hair as they rubbed in rosemary and clove oils. He cringed but held still. If he tried to dart from the bath, he'd slip or injure someone.

Yet his heart pounded against his chest, and his instincts urged him to conjure fire or summon *Calir*. Escape. Escape.

Do not be a fool, Lekore.

When the last speck of dirt had been obliterated, the hands vanished. Lekore leaned back to catch his breath while the servants disappeared with their bottles—all but the one with the cloth draped over his arm.

Rez, too, remained. He sat on one of the plush chairs near the hearth and polished his sword between sips from a goblet perched on a narrow table beside him.

The servant stepped to the tub. "Is your bath still warm enough, my prince? Shall I add more hot water?"

Lekore met the Kel's gaze and offered a dim smile. "It's fine like this. I can heat it if I need to." He lifted his hand from the water and conjured a flame. It sprang up to dance above his palm, a fire spirit flickering in its center.

The Kel gasped and stumbled back. His cheeks colored. "F-forgive me, my prince. I was warned of your...*gift*, yet I didn't expect to witness it for myself."

Lekore lowered the flame to the water as the fire spirit hissed.

Warm the water, please. "I am sorry that I frightened you. That was not my intent." The fire spirit lighted atop the water, and the water spirits swam up to peer at it near the surface. The water warmed a few degrees. "Thank you. That will do."

The fire spirit plunged into the water and vanished. Chatter welled up from the nearest sconce as the fire spirit emerged from its otherworldly realm to settle among its fellows.

"My prince, would you care for some wine?"

Lekore eyed the goblet the servant proffered. "What is wine?"

The servant blinked. "It is a beverage, my prince. Made from grapes."

"It's also intoxicating if you drink too much, sire," said Rez.

Lekore frowned. "Intoxicating?"

"It can make you lose your head. Don't drink to excess, especially if you're unaccustomed to alcohol."

Lekore grimaced. "I think I would rather keep my head."

The servant bowed and backed away, but not before Lekore caught a smile dashing across his lips. After depositing the goblet somewhere out of sight, the servant returned. "Would you like to remain in the bath a while longer, my prince?"

"No. I think I should like to sleep."

The servant clapped his hands. The other Kel servants marched in from the hallway, new bottles in hand, as well as a heap of clothes, a brush, and an assortment of other things Lekore couldn't glimpse before hands lifted him from the water and used the long cloth to dry him off. Lekore's cheeks burned, and he wrenched a second cloth away from one offending set of hands.

"I will dry myself off, if you please." He slapped aside another hand. "Forgive my abruptness, but I do not enjoy being touched so." He still felt rattled from their first attack.

The servants backed away as the lead servant clapped his hands again.

"Forgive them, Prince Adenye. They wished only to aid you, not to insult the royal person in any way."

Lekore wrapped the cloth around his waist and lowered his

eyes as his face heated more. "I know that you're right, yet I'm unaccustomed to so many people, so nearby." He ran a hand over his face. "Please forgive my outburst of temper."

Silence answered. He looked up and found every servant grinning at him. Panic toned a high note in his head, and he glanced at Rez. The lieutenant also grinned at him like an emockye who had just found his dinner.

"Forgive us, my prince," said the lead servant, bowing low. "Our behavior is improper, yet our feelings cannot be restrained."

Lekore canted his head. "What do you mean?"

The servant glanced at his comrades, then smiled at Lekore. "I am Ginn, your manservant. I requested this post as soon as I learned of your return. I..." His eyes drifted up and down Lekore's frame. "Perhaps you would prefer to towel off and change into new clothes before we discuss this further, my prince?"

Lekore shivered. "Yes, so I would." He went to work drying himself off as a servant set a bundle of fine silk clothes on a stand beside the bath. Lekore slipped into the strange apparel, soft as water to touch, lighter than the clothes Ter had brought him from time to time. His outfit, muted in color, resembled the sleepwear the Lord Captain had provided when Lekore first came to Inpizal. The sleeves were too long, and the bottoms, baggy.

"A tailor and a cobbler will arrive tomorrow to start work on your wardrobe," said Ginn. "Please forgive the ill fit of your pajamas this one night, my prince."

Another servant stepped forward and offered a soft set of shoes Ginn called slippers. Lekore accepted them and slipped them onto his cold feet. A grin spread over his lips. "I feel as though I am standing on clouds."

"I'm glad you approve, my prince." Ginn strode to a chair near Rez's seat. "You might rest here while we speak. Food has been prepared for you."

The moment Lekore sat, someone placed a narrow table before him. More hands set a tray atop that. Revealed a plate heaping with meats and cheeses, vegetables, fruit, and what

Lekore learned was bread, though it tasted light and sweet compared to the flatbreads he had baked in the Vale That Shines Gold.

While Lekore sampled his fare, Ginn said nothing as a servant requested permission to brush Lekore's hair. Reluctant, Lekore agreed after he swallowed a bite of cheos meat. As he chewed another forkful, he eyed Ginn. "If you wish, you may explain what you meant before."

Ginn inclined his head. "Of course, my prince. It is simply this: You're a legend in the palace. For many years now, servants have whispered about the lost prince. Many claimed you hadn't actually died. I thought them fools, yet the stories I heard of young Adenye filled me with sorrow. That someone would wish to kill you seemed so unimaginable. You, who did no harm and offered only kindness. It's so extraordinarily un-Kel-like but endearing nonetheless."

His smile deepened. "And now, today, word has spread of a new, dawning legend: That same young prince who vanished all those years ago has returned and brings with him the Sun Gods. I also heard that you'd chosen to come to the palace, and I requested to serve you. Until today, I served King Netye."

Lekore found the floor at his feet. *Ank*. "I am called Lekore now." He looked up. "I remember very little of being Adenye, and this place is still strange to me. All I have is the name Ter gave me, and I don't wish to lose it."

Ginn bowed his head. "Of course, Prince Lekore. That won't be a problem." He glanced toward the servants at his side. "These men, too, desire to serve you, as you've sparked a new era for the Kel. We welcome any changes you represent as the will of the Sun Gods." His smile crooked. "If I might be so bold, this is Benye." He gestured to a servant older than Nerenoth by at least twenty years. "He served your father, the late King Adelair. Benye remembers your childhood well. That was before I came to the palace to begin my apprenticeship."

Lekore studied Benye. The man smiled back, red eyes bright.

He inclined his head. "It's a privilege to serve you, my prince. You were very kind to me when you were a toddling child."

"I am sorry," said Lekore. "I do not remember your face."

A grin stole over Benye's lips. "It *was* eighteen years ago, Your Highness. I've changed a bit since then. Turned old."

Lekore leaned forward. "You knew my mother as well?"

Benye nodded. "Never have I seen a fairer lady."

A knock rattled the door. Rez stood and prowled to the exit, opened it, then stepped aside. "Sire, do you mind visitors?"

Lekore's heart twisted. "Who is there?"

"Only me," said a familiar voice, "and your cousin."

Lekore sprang to his feet, rattling the table before him. "Come in, Ademas. Come, Talanee. Be welcome."

Ademas slipped into the chamber, dragging Talanee by the wrist. The young man halted as his eyes, one ringed with black, lighted on Lekore. "Wow. You look...transformed."

Lekore slid his hand along his soft sleeve, finer even than the clothing Nerenoth had given him during his brief stay in the captain's townhouse. "It is the outfit."

Ademas nodded. "That, and you don't look filthy."

Lekore tugged on a lock of pale blue hair. "I'm afraid I've had no chance to clean myself up since our visit to the Wildwood. Back in the Vale That Shines Gold, I daily washed myself in a stream near my home."

"I'm glad the gods taught you good hygiene."

Talanee jammed an elbow into Ademas's side. "*Don't* make light of the Sun Gods, idiot."

Ademas rubbed his side and shrugged. "I didn't. Your interpretation did."

Talanee rolled her eyes. Her gaze snagged on Lekore, and her faint smirk died as she lowered her stare to the floor. Her pain writhed in a web of guilt.

Lekore crossed the room and grasped her hand. He lifted it until she raised her eyes to meet his, and he smiled gently. "I do not blame you for anything that has transpired. Nor do I think you blame me. We are not responsible for the choices of another, though it is an agony to think of that man whom we both love and weigh the wrongs he has committed against us. And against your people."

Tears brimmed in Talanee's eyes, but she pursed her lips and blinked them away. "*Our* people. The Kel are your people too. You can't shirk your new duties."

"I won't." He squeezed her fingers. "Especially when I do not yet understand what they are." He released her hand. "I understand what a king is well enough. My ignorance is in knowing what he *does*."

"Bosses people around, mostly," Ademas said.

Talanee scowled at him. "You're not helping anything."

The young man shrugged, but his smile flickered as he lowered his shoulders. "Lekore, we have a problem."

Talanee ducked her head.

Lekore glanced between them. "Why are you both afraid?"

Ademas scratched his head. "Well...we received word that Netye escaped. The most likely explanation is that Star Worshipers aided him."

Lekore's breath hitched as his fingers tingled with cold. "Will the Star Worshipers be kind to him?"

Ademas blinked, then rubbed the back of his neck. "I really couldn't say. They won't need his blood or anything, probably. But that's not the main issue. With nothing left to lose, it's possible Netye will side with the enemy. He might renounce the Sun Gods."

Concern and fear pulsed around the room. Lekore glanced at Rez, Ginn, Benye, the third servant, then turned back to Ademas and Talanee. "Is anyone searching for him?"

"Yes, Sun Warriors and the Royal Garrison are pouring through Inpizal. If he's here, they'll find him."

"Will they search the Temple of the Moon?"

Ademas grimaced. "A few brave lads might. Not many would dare venture there."

Lekore couldn't blame anyone for avoiding that place. Skye

couldn't walk there, and the Spirits Elemental hadn't been able to penetrate the darkness of that domain either.

The source of magic from that fell place is coming to this world even now. Can I combat that?

"Oh," said Ademas. "In lighter news, I sent Elekel a note. He's your uncle. Your *other* uncle. He and our father were close before everything changed. I imagine when he hears of your survival, he'll come promptly to the palace to look you over."

Talanee sighed. "Before a formal proclamation can be issued, half the city will already know about Adenye's return."

"It's true. Gossip is the fastest method of delivery."

She glowered at Ademas. "You're shameless."

The door to Mayrilana's room swung open. The physician, an older man in simple but fine clothes, stepped into the main chamber and Rez strode to his side. They conversed in quiet tones, then the physician approached.

He stopped before Lekore. "Your Highness, the young woman is malnourished and weary. A cut on her ankle is infected and will require frequent attention. More troubling is her mind. She's half-mad, and I presume that's from what she witnessed in Erokes. I can find accommodations for her elsewhere easily enough. You needn't risk yourself."

Lekore shook his head. "I will care for the Lord Captain's kin. That is no bother."

The physician sighed. "As you wish, but know that it's dangerous. The Lord Lieutenant mentioned she's already attacked you once. A second incident could result in your death."

"I doubt that." Lekore smiled and shook his head to clear it of weariness. "She has little skill with a blade."

"Suit yourself, Highness. The line of Getaal always does." A twinkle sparked in the man's eyes. He bowed and strode straight to Talanee. "Princess, how are you?"

She squared her shoulders. "Fine. Who's in the other room?"

"Lady Mayrilana Irothé. She was found in Erokes, apparently."

Talanee's lips parted. "Alive?"

"I don't treat the dead, Your Highness." The physician inclined his head and shuffled from the room. Benye shut the door after him.

The floor teetered. Lekore stared down at his feet, a thousand miles off, and wondered how he'd come to float.

"I think you need rest," said Ademas as if he spoke through a rabbun hole.

Lekore lifted his head. Found his brother's eyes. *My brother. I have a brother. Skye had a brother too, but he wasn't good.*

An arm guided him toward a new door. Drew him into a darkened room. Sat him on the bed. "Sleep, Lekore. Just rest."

Lekore curled up on the bed. Soft as a cloud. Smelling of soap and flowers and spices.

Sleep. Don't dream. Just sleep.

CHAPTER 6

All but one divine box was in good repair. The last, in the northeastern city of Kellar, required more patching. As evening settled over the sky, painting the world orange, Tora's nimble fingers cut and twisted wires until the box hummed. He rose, wiped his fingers on his handkerchief, slipped his gloves back on, and smiled. "That should do it. I'll reroute anything that doesn't draw enough power." He wobbled.

Nerenoth caught his arm. "You're exhausted, my lord."

Tora smiled. "I won't lie. I *am* tired. But we've one last stop to make. Let's return to Ra Kye. Could you bring us directly to Lady Zanah's house?"

"Are you certain, Holiness?"

Tora nodded. "Eighteen years is too long for a mother and child to be separated. After all Lekore's done for me and Rarenday, the least I can do is reunite him with his family."

Nerenoth's stomach knotted. "Can I not persuade you to wait until you've rested?"

"I'd rather collect her, restore the shield, and then rest. Please, Captain."

Nerenoth nodded and willed his concerns into silence. He

pictured the front steps of Zanah's island mansion. Though he'd only visited twice, both events remained vivid in his memory. "I am ready."

Tora closed his eyes, and in a single blink, they stood before the manor house. The structure looked as cold, as imposing, as its Kel mistress—all sharp angles and silent admonitions. A pristine walkway led up five deep steps to thick double doors, barred on the inside, unless something had changed since last the Lord Captain had been here. Nerenoth drew his shoulders back and let the memories fade, as he strode forward. He crested the stairs in a few quick steps, caught the knocker, and let it fall.

"What is she like?" asked Tora.

"A bad dream," Nerenoth answered.

Tora's brows lowered. "Her sons seem amiable enough."

"Once, she was too."

A rumble and scuff sounded inside. The door opened. An aged Tawloomez woman in simple gray garb peeked out, a frown drawing more lines in her dark, wrinkled face.

Nerenoth inclined his head. "Hello, Orra. Is your mistress home?"

Orra's brown eyes narrowed. "Why do you come here, Lord Captain?" Her gaze flitted to Tora—then froze. She shrieked and slammed the door shut. A heavy thud followed.

Nerenoth lifted the knocker and pounded the door three times. "Orra, open the door."

"Is she a slave?" asked Tora.

"A freed slave. She refuses to leave Zanah's side. Orra was devoted to Lekore in his infancy." Nerenoth knocked again. "Orra, I command you to let us enter."

"Not with a Golden Demon!" came the muffled shout.

Nerenoth scowled as a jolt of anger shot through him. "She is also traditional in her Tawloomez faith."

"I'm surprised," said Tora. "From what I've witnessed, the Kel aren't keen on deviant faiths being practiced at all."

"Indeed not. But Lady Zanah honors her husband's wishes.

King Adelair desired to free all Tawloomez slaves and restore their traditions to them. I'm not certain that included their religion, but Zanah... She's always had a defiant spirit. I'm afraid she's a little heretical."

"Ah. Will she also scream if she sees me?" asked Tora, amusement lacing his tones.

"I don't believe so." Nerenoth slammed the knocker against the door again. "Orra, let us in. It's about Zanah's son, and it's urgent."

"Liar!"

"Orra, I stand with a Sun God. If you don't let us in civilly, he will transport us inside, nevertheless. Choose."

Voices rose beyond the barrier, too muffled to decipher. A cold, low, female voice came nearer. "Open the door, *now*."

The scuff and murmur of the wooden bar sounded. The door cracked open. Orra's dark eyes glowered out at them. "See for yourself, my lady."

The door swung inward to reveal Zanah Getaal, wrapped in a white gown of silk and pearls. Pale blue hair pooled down her shoulders and back, loose and wavy. Her red eyes widened as a breath caught in her throat. A hand trembled as it rested against her heart. "Holy Light be praised. Have I at last lost my mind?"

"No, my lady," Nerenoth said. "The Sun Gods have returned."

Zanah lowered her eyes, then dipped into a low curtsy. "Forgive my companion, O Holy One. Orra is growing senile in her old age."

Orra sniffed. "I am not. I know better than to let a Golden Demon inside the house of a Kel. Have they not caused our peoples to suffer enough?" She spat on the ground.

Zanah's jaw tightened, and she whirled on the Tawloomez woman. "Hold your tongue, or I'll have it removed."

Tora stepped forward. "That isn't necessary. I'm not offended. From what I can tell, Lady Orra has every right to feel as she does. It seems my predecessors behaved in egregious ways. I won't excuse them. I will, however, attempt to atone for their actions."

Zanah and Orra stared at him.

Nerenoth's heart swelled. *Blessed is this day.*

Zanah shook herself. "Forgive me, Most Holy Light of the Sun. Please enter my home and be welcome." She glanced at Orra. "You may remain in your room if you can't be civil. This is *my* home, and I'll host whomever I wish."

Orra's mouth worked. "No. Someone should serve refreshments. I'll see to it." She hobbled across the foyer and vanished down the east corridor.

"Despite your benevolent words," said Zanah, "I apologize for Orra's behavior. She trusts few outside this house." She motioned westward. "This way, if you please, Holy One."

Tora and Nerenoth followed her into a parlor adorned in red carpets, tapestries, paintings, and elegant furniture. Tora sat on a settee and wiped a hand over his brow. His face had lost its color, and his shoulders slumped a bit.

Nerenoth sat beside him, as Zanah positioned herself in a wingback chair opposite them. The lady crossed her ankles, adjusted her skirts, and fixed her eyes on Tora. "What brings you to my home, Holy One—if I might ask?"

Nerenoth allowed himself a smile. Not being allowed to ask had never stopped Zanah from inquiring into anything. Her abrasiveness had grown since Adelair's death, but Nerenoth's friend had always been drawn to strong, stoic women, and he'd found their role model in Zanah. While Nerenoth could appreciate Zanah's personality, he had never comprehended Adelair's preference for her. He supposed that was for the best. Too many friendships ended when both men fell for the same woman.

Instead, Nerenoth had been caught in a net of his own—not one made of love. His betrothal to Lady Lanasha had been entirely political, spurred by the last wishes of Nerenoth's dying father eighteen years ago.

Tora shifted, capturing Nerenoth's focus. The Sun God leaned forward, cupped his hands, and rested them against his knees. "We need to take you back to Inpizal."

Zanah glanced at the Lord Captain as her lips tightened. "Is this about Ademas?"

"In part," Nerenoth said. "But it's more than that. Zanah..." He paused. "Adenye is alive."

Her eyes widened. She gripped the arms of her chair and drew a long breath. "It can't be. I entombed his bones!"

"But nothing else to identify him. Those weren't his remains."

She closed her eyes. "You're certain, Nerenoth?"

"Yes."

Zanah pushed to her feet and marched to the window overlooking a flower garden. "How...how is he? His mind? His wellbeing? Where has he been?"

"He grew up in the Charnel Valley."

She turned to stare at Nerenoth. "That accursed place?"

"He wasn't alone, Zanah." Nerenoth stood and strode to her side. "I couldn't tell you. I was forbidden to tell anyone...but I knew Adenye lived. I followed him and Netye from the city that night. I intended to rescue your son, and bring him here, but I was restrained by a Sun God."

Zanah's eyes flashed as they widened and flicked to Tora still seated on the settee. "But why?"

"The Sun God told me he would care for the boy, and that I must return to Inpizal, remain the Lord Captain, and serve the new king without divulging what I knew." He flexed his hands. "What could I do but obey?"

Zanah's eyes darted between his, a hunger burning in their depths. "The Sun Gods raised him?"

"Yes."

"What is he like, Nerenoth? Tell me everything."

The Lord Captain shook his head. "There isn't time. Come with us and meet him. He resides at the palace now."

A grin crept over Zanah's lips. "Does Netye know who lives in his domain?"

"Much has changed. Netye was arrested and now awaits his trial. All has been revealed, Zanah."

The woman threw her hands over her face as a sob tore from her lips. "Sun Gods be praised! At long last, Adelair, you will be avenged."

Tora cleared his throat, and Nerenoth glanced toward him to find Orra standing in the room, a tray trembling in her fingers. Tears streamed from her eyes.

"My little Nye lives?" the old woman croaked. The tray quaked. Tora sprang up and plucked it from her fingers before she dropped it, but Orra didn't notice as she shut her eyes and murmured a Tawloomez prayer.

With a click of her tongue, Zanah abandoned the window and crossed the room to take Orra's hands. The old woman looked up into her lady's face, then let out a wail and threw herself into Zanah's arms. The exiled queen held her friend tenderly.

"There, now," whispered Zanah. "Why cry over such joyous news? Our little Nye is returned to us by the mercy of your gods and mine."

Nerenoth glanced at Tora, but the Sun God stood by and watched without the slightest indication of annoyance or offense. The Lord Captain strode to him and gently took the tray. "Please, Holy One. Sit. You needn't push yourself."

Zanah detached herself from Orra to glance at Tora. "Are you unwell, Holy One?"

Tora shook his head. "I'm a little battered from an earlier crash landing, and I've not slept in almost two days." His brow creased. "Or maybe longer. I've lost track of the time."

"We must return to Inpizal," Nerenoth said. "If you intend to come, I implore you to hurry, my lady."

Zanah nodded. "Orra, ask the servants to pack whatever you think needful for our stay in Inpizal. Make haste."

Orra rubbed her eyes as she shuffled from the room.

Zanah turned back to Nerenoth with a sharp look. "What of Ademas?"

"He, too, knows of Adenye's return. He has sworn his

allegiance to the rightful king of Erokel." Nerenoth tilted his head. "Can I accept his word?"

Zanah bared her teeth in an emockye-like grin. "Oh, yes, Lord Captain. Have no fear on that account. He will remain loyal."

CHAPTER 7

Fragmented dreams slithered into the crevices of Lekore's mind, as voices dragged him from slumber. Something important, something vital, slipped like smoke between the fingers of his thoughts. One voice soared above the rest, strong, insistent. Low tones countered its clear, clipped pitch. *Thunder and lightning*, he thought as he burrowed into the warmth enveloping his weary bones.

The Spirits Elemental whispered around him, their ethereal voices like music in the still room. A wind spirit kissed his cheek.

Lekore peeled his eyes open and stretched his limbs until his frame shuddered. He turned his head to consider the wind spirit standing before his face, its tiny, translucent body shaped like a pythe. Lekore smiled. The wind spirit canted its equine head, tossed its mane, then shifted into a female Kel shape. It stabbed a finger at him in mimicry of something.

"What are you telling me?" whispered Lekore.

'Visitors. Angry. Fretful.'

The voices. Lekore dragged himself up to sit on the bed, damp hair a tangled net around his shoulders, as he rubbed his eyes and willed his muddled thoughts into order. *I'm in the palace. This is my new home.* His heart throbbed as he imagined his emockye pup waiting for him at his cave. *I must bring Lios here if he will come.*

He slid from the bed. Never had he slept in anything so comfortable, except during his brief stay at Nerenoth's estate. He'd been poisoned, so he hadn't thought much of the experience. Or anything at all, really.

With measured steps, Lekore crept to the bedchamber door and pressed his ear to the wood. The voices still rose and fell like waves in a tidal storm.

"...my own son." The clipped voice was feminine, loud, angry.

Nerenoth's calm, even tones broke over the tempest-tossed voice. "No one is trying to prevent you from seeing him, Lady Zanah. But he's resting."

"Mother, he hasn't slept in—well, possibly days." Ademas's wry tones.

Lekore's heart missed a beat. His mouth turned dry. A wind spirit settled on his shoulder, and he stared at it with wide eyes. "My *mother* is out there," he whispered.

The wind spirit nodded in mock solemnity and reached out to pat his cheek with tiny Kel hands.

Lekore shrugged the spirit from his shoulder as a jolt of fire rushed over him. The wind spirit huffed away, and guilt nudged at Lekore, but he didn't need mockery right now.

What do I need?

He raked fingers through his hair until tangles snagged them. He tugged his hand free and let out a long, low sigh. Despite a brief rest, his frame quivered. What time was it? How long had he managed to slumber?

Ademas said it would take several days for Mother to arrive.

Panic clawed at his stomach. Lekore spotted the wind spirit circling the one candle burning in the darkened chamber. A fire spirit hunkered in the single flame, afraid it might be snuffed out.

"I am sorry," said Lekore. "I didn't mean to show you disrespect."

The wind spirit ignored him as it swooped down and blew out

the flame. The fire spirit vanished in a stream of smoke, dousing the room in shadows.

Lekore turned to the door. Drew a breath. Gripped the knob and pulled the door open. The mingled scent of woodsmoke and strange perfumes taunted Lekore's nose as light tumbled into the bedchamber and painted yellow hues across his bare feet. The voices hushed. Red eyes skewered him in place.

Nerenoth, Ademas, Rez, Talanee, Ginn, Benye—and a stranger. *Mother*.

"Hello, Lekore," said another familiar voice.

He turned to find Tora standing at the fireplace, paler than before, a plate of food in his hand.

"Did it work?" asked Lekore. "Are we protected?"

Tora grimaced. "I can't test it yet. I need to return to the lab in the Wildwood first. The program forcing ships to malfunction is still running. That pulse needs to be shut down before I initiate the shield. Once activated, the shield will prevent us from leaving this city, as much as it will defend us from anything trying to get in."

Nausea swept over Lekore. "You must return to that place?"

"He won't go alone," said Nerenoth, snagging Lekore's eye. "But we will not make the journey this evening. There will be time enough tomorrow." The Lord Captain smiled. "My king, there is someone you must meet."

Lekore focused on the woman gowned in white. She stared back, tranquil as frost on the high hills above the Vale That Shines Gold in the Rainy Season. Her eyes burned with a cold fervor, and though her mouth drew a perfect line, powerful emotions roiled beneath her mortal shell. She strode forward. Her fingers flexed as her thumbs rubbed against her hands.

"You are my mother," said Lekore. His heart drummed in his head.

She halted before him, her eyes level with his chin, her frame slender like the reeds in Lekore's stream near Isiltik. She looked up into his eyes, hungry like an emockye, flecked with years of sorrow and bitter disappointment.

Her hand glided up, fingers graceful but trembling. Gently, she brushed his cheek. "How you've grown, Adenye."

That voice. Lekore shivered as he recalled lullabies, sweet whispers, tender kisses to quiet his tears. He choked on a sob as a flood of loneliness surged through his body. He flung his arms around the woman. Mother. *Mother*. He drew her close as she gasped. Clung to her bony frame to soak in her scent, sweet like the fragrance wind spirits carried in from the palace gardens. Tears shimmered in his vision, threatening to escape down his face. He didn't care.

Mother.

The Spirits Elemental chattered around him. Fire spirits hissed and cackled.

Lekore drew back and stared down into Mother's angular face. She smiled, lips trembling.

"Always so affectionate," she whispered and tucked a lock of hair behind Lekore's ear. "The Lord Captain said you grew up in the Charnel Valley. I would think such a place might change you... yet the Sun Gods have seen fit to keep you just the same."

The fire spirits chattered louder. '*Ablaze. Screaming. So bright!*'

Lekore frowned and glanced at the nearest brazier. "What do you mean?"

The fire spirits brightened at his notice. '*Fire. Burning. Blazing.*'

As their crackling voices faded, bells tolled outside.

CHAPTER 8

The Lord Captain tensed and raced into Lekore's dark bedchamber. Adrenaline spiking, Lekore sprinted after him, Ademas at his heels. Other feet followed.

Nerenoth drew the curtains aside, uncovering a glass doorway leading to a balcony. Stars winked and glittered overhead. He unlatched the doors, threw them open, and marched to the railing.

Lekore reached his side and stared out at the city of Inpizal spread beyond the palace walls. The clanging bells sounded from five or more sectors. Columns of smoke climbed above flames consuming tall structures.

"It must be deliberate," said Nerenoth. "These positions are too precise and too numerous." He stiffened and leaned out, panic careening off his shoulders. "My estate."

Lekore spotted the familiar edifice consumed by tongues of flame licking the night sky.

"Your brothers are in there," Rez said. "They took the Tawloomez prince along to keep him safe."

Lekore imagined the twins caught inside, brave but helpless, with Prince Lor'Toreth at their side, terrified. Lekore reached out a hand. "Wind, please!" The wind spirits circled him. Lifted him into the sky to arc over the ground far below.

"Wait, Lekore!" cried Nerenoth.

He didn't look back. "Take me there."

Wind obeyed, laughing, blowing its breath across the city as bells tolled danger and crowds gathered. He arced downward and landed on the wrought-iron gate of Nerenoth's manor house. Flames had consumed the lower half of the tall building, and glass burst somewhere near the roof. A few servants stood on the grounds, several sobbing. Lekore lifted his hands. "Stop, fire, please."

Fire spirits skittered along the building's shell. '*Why? We want to play.*'

"This isn't play," he answered. "You're harming people. Enough. Tell all the fires to cease. I will play with you tomorrow."

'*Promise?*'

"I vow it. Now, cease."

The fire sputtered as the spirits withdrew, robbing its strength. Wind spirits landed on the gate and walls to watch. Earth spirits crawled from holes and flowers. Lekore spotted a single water spirit in a tiny pond within the grounds. He sprang from the gate and landed near the pond. The water spirit regarded him with its iridescent fish eyes, then ducked deeper into the water.

"Won't you help?" asked Lekore.

The spirit vanished in the murky darkness.

With a sigh, Lekore stood. He trotted to the front steps, ignoring the heat curling off the blackened walls before him. Thick plumes of smoke attacked his nose and eyes until wind spirits swept ahead of him to clear the air.

He ducked inside and found the staircase, slumped, brittle, charred.

"Find anyone still alive," Lekore said as a wind spirit swooped close. It formed into a bird and soared up to the second story. Lekore's lungs burned despite the efforts of the remaining wind spirits. He tasted smoke and burnt wood as he plunged into the main level, seeking three familiar faces. Portraits hung on the walls, stained black, mere wraiths.

"Lekore."

He whirled. Skye Getaal stood in the hallway, translucent armor glistening despite the gloom.

"Where have you been?" asked Lekore.

"I left this world to find Ter. He cannot come yet but will try to get a message to Tora's father as soon as he can." The ghost tried a smile. "Why are you always endangering yourself this way?"

"Jesh and Jeth are here, as well as Lor'Toreth. I did not see them outside with the servants."

Skye nodded. "Try the roof. If they couldn't get out down here, they'd have the sense to go up."

Lekore abandoned the hallway and picked his way over debris until he reached the front door. Skye remained with him, walking just above the charred floor. The birdlike wind spirit soared down to Lekore's shoulder and chirped.

"What does that sound mean?" asked Lekore.

'Up. Go up, Lekki. Up.'

Lekore nodded and slipped outside. "Take me."

Wind spirits lifted him, and a cool breeze caressed his face and ran over his hair before he landed upon the roof. Skye stood waiting for him. Lekore scurried up the slope, then stared down the roof's backside.

There. Along the ledge, covered in blankets, three figures huddled close.

"Jesh, Jeth, Lor'Toreth!"

They looked up. Threw aside their blankets. Rose as one.

Lekore scampered down the slope, nimble despite the strange tiles under his feet. He reached the three young men. "Are you well?"

"A tad singed," said Jeth. "How did you know to find us?"

"The wind discovers all secrets."

Lor'Toreth flung his arms around Lekore's neck and rattled off words in his native tongue, while his shoulders shook. Lekore endured it for a few moments, then gently pried Lor'Toreth free.

He looked at the twins. "We had best head for the palace. Your brother looked distressed."

Jeth grimaced as Jesh scrubbed his face. Both were covered in soot and reeked of smoke, their long hair loose and tangled.

"Did you put out the fire?" Jeth asked.

"Yes. And hopefully the other fires in the city are dying as well."

Jeth's eyes narrowed. "Other fires?"

"Our home is gone," said Jesh. "Just like that. If others started at the same time, it must've been deliberate."

"*Lekore*!" Skye's voice cracked like a whip.

He whirled. An arrow struck his arm, and he spun and collided with the rooftop as pain exploded over his skin. Wind spirits roared and howled.

"Be calm!" cried Lekore. "You'll stoke up the fire!"

"Over there!" Jeth pointed to something out of Lekore's line of sight.

He lifted his head and caught a glimpse of someone hooded leaping from the far end of the roof. "Catch them," he hissed as he pressed a hand to his wound. The wind let out a shriek as wind spirits charged. Snatched the cloaked figure. Flung it back to the rooftop. Jeth sprinted recklessly along the pitched roof toward the captive as he unsheathed his blade. Jesh mirrored his twin's movements.

Jeth reached the figure and shoved his blade near the figure's throat. Jesh followed suit.

Struggling to his feet, Lekore pinched his arm near the arrow lodged in his flesh. He sucked in a breath.

Skye leaned down. "Thank the spirits you moved as you did. That aim was true."

Lekore gritted his teeth and nodded. He walked along the stone ledge toward the twins. A shadow trailed him, and he glanced back to find Lor'Toreth close by, brown eyes wide, frame trembling like a hunted rabbun. Lekore tried to smile. "I am assured that Inpizal is not always this rowdy, yet my own experiences lead me to doubt."

If the Tawloomez understood him, he showed no sign. Together, they reached the pinned captive.

Jeth met his eyes. "Shall I unveil our prisoner, my lord?"

Lekore winced at the title but nodded. "Please." He willed a flame to appear before him to cast light upon the assassin.

Jeth threw back the figure's hood. A Tawloomez girl, perhaps fifteen or sixteen years old, stared up at Lekore in open defiance, dark skin yellow-hued in the fire glow, eyes aglitter—and *red*. Lekore blinked. He glanced at Lor'Toreth, whose eyes shone brown even in the flame's light. His dark skin glowed like dusty gold. Lekore turned back to the prisoner. "You are both. You are Kel *and* Tawloomez."

The girl bared her teeth and said nothing.

Lor'Toreth spoke to her in his tongue. Her red eyes flicked to him, then away. She lifted her chin.

"Who sent you here? Why did you try to kill Lord Lekore?" Jeth twisted his blade until it flashed in the light.

She shut her eyes.

"I think we should bring her to Nerenoth," said Jesh.

"Agreed." Lekore drew a long breath. "I should like to remove this arrow as well."

The twins eyed the projectile for a heartbeat or two, then looked up at Lekore. "We apologize for neglecting your injury," they said in unison.

Lekore shook his head. "No matter." He held up his palm until a wind spirit lighted on it. "Bind the girl."

The prisoner cast him a glare, then shrieked as the spirits wound around her limbs until she couldn't move. The twins watched her body go rigid, then shrugged and hauled her to her feet.

She swayed until Lekore commanded the wind to lift her and the others. Lor'Toreth pinched his lips, squeezed his eyes shut, and made no sound, while the twins whooped as Lekore guided his companions over the roof and down to the grounds near the gate. He thanked the wind, and all but the spirits binding the prisoner flitted off to harass some unsuspecting Kel.

Lord Captain Nerenoth had reached his estate, along with the rest of those from Lekore's chambers. Nerenoth and Tora marched toward him now, relief bright in their eyes despite the pall of dusk. Crowds had gathered outside the gates, torches in hand, to observe in silence.

"Please don't leave me behind in future, sire," said Nerenoth as he neared.

Lekore tried to hide his injured arm behind his back, stifling a wince. "I am sorry, good captain. I had to act with haste. Moments more and your brothers and Lor'Toreth would have been consumed. I am afraid your house is badly damaged."

Nerenoth eyed the others. "That matters little if all are well."

"Not entirely well." Jesh shook the prisoner by her shoulder. "She tried to kill Lekore."

"His arm is hurt," added Jeth.

Nerenoth caught Lekore's arm and lifted it into the light of the torches to study the arrow jutting from his flesh. "I regret that your stay in this city is again marked with dangers. I've been a poor protector to you, and to your father before you."

Lekore shook his head. "You cannot blame yourself for my folly, Captain."

"That's quite true, Nerenoth," said Mother as she halted beside him. "Adenye was a difficult toddler to track down at the best of times. I've never seen another so inclined toward hurts—excepting his brother, perhaps."

Nerenoth smiled softly. "So I recall about the crown prince." He glanced over his shoulder. "Lieutenant."

"Yes, sir!"

"Find a physician." Nerenoth turned around as footsteps crunched along the drive. His red eyes fell on the prisoner. "I didn't think any half-Tawloomez slaves had survived."

The girl's eyes narrowed.

"It shouldn't be possible." The new voice sent a shiver up Lekore's spine. He tore his gaze from the girl to find Dakeer Vasar, still in his gold and white vestments, standing behind Mother and the Lord Captain. The Hakija looked the prisoner up and down. "Such a union is against the law. Despite that, I know there are... improprieties among the noble caste from time to time. Such results are cared for in the Sun ceremonies."

Lekore's stomach wrenched. "Is *that* why you sacrifice infants?"

The Hakija met his eyes after a heartbeat. "You know my past sins, Prince. I do not hide them. They happened."

Lekore inhaled and flinched as a cold pain pulsed up his arm. He shivered in the chill night breeze, wishing he'd thought to grab his black cloak. "I understand. And whatever you thought you accomplished by those deeds, it is apparent there were flaws in your plans."

Dakeer's brow creased. "Yes. So it seems."

"She won't tell us who sent her to the roof, or how she knew Lekore would be there," said Jesh.

"Or why she shot him if she didn't know he *would* be," Jeth said.

Nerenoth considered her. "There are ways to make her talk."

Lekore's teeth chattered. He wiped a hand across his brow as he turned toward the prisoner. "This will go easier for you if you explain yourself. I would rather they didn't hurt you."

Someone shouted from the crowd. Guards barred the way as a hand waved in the air. "Please! Please let me through. I must speak!"

Nerenoth eyed the commotion. "See to that, Jeth."

Tora slipped up beside Lekore. "You're in shock." He unclasped his short cape and drew it over Lekore's shoulders.

"Th-thank you. It isn't the...first time." Lekore smiled. "At least this isn't fatal."

Jeth bounded back to the group. "It's a boy. He claims to know our would-be assassin. He's also half Kel."

The girl stiffened as her eyes grew wide.

Nerenoth frowned. "Let him through. Perhaps he will answer our questions."

The girl started to open her mouth, then snapped it shut.

Jeth rushed off and soon returned with a boy of eleven or twelve years at his side, dressed in simple patched garb, two Sun Warriors at his back.

Tears glistened in the boy's red eyes. He spotted the prisoner and his eyes narrowed. "You fool. What were you thinking?"

She scowled and stared down at the ground.

"You are related?" asked Nerenoth.

The boy nodded. "She's my sister."

"Can you tell me why she attempted to harm a prince of Erokel?"

The boy tensed. "She...*what*?" His hands clenched and unclenched as his gaze darted between his sister and the Lord Captain. He inhaled and flung himself to the ground in a bow. "Forgive her, please, my lord. She's...she's not herself."

"Get *up*, Teyed," the prisoner growled. "I knew precisely what I was doing."

Nerenoth pinned a narrowed look on her. "Then you knew whom you attempted to kill?"

Her mouth worked, then she nodded. "The one who brought the Sun Gods. The one who betrayed his calling!"

A light caught in Nerenoth's eye. "Ah. Then you're a Star Worshiper."

"Please," said Teyed as he climbed to his feet. "It isn't what you think."

Murmurs rose from the crowd outside. Lekore turned and spotted Rez and the royal physician squeezing through the gate, then shutting it. They loped over and the physician took up Lekore's arm to examine the wound. His cool fingers startled Lekore as he prodded the discolored flesh.

The physician clicked his tongue. "This will hurt."

Lekore clenched his jaw and shut his eyes as the man broke the arrow shaft near the wound. Pain laved over Lekore until his stomach churned. He sucked in long breaths and let his mind settle on his feet. *Keep standing. Just stand.*

Voices drifted around him.

Nerenoth's low, soft tones rolled over the air like far away thunder on the plains. Familiar. Comforting, with the promise of soft rain. "Teyed, I think we should talk over there. I promise you're safe."

Fingers brushed Lekore's cheek. His eyes slid open, and he found Mother hovering close. Her eyes crinkled as she offered a warm smile. "You're very brave, Adenye."

He glanced at the wound as the physician dug a sharp point into his skin. Lekore hissed and his eyes watered. "I...do not think...this is bravery."

She stroked his cheek again. "You answered the fire alone. That was brave."

Lekore's vision wobbled as the physician drew out the barbed arrow tip. Sweat cooled his temples. "It...wasn't so...daring...a thing. I—I must sit." He crouched where he stood, and the physician followed him to the ground to patch his bleeding arm.

"It struck nothing vital," the physician said. "The bone is likely bruised, but you'll heal without any lasting damage if you're kind to yourself, my prince."

Lekore nodded as he eyed the Lord Captain and Teyed speaking several feet away from the group. Ademas and Talanee stood nearby, the latter hugging herself for warmth, both transfixed on the unheard conversation. A few moments passed before Nerenoth strode back to Lekore.

"His sister is called Nitaan. It seems a large population of half-Tawloomez, half-Kel survivors dwell in the slums near the Temple of the Moon. Star Worshipers keep them fed and utilize them for underhanded dealings. The fires tonight were lit by several volunteers. They call themselves Sunslayers."

Dakeer inhaled and traced a hand through the air. "Sun Throne protect us."

The Lord Captain continued. "Teyed appears hale of mind, less indoctrinated than his sister. Although that could well be a ploy."

Dakeer tugged on his vestments. "All this is well timed, isn't it? We anticipate threats from the very sky, as well as from the Tawloomez, and now the Star Worshipers grow more brazen, unveiling these blasphemous Sunslayers to plunge our city into chaos whilst we're on the verge of war. I cannot encourage refugees to come here if they risk being burned alive inside the *holy city*."

Nerenoth inclined his head. "It does feel like our enemies have overplayed their hand, doesn't it, Your Holiness? Yet we're not without protections." He eyed Tora.

Lekore looked up at the yellow-haired young man. Tora's troubled frown hammered home how desperate everything was. *He's not a god. He's just as helpless as we are.*

Tora ran a hand over his head. "I think I'd best return to that laboratory tonight, Nerenoth. If I can guarantee my father's safe arrival and get a message to him, I'll feel better about our more immediate threats and holding out for help."

Lekore shifted. "Skye told me Ter knows of our plight. He will relay a message to your father."

Tora's eyes brightened. "That's tremendous news. Shall we go now, Captain?"

Nerenoth clapped his hand to his chest. "As you please, Holy One." He turned to the twins. "See that Lekore is safely escorted back to the palace and keep the prisoner and her brother with you. I'm not done asking questions."

"That's a smarter move than you know, Lord Captain," said Dakeer. "Netye escaped from the cathedral dungeons. After these fires, I think we can conclude the Star Worshipers were behind his disappearance. I meant to tell you sooner, but Lady Zanah's arrival disrupted things."

A line appeared between Nerenoth's eyebrows. "Very well. Something else to address on the morrow. We will return with as much haste as possible."

Tora and the Lord Captain vanished, the latter clutching a torch.

Lekore rocked back against his heels. “It seems there will be little chance to rest in the coming hours and days.”

Skye appeared beside him. “I agree. Catch what snatches you might.”

CHAPTER 9

"I'm sorry about your home, Nerenoth."

The Lord Captain glanced at Tora, then turned to study the white-stone laboratory half-swallowed in the trees of the Lands Beyond. His gut twisted as memories of his last visit to this fell edifice returned unbidden to his mind. "It can be rebuilt, Holy One. But I thank you for your sympathy."

The song of the jungle behind him barraged his senses as the decay of dead trees blended with the wet scent of green things.

Tora strode to the door and set his hand on the smooth surface. "A structure can be rebuilt, yes, Captain. But not always what it contains. I'm glad at least that no one was hurt."

"As am I." Nerenoth studied the young god's back in the torchlight. How odd these Sun Gods appeared, from what he'd seen of them. The one called Ter had looked like a child of eight or nine years, yet his sky-blue eyes had held untold years in their depths. Tora looked perhaps twenty or so, yet while his eyes also bespoke years beyond his appearance, he *felt* younger than Ter.

The god called Rarenday looked full-grown, and strong but for his recent injuries. What years he claimed in reality, Nerenoth couldn't judge. Did Sun Gods choose their appearances like Nerenoth chose what to wear each day?

Tora sighed and fingered the panel to one side of the closed doors. The barrier hissed open. "Let's finish this."

Nerenoth drew back his armored shoulders, lifted his torch high, and plunged into the building on Tora's heels. His white cape slithered around his ankles as a breeze caught it.

Silence answered the inquiry of their footsteps. Lights flickered on ahead of them, but Nerenoth clutched his torch, nonetheless. Last time he'd come here, the lights hadn't been reliable.

"Captain?"

"Yes, Holy One?"

"I should tell you something...before everything grows more complicated."

Nerenoth arched an eyebrow as a thrill raced through him. "Anything, Holy One."

Tora's step faltered, then he strode on. "My father. When he comes, my circumstances will become clearer, and I don't want to overwhelm your people. There are things I won't say yet. But this much I should tell you now: My father is the ruler of my people."

Nerenoth halted and stared after the young god before him.

Tora paused and glanced back with a wry smile. "I know it's a lot for you to swallow." He drew a breath. "When I travel, I use the guise of Ambassador Tora, but my full name is Toranskay Ahrutahn. I don't reveal this if I can help it, ever, but under these conditions it's best you know. We're about to face the Kiisuld prince, who will immediately recognize me. And, should we survive his initial assault, my father's armada will arrive soon afterward. There won't be any secrets then. I felt it fair to warn you—and I believe I can trust you."

"Thank you, Holy Prince." Nerenoth inclined his head as his heart hammered against his ribs. "I'm honored by your faith in me. I will say nothing of your title publicly without your consent."

"I appreciate that."

They walked in silence, steps purposeful, until they reached the chamber where Lor'Toreth's retainers had fallen. Decay pricked Nerenoth's nose, as he and Tora slipped past the heap of bodies.

The Lord Captain averted his eyes. He'd seen more carnage in his life than most Kel, but he never relished it. Despite knowing these had been enemies, a twinge wrenched Nerenoth's gut. They'd been Prince Lor'Toreth's protectors; had been all he knew and trusted. Now he huddled alone and frightened among the Kel, an enemy, an outcast, hated by his own people as much as the Kel despised him.

Tora led Nerenoth into the chamber where they had first encountered Talajin as a bodiless voice. The Sun God stepped to the console in the center of the room and played his fingers over the buttons. Again, a box of light appeared in the air above the stationary console, and images flew across it in rapid succession.

Nerenoth stood in silence, watching the magic unfold, unable to comprehend it. Minutes stretched out, and the rhythmic sound of Tora's fingers tapping against the surface of the console swayed Nerenoth's thoughts into a meditative reverie.

He traveled backward to times of humor and peace. To the days of Adelair *before* he'd become king and started a family. Back when he and Nerenoth explored forbidden slums, scaled the roofs of Inpizal, and dreamed of wondrous futures, where they changed things, *really* changed things in Erokel.

The changes are coming, Adelair. Your son is ushering in the future you aimed for.

"Done."

The Sun God's voice brought Nerenoth's eyes into sharp focus, and he lifted his stare from the metal floor.

Tora offered a faint grin, a kind of weary relief coloring his pale face. "Now, approaching ships won't crash if they come too close to your world. I also sent a message to my father, in case Ter's doesn't reach him for any reason."

"Then, is it time to leave, Holy One?"

"Yes, Lord Captain. Back to Inpizal." Tora crossed to him, rested a hand on his shoulder, and transported them back to the Holy City.

Nerenoth breathed a sigh as he found himself standing in the middle of Lekore's suite, surrounded by familiar Kel. No incidents. No threats. Simple.

Something to celebrate. From here, nothing is simple.

CHAPTER 10

Prince Lor'Toreth had accepted a bath and a change of clothes, simple but fine-spun, without a word. He didn't dare speak. Didn't dare move more than was needful. Instead, he sat in a corner of the ornate royal suite and breathed as quietly as possible. How he'd ended up a *guest* of Kel royalty, he might never fathom. How he had come to be welcome in the presence of a Golden One—one of the false gods who had wronged his people so long ago—baffled him.

Yet Tora has been nothing less than kind.

How could Lor comprehend and, indeed, account for the contradictory experiences? Tora wasn't the fierce, underhanded monster he had heard stories about all his life.

It is simple enough. The Teokaka lied to me. To all of us.

Lor had been brought to the *Akuu-Ry*'s chambers, where the Lord Captain's twin brothers continued to guard him in their peculiar way. They sat cross-legged on the floor several feet away, bathed and changed, once again in matching tunics differing only in color. They inhaled a hearty meal like they'd not eaten in a week. No one else in the chamber seemed concerned with Lor's presence either. No one gripped their swords or cast him scathing glances.

The Kel called Ademas lingered near a slender, regal, white-gowned woman who resembled *Akuu-Ry* Lekore.

They might be related.

The woman and Ademas didn't speak. Princess Talanee had claimed a seat near the blazing hearth, and she stared into the flames with a deep frown.

The Lord Lieutenant stood near the large double doors, conversing with the Hakija of the Kel and a pompous-looking priest who had joined the company en route to the palace.

Servants flitted between the Hakija's group and those near the fire, stirring the foreign fragrances of the Kel palace as they offered refreshment. Few took anything. All were grim, some whispering in their foreign tongue, the rest silent.

Lor glanced toward the *Akuu-Ry*. Lekore stood apart from the rest, on the north end of the chamber, also bathed and changed from his soot-soiled apparel into silken nightclothes and a shimmering golden robe.

Lekore watched the different factions like an outsider, a hand pressed against his arm. His damp hair shifted in a private breeze, and his red eyes burned with an inner flame. His head tilted to one side, as though he listened to something no one else could see or hear. Perhaps it was so. Favored of the gods, Lekore behaved like no Kel Lor had ever seen or heard tell of.

Does he feel as out of place as I do? He grew up apart from other Kel, didn't he?

Lor had heard stories of the *Akuu-Ry* for many years: That ghostly specter who dwelt in the Valley of Bones. He who frightened the Tawloomez warriors away from the northwestern route into Erokel each time they marshaled an attack. He who walked with shades and feared no mortal being.

Were the stories true or exaggerated?

The Tawloomez prince studied the fine, angular features of Lekore's face as he reflected on what he'd witnessed in the Wildwood. Lekore could command fire, just as rumors claimed. He saw and spoke with the dead. He could even fly.

"He is a strange king, is he not?"

Lor choked back a yelp and snapped his head around to find the creaky voice who spoke in his tongue: An old woman, Tawloomez born, wearing the threads of a Kel servant. She offered a dusty smile, crinkling her worn face.

"Who are you?" Lor asked. "Why do you speak to me?"

"I am called Orra. What my full name once was, I do not know. I speak to you now because I wish to."

Lor narrowed his eyes. "You are more Kel than Tawloomez in your heart, are you not?"

Orra's lips pulled into a wry grimace. "I am *Orra*, young fool. I am *me*. I grew up in Erokel under the reign of King Erodem—may his spirit walk proudly in the vale of death. I have served House Getaal these many years since. Yet I know the paths of our ancient faith. I know the Sun Gods are not the true gods. I am not a traitor to truth." She jabbed a finger against his chest. "I also know better than to think the Kel are *evil* simply because they are wrong."

Lor bowed his head as shame burned his cheeks. "I...do not know *what* to think."

"Good. The first glimmer of wisdom sparks within you now. What is your name, young Tawloomez?"

He inhaled. "Lor..."

"Lor what? Who is your sire, boy?"

"Toreth."

Orra drew a sharp breath. "*You*. You are the prince of Tawloom."

"No longer." He laced his fingers together and wrung his hands. "I am banished. The Teokaka rules the Firelands now."

Orra grunted. "I have heard plenty of this Teokaka: She who thinks she can bury the old ways."

Lor frowned. "She is chosen by the Snake Gods to guide us."

"Do you believe that in your heart, young prince?"

"I..." Lor stared at his hands. "I do not."

"Good. You're not so much a fool." Orra groaned as she

climbed to her feet. "I must go. I have waited with wondrous patience to speak with my king—and now I wait no more." She smoothed her plain gray dress and hobbled toward the *Akuu-Ry* across the plush rugs covering the polished marble floor.

Lor's eyes widened. "Your king?"

Orra glanced down at him. "You didn't know?" She waggled a gnarled hand toward Lekore. "He is the lost prince, Adenye Getaal, returned to us at last."

Lor's heartbeat accelerated. "He is the lost prince?"

Orra scowled. "Did I not just say so?"

Lightheaded, Lor drew his knees close and buried his head. "He is the new king of Erokel. The *Akuu-Ry*. Wait until the Teokaka learns of that." *Why am I grinning? This is not good news for the Tawloomez. He has powers we cannot fight.*

But then, Teokaka Susunee also had powers. Lor had seen her accomplish terrible things with them. He lifted his head and watched Orra approach Lekore. The young king eyed her, a question in his eyes.

Orra curtsied in Kel fashion. "You will not remember me, I think, but I once cared for you like you were my own flesh, Adenye."

Lekore studied her. "What is your name?"

Lor started. How could he understand the Kel king? *They aren't speaking in my tongue. They can't be!*

The old woman spoke. "Orra, my king. But you called me 'O.'"

Lekore blinked. His eyes widened. A grin slipped over his face, and he flung his arms around Orra. "O! I remember you, O! How had I forgotten?"

Orra laughed, her small, frail frame swallowed up in the young man's embrace.

The regal, white-clad woman marched across the room, steps precise and clipped, though a smile graced her lips. "I forgot to reunite you, Orra. Forgive me."

Orra batted at Lekore until the young man released her with a sheepish grin. The old woman laughed. "Quite all right, milady. I'm able to handle my own wishes." She reached her hand up and stroked Lekore's cheek. "Ah, how I've missed your pretty face."

He laughed. "And I, yours, O."

The old woman swatted his hand. "*Orra* now. You're to be king. No pet names."

Fear brightened Lekore's eyes, and his mirth tumbled from his lips. "Yes. King."

Lor shifted to better study the fear in the Kel king's countenance. *I can truly understand them. Yet moments ago, I couldn't. How?*

Orra patted Lekore's shoulder and whispered soothing words. An ache throbbed in Lor's chest. No one showed him such tenderness. No one ever had. Not even Father before the man's death. He had demanded strength, silence, with no sign of feebleness. He had never listened to Lor's petition to escape Teokaka Susunee's clutches; her torture and neglect in their turns; her gleeful whispers of his worthlessness.

And then, how King Toreth's pride had been hurt when Lor first broke under the Teokaka's relentless abuse. He'd never looked Lor in the eyes again. Shame drove the man to heed the Teokaka after that, and she coaxed him into the Wildwood to prove his mettle against the dread realm. And there he fell.

Lor had cried when he'd heard the news. He didn't know why. Perhaps it was because of what King Toreth *should* have been to him. Perhaps it was because Teokaka Susunee no longer needed to hide her abuse after that.

"Prince Lor'Toreth is mad," she had told the people. "He requires peculiar attentions to keep his mind steady."

Few took Lor's side. Few dared.

The Teokaka was the Voice of the Snake Gods. She knew best...and anyone who opposed her ended up insane or dead.

"Holy Onc, were you successful?"

Lor blinked and turned from Lekore and Orra to find the Sun God and Lord Captain standing in the center of the chamber, their rich apparel glinting in the firelight. The Hakija and priest had moved to stand with them.

Tora offered a drained nod. "Yes, Hakija Dakeer. I think now I can turn on the shield, if trapping us inside is still the safest choice."

The Hakija rubbed his chin as his lips curled down. "It is incomprehensible that upon seeing your luster, Holy One, *anyone* would deny your divinity. But Star Worshipers prefer darkness and secrets."

The Sun God's smile strained further. "Yes, well...I think...I should like very much to sleep."

Lekore strode to his side, cradling his arm. "Take my chamber. I shall not sleep longer tonight."

"You should, Lekore," Tora said. "You and I stand the best chance against our foes, and we need to rest, or we risk all of your people." His blue eyes dropped to Lekore's arm. "That injury will be hindrance enough."

Lekore squeezed his arm. "I know you are right, yet my mind is bright with questions and, I suspect, will not be soon silenced."

Tora laughed. The sound rang out like a clear chiming note, filled with sunshine and green, growing things. He rested a hand on Lekore's shoulder. "We'll be great friends, you and me. Our minds are a lot alike. But mastery of our thoughts will serve us well, so let's attempt to rest no matter the mysteries around us. They'll still be present in the morning."

A grin stole over Lekore's lips. "Very well. You speak sense."

"There are several available bedchambers, Holy Light," said Dakeer. "You may choose whichever you wish."

"Except that one," said Lekore, pointing. "Lady Mayrilana slumbers there."

Tora slipped to a polished chamber door on the far side of the grand fireplace and glanced inside. "This will do well." He glanced behind him. "Hakija, would it be possible to have my people brought to the palace tomorrow? I'd feel better to have them close, especially with arsonists on the loose."

"Anything you wish, Holy One." Dakeer dipped his head as his hand settled over his heart.

"Thank you. I'm grateful." Tora's eyes flicked to Lekore. "Sleep, my friend. Try. Good night."

Lekore smiled an answer as Tora shut the chamber door. The room issued a collective sigh, then the Lord Captain stepped to Lekore's side.

"Rest, my king."

Lekore eyed Nerenoth as he swayed. Lor batted down a strange urge to leap up and steady him, even as the Lord Captain caught Lekore's uninjured arm.

"I shall, I think, despite myself," Lekore whispered.

"Good." Nerenoth steered him to his private chamber. "I will be at the door."

Lekore shook his head. "You need rest, too, good captain."

"I will, nearby."

Lekore drifted into his room, and Nerenoth shut the door after him. The Lord Captain turned to face the main room, and his gaze collided with Lor's. The Kel smiled his somber smile, nodded his head, then scanned the rest of those assembled in the chamber. He settled on his twin brothers.

"Both of you catch a little sleep."

The twins shrugged and rose in unison. "We'll be in the next suite. Rez arranged it."

Nerenoth nodded. "Very well."

The twins trotted to the exit and slipped out, while the Hakija and his priest watched. Then the Hakija strode to Nerenoth's side, red eyes vivid in the myriad candle flames.

"We've certainly moved into a new era, Captain."

"So we have, Dakeer." Nerenoth sighed and unlatched his cape from his shoulders. He slid the white cloth loose and draped it over his arm. "I can't quite fathom what it will look like."

"Nor I." Dakeer angled himself to stand beside Nerenoth, both facing the room at large. "But we must be ready to face whatever comes."

"Obviously." Nerenoth's eyes found Lor's again, and his brow wrinkled. "What does the Tawloomez prince have?"

Dakeer Vasar tracked his glance. He frowned. "I don't know."

Lor tensed as they approached.

Nerenoth pointed toward his feet. "This. What do you have?" He pointed, repeating the question.

Lor glanced at his bare feet. A single piece of parchment lay under his toes. Circles and runes covered its surface, familiar. Lor looked back up and shook his head. "I didn't do this."

The two Kel started and gaped.

"You speak Kel?" asked Nerenoth.

Lor shook his head. "No. I...I did not understand you before, but I do now."

"That's my fault."

Nerenoth whirled, sword scraping free of its sheath. Dakeer turned with him, drawing a dagger from within his voluminous robes.

They faced Keo leaning against the wall near the fireplace. The green-haired man held his arms up in a sloppy kind of surrender, a smile like a barren desert pressing his lips up. "Easy there, Captain. No sense wasting effort on the likes of me."

Nerenoth lowered his sword. "Hello."

Dakeer stared between them. "Who *is* this—this unholy creature? I saw him once before, speaking with the Sun God."

"I'm Keo. Greetings, Hakija."

"He aided us in the Lands Beyond," said Nerenoth. "We met him at the same time we encountered Lor'Toreth. They're acquainted."

Dakeer Vasar glanced between Keo and Lor, brow creased, eyes narrowed. "The Sun God trusts him?"

The Lord Captain blew out a breath. "It's a tentative truce."

"Relax, Your Tenseness," said Keo, smoothing his rumpled, long, green and black tunic.

"We'll vouch for him." The new voice belonged to Ademas. He approached with a hand on one hip, near his sword hilt. The pink-clad princess walked with him. "He helped us against the Teokaka as well."

Keo shrugged. "Against her, I'd help the Devil himself."

Lor wondered who this *Devil* was. No one else inquired.

"Why are you here?" asked Talanee.

Keo shrugged. "I came to make sure my charge is still alive. Seems he is." He winked at Lor. "I also decided to try out my spell." He stepped toward Lor and bent to tap the paper under his feet. "This is a translation circle. As long as Lor touches it in some way, he can understand you, and you can understand him. It works like a Void or Hollow portal in that regard, but for non-magic users. Pretty nifty, hm?"

Lor stared at it. "But how did it get under my feet?"

"I magicked it there." Keo straightened. "Keep it in your pocket. If you're stuck in Erokel for a while, might as well know what's going on. Not knowing a language can be unsettling."

Lor slid the parchment from under his feet and stared at the strange symbols inked across the page. He carefully folded it and tucked it into his tunic's inner pocket. "I will take good care of it."

"Good." Keo rubbed his stubbled chin. "Any chance I could get a bite to eat while I'm here?"

"Yes." Nerenoth turned to a servant. "Bring him a plate of food. Be generous."

The servant bowed and scurried off.

Nerenoth strode to the chairs near the fire. "Have a seat, Master Keo."

The green-haired man complied and sank into a plush chair with a sigh. "Feels good to get off my feet."

Nerenoth took the chair opposite. "You mentioned protecting the Tawloomez from our impending threat."

"Yes. I've done what I can. Any invaders stepping into the Firelands will trigger an alert—and I can face down the enemy. The Teokaka won't like that. No doubt, she's planning a big welcome party."

Nerenoth's brows creased deeper. "For her dark gods."

Keo's smile turned brittle. "For her father."

The pop and hiss of the fire dominated the chamber.

Lor shivered and curled into himself. He pinched his eyes closed as a hundred fleeting memories surfaced, taunting him. *She's a goddess. She's a Snake Goddess!*

"Wow." Keo's voice carved the room like a knife through cheos meat. "Didn't mean to dampen the mood quite so much. Relax. She's still nothing compared to what's coming...and I'm willing to fight alongside you."

"Why?" The Hakija's voice held venom.

The chamber door clicked as the servant returned, a platter heaped with food in hand. He padded to Keo's chair, proffered the platter, and backed away. Keo took a few bites as everyone waited in silence.

The tall, regal woman had crept closer, along with Orra. Neither spoke. No one dared do more than breathe.

Keo swallowed a third bite. "Simple, Hakija. I don't want the Kiisuld coming here anymore than you do. I'm *very* aware of their ways, and I don't like what they're after. This is my home as much as yours. I've lived on this planet for several centuries, and I've grown fond of its people—and that means you." He scraped up another mouthful of food.

"Centuries?" Ademas asked.

Keo swallowed and wiped his mouth with his black sleeve. "Yeah. I guess I should clarify something. The invaders coming in three days are called Kiisuld. I know a lot about them for a very specific reason. *I'm* Kiisuld, too." He scooted vegetables across his platter with a fork. "That doesn't make me their ally. On the contrary, I despise Kiisuld as a rule. I'll do all I can to thwart them."

"Why?" The Hakija folded his arms and glared at Keo with undisguised hatred.

Keo stuck his fork in a mound of meat. "Because they rejected me."

"You were cast out?" asked Ademas.

"Why?" asked Talanee.

Lor sent Keo the same silent inquiry.

The man smiled dryly. "That's private. Sorry."

Nerenoth stood from his chair. "It's enough to know you'll help us. We can discuss more when Lord Tora and Lekore rejoin us tomorrow morning. For now, those who can should sleep. Will you remain here, Keo?"

"For now. I'll check on my alarms closer to our enemy's arrival." He settled back in his chair, half the platter emptied. "I'll just sleep right here. It's more comfortable than my matt in the *Ava Vyy*."

"If it suits you." Nerenoth moved toward Lekore's door, and the Hakija joined him. They spoke in low voices, the former in tranquil tones while the latter hissed out his words like a snake.

Lor gingerly rose and tiptoed to Keo's side as the other Kel retreated to adjacent chambers or corners. Lor knelt beside the chair. "I'm glad you're well."

Keo snorted. "Hard for me not to be."

"I'm also glad you came to check on me."

Keo considered him, green eyes searching for something. "By Suld, you actually *are*. Wonders will never cease." He ruffled Lor's hair. "Guess I can't stop a boy from imprinting on what he looks up to, but bear this in mind, young prince: I'm not your best role model. Better to take your cues from the Lord Captain." His hand retreated.

Lor grimaced. "From a Kel?"

"From *that* Kel, yes. Don't be a fool. Now get some sleep." Keo flopped his head back against the chair and shut his eyes.

Lor curled up beside Keo's chair, grateful for the warmth of the fire and the comfort of a solid room surrounding him. *Just focus on that. Don't think about the morrow.*

CHAPTER 11

Toranskay Ahrutahn bobbed to the surface of wakefulness with weary reluctance. His mind conjured up a half dozen excuses to stay asleep, but a dozen more powerful reasons lured him upward until his eyes betrayed him to the dawn.

He lay in a strange bed, in a foreign room, muscles sore and bruised. A cut on his leg throbbed. A dull headache played percussion against his skull. He let out a faint groan. A new day, with looming problems.

He longed to find Rarenday and commiserate together; how they'd come to crashland on this strange world, with its peculiar, primitive people, *who thought him a god...*

Ter might be to blame, but that was true of many things. Toranskay had deep rooted suspicions that the childlike Ephe'ahn enjoyed steering people into necessary danger.

But it's always necessary.

An image of Lekore fluttered into Toranskay's mind. The young man wielded a sword forged by the same magic that had crafted *Calisay*. Twin blades, if Toranskay judged right. But how?

Ter will know.

Yet the wise old child wasn't here, nor would he soon come, according to Lekore's ghostly companion.

Toranskay sat up and ran a hand over his face. A beam of light pierced the ground near the bed. He followed its path to the crack between the deep green window drapes and stared into the blinding splendor until water gathered in his eyes. Ghosts. Prophecies. Sun Gods. Twin blades.

What have you shoved me into now, Ter N'Avea?

Amusement tugged at his lips but died as he recalled the hovering threat coming closer with every second.

Kiisuld.

Toranskay's shoulders hunched. His breath hitched.

Be calm. Stay calm. You're not alone.

While the Kel could do little against the Kiisuld, Lekore wielded powers like few people Toranskay had known. *He should come to Raal Corenic and learn to master them.*

If we survive this, I'll suggest it to him.

It begged the question: Why hadn't Ter already taken Lekore there?

So many questions. Always. Toranskay usually didn't mind them.

He threw the forest green brocaded coverlets aside and slid from the bed as his muscles thrummed a protest. He ignored them and reached for his battered clothes before his mind registered the soiled things had vanished. In their stead, an assortment of Kel-style gold and white raiment hung from a hook near a washstand, soft white leather boots nearby. He smiled at the novelty as gratitude surged through him.

They do this because they think you're a god, Toranskay.

Guilt stabbed at his gut, dampening his pleasure. He'd experienced such worship before. Father had experienced it far more often, but never on this level. To find himself woven into the theological tapestry of a race manipulated by Ahvenian dissenters rocked Toranskay to his center.

Why were they here, and why did they build themselves up as gods?

He ached to dig into the archives stored within the old technology of this city, but a preliminary inspection showcased extensive damage—likely caused by Talajin or his colleagues to hide their plots from all prying eyes. If the Kiisuld really had come here before, they'd be just as curious about the dissenters as Toranskay found himself.

I'll need to bring in a team to recover the deleted records.

Dressed and groomed, Toranskay paced to the curtains and drew them aside. Light filled the room, and birdsong greeted him from a private garden below. The palace walls stood a long way off, and beyond that, the little Kel city. Even so early, the faint din of carts and market calls wafted on a fragrant breeze. A chime sounded the hour; perhaps seven o'clock. Toranskay closed his eyes and let the music of the morning settle over him: The buzz of insects, the errant wind, the distant merchant calls, rattling wheels, pythe braying, a trickling fountain.

A world without machines, without engines and the whirring of technology, without hovercrafts veering by, or starships soaring toward space.

He drank it in, along with all its accompanying aromas. Let it all settle into his blood.

His fingers danced over a teasing melody. Such music he could make of these pastoral sensations, like a favorite dream of lost worlds in a bygone age.

"May I join you?"

The forming notes shattered. Toranskay started and turned his head to find Lekore clinging to the windowsill in an effortless crouch. His long, loose hair danced like a streamer and shimmered like water in sunlight. He wore a silver tunic and charcoal breeches with matching boots, all better fitted to his slender frame than the previous night's pajamas. If Lekore's new servants had adorned him in any baubles, he'd already abandoned them.

Toranskay smiled. "I'd welcome it."

Lekore shifted to sit on the window ledge, feet dangling down the outer wall. "The spirits told me you had woken."

"Ah. They're a talkative lot, I understand."

Lekore laughed. “Most especially the wind.” He turned his red gaze on Toranskay. “Water is rather secretive and aloof.”

“So I’ve heard. How is your arm?”

“It hurts, but that is to be expected.”

Toranskay searched the young man’s face. “I suspect with everything else on your mind, a flesh wound is nothing. You’ve been reunited with your family amid a period of civil and religious unrest, in large part caused by my arrival.”

“You could not help it.” Lekore twisted to face Toranskay. “Do you sail the stars often?”

“Sometimes. It depends on my duties. But I do enjoy space travel.”

Lekore sighed and tipped his head back to stare at the golden hues of the morning sky. “I long to travel there one day. Ter said I might.”

“Did he?” Toranskay leaned his arms on the windowsill. “That’s good news for me. I’d like to take you to Raal Corenic. Your gifts should be known and honed.”

“Ter has spoken of Raal Corenic. It is where Skye once studied.”

Toranskay blinked. “Your ancestor?”

“Yes. He spent a year there when he was younger than I.”

“Indeed?” Toranskay grinned. “That settles it. I’m certain I can bring you there.”

“Not yet.”

Toranskay’s heart plummeted as his chest tightened. “True, not until we’ve faced our adversary.”

“They are coming fast.”

Toranskay sighed. “Faster than anticipated?”

“No. But is that not fast enough?” Lekore’s eyes dropped to the garden. “Will the shield hold?”

“It will buy us time. That’s all. It’s not invincible, and the generators aren’t up to current standards.” Toranskay traced a grain of wood in the polished sill. “I’ll try to activate it today. That’ll give me a better idea of its strength.” He studied Lekore’s profile. "You're a Seer and an Elementalist True. It's quite the potent combination. If your blood was used to summon these Kiisuld, the prince must want that power a *lot*, and I can understand why. Someone of your unique skillset would be quite formidable in one's arsenal."

"There is more." Lekore's brow drew together. "I—I feel things from other people. Emotions. Secret fears and wishes. Hatred. Sometimes I *see* their memories, their pain."

Toranskay inhaled. "An Empathist as well?" He leaned his chin against his knuckles. "You defy the rules of magic. Few times in history has such a powerful assortment of magic been born inside a single person. It's not unprecedented; but rare. Very, very rare."

He straightened up. "I'm certain Ter knows more about it, so I'd best not speculate. He's got a knack for finding rare magics and those who wield them." He smiled and rested a hand on Lekore's shoulder. "I hope we can become good friends. My position on my home-world is such that I can call few people my peers, but I'm confident you're one of those rare exceptions. I'd like to know you better, assuming we survive the coming days."

Lekore tilted his head. "And I should like the same. I feel as though somehow I already know you. Perhaps it is because we are both acquainted with Ter."

A laugh slipped from Toranskay's lips. "No doubt that's part of it."

Lekore stiffened and stared into the sky, tipping his head more. "What is it?"

Toranskay followed his intent gaze. "Is Skye here?"

Clouds gathered on Lekore's brow. "Yes. He says an army has appeared outside the walls of Inpizal."

As Lekore's words died, the bells of Inpizal tolled like thunder in the heavens. He sprang up and lifted a hand into the air.

Toranskay snagged his pant leg. "Take me with you."

Lekore glanced down at him, nodded, and clutched at a breeze. "Take us to the wall, please."

Wind swirled around Toranskay's legs and hefted him from the floor and out the window. They rode the air, steady, embraced by the spirits Toranskay couldn't see. The spirits guided them due north toward the main city gates, past a parade of birds flying west, across the rooftops and cobbled streets, to land upon the white stone battlements beside the gates. Lekore peered over the wall.

Toranskay leaned out to study the army of green and brown clad Tawloomez warriors spread across the vast plain. The faint remnant of a Hollow portal tinged the air. At their head, gowned in shimmering snakeskin, the half-Kiisuld leader, Teokaka Susunee, eyed the gates. Her lean, tall frame tensed, then she swiveled to spot Lekore and Toranskay. Her dark face, angular and beautiful, stretched into a wide, feral grin.

"Ah, the *Akuu-Ry* and Golden One have blessed us with their notice!" Her voice rang out across the grasslands, strong and clear. "Surrender yourselves before the Snake Gods arrive, and we'll have no cause to burn your city."

"Heed me, Teokaka!" called Toranskay. "When the Kiisuld arrive, they'll show no mercy to anyone. You, least of all."

She laughed over him. "Fool! I am a Snake Goddess, born of the Snake Prince himself! He returns as he promised to take his heir into his pantheon where he dwells on high—and to claim his prize." Her tongue darted out to lick her lips. "The *Akuu-Ry* has come into his power, and that has drawn the attention of my father!"

Lekore trembled.

Toranskay rested a hand on his shoulder. "I won't let them take you."

The young man glanced at him with a weak smile. "I, too, will fight." He turned back to the army. "I could open up the earth and let it swallow your army, Susunee. Why face us now, ahead of your father's arrival? Why not wait?"

The Tawloomez woman's red lips split in a wide, toothy grin. "I wish to deliver both of you personally to my sire!"

Lekore's mouth twitched downward. "Scare her a little, please."

His words were soft, yet the ground rumbled at once, not enough to rock the city foundations—but the army cried out, and the Teokaka's brown eyes narrowed as she stumbled.

"Enough, *Akuu-Ry*! You would not risk damage to your precious city."

"Stop a moment," Lekore murmured. The ground ceased to rock, and the Teokaka laughed.

Toranskay leaned close. "It's odd that she boldly appeared here. She's probably distracting us from something else."

Lekore blinked and whirled. "Do you think she has agents within Inpizal?"

"Possibly. But if she can come here so easily, and infiltrate, why hasn't she tried to demolish your lands well before now?"

"Two reasons."

Toranskay's heart stuttered as his eyes found Keo standing beside Lekore, the crackle of a Hollow portal fresh on the air. He scowled at the Kiisuld. "Oh?"

Keo nodded. "I usually discourage her from using her power if she's too eager."

"Ah!" called the Teokaka. "The treasonous wretch joins the enemy upon the wall, does he?"

Keo didn't so much as blink.

Toranskay lifted an eyebrow. "And the second reason?"

The Kiisuld patted Lekore's shoulder. "This one scares the Tawloomez spitless. *Akuu-Ry* means *demon child*. He's prevented more attempts to invade than I can count—or care to." He glanced at the army. "But her blood stirs with the nearness of her sire. She'll be hard to contain now."

"Is she a decoy, do you think?" asked Toranskay.

"Probably. To what end, I can only guess, though I think they're good guesses."

Lekore looked between Keo and Toranskay. "Is she in league with the Star Worshipers?"

Keo shoved his hands into his pockets. "I suspect so. Makes

sense they would be, seeing how they both worship the same two *gods*."

Toranskay absorbed the city view, then turned back to face the army outside. "I'll warn you one last time, Lady Susunee: The Kiisuld on their way here have little tolerance for their illegitimate offspring. You'll not be accepted or elevated by Prince Vay-Dinn Fyce. He'll probably kill you. If you surrender to us now, we'll agree to harbor your people during their invasion."

The woman threw her head back and belted out a deep laugh. "So condescending! So noble!" Her grin stretched until her eyes burned with madness. "We'll take our chances—better that than anything a Golden One might try!" She beckoned. "I speak now directly to the *Akuu-Ry*: rightful king of Erokel."

A Tawloomez warrior separated from the army and dragged a man forward. A cloth sack covered the prisoner's head, but he was dressed in noble Kel fashion.

Lekore stiffened and leaned further out. "No..."

Susunee ripped the sack away, revealing King Netye, disheveled, cheeks discolored. The Teokaka kicked the back of his leg, and the king stumbled to his knees with a cry.

Violet sparks played at Susunee's fingers. "I understand he's dear to you. Let me be clear: Your lord uncle faces death, *Akuu-Ry*, unless you surrender your city and yourself to *me*. Believe me, I would relish the chance to ravage his body, peel back the layers of his flesh, and watch him die very slowly—but I shall refrain if you comply."

Toranskay brushed his fingers against Lekore's arm. "Even if she's telling the truth, the Kiisuld prince won't be so generous. You can't negotiate with her."

Lekore's red eyes flashed as his jaw set. He stared down at the Teokaka, shoulders trembling, fists clenched. "She is lying; that much I know."

Relief flooded Toranskay's body like cool water. *He's no fool.* He glanced toward the palace as the city bells rang on. The city watch upon the wall also eyed the bells, but none left their station.

Several watched Toranskay from a safe distance as he fisted his hand. "If this is a diversion, what does she intend elsewhere?"

Lekore caught the edge of the merlon and sprang up onto crenelated stone to stare down the army below. "Susunee, this is not a fight we must wage. Do not force my hand. It will not go well for either of our peoples. Nor will I subject Inpizal to your wrath and ruin, even to spare the life of my uncle. Let us come to a different understanding."

The woman's laugh rang out again. "What a creature you are, *Akuu-Ry*! Neither Tawloomez, nor Kel, nor god. What *are* you, to be so naïve?" Sparks flew from her fingers and struck Ank. The man screamed and crumpled to the ground, frame quaking. Susunee lifted her fingers and allowed sparks to envelop her hand, again.

Nausea washed over Toranskay as the tainted magic fouled the air. His bones throbbed and his heartbeat quickened.

"Do you condemn him to his death?" Susunee cried. "You have mere seconds to decide, Kel King!"

Heat rolled off Lekore, as though he carried fire in his blood. Perhaps he did. Fire Elementalists could alter their temperatures with a thought. Even molten lava couldn't harm them if they were strong enough. The Seer's pale blue hair fluttered around his ankles, caught in a private draft, dancing with his silent fury.

"Release him, Susunee, or things will not go well for you." Lekore's voice carried, clear as a bell, though he didn't shout to reach the woman. Flames bloomed on his fingertips and the wind howled overhead, lashing his hair around his legs.

Toranskay summoned *Calisay* from its otherworldly realm, and the sword's familiar weight lent strength to his will. His gaze flicked to Keo, who leaned on the raised crenel, staring out at the enemy army, a faint, wry smile playing at his mouth.

Can we really trust you, Kiisuld? Toranskay wondered.

Susunee spoke. "You'll make no more demands upon me, *Akuu-Ry*. You, who stole our slaves while keeping your own despite your promise."

Lekore's eyes narrowed. "It has been less than a full day. I've not had time to release them."

The woman's grin stretched impossibly wide. "No, indeed. Which is just as well."

The bells clamored loud, wild, pealing over the sky—then fell still.

Lekore whirled toward the Kel cathedral, and Toranskay followed his eyes as a chill spidered up his spine.

Keo swore and vanished on the spot.

"Ah," breathed Susunee. "It is done!"

Like breaking thunder, cries rolled over the city, some desperate, others angry. Soldiers on the wall and in the guardhouse below unsheathed their blades as Lekore summoned his sword, *Calir*, from its resting place on some other plane. *Calisay* chimed a greeting to its twin brother, and *Calir* replied with a harmonic song of its own.

"Too late to fight, Seer!" screamed Susunee. "My people—your so-called *slaves*—have taken Inpizal!" Her eyes speared Toranskay. "And *you*, Golden One—I shall relish watching my sire brutalize you in every imaginable way!" She licked her lips. "Ahh, if only he would hurry."

Lekore's eyes blazed. His sword quivered in his white-knuckled grip. "Tora."

"Yes?"

"Please do what you can for those within Inpizal. I must rescue Ank, which means I must take Susunee down."

Toranskay stiffened. "She's powerful, Lekore. *Very*. Kiisuld absorb the lives of those they kill, which means she can regenerate. She won't die. Not easily, anyway."

"Then I'll simply have to incapacitate her." He sprang from the wall, wind slowing his descent as he swung his blade at the Tawloomez woman. She laughed, hurling bolts of violet lightning at him as Toranskay staggered backward on the wall, blood throbbing against the taint.

Calir swallowed the magic threads. Lekore struck the earth with his blade as Susunee leapt several feet back, her dark leg showing through a slit in her green gown, a wild glint burning in her dark eyes. Laughter trembled on her lips.

Toranskay gripped *Calisay* and lurched forward to spring from the wall and follow Lekore into battle, but his mind scuttered over the Lord Captain, Talanee, Ademas, the twins. *What should I do?*

Lekore needed help, yet no one else within the city wielded the power Toranskay could, except his companions, all too injured to quell an uprising.

She's trying to take the city hostage. I must thwart her.

He darted for the stairs and took them four at a time, eyes sweeping the street for a mount. There. A pythe stood secured to a post near the guardhouse. He reached the road and sprinted to the reptilian equine creature as he lamented its stubs where wings should be. Never had he seen pythe without wings before, yet all on this world appeared to have been stripped of flight, genetically altered in years past, devolved by Ahvenian scientists, if Toranskay didn't miss his guess.

Think on it later. He untethered the beast, swung into its saddle, and urged the pythe south toward the palace glistening under the rising sun. It dug talons into the cobblestone cracks as it loped ahead.

CHAPTER 12

Lekore dodged strands of violet lightning and pivoted to face Susunee as the air crackled and wind spirits swooped away from near-death.

The Tawloomez army backed up as flames danced along Lekore's fingers and Susunee raised her arms to summon magic. Lekore whipped his hand out, arrow wound throbbing as he unleashed a stream of fire. Flames arced around Susunee and encircled Ank at Lekore's silent command.

Susunee let out a scream and tossed magic at the flames, but wind spirits threw Lekore in front of the attack and *Calir* staved off the bolts. Magic shrieked as it dissipated on the air, and Lekore slid into a defensive stance, curved blade held before him, eyes narrowed on his enemy.

Calir toned a note. Lekore shifted his heels at the sword's urging.

Beside him, Skye Getaal materialized, translucent armor glimmering as daylight grew. "Be careful. Her mind is untethered. She'll not care if her army stands in her way."

Lekore offered a single nod and imagined his flames growing, stretching to block the Tawloomez from their unhinged leader.

The fire spirits encouraged the fire to expand, reading his will, glad he had fulfilled his promise to play with them.

Several warriors cried out and broke from the ranks to dart northeast. Lekore let them go.

The Teokaka laughed. "Cowards! Wait until my father arrives. He'll not spare you!" Her eyes swung back to Lekore. "*You*, I can't destroy. But I can maim you!" She leapt at him, hands stretched before her, violet threads weaving along her fingers. The air crackled, tasting of lightning in a storm, and blood, and fear.

Lekore hefted *Calir*, but the threads of violet light struck at his feet, jolting his bones, scalding his blood. He cried out, stumbling. Nearly dropped his sword. Caught himself and tightened his grip as he searched for Susunee in the dust rising from the dry earth. Wind spirits rose to sweep the dust cloud away.

There.

She lunged at him from the left, and he whirled to swing his blade. She danced aside, tossed magic threads out in all directions, and summoned a blade made from violet light at the same moment. Swung.

Lekore caught the crackling sword with *Calir*. Lightning marched up and down his curved blade, sparking against his fingers as he gritted his teeth and pushed against the blow. His wounded arm throbbed again, but he ignored it.

Susunee's eyes darted toward the wreathing flames protecting Ank. Her tongue raced over her lips.

Lekore leaned harder against her sword until her eyes met his narrow glare. "Do not try it."

She flashed a grin and pulled back, dislodging their swords. Her long, brown hair slithered around her back and arms. "Give up, *Akuu-Ry*, and I'll have no cause to harm him. You're what we want."

Lekore shifted his grip and lunged, summoning wind and fire to encircle him. Susunee's eyes widened. Her guard dropped, and she whirled to sprint away from the Spirits Elemental. Lekore unleashed his will into the earth, and its spirits reached up to snatch at her feet. Susunee screamed as she swung her sword against the spirits she couldn't see. Finally, she whirled to face Lekore as he let fire ring her.

"Surrender," he said. "Pull your followers from my city but let all remain who would prefer the protection of Tora's shield against your father's coming."

Hatred stormed in her brown eyes, raw, bright. "You win for now, *Akuu-Ry*, but a reckoning will soon come." She barked strange words at the Tawloomez huddled away from the battleground. "Release me, and we'll pull back for now."

Lekore shook his head. "Not until the city is secured."

She narrowed her eyes, then sniffed. "Do as you please."

"I intend to." Lekore gestured, and the fire crawled over the air to form a ball of heat around Susunee, containing her without cooking her. "Stay there. I will return soon."

He eyed his uncle kneeling on the plains, trembling. With a gesture from Lekore, flames encircled Ank, protecting him from Tawloomez and Kel alike.

"I will come back for you, Ank."

The gaunt man flinched and stared at the ground before his knees.

Lekore called to the wind spirits, and a band of translucent butterflies lifted him up and over the city wall into Inpizal. Midflight, the Teokaka's bloodlust and a burst of glee rolled over his soul, malicious, far from despairing. Lekore landed on a rooftop and glanced at the wall hiding the woman from view.

He lifted his hand, and a wind spirit morphed into a bird to land upon his finger. "Watch her. Tell me if she tries anything."

The spirit nodded its birdlike head, fluttered its transparent wings, and took flight. Lekore turned south toward the palace and started as Skye materialized before him.

"She's up to something," said the ghost.

"Yes, I feel it. But what am I to do? Even should I choose to kill her, Tora said she cannot die."

Skye tipped his head sideways. "To a degree that's true. She's *hard* to kill, but it's not impossible. For now, best you keep her contained and assess the extent of her plot. I looked within the palace and cathedral, and Tawloomez slaves have risen up to attack their masters, particularly within the latter. Tora is heading for the palace, where Nerenoth and the rest are locked in combat. Will you join him?"

Lekore eyed the golden dome of the cathedral as a voiceless whisper tugged upon his mind. "He must tend to the palace. I am needed elsewhere."

He spread his arms wide, and the wind spirits swept him upward and across Inpizal as a bird would fly. Rooftops glistened under his feet, far away. Kel struggled in the streets against drab clad Tawloomez. The clatter of swords, the thud and grunt of bodies, the cries of wrath, pressed against Lekore's skull, but his fear had died. Quiet settled under his bones.

He lighted upon the cathedral's outer wall and surveyed the Kel and Tawloomez bodies lying across the manicured lawn as his heart twisted. Chills marched up his arms as his eyes pricked, but he steeled himself, set his shoulders, and adjusted his grip on *Calir*.

Wind spirits caught him as he sprang from the wall and landed lightly on the grass. He raced to the front steps and took them three at a time, flew into the cathedral, and staggered to a halt in the massive vestibule.

Bodies lay before him, strewn like carpets, blood puddled around them. For every fallen slave, four Kel lay dead around them, gold and white robes bespeaking their priestly rank and race. Grand pillars rose around the fallen like guardians of the dead. Stained-glass windows painted eerie colors on the flat, staring eyes and rumpled robes.

It's a massacre. His pulse galloped through his veins as his ears pounded like waves crashing against the northeastern coast. *Such waste. Such hatred.*

An image of Dakeer Vasar settled into his mind's eyes; a man filled with venomous hatred for those who had slaughtered his family in his youth. Yet Dakeer was trying to be better, wasn't he?

"Take me up, please." The wind spirits carried him over the bodies and to the sweeping stairs, where he ran under his own power to the second story. The upper landing cradled more fallen warriors, but not so many as below. The crash of metal rang out at the end of the long corridor, and Lekore fled up the passage, tapestries and portraits a blur in his periphery.

He reached a door left ajar, flung it aside, and found a prayer room. Within, more than a dozen Tawloomez slaves wielding swords surrounded five Kel priests. Among the pinned priests, Lithel Kuaan, high priest of Erokel, held his blade before him, eyes raging.

Flames sparked across Lekore's fingers as the slaves whirled to face him. Eyes widened, bright in the fire glow.

"Drop your weapons and leave this building peacefully, and I shall not harm you," said Lekore. Motion from the Kel snared his attention, and he lifted a hand. "Do not provoke them. All of you will stand down."

The Kel blinked, but Lithel lowered his sword. "Do as he says. He's our new liege."

The slaves glanced between Lekore and the cornered Kel.

A Tawloomez woman clad in plain breeches and a coarse blouse turned to Lekore. "*You* are the new king the city speaks of?"

Lekore's stomach fluttered. "I am, it seems."

She looked him up and down. "There are whispers you are King Adelair's son—he who stood for the slaves."

A scent like clean air after rain and the warmth of large hands lifting him high filled Lekore's mind. "I am told as much. I think it must be so." Fire spirits danced flames over his hand. "I intend to free all of you, but first, we must defend against a coming threat from the heavens. The safest place to stay is Inpizal. Will you and your companions lay aside your weapons?"

She eyed her companions. One shook his head.

"They can't be trusted, Your Majesty," said Lithel, taking a step forward. A Tawloomez man lifted his blade toward the priest, who stopped and studied its tip, eyes crossing as he slid backward a pace.

The woman sighed. "We do not trust you, Kel King. Too long we've suffered at the hands of your people, made to undertake the grueling labors of your cities and fields."

Heat climbed Lekore's face. He squeezed his sword hilt tighter. "I *do not* own slaves, nor have you worked *my* fields. Until mere days ago, I knew nothing of these horrors. While I can imagine how angry you must feel, having no freedom, forced into slavery, the taking of lives and wanton destruction of Inpizal will only beget further hatred. And do not forget, your people have likewise taken slaves. The pain goes both directions. This violence solves nothing. Let us find a solution that mollifies all hurts."

The woman's jaw hardened. "So you say, yet the Kel began this cycle. Let *them* end it with the price of their souls."

Fire curled up Lekore's arm as a fire spirit settled on his shoulder, its frame Kel-like, hair a fiery cascade dancing down its tiny arms. Lekore let its heat wash through his veins. "Unacceptable. I will not let genocide stain the good earth over hypocrisies."

The woman scowled. "There is little you can do to—" Her eyes widened as the fire spirit sprang over Lekore's head to land on his other shoulder, taking the wreathing flames with it. Her sword arm trembled. "You cannot be *Kel*."

"He is the *Akuu-Ry*," said a slave nearby. "I've heard of him in the slums. He's the demon who rides the wind and tames the prairie fires at will. The lost heir of Erokel."

Lekore let the man's words penetrate those in the room. He allowed the fire to race up *Calir*. "I do not intend to harm either the Tawloomez or Kel, but neither will I let you tear this city apart, even should that mean employing every spirit to my cause."

As he spoke, the Tawloomez slaves tensed, and a chill crawled up Lekore's bones.

Lithel let out a stifled cry even as a Tawloomez swiped at the high priest with a blade.

"Stop!" shouted Lekore, then yelped as hands gripped his shoulders, vise-like, cold.

Someone spun him around, and he glimpsed the huge Kel called Teon before the towering man rammed a large fist into his ribs. Lekore gasped as he folded into the fist, vision flashing, then bleeding to white.

Reality slipped away as fire spirits crackled a question.

'Lekki, are you hurt?'

CHAPTER 13

A ringing sound dragged Talanee from sleep.

She sat up and raked blue hair from her face, blinking away sleep with increasing frustration. *If Ademas is trying to goad me this early in the morning—*

The city bells tolled. How long had they been pealing? She slithered from under her coverlets, pulled on slippers, threw a pale green robe over her matching nightgown, and plucked up the dagger she kept on her nightstand. She then darted across the plush carpets of her darkened bedroom.

After tossing aside the swaths of burgundy curtains hiding the balcony, she trotted out into the open air, heavy with last night's smokey scent, to survey the city as the bells fell silent.

Figures raced in the streets, some Kel, others Tawloomez slaves dressed in their drab colors. The morning light glinted off the Cathedral of the Sun's golden dome, stunning her eyes until they watered. She blinked fast and tried to spot the threat.

A gasp tore from her lips as a Kel soldier on the palace steps stumbled and fell beneath a slave's blade.

"They're in revolt?" Horror ripped down her arms as she leaned over the stone balustrade, letting her feet lift off the stone floor.

"It is time, Tala."

Talanee dropped her feet and whipped around, heart thudding against her ribs. She lifted the dagger. Upon the stone balcony, blocking the door, stood the young Tawloomez servant called Khyna. She'd been kind to Talanee in the princess's brief captivity in the Firelands. The girl smiled sadly at Talanee; long brown hair pulled back in a simple braid; dressed in the lumpish gray garb of the Teokaka's servants.

"How did you get in here?" Talanee asked.

The girl's smile wobbled. "Told to. Now is the time." The words came out halting but much less broken than she'd let on in their past encounter, and she appeared to understand Talanee well enough. Khyna lifted her hands. "Come."

As though invisible hands seized her limbs and shoved her, Talanee slipped the dagger in her robe pocket and strode toward Khyna, heartbeat growing into a frenzied drumroll. Her feet halted mere inches before the ten-year-old girl.

"What happens now?" asked Talanee, glad her voice held none of her pounding fear.

"Come." The girl turned and slipped from the balcony to enter Talanee's bedchamber, bare feet quiet on the plush carpets covering most of the polished marble floor. Talanee's legs led her after the girl though she willed herself to stay still. She opened her mouth to cry out for help, but the words caught in her throat, and she choked.

Khyna glanced back at her and shook her head. "Cannot. Do not try."

Wrath burned through Talanee's veins. She glared at the girl and tried to demand what she wanted, but again the words stuck, wedged like a chunk of meat too large to swallow. She tried to stamp her foot instead, but her limbs held fast, snared in whatever profane magic Khyna had used to bind her.

"This way." The girl crossed the room to reach the bedroom door, Talanee on her heels.

The princess's handmaid Keerva was nowhere in sight; perhaps she'd been waylaid by the city bells en route to Talanee's chambers.

She never came last night either. I hope she's alive.

Tawloomez in the palace and in the streets, slaves in revolt... and Star Gods descending in a few spare days from the heavens.

Will any of us survive?

Her mind flitted to Tora, his companions incapacitated, his sky-sailing ship broken. Could he help the Kel, or did he await a worse fate than Talanee's people?

Khyna cracked the door open and peeked out into the antechamber. The air hummed with an unsettling stillness. Khyna slipped through the gaping doorway, and Talanee followed against her will. The hearth held no flame, only the pulsing embers of the night's fire. No servants bustled about dusting, polishing, scrubbing, lighting candles. No sounds came from the corridor beyond the antechamber.

The Tawloomez girl padded to the door and peeked out at the solemn hallway. She glanced back at Talanee. "Come. Hurry."

Talanee obeyed, teeth gritted. They traveled up the palace passageway, undisturbed by the usual occupants, all missing. Several turns brought them to the main thoroughfare that connected Talanee's suite and several other halls to Lekore's wing. Here, guards lined the passage, spears gripped tight, shoulders squared, eyes vigilant.

"Take us to the Golden One," murmured Khyna.

The corridor tipped in Talanee's vision. *She wants to use me to kill the Sun God!* She curled her fists and tried to halt her steps, willed herself to whirl around and strike down the girl instead, but her feet moved, unfaltering. The guards eyed her, not with caution; one dipped his head. If they found her nightclothes surprising, they were too diplomatic to show their alarm.

"Smile and go into the king's suite. Do not give away." The girl's voice was the barest whisper. The strength of her broken words carried Talanee ahead, a smile tacked to her lips, far too natural, too nonchalant.

"Is my royal cousin up yet?" she found herself asking.

The guard nearest to the door stepped aside with a cursory glance at Khyna. "No one has stirred yet, Your Highness."

Talanee stepped into the large chamber where Lekore's morning bath awaited him, steam rising over the lip, a fire blazing. Despite the panic in Inpizal, the king's routine must be established and maintained. It made sense. None of Lekore's servants were Tawloomez. Even Father had refused to let slaves serve him personally, likely due to his growing paranoia.

Khyna shut the door behind them. Across the vast room, the servants Ginn and Benye, impeccably groomed, stood outside Lekore's bedchamber, speaking in muted tones. They looked up from their conversation and bowed to Talanee, then Ginn left the door to approach. His red eyes slid to Khyna, and his brow creased.

"A new slave, Princess?"

Talanee barked out a laugh. "An unconventional one, you might say. Is Lekore up?"

"Not that we can tell, but I..." Ginn glanced toward the bedchamber door. "I'm not certain he's *in* there. Even as a toddler, he often escaped through his window, from what Benye recalls. King Adelair and Queen Zanah had his chambers moved to the first floor to prevent an accident." He sighed. "And we may have made a mistake in setting clothes within for him to wear."

Clenching and unclenching her fists, Talanee quirked a smile. "Sounds just like my newfound cousin."

"Indeed, Your Highness. The bells might have lured him out—but we dare not check."

She speared the other bedchamber doors with a glance. "Is anyone else awake? Lord Ademas or the Sun God?"

"None, despite the clamor," said Ginn. His gaze drifted to her hands and down her dress, only a faint crease drawn in his brow. "Are you hungry, Princess Talanee? We've food."

Talanee's nails dug into her palms. *Blast you for being too tactful to ask after my wardrobe.* A smile wobbled over her lips. "Ah, no. Thank you, Ginn. I'll wait here for everyone to awaken if that's acceptable. Has anyone come to report on the trouble?"

"Not yet. The Lord Captain left to investigate." Ginn led her to the hearth and the velvet chairs angled toward the cheery flames. "Please sit, Your Highness. Perhaps a glass of wine?"

Talanee shook her head and sank into the plush wingback chair. Khyna stood beside her, silent. Despite that, an overpowering urge to dismiss the servants fell over Talanee. She set her jaw, but the words tumbled out all the same. "Perhaps you should send Benye to learn what's caused the bells to sound."

Ginn prodded at the fire with a poker. "We were just discussing that, Your Highness." He glanced at the older manservant. "Go ahead, Benye."

The man inclined his head and moved to the doors, then slipped out.

Talanee glanced around the chamber shrouded in shadows, none of the curtains drawn aside for the day. "Where are Lor'Toreth and Keo?"

"The man called Keo vanished not long ago from the very chair you sit upon." Ginn pointed to a corner near the hearth. "The Tawloomez prince slumbers just there. He's quite soundly sleeping. Benye dropped a candlestick, and the lad didn't so much as twitch."

Talanee eyed the Tawloomez prince curled up under a blanket on the floor. "After everything he's been through, I don't fault him."

Her mind skittered over the events of the past several days, culminating in the arrival of Sun Gods. She'd often imagined what their arrival might be like, but she hadn't expected Tora. He was beautiful, youthful, no older than Lekore in appearance, with flawless features. Yet he could bleed. She should've expected it, she knew that. After all, the Sun Gods of old had died in the War of Brothers, hadn't they?

Priestly scholars argued that the Sun Gods entered mortal shells to descend among their worshipers, and those shells could be slain. Add to that, gods fighting against gods, and it stood to reason they could be destroyed both temporally and spiritually.

The click of a door opening brought Talanee's gaze from Lor. Ademas staggered into sight, clothed in his disheveled breeches and green tunic of the day before. The chain strung around his neck glittered in the candle flames, the Getaal crest flashing against his chest. His hair stuck up in all directions, suggesting a restless night. He rubbed his eyes, then draped his wrist over the sword strapped at his hip. An absent smile tugged at his lips.

"Good morning, cousin."

Talanee offered a flat smile of her own. "If you'd heard the bells, you would know it's not really a good sort of morning."

He grinned wryly. "Ah, so that's what woke me." He ran his fingers through his short hair, tugging strands into a kind of carefree style. "Do we know what's happening?"

"Not yet." The taste of her lie sat like a bitter herb on her tongue. "Benye went to investigate."

He nodded and shuffled toward the windows as he tugged his tunic straight. A yawn escaped his mouth, then he shook sleep away and peeked between the curtains. "Who's your new friend?"

Talanee stiffened. "This is Khyna. She's in training. I couldn't find Keerva this morning, so she's attending me instead." The words burned, but she said them anyway. Her nails dug into her palms, tearing flesh.

"Pardon, Princess," said Ginn. "Lady Keerva resides in the dungeon. Those were your father's orders when she let you escape your carriage. She's awaiting your lord cousin's judgment."

Guilt gnawed at Talanee's stomach. She'd have to talk to Lekore about freeing the poor young woman.

Ademas glanced over his shoulder, then turned to Ginn standing at the hearth. "Is Lekore up?"

"That, I don't know, Your Highness. Perhaps you might check?"

Ademas nodded and strode to Lekore's closed door, his steps certain now. He knocked. Paused to listen. Shrugged and slipped into the chamber. The door shut. Moments passed, drawn out like the quiet before an ocean storm, then he peeked his head out. "Talanee, he wants to talk to you."

She rose and Khyna started to follow.

Ademas held out his hand. "Sorry, just the princess." He stepped into the hall and motioned Talanee into the room. As she slipped inside, he whispered, "Take your time," and shut the door after her.

She stood in the empty room; the balcony doors open wide, golden curtains floating on the airy morning breeze. The bed had been made, its pale gold coverlet smoothed, while folded sleepwear sat neatly on its end.

The hiss of an unsheathing sword sounded beyond the door behind her.

Ademas's voice came through the barrier, muffled but loud enough to understand. "Whatever you've got on the princess to make her obey you, I request you to hand it over."

Talanee slumped against the polished door and let out a low gasp, muscles loosening. *Thank the Sun Throne! He saw through my lies.*

ADEMAS GETAAL POINTED HIS BLADE AT THE TAWLOOMEZ GIRL, cool anger pumping through his veins.

The girl sighed and lowered her eyes. "This I cannot do. I am under orders."

"To do what, precisely?"

The girl looked up, brown eyes bright with pain. "To destroy the Golden One. Tala must obey. She must end the god's life, that is all."

He snorted. "Right. Just that, only end the life of a Sun God. Sure." He took a step toward the Tawloomez. "But I won't let you succeed."

She held fast. "You cannot stop me. Tala, come."

The door behind Ademas opened, and Talanee came out, eyes

burning with silent fury. She clutched a dagger and held it against her own throat.

"You must choose," said the Tawloomez girl. "Your god or your princess."

Fury clawed at Ademas's chest like wild beasts begging to be unleashed. He ignored the beasts and shrugged. "Fine. Slit her throat. I'll not risk my soul over a mortal princess."

The Tawloomez girl's brow twitched downward. She stared into his eyes, searching. He eyed her back, confident he would give nothing of his feelings away. Mother had taught him too well for that. He allowed a smile to curl at the corner of his mouth, and the girl staggered back a step.

"You would not sacrifice your own kin..." She caught her lip with her teeth and stared at Talanee.

"Better that than let you have your way," Ademas said. "Trust me, the princess will be glad I chose to sacrifice her life rather than risk a Sun God. If you don't believe me, just ask her."

He caught motion in his peripheral view, but he didn't glance toward it. Likely, the Lord Captain crept toward the little girl, ready to cut her down to spare the princess. Ademas waggled his sword to keep the girl's attention.

"Looks like we're in a deadlock," he said.

Her mouth worked, eyes dancing between him and Talanee. "I must succeed. Tala, kill your cousin."

Talanee let out a choked cry as she turned her blade on Ademas, who parried with his sword. The dagger thudded to the floor, and Talanee's fingers twitched as tears rolled down her cheeks.

"It's all right, cousin," he said. "I'll never let you hurt me."

She darted forward, hands stretched before her, aiming for his throat. Ademas dropped his sword and wrapped his arms around her, pulling her tight against his chest to pin her arms. Talanee's body trembled, despite her tense muscles. Her tears dampened his shirt as she pressed her face into his chest.

"Kill him, Tala!" cried the girl.

Ademas gripped Talanee tighter and glanced at the Tawloomez girl as the figure in his periphery crept up behind her. Not the Lord Captain.

Mother.

She plunged a knife into the Tawloomez's back, red eyes storming. The girl's eyes bulged, then glassed over. She stumbled and slumped forward. Fell to the ground, the knife lodged in her ribs.

Talanee's tense muscles relaxed at once. She drew back and turned her face to stare down at the body. Tears sparkled in her eyes. "She controlled my limbs, Ademas. I couldn't fight her. The same thing happened while we were in the Firelands. She controlled me then, but only for a moment."

"That's a nasty bit of sorcery." Ademas wrapped an arm around Talanee's shoulders. "But it's over now. She's dead."

"No." Lor's voice drifted from where he sat in his blanket. "She's not."

The girl's body twitched. Her head lifted, and she stared unseeing before her, then blinked light into her eyes. The knife clattered to the floor as her wound closed. Her brown gaze flicked up to meet Ademas's, and her gentle smile reappeared. "That was painful."

Chills sprinted over Ademas's flesh. "What are you?"

The girl's smile broadened. "I am part god. The Teokaka is my mother."

CHAPTER 14

Barking orders, Nerenoth marched up the palace corridors, armor clanking, as the cathedral bells thrummed in his ears. Palace guards scrambled to attention, saluted, then raced off to fortify defenses, as Nerenoth paced toward the front doors.

He met Lord Lieutenant Rez Kuaan halfway as the bells fell silent.

"Sir," Rez said without preamble. "The slaves are in revolt."

A weight settled in Nerenoth's chest. "You're certain?"

"Yes, sir."

Nerenoth whirled on the nearest gaggle of guards. "Secure the servant corridors. Keep all Tawloomez servants and slaves from coming into the main palace hallways. Understood?"

"Sir, yes, sir!" They snapped off hasty salutes and tromped off to obey, dark green capes billowing after them.

Nerenoth squeezed his eyes shut. *Why now, so close to reform?* He opened his eyes and headed again for the front doors. "With me, Rez."

"Sir, shouldn't you remain with the king?"

Nerenoth sighed. "I sincerely doubt he's still in the palace. He ran off alone to stop that fire last night. Despite anything we might say, Lekore is accustomed to his independence. I doubt he thinks before he leaps into action."

Rez grunted agreement.

They reached the double doors as the sounds of combat rang out beyond the closed barriers. A dozen guards stood at attention, blades drawn.

Nerenoth unsheathed his sword. "Open them."

The guards pushed the doors aside to reveal several dozen Tawloomez slaves battling against the palace watch on the front steps. Metal clanged and scraped across the courtyard. Several bodies stained the stone stairs, Kel and Tawloomez alike. Screams tore the air in Inpizal proper beyond the palace walls. The gates had been broken and hung on their hinges, splintered, the ornate workmanship of the wood destroyed.

Nerenoth sprinted down the steps and stabbed a Tawloomez through the arm. He pulled his sword free and swung to knock aside the cudgel another Tawloomez held in clumsy fingers.

"Cease your fighting!" His voice rang out over the palace grounds. "Full quarter will be given to all slaves who lay their weapons aside without further violence. If you continue to resist, I will cut you down."

Several Tawloomez dropped their makeshift weapons at once. Others maintained their struggle against the guards.

"Take those who surrender to safety, lieutenant."

"Yes, sir." Rez moved off to comply.

Nerenoth blocked a Tawloomez's swinging spear, then dodged right and slashed at the man's chest. Blood spurted from the wound, and the slave collapsed against the steps.

Such a waste. They were nearly free.

He cast a glance skyward, wondering where Lekore had vanished. *What would he do here? Surely, he would hate to lose so many lives, no matter their race and creed.*

How could Nerenoth prevent unnecessary bloodshed?

He spun and deflected a slave's sword. Sidestepped. Caught the enemy's blade and shoved, forcing the slave to lose his footing.

Nerenoth lopped the man's head off with a powerful stroke. The severed head rolled down the steps as slaves backed away, eyes wide. Several more dropped their weapons.

"Is this not enough?" Nerenoth eyed the rebel slaves.

Not slaves. My king would not call them that. They're people, not property.

He strode down the steps, glancing between the frightened faces of Tawloomez men and women. Some were old; some too young to lift the weapons they clutched. He drew a breath. "The new king of Erokel intends to free you—to let you return to the Firelands or to give you a parcel of land all your own outside the rule of either nation. This bloodshed serves no purpose but to waste the lives of good Kel and good Tawloomez."

"Lies!" cried a Tawloomez man.

Nerenoth wheeled on him, white cape flaring. "*Truth.* King Adelair's son has returned to claim his birthright. He's not like other Kel; he's not subject to your prejudice or mine. He wishes to make amends."

Murmurs swelled from the ranks of the plain garbed rebels. They eyed one another. Most knew of King Adelair. Many revered him for his kindness before his death. Legends of his lost heir had taken root among the slums where slaves made their homes; that he would return; that he would set them free.

Nerenoth read the fragile hope in their faces. They clustered together, most of them. A few stood apart, hatred scarring their faces, unmoved by the promise of freedom. Likely, that hatred had been festering for decades under the rule of their masters.

It's like Adelair said. Slavery is wrong.

Nerenoth had never known what to believe. Had never thought about it until Adelair brought it up in private conversations. The practice of slavery had existed so long in Erokel, and the Tawloomez had practiced it in their own lands. It had been a matter of course. A consequence of war against a heathen race.

But Lor'Toreth was more than a savage who worshipped Snake

Gods. He was an adolescent, younger than Lekore by several years. Frightened but determined. Made of flesh, bone, blood, just as any Kel.

They're people.

Why did the fact surprise him?

I have much to learn.

The clack of a pythe's taloned feet brought Nerenoth's eyes to the broken gates. Between the hanging barriers, the Sun God appeared on the back of the reptilian mount whose green scales flashed in the climbing sunlight. The slaves whirled. One shrieked. Others backed away from the Golden One.

Nerenoth strode toward him as Toranskay loped closer, slitted eyes of blue surveying the carnage in the courtyard and upon the steps.

The Sun God halted his pythe. "Lekore is dueling the Teokaka outside the city gates. She has your former king and tried to use him as a hostage. Lekore asked me to return and help you. The entire city is locked in combat, slaves against their masters." His frown deepened, and he shifted in his saddle. "Those who saw me along the main road ceased to fight. Many followed me here."

Nerenoth noted the Kel and Tawloomez peering through the smashed gates, then laid a hand on the pythe's scaly muzzle. "Might you proclaim your will to the city and compel all fighting to cease, Holy One?"

Toranskay shifted again, something like pain flashing in his pale eyes. "I can, I think. I'll need access to the throne room. Is it secure?"

Nerenoth hefted his sword. "If not, I shall clear the way."

The Sun God swung gracefully from the pythe, tugged his borrowed clothes straight, and nodded. "Lead on, Lord Captain."

A silent throng followed the Sun God and his escort through the palace until they reached the throne room. No one intercepted them. Again, Toranskay positioned himself upon the sun motif and drew a console from the floor. His fingers flew over symbols, a blue-stone signet ring flashing as he worked. A window of light flickered and scrawled upon the open air above him. The wonder of it was no less for Nerenoth now than before. Perhaps it only grew, knowing others looked on the scene for the first time.

Behold the power of a Sun God.

Toranskay's fingers halted, and he stepped back a pace as a sound chimed from the console. The god's visage appeared on a new, larger window of light at the head of the chamber, his appearance enlarged yet pristine as though his head and shoulders hovered there. He drew a breath and spoke. Toranskay's words flooded the throne room like they thundered from the heavens, filling the space between the domed ceiling and the marble floor.

"Citizens of Erokel, Tawloomez guests, and all else within the sound of my voice: I am Tora, ambassador to the Sun Throne of Ahvenia. Your two nations stand in crisis, but this isn't a crisis of two countries alone. A terrible threat will soon descend from the stars. When that threat arrives, it means no good will to anyone. It is a domineering, deadly evil, intent upon destruction for its own sake. To this evil, your lives are an amusement, nothing more.

"I ask each of you to set aside your differences, no matter how hurt, frightened, or angry you may feel. If you live in the outer cities of Erokel, head for your capital, where I will erect a shield to protect you. If you're from the Tawloomez lands, remain here just the same, so that the shield will protect you as well. Those within the Firelands will be protected by a man called Keo, so rest your worries in that knowledge. Your families are safe."

Toranskay hesitated. "Should you feel the coming threat to be your ally, depart from our protection if you choose, but know that it will likely end in your suffering. These beings are cruel and deceptive and very hard to destroy."

His strange eyes narrowed a fraction. "To those within the city of Inpizal, I say again, cease your fighting. The new king of Erokel intends to free all Tawloomez slaves. He's already freed all Kel slaves from the Firelands. Do not begin his reign with needless bloodshed. Work to establish peace between your lands. No matter the coloring of your bodies, your souls are the same."

He stepped forward and pressed a button. The large window vanished, and his voice echoed the last phrase once more before all fell into silence.

Nerenoth strode forward to halt beside the console. "Did everyone hear your words?"

"Everyone within your Sun Cities. Not the villages. But word should spread quickly." Toranskay leaned against the console, golden hair falling into his face. "It's the best I can do."

He's still young. Nerenoth rested a hand on the god's shoulder. "It will be enough, Holy One."

"I hope so." Toranskay tapped a few buttons, and the console slipped back beneath the marble floor, leaving no sign it had ever risen. "The Teokaka's still a problem if Lekore can't contain her."

Nerenoth eyed the commoners standing around the chamber beneath the fluttering sunburst pennants. Lord Lieutenant Rez stood at the doors, troops of red and green caped soldiers behind him, all with eyes pinned on the Sun God.

Nerenoth suppressed a smile. "Lieutenant, report."

Rez saluted. "Sir, we heard the Sun God's message. And that—that's all. Request permission to assess the situation in the streets, sir."

"Permission granted. Report back soon."

"Yes, sir." Rez clapped his hand to his breastplate, then pivoted and marched between his men to head for the streets, long hair whipping behind him. His troop followed.

Nerenoth turned back to Toranskay. "If it's all right, I should check on those remaining in Lekore's suites. Prince Ademas is likely as reckless as his brother, and their cousin is little better. I should also like to make certain our half-blood guests from last night remain quartered and under guard."

"Certainly. I'll accompany you."

They strode across the throne room to a side door, Nerenoth noting the worshipful eyes tracking them in silence. No one stirred. At the door, Nerenoth turned around to face the crowd. "If you need something to do, I'm certain there are wounded who need tending."

The Tawloomez woman who met his gaze blinked. Nodded. She motioned to her companions. "Let's help out."

Kel guards followed them. Swords remained sheathed. They all walked together.

CHAPTER 15

Khyna climbed to her feet.

Talanee drew back, bones shuddering as her chest constricted.

Ademas reclaimed his blade though he still held her close. "Now what?" he asked Khyna. "I won't let you achieve your goal, no matter how many times we have to kill you. That leaves us few options."

"I am under orders," said the girl. "I will not surrender." Her chocolate eyes slid to Talanee. She said nothing, but Khyna's will seized Talanee again. The princess lunged for Ademas's sword, but he swung his hand out of reach and pressed her nearer to keep her from her lethal mission. His cinnamon scent tickled Talanee's nose.

In the same moment, Lor leapt onto Khyna, and the two crumpled to the floor in a heap. Limbs thrashed as Lor tried to plunge a bone knife into the girl's chest. Her nails caught his cheek and tore skin; he snatched and pinned her wrist, then swiped the knife across her throat. Foamy blood bloomed on her lips as her body thrashed, then fell still. Lor remained atop her, holding down her arms with a foot and one hand.

"Will she come back?" asked Ademas. He still held Talanee,

though she'd stopped wrestling against him when the girl died, the irresistible urge to murder him gone.

"Yes," Lor said through gritted teeth. As the girl twitched to life, he slit her throat again. "I do not know what might happen if I keep killing her, but what else can I do?"

Ademas released Talanee and moved to the girl's side.

Talanee stayed back, gripping her disheveled robes close, fear weighing down her legs. *How do I free myself from her control?*

Khyna moaned. Ademas sank his blade into her heart.

An ache grew in the back of Talanee's throat. She looked away, dragging strands of long hair from her face. *Why does this bother me? I don't care about Tawloomez. They're heathens!*

When she'd first met Khyna, the girl had stopped to rescue a spider stuck inside the Tawloomez palace. She'd spoken kindly to Talanee, led her gently, not treated her like a lesser being.

But she's part Star God. She's fallen.

Talanee took a step. Faltered. *Even if she is kind, she intends to kill the Sun God. She means to use me.* Talanee backed up. "I can't stay here, Ademas. She'll try to control me again."

He looked up from the captive girl. "You're right. But you need to avoid Lord Tora as well, just in case she can command from afar." His eyes scanned the room and paused on the door where the god slumbered.

A chime tolled over the air, and a window of light flickered into life near the chamber's main doors. Tora's fair face appeared, and he spoke, words steady and calm as he asked for the fighting in Inpizal to stop. Talanee held her breath as she listened until dizziness caused the floor to wobble, and she gulped in air. The hovering window faded after he finished, and the room fell still.

The Sun God's words echoed through Talanee's head. '*No matter the coloring of your bodies, your souls are the same.*'

Lor slit Khyna's throat again.

"How many times is that?" Ademas asked.

"Six," said Lady Zanah, keeping vigil over the morbid affair.

Talanee groaned. "How do we end this?" Her stomach twisted.

If Tawloomez are equal to Kel, does that apply to Khyna as well, even though she's partly a fallen goddess?

Her stomach twisted more as she thought of the Blood Rite. Of all those Tawloomez infants sacrificed. Of Lekore's reaction to that event.

How could our doctrine be so wrong? Why did the gods not correct us sooner?

"Let me take her."

Talanee choked down a scream as she whirled. The man called Keo stood behind her, green eyes locked on the Tawloomez girl.

"I can keep her unconscious for a while, far from Inpizal," Keo said. "That should help. She's only quarter-Kiisuld, so not much of a challenge for me."

"Thank the blessed earth," said Lor. "I'll be tired before too long."

Keo strode past Talanee and knelt before the body. "Don't think the Kiisuld on their way here will be so easy to overpower."

Talanee scowled. "Of course not. They're full-blooded gods; she's not."

Keo glanced at her with a crooked smile. "Something like that." He gripped Khyna's arm as breath fluttered through her lips. He eyed her. "Time to go, little girl."

Khyna whimpered. "No, please—"

They vanished on the spot.

Ademas sighed and scratched the back of his head. "Well, that's two crises averted, assuming the people listen to Holy Tora. Now we just have to face the greatest hurdle head on. Good thing we've got three days to figure it out."

Talanee rolled her eyes. "Your humor is in bad taste, cousin."

He shrugged as Lady Zanah gave a faint nod.

A knock sounded on the doors.

"Come," called Ademas.

A soldier poked his head inside the room. "Beg your pardon, Your Highnesses. Lords Jesh and Jeth have arrived and request to see you."

"Show them in."

The guard stepped aside and admitted the Irothé twins, both disheveled, sweat stained, with their long blue hair half unbound from their tails. The twins' red eyes scoured the room.

"Where's Nerenoth?" asked Jeth—it was probably Jeth.

"We don't know," Ademas said. "We've been a bit preoccupied."

Jesh elbowed his brother. "It doesn't matter. We came because the cathedral fell under heavy attack. Jeth and I rushed there but got a bit sidetracked." He lifted his left hand to reveal heavy bandages. "By the time we reached the chamber where the Sun Gods slept, one had awakened and...and, well, slaughtered all the Star Worshipers who tried to kill him. The room's a mess. You should see it."

"That's not the point though," said Jeth.

Jesh grimaced. "No. It's not. Point is, the Hakija is missing. He was reported heading for the same chamber ahead of us, but he never arrived. Likely, the Star Worshipers took him. No sign of His Holiness's body anywhere."

"That's not all." Jeth scratched his neck where a trickle of blood had dried. "A servant found High Priest Lithel badly wounded. Still alive but no one knows if he'll pull through. Other priests with him were all dead. Lithel woke up long enough to tell the servant that Lekore had been there but—"

"Got taken," Jesh finished.

Jeth nodded. "Yeah. Exactly."

The door swung open and Nerenoth strode into the chamber, Tora at his back, a slew of guards behind them.

"I just received word that Lekore is in the hands of Star Worshipers," said Nerenoth, eyes ablaze like the sun. "We must organize a troop to take the Temple of the Moon."

CHAPTER 16

The drip, drip, drip of water lifted Lekore's thoughts from deep ravines. As his mind settled into his body, his ribs throbbed. His heartbeat pounded against his skull. A hiss slipped from his lips when he tried to shift. The odor of mildew and dust stirred under him.

"Steady, Your Highness."

Lekore cracked his eyes open. A shaft of torchlight from beyond the closed door illuminated a strip of the otherwise darkened chamber, revealing Dakeer Vasar kneeling beside him on the cold, moldering stone floor. A dark bruise stained Dakeer's cheek, and he clutched his side with one hand over his soiled vestments.

Lekore sat up and gasped, ribs protesting. As Dakeer caught his arms to hold him still, stars flickered in Lekore's vision.

"The brute who brought you here was anything but gentle, Your Highness. It is likely you have a few cracked ribs, and your legs are a bit torn up. He may have dragged you partway."

Partway to where? Lekore let the Hakija ease him back until he could lean against a dank stone wall. His ribs burned. He lifted a hand and willed fire to roll onto his fingertips—but the spirits didn't answer. He frowned through his muddled thoughts until, like a breaking bone, knowledge snapped into his mind.

I'm back in the Temple of the Moon. Chills needled up his arms until his neck hairs bristled. His eyes settled on Dakeer.

"Why are you here?"

Dakeer shrugged. "Apart from you, I am perhaps most significant to them. Certainly, I'm least loved by their order."

"They have a Hakija, too." Memories of the man danced across Lekore's eyes, dark and soft like silken death.

Dakeer frowned. "Yes. I know of him." He shifted to stare at the rough-hewn door where the torch beyond danced through the bars of the window slot. "We must find some means of escape, if possible. Might the wind help us?"

Lekore sighed. "My communication with the Spirits Elemental is severed in this unhallowed place."

The Hakija nodded. "Well, we'll have to seek other avenues until the Lord Captain comes to our rescue. Better to try than sit here waiting." He stood and strode toward the door, then halted as the faint scuff of boots approached down the outside corridor. Swift and silent, the Hakija padded back to Lekore and knelt beside him.

The scuffs stopped outside the dingy cell, and red eyes peered inside through the window slot. "They're awake, Your Holiness."

"Open it. Stay vigilant."

Keys jangled, then shrieked in the lock. The door swung open and the slim figure of the Dark Hakija stepped inside the cell. Behind him, Teon entered clutching a torch to illuminate the ruins of the dank chamber.

Dakeer stiffened. "*You?*"

The young man smiled, face contorted in the firelight. "Greetings, Dakeer Vasar. It's a pleasure to meet you as equals at long last."

Dakeer's lips lifted in a sneer. "We are not equal, Farr Veon. You serve fallen gods."

Farr Veon chuckled. "According to *your* doctrine, perhaps. But let's not haggle over such small matters. You and" —his gaze slid to Lekore, smile growing— "Lekore Adenye Getaal are my guests. I welcome you warmly."

Lekore shrank back as his arm throbbed where this man had cut it to summon the Kiisuld using his Seer blood.

Dakeer scoffed. "This chamber is hardly warm or welcoming."

"A temporary measure, Hakija. I assure you, once our gods have arrived, you'll be made much more comfortable above ground. At present, we know the Lord Captain will attempt to save you. We had to be certain he couldn't easily manage the deed. Never let it be said I underestimated that man."

Farr Veon stepped closer to Lekore. "I was distraught to find you gone so soon after our first meeting, but I acknowledge that my haste must've scared you. For that, I'm truly repentant. My strongest failing is often my zeal, though it serves me well in church matters."

He crouched before Lekore. "Forgive me for frightening you, Your Majesty. I knew then you were special, but I didn't grasp the extent of your position. You are the first king since Skye Getaal who bears the favor of the Star Gods. I should have guessed. I should have felt it. I shall do all I can to make amends henceforth, my beloved king."

Staring into those eyes, chills prickled at Lekore's flesh like the poison barbs of the Wildwood. He tore his gaze away. "Please let us go. Do not keep us in this fell place."

The Dark Hakija sighed. "Alas, that's not a command I can yet obey. It's for your sake I keep you here, away from the battles above. Inpizal has gone mad. Best to protect you. Soon, my king, your gods will come to claim you." Farr Veon reached out and stroked Lekore's cheek. "Bear up under these conditions a little longer. They arrive in just three days' time."

Lekore pressed his eyes shut. "They will only kill me."

"Ah, no. Not that." Farr Veon pulled his hand away, and his dark clothes rustled as he stood. "They *need* you. It's part of our scripture. Fear not, young king; you are greater than you know."

His footsteps retreated to the door, followed by the heavy thud of Teon's boots. The door swung shut, and the lock tumbled back into place.

Lekore opened his eyes to stare into the fresh darkness.

Dakeer's hand gripped his shoulder. "Hope is not lost yet, Your Highness. The Sun God will guide the Lord Captain here much sooner than three days. We'll yet be freed."

Lekore drew his legs to his chest and hugged them. He buried his face against his knees. "I pray you are right, Hakija. But that will not stop the Kiisuld from coming, and my fate may yet remain the same." His thoughts flicked to Ank, captured by the Teokaka. She'd been encircled by Lekore's flames, but that must have ended the moment he reached the Temple of the Moon. She'd be free again. Would she kill Ank? Would Lekore ever see him again?

"Skye..." His whisper trembled on his lips.

The Hakija's fingers dug into his shoulder, then retreated. A faint sigh sang in the air. "Tell me about him."

Lekore looked up. "What?"

The Hakija's eyes bored holes into the floor, brows drawn low, mouth twisted down, like he carried a tremendous weight. "All my days, even as a youth, I've heard dread stories of Skye Getaal—he who betrayed his people and sold his soul to the Star Gods. Never have I doubted them...until you. Until all this." His hand circled the air. "Now, my faith, though strengthened by the Sun Gods' presence, knows not what to believe of our tenets. 'Twas Erokel the Second, brother of Skye, who declared enslavement acceptable, even preferable. He slew the first infants born of Tawloomez slaves as our founding Hakija and king."

Dakeer drew a deep, shuddering breath. "But now...both you and His Eminence the Holy God Tora say that Erokel deceived us, that Skye was worthy and..." His head dipped further. "Tell me about him. Please."

Lekore shifted as his ribs ached. "He is a solitary fellow, often sad. He seldom speaks of his wife and child, stolen by his brother. Only twice has he mentioned Naal, describing her like a wild storm none but he could calm. He speaks most of the early days with his brother, Erokel. The good days, when they traveled the deep woods together before the trees grew too wild and dangerous —before the Ahvenians tainted them. Back then, our people dwelt within the forest."

"Did we?" Dakeer's eyes fell on him. "That I've never heard."

"After the Kel claimed these grasslands and the Sun Cities for themselves, Erokel rewrote much to bury his guilt. He burned records under the guise of rebellion. Yet Skye has witnessed *all*."

"Why does he remain? To exact revenge upon we who followed his brother?"

"No." Lekore smiled. "He is not a vengeful specter. He seeks to right his brother's wrongs. To return truth to our people."

"There are no portraits of Skye within the kingdom. What does he look like?"

Lekore closed his eyes. "He is built on slender bones, much as I am, though he is taller. His hair, too, is an almost-white blue, though shorter than most Kel men I've encountered. He wears the armor from the moment of his death, much like the armor littering the Vale That Shines Gold. You call it the Charnel Valley."

"I know the style of that armor, though I've never been to the Charnel Valley."

"You should see it." Lekore opened his eyes. "It is not a bad place, though sometimes it is sad. Skye's ghost is not alone. Many more wander that realm, silent, waiting. Some are Kel, others are Tawloomez, others still are Ahvenian."

"Ahvenian." Dakeer spoke the word gently. "Is this the holy name of the Sun Gods?"

Lekore dropped his gaze as his gut twisted. "It is what Tora's people are called."

"How wondrous these days are."

"Hakija?" Lekore shifted, curious but wary.

"Yes, Your Highness?"

"Do you despise me?"

Dakeer changed position, grit grinding under his weight. "No, my prince. I...harbor conflicted emotions, many I've yet to sort. Some regard you; all regard myself. Long have I let hatred steer my course and, as a result, the course of the church. I've allowed many to die for my private causes—including your good father. I saw him as a weak man. Only now can I honor his strength for what it was, as I witness my own terrible weakness. My *blindness*." He rubbed his face. "Greater truth than I have ever known stands before me and all Erokel, yet I feel more lost than I have since..." His eyes narrowed as sorrow teemed from his frame. "You saw my past once. You described it."

"I also dreamt it," said Lekore. "I dreamt I was you, bound to a well, your family rotting beneath the hot sun."

"Ah." Dakeer trembled. "Then you know my secret pains. You understand my motivations."

"I think I do, yet I do not understand revenge. I do not understand how such actions might help to heal a soul. Nothing is brought back."

"No, indeed. Yet the feelings come, nonetheless. I pray you never understand, my prince. It's best if you do not."

An hour or longer passed in somber silence. Lekore's ribs sent stabbing pulses through his body, each drip of water agitating the pain. Dakeer nursed his own wounds between snatches of prayers muttered under his breath.

The scrape and scuff of boots and lighter steps outside the cell lifted their heads as one. The brattling of keys followed, and the door opened. Light pooled over the floor, revealing Teokaka Susunee. Beside her stood Hakija Farr Veon, a smile tacked on his lips, eyes like blood in the guttering flames.

"Nerenoth Irothé has begun gathering a force to storm our temple," Farr Veon said. "You should know he will not succeed. Not before our gods have arrived. Not even with the Sun God who walks with him." Farr gestured to Susunee. "I'm certain you're acquainted with one another but let me be clear: We acknowledge the divinity of the Snake Goddess, sired by the Moon Prince when last he descended to this sphere. We are allied." His eyes speared Dakeer. "She has asked for your blood, Hakija of the Sun."

Dakeer lifted his chin. "I will resist."

Lekore stood with one swift motion, ribs thrumming. "Do not touch him, Susunee."

The woman's smile stretched. "Defy me at great risk to your precious *Ank*'s health, Kel King." The notes of her words hummed a false tone.

"You're lying." Lekore took a step forward.

Beneath his gaze, Susunee slinked backward, a quiver of fear strumming over her heart. "Are you willing to risk that, *Akuu-Ry*?"

"There is no need for all this," Farr cut in. "The Snake Goddess shall have the Hakija, but not yet. His life is required to keep your sun worshipping Kel from doing anything rash. She merely wanted to confirm you were both well contained."

Susunee's tongue darted over her red lips. "I understand your powers are stifled in this temple, dear little king. How uncomfortable that must make you." She shifted her slim shoulders, only partially covered by her snakeskin gown, and held his gaze. "I wonder what renders you so utterly powerless."

Farr Veon waved his hands to encompass the cell. "A blessing from the Voice of the Stars, he who was our first Hakija, even Skye Getaal."

Faint lines appeared between Susunee's brows as waves of disgust pulsed from her frame. "Perhaps. More likely it was the blessing of my holy father."

Lekore looked between them. *Allies, they may be. But their doctrine does not align as much as they pretend.* Could he use that? Should he agitate the fragile bonds of their cooperation? *It may cost both Ank and Dakeer if I anger them too much.*

What should he do?

"I see the wheels of your mind turning," breathed Farr, a smile sparkling in his eyes like frost. "Best not to act with haste as you're wont to do. A burning building may not offer much risk to one with your talents, yet this situation is far different. Many lives are at stake should you choose a wrong step."

Lekore bowed his head. "This I know well."

"Good. Now, answer one question. When last you came to this temple, one of my men took you to your room. Teon can attest to that much. *Someone* helped you escape after slaying your guard. Who was that?"

Lekore looked up. "I will not tell you."

"Not even to spare Netye's life?"

Lekore shook his head. "You would be supremely foolish to waste your leverage on one thread of information. Reconsider."

Farr chuckled. "A fair point. I'll leave it be for now, but when our Star Gods arrive, rest assured, I will learn all."

Lekore let out a faint sigh. "Beware, Hakija of the Night. *All* may be more than you wish to know."

CHAPTER 17

"I know a secret way in, Lord Captain."

Nerenoth looked up from the maps strewn across the table of the War Room to eye Ademas.

The chamber had been stuffed to capacity, from Lord Toranskay; the Getaal royals—including the newly arrived Elekel, intent on rescuing his nephew—and Rez; a handful of other officers; and several high-ranking Sun Priests.

Ademas leaned over the table, waiting for Nerenoth's response.

Nerenoth stifled a grimace. "What a curious piece of knowledge to have, Your Highness."

Amusement glinted in the young man's eyes. "I like to be prepared." He leaned closer. "Use the troops as a distraction while we lead a handful of skilled fighters into the temple. We'll locate Lekore and His Holiness and get them out."

"A simple solution in theory."

Lady Zanah, gowned in deep red, tapped her fingernails against the tabletop where she sat to Nerenoth's left. "Do you find too many flaws in his plan?"

"There are always flaws in any viable plan," Nerenoth said. "Yet I'm excruciatingly aware that the cost of failure is of the highest caliber. We *cannot* fail." He leaned back, eyes tracing the inked lines depicting the unholy temple on the city map. "Likely, Prince Ademas's plan is our best option. Even so, my heart rests uneasy."

"Surely," piped up Priest Het, a man of considerable girth but a swift blade, "from what we've seen of our restored king, he can get himself *and* the Holy Hakija out of that abominable place. He wields fire and tames storms! What reason do we have to march upon that accursed temple?"

Ademas shot him a scowl reminiscent of his father's scalding gaze. "Once already, Lekore has been a prisoner in that place. Could he have escaped on his own, he doubtless would've—which leaves me to surmise somehow he can't."

"Perhaps light and goodness cannot dwell in such a domicile," another priest said.

"There are stretches of land where only vile darkness can thrive," Toranskay said, hushing the room at once. "If the ground beneath that temple was blighted by Kiisuld magic, it's possible the Spirits Elemental would never have the strength to breach its borders. Likely, wholesome ghosts would also avoid it at all costs."

Nerenoth sighed and tapped a gloved finger on the table. "That settles that. We cannot assume Lekore capable of freeing himself, let alone the Hakija. We must act accordingly." His mind turned over his options. "We cannot—"

Someone knocked on the chamber door. A priest opened it and allowed a liveried servant to enter, gripping a platter, a sealed scroll resting on its polished silver surface.

"Lord Captain, for you." The servant's voice quavered.

"Bring it here."

The servant plowed through the crowd of officials, then faltered as he noted Toranskay on Nerenoth's right. To his credit, the servant squared his shoulders and stepped near enough to offer the platter to Nerenoth.

The Lord Captain plucked the scroll up and broke the seal. He unrolled the heavy parchment and devoured the scrawl, then read it again. Looked up. "We've received terms from our enemy. The Hakija of the Night knows better than to threaten Lekore's life.

Instead, he holds our Hakija under threat of torture and death if we attack them before the Star Gods arrive."

Murmurs swept the room. Nerenoth read fear, indignation, fury, hatred across the Kel faces. Toranskay stirred beside him. The room fell still enough to hear the hiss of the torches set in sconces between the wall tapestries.

Toranskay tapped the map. "Then our only option is to sneak into the temple as Lord Ademas suggests. We'll need to create a diversion other than brute force to avoid provoking your enemy." His frown deepened. "I'm afraid I'll be of little use in this. If the Kiisuld taint is strong enough to repel Spirits Elemental, I'll likely be incapacitated should I get too near. I'd best remain here and get the shield operating at full power."

Ademas rapped the table with his knuckles. "Let me lead the team, Lord Captain. I'll select a few skilled and trustworthy Kel. You'll need to be seen in the city, supervising the refugees' arrival and the aftermath of the slave revolt. Let me manage this, and I swear, I'll get them out."

Nerenoth tensed and turned his gaze to the table, vision blurring. With a sigh, he nodded and let his eyes refocus. "Your arguments are valid, though I wish they weren't. Will you agree to bring Jesh and Jeth?"

"Already planned to." Ademas's smile brightened his eyes. "I'd like to request the Lord Lieutenant as well, in your stead."

Another knock struck the door. The same priest answered it, listened, then shut the door. The messenger never came in. With a drawn brow, the priest approached the table. "O Holy God, your fellows have arrived and are resting in the wing set aside for your use. One called Raren demands to see you."

Toranskay inclined his head. "Thank you." He looked at Nerenoth. "I'll speak with you again soon. I shouldn't keep Raren waiting." He slipped through the crowd as all parted for him, then stepped out into the corridor. Nerenoth signaled two guards to follow.

Motion snared the Lord Captain's attention. He found Talanee, draped in a green sleeping robe, staring down Ademas with a sort of frenzied determination glowing in her red gaze.

"Out of the question, Princess," said Nerenoth, fingers curling against the table's surface, his chest taut.

Talanee scowled. "But I—"

"Under no circumstance will you enter that temple to become another possible hostage. That I send your lord cousin hurts too much already. I shan't risk you."

She scowled as her cheeks reddened. "Very well."

Ademas cleared his throat. "You have a good soldier in your ranks, Lord Captain. Carak, by name, yes?"

Nerenoth nodded. "He is that."

"Do you need him?"

"Take him, if you wish."

Lady Zanah stood. "And one more. Ademas will take one of my own contacts."

Ademas inclined his head. "As you please, Lady Mother." He stood up. "I'll collect those I've requested, and we'll begin planning our strategy this moment. Jesh, Jeth, Lord Lieutenant." He glanced at Zanah. "Mother?"

The five moved out of the room, allowing a little more breathing space. Nerenoth resented handing such a dangerous mission to Ademas and the twins, but what could he do? With a sigh, he tapped the map where the palace gates had been inked. "We must start with repairs, as well as continue to clean up the carnage left from today's revolt, and we should double the watch on the city walls until that Tawloomez camp retreats."

As voices lifted to pour out suggestions, Nerenoth leaned back and willed his face to reveal nothing, even as his legs ached for action. His fingers drummed the arms of his chair. Voices grated against his nerves.

Be calm and trust others to do all they can. You cannot be in every place at once. Ademas will rescue Lekore and Dakeer. Best you remain here to defend your city—and your Sun Gods.

ADEMAS STRODE ALONG THE PALACE CORRIDOR, MOTHER AT HIS side. "Whom do you wish to send with me, Lady Mother?"

"Myself."

His heart missed a beat, though he'd anticipated her answer. He nodded. *I'd be a fool to argue with the will of a woman obsessed.* "I'll agree, but only if you act under my orders."

"I've no issue with that," she said.

Firm steps behind Ademas resounded in his head like the reassuring beat of war drums. "Lord Lieutenant."

"Your Highness?" said Rez.

"Send for Carak if you would. We'll meet up in Lekore's suite and plot our move there. I've a few things to gather, myself. Mother, will you and the twins go ahead?"

She nodded and turned off at the next corridor, Jesh and Jeth on her heels. Ademas and Rez split at the next passageway, leaving Ademas alone with his thoughts.

He marched toward the small chapel tucked into a corner of the palace near Father's old study—the room where he'd fallen to his death eighteen years before. The chapel had been the king's private sanctuary, a place he hid to work out his deepest feelings as Erokel's ruler. Mother spoke of it like a place more sacred than the Cathedral of the Sun, and to her, that might be true. Queen Zanah worshiped her husband's memory like he'd been a god.

When Ademas first arrived in Erokel one month ago, he'd come in secret to acquaint himself with the streets of the city, its people in their several castes, Uncle Elekel with his eccentricities and concealed disdain for King Netye. Ademas had also sneaked into the palace to find the study where Father had been murdered and to locate the secluded chapel.

He entered the tiny chamber now to find it glowing gold through the stained-glass as the sun outside reached its zenith. The musty scent of dust whispered on the stale air. Soon the Zen Hour bells would chime. Prayers would lift to the heavens, perhaps more heartfelt than ever before. The Sun Gods were real. Some had come down from their eternal throne. The days prophesied by Erokel the Second had come at last.

But the Star Gods were just as real, and they were coming too.

Ademas marched up the aisle between the few polished pews painted orange in the dim light, boots sinking into the plush carpet. He reached the altar at the far end of the chapel and stooped to tap the hidden door inside the base. Inside, the pendants of Star Worshipers, Sun Worshipers, and various other keys into parts of Inpizal, lay upon a velvet covering, where he'd placed them yesterzen upon returning to the palace.

These pendants had belonged to Father. In his youth, the king had used them to spy, alongside Nerenoth Irothé; to uncover the ugly truths of his kingdom. Ademas had since put them to use himself. Time to do so again.

He strung the pendants around his neck, tucked them out of sight, and traced the rising sun before he left the chapel. As he made his way to Lekore's suites, his thoughts flittered between his long-lost brother and Princess Talanee, the two unforeseen challenges in all his plans. A smile brushed his lips.

Keeps life interesting, doesn't it?

He'd come to Inpizal last month with two goals in mind: Kill Netye along with his heir, and then take the throne for himself.

Mere weeks later, he'd failed at both goals, yet he couldn't recall a time in his life when he'd felt happier. *Except for the impending threat of Star Gods and Lekore's capture.* But these were minor setbacks if the tradeoff meant family. He would rescue Lekore or die in the attempt.

He'd always wanted to know his brother. Dreamt often of what life might've been like had Prince Adenye lived. Even above the king's death, it had been the toddler prince's disappearance that altered Mother from a stern but devout woman into a creature in Kel skin. Ademas had never been good enough; he'd understood that early on. Mother's vengeance became his single purpose in living.

Though he doubted he and Mother would ever become close beyond their mutual respect for King Adelair, now the woman might have some hope of healing.

Ademas smiled. *That's enough for me.*

He'd never hated Mother. He'd only ever pitied her.

Talanee had become his real problem. Though meant to die at his hand, she survived. Not because Ademas hadn't tried to end her life. He'd encountered her well before the Sun Ball, once in the dead of night, when he'd sneaked onto her balcony and into her chamber to stab her through. It had seemed a fitting end, crowned by throwing her off said balcony to the courtyard stones below.

But he'd not been able to finish the deed. As she'd lain beneath his blade, asleep, oblivious to his presence, he'd studied her troubled face framed by tousled hair. Even in slumber, her lonely life wrote lines across her young, solemn face.

She's like me, he'd realized in that singular moment.

He left the same way he'd entered, making no noise, causing no scene. Talanee still breathed, lost in her private torments.

He'd watched her since and convinced Uncle Elekel to introduce them at the Sun Ball. Talanee's stifled temper and intelligent, sly retorts, had delighted Ademas. Somehow, he'd expected a different sort of princess; someone sullen, or bashful, or a hundred-thousand other things. Not beautiful, stubborn, and courageous.

He reached the corridor where guards in deep green capes lined the walls, an imposing force of arms, as though the rightful heir still dwelt in the rooms beyond the secured entrance. Ademas strode between the flanking soldiers, opened the door, and slipped inside.

The twins and Mother waited in chairs scattered around the chamber. Lord Lieutenant Rez hadn't arrived yet. Ademas made for the hearth, near Lor'Toreth who huddled in his blankets and watched.

Ademas turned toward his team and waited in silence. No one spoke. The whispering flames in the fireplace spread heat up his back, but he didn't move as he wondered why Ginn and Benye had bothered to light the fire. Already, the day promised to be hot.

Moments later, Rez knocked, then entered with a tall, lanky soldier at his back, like Rez, wearing the red cape of the royal garrison. Carak. Ademas nodded curtly as the soldiers saluted.

"Thank you for your promptness," he said. "We'll start at once. Please be seated."

The shuffle and thud of chairs disturbed the quiet as everyone moved their seats into a circle around Ademas.

He drew a breath, then slipped one pendant from under his shirt. Eyes widened as the twins shifted in their chairs. Ademas waggled the starburst in his hand. "I've infiltrated the ranks of the Star Worshipers. Besides my lady cousin, none knows the truth outside this room. I expect it to stay that way."

He searched each earnest face. "For the most part, I trust each of you. Should you shatter that trust, matters won't go well for you. That's a promise."

He caught the arm of the vacant armchair and dragged it closer, then sat on its edge and leaned forward, elbows propped on his knees. "Listen carefully and we'll be able to rescue Lekore and the Hakija without any casualties. No mistakes. *None*. Understood?"

CHAPTER 18

Skye Getaal stood on the city battlements, wind whistling through the crenels and whipping through the grasslands beyond Inpizal's wall. His long red cape hung still against his ghostly frame, while his short hair never stirred.

Clouds plumed in the sky, carried by the spirits' tantrums. Once, he'd been able to calm the Spirits Elemental.

No longer.

They could see him; he could see them. But his reach didn't extend to the realm of life anymore. The spirits might heed him on a whim, or they might not.

With a sigh, Skye held out his hand. A wind spirit dropped from its air current to hover above his palm, its form like the down of a dying weed until it transformed into the prismatic outline of a Kel woman.

"Any sign?"

It shook its long mane of translucent hair.

Skye sighed and eyed the Temple of the Moon. "Well, we already guessed where he is."

The wind piped a high note.

"Yes, I know. But he'll manage, he always does." Skye's gaze drifted upward until he stared into the sun beating down on Inpizal. "Star Worshipers aren't our greatest concern."

The wind spirit tossed its head as it shifted into the likeness of a bird, hopped off the air above his hand, and winged away. Skye knew the tiny guardian spirit cared nothing about Kiisuld invaders or potential genocide. Wind cared for little at all but freedom and flight.

The ghost turned to face the golden domes of the palace and cathedral. Despite the indifference of the Spirits Elemental, a reckoning had fallen upon Erokel. Skye had longed for centuries to witness this age, but now it had come, and he feared for Lekore.

Did I place him in this position by my prophetic words, or did fate decree his destiny long before I existed?

The question had plagued Skye since Lekore let out his first cry twenty-one years ago. The Spirits Elemental had ceased their flitting and flowing; the hum of life stilled to near silence as the earth slowed; the flames in the candelabra and sconces guttered to a mere spark; then it all leapt into a life more vibrant than the moment preceding his cry. Skye had known as surely as the spirits: His one hope had been born at last.

He'd spent the first three years of the prince's life torn between wonder and guilt at all the child might become.

Ter had come to Skye just before King Adelair died. "Adenye will be great, no mistake," the diminutive Ephe'ahn had said. "But Skye, if he should fall to darkness, more than your world will become wasted in the path of his ruin."

How well Skye knew it. Once, his own brother Erokel had been someone kind and honorable. They'd been inseparable.

Until Erokel succumbed to his greed.

Such wouldn't be Lekore's fate; the boy hadn't any tendency toward greed.

If he falls, it will be by something far worse.

Wind spirits settled on the battlements like a flock of birds resting from a long flight. They eyed the earth spirits far below as though weighing the plumpness of worms. One swooped from the crenel to snatch an earth spirit shaped like a flop-eared rabbun. The wind carried the spirit high, high overhead, then dropped the hapless earth spirit toward the distant ground.

A second wind spirit dove to catch it just before it collided with the ground, carried it high, and dropped it again. The earth spirit endured its ill treatment like a long-suffering parent tolerates the torment of toddlers at play.

Skye turned west to eye the shadows of the slums where the Temple of the Moon lurked in its long decrepitude. *If he falls, it will be to hatred and fear: far more dangerous than greed, for they are more reasonable and less selfish feelings.*

CHAPTER 19

Tahomin Harrulay moved his chess piece and collected the pawn he'd defeated before settling back in his chair to wait for his partner's move.

Prince Vay-Dinn Fyce tapped his clean-shaven chin with one manicured nail, then sighed and flopped back against his wingback chair. He sank into the plush cushions, a pout touching his lips as his blue eyes darkened. "I don't see the point in playing you anymore. There's no challenge in it: I always, always lose, curse you."

Tahomin shrugged. "You're the one who insisted on a second round, Your Highness."

Vay-Dinn's pout pulled down into a grimace, and he stretched his long, aristocratic finger out to flick chess pieces off the board, one by one. "Only. Because. You're. Always. Bored." The ivory pieces clattered onto the gleaming black floor and rolled.

Tahomin suppressed a sigh. "That's really not my fault, Your Highness."

"Not really mine either, which is even more important, hm?" The Kiisuld prince glanced toward the nearest console with its flashing lights. "Shayra, what's our ETA?"

The crisp 3D image of a voluptuous woman with long, dark

hair flickered into life. The AI stood in an alluring stance, dressed in a sleek, low-neck, deep crimson gown, as she said in monotones, "Two days, twelve hours, fourteen minutes, six seconds, forty-two—"

"That'll do, pest."

The AI vanished.

Tahomin lifted his brow. "Is that really necessary?"

Vay-Dinn shrugged one shoulder. "You wanted to know too."

"Debatable, but I'm not talking about our estimated time of arrival. I meant about Shayra."

Vay-Dinn's lips twitched upward. "I thought it was a pleasant upgrade."

"Really? That's three different risqué outfits in the past ten hours."

"Still doing nothing for you?"

Tahomin glowered at the goblet resting on the edge of the chess table. "Give it a rest, please. I'd rather we concentrated on what's ahead."

"Ah, yes. Boredom—for the next two days, twelve hours, thirteen minutes, blah blah blah." Vay-Dinn's fingers caught the chessboard and flipped it onto the floor as the rest of the pieces skittered across the room.

"We'll just have to put up with it," Tahomin said. "We'll blow an engine if the captain or I try to eke any more speed out of the blasted thing."

"That's not good enough." Vay-Dinn sighed and plucked up his wine goblet. "In this, I can't be patient, Tahomin. It's almost in my grasp, after...how long's it been?"

"Four, maybe five hundred years." Tahomin knew the exact timeframe, but he wouldn't admit that.

"That's a long time to wait for one prize."

Tahomin tipped his head to one side, a dry smile on his lips. "Is it?"

The prince blinked, then sighed. "That was insensitive." The man set his goblet down and swept back strands of his shoulder-length Prussian blue hair. "You know I didn't mean *that*."

Tahomin waved his hand. "No big deal. I get it, I really do. Honestly, I feel the same way, if only because we keep failing." He stood and ambled to the panoramic window showcasing a dazzling array of stars and planets outside the yacht. Cupping his hands behind his back, he stared into the black void. "You need to be prepared for another."

"Another failure?" The prince growled under his breath. "Not this time—not again. If those bucolic peasants made a mistake, I'll wipe that planet from existence, notwithstanding its nearness to the border."

Tahomin's eyes flitted to the imaginary line between Kiisuld and Ahvenian space. Nearness was a loose term. The planet of Erokel—was that its name? he couldn't quite recall—lay right on the line between the two empires. No one noticed; no one cared. Vay-Dinn knew better than to vie for a claim to the backwater world, or the Ahvenians would discover its existence.

Fortunately, the rebel Ahvenian faction who had inhabited Erokel made a point of erasing themselves and the remote planet from the empire's database to preserve their schemes.

All the better for Tahomin and Vay-Dinn when they'd stopped by for a respite five hundred years ago and discovered the rebels—and a *Seer*.

That Seer died in an unanticipated moment of martyrdom. But magic will always find a way, and Vay-Dinn had banked on heredity producing an heir to answer the Seer's final pronouncement.

If the recent summons wasn't a mistake, the time had come at last.

Chances of an error were slim; blood alone could awaken the stone's power. The only risk was whether the Seer had deluded scrying powers or the genuine gift. Too many subpar seers dotted the Universe, mere shades of the ancient scryers of yesteryear: the extinct Star Seers.

Skye Getaal's gift had been indisputable.

His successor had better be as gifted.

If not, Tahomin's traveling partner and prince might lose all patience. That he'd been patient this long demonstrated how much it mattered.

A chime sounded across the chamber. Tahomin turned as Vay-Dinn looked up from his goblet.

"Come," the prince said.

The ship's captain entered, bowed, then straightened. "Your Highness, an Ahvenian armada has departed from the Starburst Station. I can't determine its course yet, but its general movements suggest a potential border inspection."

"How large an armada?"

"Several hundred cruisers. It includes the *Daybreak*."

Tahomin's shoulders tensed. *Emperor Majentay's flagship, heading this way?*

"That *is* curious." Vay-Dinn swiveled in his chair to meet Tahomin's eyes. "We haven't provoked them recently, have we?"

"No more than usual. Not enough to draw Majentay's personal attention."

Vay-Dinn angled back around. "Keep an eye on it, captain. Maybe they detected our ship and mean to intimidate us. Unless they come close to our destination, there's no need to react. Besides, if they've just left the space station, we're days ahead of them. We'll be on and off the planet before they notice us."

Tahomin turned back to the window. *I hope so.* If the threat of an underpowered seer wasn't enough to upend his prince's patience, the arrival of Emperor Majentay would be.

CHAPTER 20

The light of a cheery fire bathed Toranskay's feet as he entered the guest room set apart for the injured Ahvenians. Four imposing beds had been crammed into the chamber, and Kel healers draped in white and gold bustled about, trays, bandages, and pitchers clutched in their hands. One Ahvenian occupant sat on propped pillows in his bed. The others lay still and silent, one pale, his face wrapped in stained bandages.

The chamber windows stood wide open to beckon any stray breeze in to combat the stifling heat of the room. With the faint currents came the combined aromas of the plant life outside to blend with the strong scent of herbs within.

The sitting Ahvenian looked up from a sheaf of parchment he'd been scrawling on with a genuine quill pen. Rarenday straightened, light catching in his orange eyes. He smiled at his prince and rested the sheaf beside him, shifting the blue brocade coverlet.

"Don't you dare get up." Toranskay moved across the room at a quick march.

Rarenday eased back against his propped pillows and waited to speak until Toranskay reached the bed. "I'm glad you're well, Tora. Several people assured me you were, but I had to see for myself."

"I know. That's why I've come. We've landed in quite a muddle, Raren."

The man sighed and nodded. His long, pale blond hair, customarily bound in a tail, hung loose down his shoulders. He wore white robes, slit on one side to let his splinted leg lie free of the blankets. Despite the bad break, and a dozen or more bruises and lacerations, Rarenday looked well. The man had an indomitable spirit.

Toranskay's smile crooked. "I understand you took out several eager Star Worshipers earlier."

Rarenday's brows shot up. "Sounds accurate. I did clock a few overeager idiots. So, what are Star Worshipers?"

Toranskay sat on the bed's edge and lowered his voice. "According to Kel theology, *we* are Sun Gods and the Kiisuld are Star Gods. I think you can fill in the rest."

Rarenday blew out a breath and stared at the blankets, brows scrunching together. "Great. Marvelous."

"My thoughts precisely. Raren, this world was colonized by a group of Ahvenian scientists bent on creating bioweapons. You should see the jungle they grew for their experiments."

"Bioengineering, on a backwater planet? That couldn't have been sanctioned by the emperor."

"No." Toranskay traced his finger over an embroidered wave pattern on the coverlet. "The lab was still operating five hundred years ago, so, during Emperor Farelin's rule. Apparently, it was run by a dissident group intent on overthrowing the Royal House. I met one of them: A man named Talajin. He despised the House of Ahrutahn."

Rarenday's eyes narrowed. "That's disturbing. You use past tense. Is he dead?"

"Yes. A worthy fellow named Nerenoth—the ranking military leader of this kingdom—ended his life."

Rarenday scanned the room. "What can you tell me about our hosts beyond their religious, uh, leanings?"

"We're in a kingdom called Erokel. It's one of two, so far as I can tell, which fits with the numbers I scanned right before we crashed. The population density of this world is shockingly small. The Kel—so they're called—live in a type of feudal society, led by three governing heads called the Triad. Their king has been lately ousted, and the rightful heir returned to the throne. We may have had a hand in that."

His protector winced. "Great. Upending feudal systems using our *divine* station is definitely going to go over well with," his voice dropped, "*your father*."

Toranskay sighed. "I know. It's problematic." He tapped his hand on his chin. "Every movement we make is analyzed and canonized, but we can't uproot their entire theological system. Not abruptly, at least. The worst of it is that their doctrine is made up of examples of insurgent Ahvenians, corrupted and cruel. From the look and sound of things, those scientists experimented on animals and people alike."

Folding his arms, Rarenday tracked a Kel woman as she leaned over a sleeping patient. "Five hundred years or more. That's a long time for a race with an average lifespan. We'll have to handle all this delicately."

"Raren."

The man met Toranskay's eyes.

"Kiisuld are on their way. They'll be here in three days. Vay-Dinn is coming, *personally*."

Color bled from Rarenday's face. His lips parted, and he mouthed a word Toranskay didn't catch. "You're certain?"

"Yes."

The man dragged a hand down the pale stubble on his jaw. "Great. Even better. I dare say this is the most exciting diplomatic mission we've ever experienced."

Strain pulled at the corners of Toranskay's smile. "Possibly, that's true."

Rarenday cringed and dropped his hands. "I apologize, Your High—Tora. That was insensitive of me."

Toranskay batted the air with a hand. "I understand what you mean. Vay-Dinn is worse by far than anyone from the House of Shimm, despite what the Kiisuld might claim otherwise. You should be warned, there *is* a Kiisuld living on this planet, alone. He claims to be a Keeper of Memory, and he knows Ter. I'm inclined to believe him, despite myself."

"A *Kiisuld* Keeper of Memory? I mean, sure, it's possible. They'd have one, too, but what's he doing here?"

"He had a falling out of some kind and was banished, apparently." Toranskay stood to investigate a pitcher on the stand beside Rarenday's bed. He poured water into a goblet and offered it to Rarenday.

The man took it with murmured thanks and gulped down a long drink.

Toranskay sat on the bed again. "That's not the end of our troubles." He summarized the past days' events as succinctly as he could.

Rarenday listened, asked a few clarifying questions, then leaned back and tapped his fingers against his empty goblet. "I'm gonna skin Ter when next I see him."

Toranskay chuckled. "I doubt he foresaw half of this."

"Yeah, maybe, but one half is enough. Why is he always, always plunging people into peril? He's got a misshapen mind."

"He's wise and eccentric, that's all."

Rarenday snorted. "We'll never see eye to eye regarding him. Don't mistake me, I like the dratted fae. I just don't like his methods."

Toranskay's smile deepened. Cool relief trickled through his limbs, and he clutched the coverlet. "I'm glad you're well, considering. I'd like things better if you had a real doctor to look at that leg and be certain you're not bleeding internally."

The man slapped the bed as he grinned. "By now, I'd be dead if anything were really messed up inside. I'll recover, don't worry. And if your ghostly contact is right, a real doctor isn't too far away. Knowing your father, he'll stretch those engines past their max capacity and get here ahead of schedule."

"No doubt of it." Toranskay stood. "I'd best get back to work on that shield. I've repaired all the ports but somewhere I'm losing power. The shield will still activate and umbrella most of the kingdom, but unless I track down that short, the Kiisuld will be able to puncture the shield in a matter of hours. We need days."

"Hop to, then," said Rarenday. "I'll be right here when you're done."

Toranskay slipped from the chamber and headed for the throne room. As he walked, his light steps grew heavier. Kiisuld, coming here. Could he manage to keep the shield running until Father arrived? Or would Vay-Dinn Fyce claim Toranskay at last?

CHAPTER 21

Lekore started and sat up, ribs twinging. He sucked in air and waited for the pain to pass.

Dakeer lay somewhere nearby, wrapped in his besmirched robes, breaths steady and deep.

Wincing, Lekore staggered to his feet and followed the rough, lichen-covered wall with his fingers until he reached the door. The torch beyond the cell had died hours before, plunging all in pitch darkness. He peered through the peephole out into the blackness, willing his eyes to adjust.

Nothing.

Lekore rested his forehead against the wooden door as panic crawled across his skin and formed a pit in his stomach. A mad urge to scream rolled through him, deep, bubbling up to snag in his throat. He drew a shuddering breath and pinched his brows together as he squeezed his eyes shut.

All will be well. The good captain will not leave you here. You're not abandoned.

Ademas and Mother were out there as well, and they appeared to care about him.

Ank is out there too. Does he worry for me?

The memory of the king's knife against his throat twisted Lekore's stomach. A sob escaped his lips.

Dakeer's breaths shortened. Scuffing noises sounded behind Lekore.

"Are you crying?" asked the Hakija.

Lekore scrunched his eyes shut more. "No." His voice scratched his throat, tight, low, with a faint tremor. *Why are you so weak?* He'd thought himself immune to these feelings after so many years in the company of ghosts and spirits. Now, in a Kel city, surrounded by life, his loneliness ran deeper.

The scuff and rustle came close. A hand fumbled, knocked into Lekore's injured arm, then found his shoulder. "There now, my child. All is not lost."

Lekore nodded. "They will not leave us here."

"No, indeed not."

Lekore circled around to face the darkness and the man enveloped by it. "I am no less frightened, even knowing that."

Silence. A sigh. "Nor am I."

Lekore hugged himself as a shiver traced his spine. "You're afraid as well?"

"The Star Gods will soon come, and we are at the mercy of their dark followers. You and I shall not fare well should Nerenoth fail to free us. Indeed, even should we escape, the history of the Star Gods promises an ill fate nonetheless."

Lekore hunched under the weight of Dakeer's words. "We must not let them succeed. It would mean more than your suffering or mine. They will want to harm Tora as well, and all others may die. Skye once described to me a few of their atrocities." He clenched his hands into fists. "They are responsible for the corruption of his brother Erokel. They recognized the secret darkness in his heart and exploited it for their amusement."

The hand retreated. A heavy sigh followed. "I knew you would upset the balance of our kingdom, Lekore. My instincts were good enough to feel that. But I had no notion how much. Rather than prune back trees, you're uprooting them."

Lekore canted his head, sensing and hearing no malice. "Are you angry?"

"Resigned, I think." The crunch of Dakeer's boots moved away. "A day after the Tawloomez massacred my family, leaving me to die for whatever twisted reason, a Sun Priest arrived and freed me. He took me in. Fed my ravaged soul on King Erokel's many laments. His anguish matched my own. Rather than turn my hatred toward the Sun Throne, as I'd been wont to do at first, I directed it rightly at the Tawloomez who robbed me of my home and kin. I drank in Erokel's words of vengeance and made them my own.

"Have you ever read his words, Lekore? Have you ever heard more than the fragment of his lament I recited during the Rite of Blood?"

"No." Lekore used the door as a guide to sink to the floor, then crossed his legs before him. His ribs ached. "I've no desire to hear the poisoned justifications of a man consumed by want and guilt."

Another sigh fluted from the darkness. "Just as well. He is a man of great eloquence, a man whose words can move one to act upon what he desires. Erokel laid the foundation of our faith and culture."

Lekore shifted his knees up to lean against them, dragged his hair free behind him, and flinched as his ribcage protested again. "Had I been raised as one of you, might I not feel the same? Why did I frighten you as a mere toddler?"

"Ah. You little understand your disposition, even back then. Already, you were different. Your father began it. He'd been a strange boy himself, prone to debate points of doctrine, points of caste. He despised the slave trade. But he also knew better than to push for reformation all at once. You... I knew you would be different. As a three-year-old, you stood within the throne room, observing the debates at court. More than once, you stood up, pointed your finger at an aristocrat during his heated argument and declared him a liar."

Lekore tensed. "I...did?" A tight laugh tumbled from his lips. "What did he do? What did they all do?"

"The first time, no one took you seriously—except the king. He seized the man's holdings, ordered an inquest, and uncovered a smuggling ring affiliated with Star Worshipers. The second time you accused a noble of the same offense, the man took off running then and there. His crimes were treasonous." Dakeer chuckled. "After that, none dared request that you not attend court for fear of sounding guilty, and far fewer arguments and accusations flew around the chamber. Doubtless, your lord father had never experienced such tranquil sessions in his years as king."

Lekore's heart warmed as he imagined a gentle hand on his head. "He became king very young, didn't he?"

"Yes, his father died of a lifelong illness when Adelair was a mere adolescent. But he'd been well groomed by then, since all had recognized his father's failing health for years. I think his early rise to the throne inspired Nerenoth and myself to earn our positions young as well."

"I wish I remembered more of my father," said Lekore, "but there are only snatches. Somehow, it's sad to better recall Ank."

"You were very fond of each other, you and your uncle."

Lekore stared into the darkness. "Why then did he abandon me?"

"Fear. Greed. Madness. Most of all, grief. Netye has always been a weak-willed, short-sighted creature, but he fell in love with Naveena of House Benaal and grew better for it. For some reason, she returned his affections. I understand love can make fools of even the most sensible Kel." Dakeer drew a breath. "She died giving birth to Princess Talanee. Naveena's constitution had never been strong. Her death unhinged Netye."

Lekore gripped his legs. "The loss of a loved one hurt him so much that he would choose to abandon all others? To kill his brother? To leave me in the wilds to die? I do not understand."

"Pray you never do, my son."

Sleep eluded Lekore, long after Dakeer had fallen into silence and slumber.

He leaned back against the door and hummed the one lullaby he knew. The scuttle of rodents in the corridor outside scratched at his ears as he willed his mind to concentrate on anything but his imprisonment.

Nausea stabbed at his insides. He drew a long breath and mouthed the words to the lullaby.

'Sleep, O restless child, sleep.
Let the stars thy vigil keep.
Hear them sing of morning's light,
Hear them pray all through the night.

'Fear not darkness, babe in arms,
Stars will shelter thee from harm.
In their light, be thee embraced
Like a kiss from sun's warm face.

'Journey now to what's beyond.
And then return by starlet's bond.
Tell me all thou seest there,
With thy smile, sweet and fair.'

He hunched into himself and repeated the words in his mind again and again as his throat closed. Blood pounded in his ears. He rocked back and forth, eyes burning, fingers numb.

I am well. I am not alone. Nerenoth and Ademas will come for me. They will bring others.

The image of Tora tumbled into his mind, and with it, the chiming toll of *Calir*. He straightened and summoned the sword. It hummed as he gripped the familiar hilt, and the fire gem flashed with a light that scattered shadows.

Dakeer sat up, eyes wide and wild, hand groping in his robes, probably seeking a weapon.

The gem's glow remained, perhaps sensing Lekore's desire for light. He clutched the sword close and smiled softly. "All is well, Hakija. I merely answered *Calir*'s inquiry, and it gifted us with light."

Dakeer arched his brows. "You might've thought to do that a little sooner."

Lekore laughed. "I did not know it could, or I surely would have."

The Hakija grunted. The light illuminated bruises and scrapes across his face, and blood splatters staining his white vestments. His red eyes glowed as he followed Lekore's gaze, and his hand settled over a patch of blood. "It's not mine, not most of it. Though I'm not as able a fighter as your Lord Captain, I'm no slouch. Those heretics took me at a costly price." His lips lifted in a grim, satisfied smile as his eyes flashed with pleasure.

A twinge wrenched at Lekore's stomach. He stared down at his hands, and the sword resting in their grip. "I have killed before, Hakija. To defend myself, to feed myself, and to keep the Tawloomez from invading Erokel. But I have never relished the taking of a fellow life. It does not offer any pleasure. Even when a death is warranted, I regret that I must make that choice."

Dakeer stared at him, eyes dimming. "Are you even Kel at all?"

"Must I conform to your ideal of a Kel to be accepted as the same race?"

The man bowed his head, hands trembling as he gripped the cloth of his robes. "I hardly know. What am I to believe, Lekore? The words of Erokel the Great swarm my thoughts, prejudicing my soul against all that you are—but the Sun Gods stand with you, declaring my faith to be false. Yet most firmly, I believe in the Sun Throne."

Lekore swallowed bile as he looked away, stomach churning. *What can I say? The Sun Gods are not what he perceives, but to tell him so would likely break his spirit.* He inhaled and clutched *Calir*. Skye had told him more than once that people are fragile. "Dakeer, is it necessary to know all the answers now?"

The Hakija looked up, brows knitted. His lips parted but he said nothing.

Lekore rested *Calir* on his lap, holding it with one hand in case the light faded should he let go. "If it were so easy to learn all things and accept them, would we not die sooner than we do? Yet Skye has told me that a Kel lives over one hundred years, barring illness or accident. Or murder, I suppose." He chewed the inside of his lip. "I feel that we are given so many years to learn, to experience new, strange circumstances, in order to discover truth: not what we *think* truth is."

Dakeer's brows smoothed as he sighed. "So young, yet you see things much clearer than I do."

Lekore played his fingers over his sword hilt. "I think my vision is unclouded merely because I've seen so little yet. My field of sight has been limited to a vale and the Wildwood—not to people and their perspectives and problems. What do I know of the world, Dakeer, beyond my opinion of it? What good will that do me as I wrestle the duties of kingship or the nuances of your faith? I know nothing of these matters. I'm likely to make a fool of myself."

The man scoffed. "Knowing that, you're already far more prepared than most rulers. You'll do well if you live long enough. But Lekore, you'll make enemies. Many. No one with so kind a heart could do less."

Lekore held the man's trenchant gaze. "If that is the price to learn truth and defend it, so be it."

He rose to his feet, flinching as his wounds complained. Jaw set, he turned to the door, flexed his grip, and swung with all the power he could muster.

Time to escape.

SKYE SPRANG UP FROM HIS HOVERING CROUCH ON THE CITY wall, soul tingling. His eyes speared the beacon of light rising like a pillar from the Temple of the Moon. Sunset had painted golden-red fingers across the white stones of Inpizal's buildings, but where the pillar shone, silvery-white tendrils of light overpowered the hues of gold and crimson.

A cluster of wind spirits riding a warm breeze paused in their play to examine the light.

"It's *Calir*." Skye laughed. "Not as powerless as you supposed, eh, Farr Veon?"

TORANSKAY BOLTED FROM THE THRONE ROOM AS *CALISAY* chimed an answer to its twin brother's call. The prince's arms tingled as he sprinted down the marble corridor toward the front doors of the Kel palace. Soldiers stumbled aside to give him passage, and several followed without a word.

Near the doors, Nerenoth appeared, striding from down a separate passageway. His midnight blue hair and cape settled against his back as he slowed his pace. "Is something amiss, Holy One?"

Toranskay motioned as he caught his breath, and the guards stationed at the doors pulled them aside to let him pass. He paced out onto the stone steps painted red in the eerie sunset and stared at the beam of light stretching above the northwest end of Inpizal, beyond the golden cathedral dome.

"That's Lekore's sword," Toranskay said. "I think he's causing his captors some difficulty."

A smile spread over the Lord Captain's face. "He's his father's son." His eyes probed Toranskay.

The Ahvenian prince met his red gaze. "We should head that way. If he's acting now, we can't wait on Ademas's plan to offer backup. Your Hakija's life is in peril."

Nerenoth nodded. "I agree." He clutched his sheathed blade. "I dislike waiting anyway."

CHAPTER 22

Footsteps hammered the stone floor ahead of Ademas. He willed his shoulders not to tense as he strode through the ruined Temple of the Moon, shrouded in black velvet, his starburst pendant bright beneath the torches lining the wide corridor.

A crowd of Star Worshipers appeared in the arched passage ahead, lit by the orange glow of the flames, cloaked and hooded, their pace rapid.

He stepped aside to let them jog past. "What goes on, brethren?" he called out.

Several slowed their steps, and one answered in a decidedly female voice. "The accursed Sun Hakija and Prince Lekore have escaped from their cell."

Ademas tensed and staunched an overwhelming urge to grin like a maniac. "Any idea where they went, or are we scouring the entire temple?"

"They vanished. Look everywhere." The stragglers raced off to catch their fellows.

Ademas turned and made his way to the front of the temple. He'd wondered if Lekore might be too passive to rescue himself, especially if he risked the Hakija's life. *I should've guessed better of a man willing to plunge into the Lands Beyond, emockye pet in tow.*

His grin surfaced, wide and proud. He couldn't help himself as he trotted toward the room where he'd found Lekore mere days before, upon their first meeting. If Lekore had the sense to escape his cell, he'd track down the tunnel Ademas had led him to before, if he possibly could.

Good thing I didn't wait to infiltrate until nightfall.

New steps echoed ahead, and Ademas wiped the grin from his lips with practiced ease. The cloaked figure rounded a corner: Farr Veon, an illustrious and wealthy nobleborn Kel. Despite the panic of his followers, the young Hakija showed no hint of distress.

Ademas slowed and inclined his head. "Holy Hakija."

"Ah, my fledgling disciple. Aiding in the search?"

Ademas frowned. "I've just heard about it, but I'd like to help."

"Good. The southern side of the temple is being combed. Come with me. I know what path he's most likely to take."

Ademas nodded. "As you wish, Holiness."

He trailed after the Dark Hakija, pleased by his good fortune. Whether they ran into Lekore or not, Ademas might thwart the Hakija's efforts either way.

Moments later, the young nobleman plucked a torch from its sconce and led Ademas down a passageway narrower than the rest, its torches cold, its shadows deep. The skittering of rodents pattered against Ademas's eardrums to contrast the firm footfalls of Farr Veon and himself. He suppressed a grimace; even a religion that worshiped the night might consider cleaning house now and then. The temple's filth threatened disease.

The passage gave way to a circular space whose stained-glass skylight filtered in the sunset's glow, wrapping the chamber in hues of red. Strange doors bent to the will of the walls, adding to the circle's effect. Starbursts carved into the wood burned like bright red fire under the light's influence. A round rug carpeted the room, black with embroidered stars whose silver threads glittered as Ademas's shadow brushed them.

Farr Veon strode to the door straight across the chamber. "This way, Lord Ademas." He slipped past the barrier and down a flight of steps.

Ademas joined him as understanding blossomed. *We're headed to the tunnels, are we? So, Veon, you know that's how Lekore escaped last time.*

The stairwell charged downward into inky blackness, the steps steep and unpolished. Ademas took care to find his footing before he slid his boot down to the next stair. Farr Veon moved with equal deliberation until the stairwell ended and a dirt passageway sprawled ahead, the ceiling rounded to gape like an open maw before them.

Ademas studied the branching tunnels. "He'll be hard to track down here, Holiness."

"There are only a few entrances into this network he could have discovered, and all of them lead to one of three exits. This way." The Hakija of the Night strode ahead, boots grinding dirt.

Blowing out a breath, Ademas shadowed the man, one hand draped over his sword hilt. The steady drip of water beckoned from a side passage as he conquered the main thoroughfare, and tiny paws scurried over his boot to scamper away.

Not for the first time, Ademas debated stabbing Farr Veon in the back. When he'd first arrived in Inpizal, he'd intended to ingratiate himself to the Star Worshipers. It hadn't taken long to earn their trust, as he'd begun his efforts on Ra Kye years before. With a smile, he'd delivered a letter of recommendation from the dark order's island priest to the Dark Hakija himself. Farr Veon had been impressed and welcomed him with a ravening warmth.

A few carefully chosen heretical words now and then, followed up by confessional prayers for forgiveness, had sealed everything. The Hakija of the Night had been delighted by the idea of controlling the line of Getaal, even if it came through an illegitimate heir.

Ademas had been faithful in attending nocturnal worship meetings twice each week, and he fed information to Farr Veon's disciples to maintain the façade. Most of it was rubbish, but he offered up enough verifiable truths to instill trust in his word. If a few rumors fell flat, well, that was to be expected.

"How has the princess been coping with the shift in power, Ademas?" asked Farr Veon as he stepped around a puddle of stagnant water. Its stench curled the man's lips into a sneer.

Ademas shrugged. "She's understandably downtrodden. She'd been counting on her father's early death to secure her crown, but now she recognizes her unsteady standing. She even considered tutoring Lekore, likely thinking his mind malleable."

The Hakija snorted. "An easy error in judgment to make of that one. Alas, I'd been under the same impression at first. He's sharper than he first appears."

"I discovered the same. Good news for me is that he means to overlook my unconventional standing. We could use that if we can only find the heir."

Farr Veon sighed. "No, Ademas. That's not possible, though I would relish it under different conditions. The Star Gods are nearly here. They intend to claim Lekore for themselves." He turned, eyes burning in the torchlight. "That means a new monarchy must be organized, and as in the days of Erokel the False, we shall have a king and Hakija in one form—but not a blaspheming worshiper of the Sun Throne. The Triad will be dissolved. I will rule Erokel, and I shall need my most loyal supporters at my side."

Ademas smiled and dropped to one knee as he bowed his head. "I would be honored if you considered me among them, O Holy Hakija."

Fingers brushed his hair. "Faithfulness shall be well rewarded, Lord Ademas. Arise, and we can further discuss matters after Lekore is brought back under my control. He cannot escape. We have mere days before the Star Gods reach us."

Ademas straightened and nodded. "As you wish, Hakija."

Their pace quickened. Ademas's smile deepened. *Plot all you like, Veon. You're not the only one scheming.*

CHAPTER 23

Lekore stumbled over something in the dark earthen tunnel. He shifted his balance to catch himself before he struck the ground with his face.

Dakeer slammed into his back and hissed. "What is it?"

"Something in the path." Lekore resisted a desire to ask *Calir* for light. He and the Hakija had agreed to travel the underground tunnels in darkness to keep their presence unknown, but he didn't relish breaking his neck instead.

The Hakija's clothes rustled and Lekore imagined him stooping to locate the object. The man sucked in air. "Bones, unless I'm mistaken."

Blood drained from Lekore's face. The memory of striking down his guard outside the cell resurfaced, another kill to his name. He pawed loose hair from his face as needles stabbed his stomach. "We must keep going."

Minutes later, as they padded down the dank corridor, Lekore froze as a faint scuff reached his straining ears. Dakeer didn't bump into him, so perhaps he heard the same thing. Neither dared to breathe as they listened against the *plip* of water close by.

"Ah *ha*."

Lekore's blood chilled. *That voice.* He backed up as footsteps pattered against the dirt floor.

Oozing, sludgy delight swilled off the familiar aura. "Don't run away, *Akuu-Ry*. We've a duel to settle." The swish of cloth whispered in Lekore's ears as Susunee's steps neared.

His heart thudded against his tender ribs. Fingers prickling, he summoned *Calir* with a thought. The sword blazed with fiery light, chiming a note as clear as crystal bells; the glow illuminated Susunee's angular, grinning face, and her snakeskin gown glistened.

"Let us pass, Teokaka."

She coughed a laugh. "You're becoming increasingly dull, you know that?"

If only Lekore had made it a little further along the tunnel, he might've reached the end of the temple grounds. There, the Spirits Elemental could find him, and he'd be able to ask the earth spirits for help. Instead, he must rely upon his skill with a blade against someone nearly impossible to kill.

A grim smile banished his scowl. *Even so, the odds might be worse.*

He lunged. Susunee sprang back as his sword swung through the space where her throat had been. The woman threw violet sparks at him, and he slashed them aside. Leapt right, feigned, and danced left as Susunee retreated from his false path. *Calir* caught another thread of violet magic as she shielded herself.

He swung again. Again. Susunee stumbled back as she tossed bolt after bolt. Lekore gained ground and steered her into a side passage. Hopefully, Dakeer would understand and move ahead in the main tunnel.

A few more swings, and Lekore retreated under a barrage of violet lightning. Strands singed his hand as he staggered away from a concentrated bolt. The Tawloomez woman laughed and charged him.

Lekore broke free of the narrow tunnel and whirled to find Dakeer gone. *Good.*

He pitched himself up the passage as magic chased his heels.

Sparks nipped at his legs, and the odor of burning hair wafted into his nostrils. *Run*.

He fled, halted to deflect another barrage, then whirled and scrambled on.

Get to safe ground. Find the spirits!

Hot blood flooded his limbs, and he ran when he knew he should give out. Susunee followed, laughter hounding him, urging him onward.

He had no way to tell if he ran the right way. Perhaps he plunged deeper into the temple's clutches, where the Hakija of the Night awaited him.

"This way!"

A strong hand snatched his wrist and yanked him into a new passageway. Dakeer.

They ran on, Susunee at their heels, the world a blur of violet light and dank, moldy scents.

Wind laughed at him. Snatched at his trailing hair. Earth spirits leapt alongside him, shaped like rodents, rabbun, emockye, a tiny, hand-size pythe. He grinned, stumbled to a halt, and swiveled.

Wreathing fire burst around him and Dakeer, encircling them, as Susunee raced into view, hands glowing with violet light. The earth trembled and asked a question.

"Only around the temple grounds," Lekore whispered. "Nowhere else."

The earth spirits nodded their understanding as the ceiling cracked like drumming thunder. Susunee jerked her gaze upward as clods of dirt rained down. She shrieked and flung her arms up as the foundations above crushed her body.

Lekore staggered as the quake rumbled up the passageway. Cracks webbed along the ground and the ceiling spit dirt. Willing the fire to ebb, he caught Dakeer's arm as the man swayed, and they stumbled away from the epicenter. Spirits raced under their feet, excited by the noise and crumbling debris.

"Show us the way." Lekore tossed his command at a cluster of wind spirits. They saluted in mock Kel fashion and swept up the tunnel. Lekore chased them, keeping hold of the Hakija, afraid the earth spirits might swallow him in their fun.

The wind spirits veered into a passage less cluttered by debris.

A figure lurched into view, this one enormous, a broad grin stretching over his face. “Gotcha!” Teon snatched at Lekore, who danced backward, dragging Dakeer with him.

The wind fluted a warning. Too late. The bite of a dagger caught Lekore’s side as he tried to dodge the second attacker. He whirled, dropping Dakeer’s arm to clutch at his side. *Calir* toned an angry song, as Lekore’s eyes collided with the familiar, ragged face of Ank. The mad king slashed at him again. Lekore couldn’t fight him—*he couldn’t do it.* Heart throbbing, he retreated.

With a guttural cry, Dakeer launched himself at Ank. They tumbled to the ground, wrestling over the dagger.

Teon’s massive arms wrapped around Lekore, pinning him, hot breath tickling his ears. “Knew you’d be down here. Got you now, little king.”

Lekore strained against him. “Let me go. I’ll torch you if I must.”

“Can’t torch us both.”

Lekore’s eyes narrowed. “Fire won’t harm me. Release me, and I will spare your life.”

A cold, rumbling laugh sent spidering chills up his arms and down his spine. “Try it, just try. I’ll snap your neck before I expire, ’cause if *I* die, I won’t care what happens to you.” The grip tightened until Lekore’s ribs screamed. He choked out a gasp, vision wobbling. Fire spirits hissed and sputtered, drawing close upon the air.

“B-back!” Lekore’s cry hobbled them, and they retreated, embers floating above their flaming shapes, smoke curling on the stale wind. Several hissed at Teon as they clumped together to form a large flame.

“Dakeer Vasar,” Teon called. “Unhand Netye and back away, or I’ll pop the boy’s head off like a wine cork.”

Scuffling increased, and a grunt followed. Dakeer’s voice rose over the hissing flames, cold as the frigid heights of the Nakoth mountains. "You would risk the wrath of your gods?"

Teon chortled. "Maybe I will, maybe I won't. Don't test it."

Lekore flinched as the man squeezed tighter. "Can't...breathe."

Teon loosened his grip a margin. "Don't resist. Don't you dare." His voice boomed out. "You alive, Your Majesty?"

"Unfortunately," murmured Dakeer.

A cough sounded out of Lekore's sight. Ank's feeble voice drifted up from the ground. "Yes, I—I'll survive, no thanks to *you*, Dakeer."

A grunt followed and Lekore wondered if the Hakija had kicked Ank.

"Get up, or I'll finish what I began," the Hakija said, tones rasping.

Dakeer rounded the large flame, followed by Ank. The latter man wore bruises over his hollow cheeks, and his short, thin hair stuck out. He brushed dirt from his black clothes.

"Now what?" Ank asked.

Teon jerked his head, tightening the pressure on Lekore's ribs. "We go up. See what happened to the temple in that earthquake. Find the Hakija."

Dakeer's scowl deepened, but he said nothing.

Ank tugged his sleeve down. "Right. Upward."

Lekore's stomach clenched. "You're one of them?" His tones hung low, gruff.

Ank's lips fluttered upward. "By necessity. Better to sell my soul than die for the Sun Throne."

Dakeer scoffed. "I always *knew* you for a coward. It's strangely satisfying to witness the proof."

"No chitchat." Teon loosened his hold to wrap one hand around Lekore's throat; long, thick fingers connecting. "Walk and do it fast."

Lekore led the way, collared by Teon, fire spirits spitting and hissing at a safe distance. Dakeer walked in the middle, with Ank at the rear, judging by their footfalls. Dakeer's stride maintained a smooth clip even on the soft dirt, while Ank's gait carried an uneven pattern, suggesting a faint limp.

Teon must've known the tunnels well, for he led them to a set of stone stairs within a few moments.

"Majesty, go ahead," the man-giant said. "Make sure the way is clear."

Without protest, Ank slipped past Teon and Lekore to scurry up the steps. As the unseen door squeaked open, pale light poured down the stones. "It's safe."

Teon urged Lekore up the stairs to a tiny landing, an open door, and a derelict street beyond. Dusk had laid a gloomy shroud over the sagging townhouses, empty of Kel or Tawloomez, pythe or flowerpot, streetlamp or carriage. The musty hint of dust and decomposing rubbish lingered like a ghost in the barren streets.

At Teon's insistence, Lekore padded out into the silent open. Dakeer joined him, expression hard as chiseled stone, though fear rolled off his frame, twining with confusion and doubt.

Teon urged Lekore into the middle of the thoroughfare, as Ank closed the passage door. Lekore craned his head to catch where the tunnel came out, but Teon struck his cheek, and he jerked back around, seeing stars. A coppery taste filled his mouth. Lekore swallowed and set his jaw as the world settled back into place.

"Walk," growled Teon.

Lekore obeyed, and they moved through the slums as quietly as a herd of pythe. Lekore's ears thundered with their footfalls. Did Kel not know how to sneak?

His mind caught on Lios, alone in the Vale That Shines Gold, awaiting Lekore's return. The half-grown emockye could fend for himself, but what if Lekore never went back? Lios had no pack of his own; he relied on Lekore for company, as Lekore relied on him.

Please be all right. I'll try to get back to you.

The odor of charred wood tickled Lekore's nose, and he lifted his eyes from the road to find blackened buildings, crumbled, abandoned. The damage was too old to belong to the fires of the previous night. "What happened here?"

"A purging," Dakeer said. "Ten years ago, the Star Worshipers rose up to dethrone Netye. He ordered this quarter burned. Sun Warriors led the attack." Dakeer's tones dripped with derision. "Now look at him: the lackey of a lackey."

"I did what I must to survive, Dakeer," said Ank's voice somewhere behind the hulking Teon.

Dakeer scoffed. "Might as well have left Adelair on the throne, for all you've done since. I see now how deep my folly has burrowed. All you've done is forge chaos and delay the inevitable. How much sooner might the Sun Gods have returned if not for your choices?"

"And *yours*," Ank said.

"And mine, yes." Dakeer stared ahead, brows pinched together. "Most certainly that."

Teon rumbled a laugh. "Too late for regrets; both of you finished your reigns. Time for the Moon Throne to ascend."

"Don't be so quick to relish that idea, Teon Keela," Dakeer said. "Five hundred years ago, the Sun and Star Gods fought for dominance upon this world, and we lost half our population in the battle. The cost of waging a holy war is unfathomable."

Teon snorted. "Well aware of the numbers, priest. We intend the same thing to happen again, but this time, only Sun Worshipers will have to die."

"Death doesn't pick a side, my wayward son."

Teon's arm shot out, and he struck Dakeer hard. The Hakija staggered sideways and sank to the ground.

He shook his head, then turned his red eyes on the man-giant, lip bleeding. "An eloquent argument for a brute."

Teon chuckled. "Brute, am I? Just 'cause I like to break things?"

Dakeer struggled to his feet. "Yes, that's one reason."

The faint crunch of stone on stone arrested Lekore's attention. Wind spirits fluted at him from a roof across the square ahead. Did a figure lurk there, atop the roof?

"Keep moving," Teon said and tightened his grip on Lekore's neck.

Lekore flinched and drew a sharp breath.

Dakeer tugged his vestments straight. "If you wish to keep moving, perhaps don't strike me down."

They strode into the square. The dark shape moved almost imperceptibly. The husks of burned-out buildings hunched in the plaza, though a few remained intact, barely scarred by the purging. The building opposite, where the wind spirits danced, bore damage on its south corner, where a broken window had been stained with black smoke.

Teon turned south, and Lekore's eyes lifted to seek the Temple of the Moon's shape against the dusky sky. It no longer loomed above the derelict structures surrounding its grounds. Had collapsing the tunnels surrounding the temple been enough to topple it?

Wind whistled in Lekore's ears as a faint twang sounded from the rooftop. His eyes widened as his heartbeat galloped up his throat. "Ank, move!"

Too late. The arrow struck the thin man, and he jerked sideways, then collapsed to the ground. Lekore screamed and wrenched against Teon as the man's grip slackened in his surprise. Lekore stumbled free and darted to Ank's side. Slammed his knees against the cobbled road. Lifted the man's head.

"Ank?"

The man's red eyes looked like pools of blood in the dying light. "Nye. My little Nye."

Lekore pressed his forehead to Ank's sweat-soaked skin. "Do not leave me, *please*."

Teon's fingers dug into Lekore's shoulders and yanked him upward.

"No! Leave me with Ank!"

"Little fool! They're trying to kill us."

An arrow clattered against the stones mere inches away. Lekore willed the wind spirits to capture the figure on the rooftop, and the spirits fluted their understanding.

Dakeer knelt on the king's other side and leaned over the

arrow jutting from Ank's chest. "He's dying. There's nothing to be done." His eyes lifted to scan the rooftops.

Hot tears burned Lekore's eyes. "No. No, Ank!"

Fire surged through his body, warming his flesh until Teon jerked back, releasing him with a curse. Lekore flung himself beside Ank again and caught his hand. "Please, stay. Please."

Blood trickled down the man's lips. His eyes stared unseeing. "Poor lonely child. I can't...stay... Leave me. What does my life matter any...more? You should—should hate me."

"I cannot hate an ailing man," Lekore whispered, pressing Ank's hand to his cheek. "Stay, Ank."

The king's body convulsed. Blood seeped faster from his lips. "Goodbye, dear boy. Do...not mourn...the man who killed your... good father."

Teon's hand slammed into Lekore's head, knocking him sideways. The ground slapped Lekore, and he lay stunned, staring at Ank's leg as the man's body jerked a final time. Tears stung Lekore's cheeks and dripped off his chin.

"Were you anyone else," Teon growled, "I'd *kill* you for singeing my hands."

Lekore shook his head to clear the growing ache, his hair rippling down his shoulders. "Were I anyone else, you'd not be singed."

Teon seized his collar and dragged him upward to dangle above the cobbled road. The man's breath wafted into Lekore's face, rank, stale. "One of these days, I'll pound your eyes in, little king." His voice shook with blistering wrath.

Lekore glared at him through watery vision. "Your *gods* would not like that."

Teon's teeth ground together. He released Lekore's collar with one hand and snatched a handful of hair at Lekore's scalp, yanking his head back. Lekore hissed in a breath between clenched teeth and pinched his eyes shut.

"Enough!" Dakeer's voice rang across the square. "Have you forgotten we're exposed, and *someone* shot Netye?"

Teon dropped Lekore to his feet and shoved him forward. "Move, little king."

Lekore righted himself and squared his shoulders. "I will not leave Ank here."

"You'll do as I say, or I'll break your legs and drag you."

Lekore clenched his fists. "I've asked the wind spirits to apprehend the one who shot Ank. We're not under attack now." He took a step toward Teon. "Bring Ank."

Teon sneered and lifted his eyes to scan the rooftop. "Maybe you're telling the truth, maybe not. We can't bring the body. He's dead anyway."

Fury bloomed like a spark on dry tinder, crawling through Lekore's flesh until the cool evening air turned warm. "You're an evil man."

Teon's lips parted in a canine grin. Malicious glee spilled from his soul, thick and malodorous like a noxious bog overflowing. "What of it?" He swiped an arm out as he strode toward Lekore, eyes gleaming. "I enjoy pain. I like the melody of screams. The pleasure of blood under my nails."

Lekore darted back, instincts blaring. *Run. Flee!* "Stay back!" he cried. Flames nipped at Lekore's fingers. He let them grow until a blaze danced over his open palm.

Teon's barking laugh shattered the stillness of the street. "Or what, you'll crisp me?"

"I do not long to kill as you do, but do not test my fortitude."

"Long to kill?" Teon's eyes danced. "Oh, no, that's just a result of my actions. A consequence of my fun. I prefer my victims to stay alive as long as possible." He flexed his fingers until the knuckles popped.

A wall of fire sprang up between Lekore and the man-giant, fire spirits spinning and dancing upon the wind as they helped the flames to grow with hissing cackles. With a thought, flames leapt up around Dakeer, shielding him from Teon's wrath.

Teon sighed and scratched his head. "Listen, little king. You can defy the will of our order all night long, but you'll only tire yourself out. When the Star Gods arrive, it's all over for you."

"Forgive me if I choose to chance that," said Lekore, willing the flames to burn hotter.

Teon exhaled through his nose. His hand flew to his side, and he hurled a dagger at Lekore. A wind spirit snatched and tossed it back, and the man lurched aside, evading damage.

Teon's eyes brightened as a sneer curled his lips up. "Can't keep this up forever."

"He won't have to." Tora's voice rang out from the heavens. The Ahvenian's sword chimed and *Calir* answered, as Tora soared down from the nearest rooftop, sword in hand, the naked blade glistening under the light of the rising moon. He aimed for Teon, who fumbled back and dragged a sword from its sheath in time to block the smaller man's attack. Tora retreated several steps as another sword gleamed in the dim light, swinging at Teon, who cursed and stumbled aside.

Nerenoth stepped from the shadows, broadsword unsheathed, expression grim. His armor glinted in the twilight. His eyes skimmed Ank's body sprawled across the paving stones, and the line of his jaw tightened.

"Excellent timing, as usual, Lord Captain," Dakeer said through his fiery shield.

A smile flickered and died on Nerenoth's lips. "Glad you're well, Hakija." His gaze slid to Lekore, and the hard lines of his face softened. "And you, Your Majesty."

Tears brimmed in Lekore's eyes as relief flooded his scorching veins. "Captain, thank you for coming."

"Always." His attention turned to Teon, whose face had paled several shades. "I will dispatch this heretic. Please take Dakeer and hide far from the temple."

"Can you handle him on your own?" asked Tora.

"Yes, easily."

"Then I'll stay with Lekore and the Hakija. I don't want to lose track of them again."

Nerenoth nodded. “Thank you, Holy One.”

Tora turned to Lekore. “Come.” He raced toward a dark alley off the road.

The flaming walls fell, and Lekore sprinted toward the backstreet on Tora’s heels, then faltered and spun. “What about Ank?”

Nerenoth didn’t turn around. “I shall care for his body once I’ve slain Teon. That is a promise. Go, please, Your Majesty.”

Lekore’s eyes lighted on Ank, then he nodded. Dakeer brushed his fingers on Lekore’s arm, their eyes met, then they fled into the shadowed street, leaving the Lord Captain to fight alone.

CHAPTER 24

Left behind, frustrated that she couldn't disagree with the Lord Captain's decision, Talanee stalked the palace halls, adorned in her plainest gown, graceful sword clutched in her fingers, hair caught back in a braid. Keerva would die of shame to watch her princess, stripped of title, looking for all the world like a disjointed noblewoman itching for a fight.

But it's exactly what I am.

She'd considered following Ademas's group to the Temple of the Moon but thought better of it. Until she understood how the Tawloomez girl Khyna had managed to control her, she couldn't risk others' lives, and the city might still be stuffed with slave insurgents.

Still, she had to do *something* useful. Everything she'd been born to do, to be, had been ripped away. What became of a princess with no throne?

She's married off to political advantage, what else?

Talanee swept through the hallways faster. Guards eyed her, unmoving, still tense from the day's battle. Even the presence of Sun Gods couldn't spare them the fear of attack. Perhaps it made them even more uptight.

Talanee's steps stammered. She turned and blazed a trail east, toward the wing set aside for the wounded Sun Gods. *We know they can be killed. They're not invincible.*

Khyna had meant to use Talanee against Tora. Whether killing him would have been simple or not, she'd intended to try. Nerenoth and Tora had run off to investigate the light shining over the unholy temple, and Ademas and his company had sneaked out ahead of them, leaving Kel guards and a few priests, servants, healers, and no one else to protect the other Sun Gods resting in a chamber.

Except for me.

Surely, Nerenoth had fortified the chamber's defenses. But would that be enough if the slaves revolted again? Princess Talanee knew how to duel; she led every woman's tournament in fencing and knife-throwing, and she had no qualms about killing an enemy. Here, she could tip the scale if the situation required it.

As she neared the east wing, the clatter of footfalls sounded ahead. Talanee peeked around a corner and found several healers conversing in soft tones. Letting out a breath, Talanee shook her plain lavender gown straight, then walked into view. The healers looked up and straightened.

"Your Highness," the female healer said, dipping into a curtsey.

The male healer bowed. "May we help you?"

"I'm just checking on our holy guests. How are they mending?"

The healers exchanged grim looks. The woman spoke. "Most are well, Your Highness. One fares ill. He might not survive."

Talanee pursed her lips as her chest constricted. "There's nothing you can do?"

The healers shook their heads.

"Nothing beyond what we're doing now, Your Highness," the man said. "Divine blood is different from ours. Even should we attempt a transfusion, it could pollute the Sun God with our impurities. We don't have the skills necessary to do more than make him comfortable and staunch the bleeding."

The woman squeezed her hands. "The Sun God with the broken leg—Holy Raren, he is called—he said other Sun Gods will soon descend to heal them and asked us to keep his companions comfortable meanwhile." Her eyes brightened. "He thanked us for our efforts."

Talanee excused herself and slipped past them to peek in on the Sun Gods. The one called Raren slept propped up against a handful of feather pillows, his mouth slightly open, breaths deep. The other three Sun Gods slumbered stretched out, breaths floating above them, the only noise in the chamber.

All looked comfortable, considering their conditions. The air, smelling strongly of fresh herbs, felt warm, but not stifling as evening dropped into night. Blue drapes had been drawn, shrouding the room in semi-darkness.

Satisfied, Talanee withdrew from the room and started to close the door, but a tingle spread up her spine and she halted. Her eyes scoured the chamber until she spotted a misshapen shadow against the glow of the hearth fire.

Think fast. Account for your hesitation.

She thumbed a ring from her finger and cupped it in one hand. With a curse, she made a show of her bare hand and stooped to pat around, working her way into the chamber on her knees. She left the door ajar. With stealthy fingers she rolled the ring to the edge of the nearest bed and crawled toward it, padding around on the floor.

Should I call the guards or am I imagining things?

If she called for one under the pretense of seeking her ring, the action might encourage the hidden assailant to lash out. Talanee nibbled the inside of her lip and brushed stray locks of blue hair from her face as she groped for the ring.

"Ah ha." She snatched it and rose, slipped the ring onto her finger, and shook her gown straight. She casually draped her hand over her sword hilt, mirroring Ademas, and turned toward the open door.

The faintest scuff of a foot against the floor pricked Talanee's ears and she spun, unsheathing her blade. The point came just shy of a half-Tawloomez girl standing before her, red eyes wide, a boot knife clutched in her hand.

"*You*," Talanee growled. This was the same girl who'd tried to assassinate Lekore on the Irothé roof. Talanee scanned the room. "How did you get away from your guards?"

The girl's lips slid up. "I killed them. Unless you wish me to do the same to you, stand back and let me fulfill my duty."

Talanee scoffed. "Let you slay the Sun Gods so that my soul can be condemned alongside your own? Absolutely not."

The girl's eyes narrowed. "Getaal scum." She lunged right to evade Talanee's blade, but the princess swung to follow her path. The girl—had Nerenoth called her Nitaan?—sprang back, scowling. She whirled and raced to the nearest bed, knife glinting.

"Not on my watch!" Talanee sprinted after her and jabbed her sword at the girl, who narrowly dodged and staggered away from the bed. Talanee positioned herself between the intruder and the bed, heart clattering against her ribs, breaths shallow, eyes narrowed. "I'll never let you slay them, *heretic*."

"Nitaan, stop!" A boy's voice rang out from behind the drapes.

The girl started and glanced toward the noise without dropping her guard. "Teyed, stay out of this."

The drapes flung aside, letting in the last vestiges of daylight as Nitaan's brother stepped away from the open window. A breeze curled around his face and tugged at his patched clothes. His red eyes looked strange in his dark face, flashing crimson in the firelight.

"I won't let you do this," Teyed said. "We're not minions of the Star Gods any longer. We can escape that life. Please, Nitaan."

The girl's lips curled into a snarl. "Silence. You don't understand. The Sun Gods used us before—they'll use us again! Hurt us and then kill us!"

A new voice, deep and male, spoke. "I can understand your fear, but we're not like those who came before us."

Talanee found the Sun God Raren sitting forward, one hand

resting on a blade set beside him. She hadn't noticed the weapon before.

Raren smiled sadly, orange eyes rooted on Nitaan. "You're too late to kill us. If I chose, I could slaughter every person in this room before you could reach the door. But I won't. I don't enjoy murder. That doesn't mean I wouldn't defend myself and my companions if necessary." He nodded toward Teyed. "Heed your friend's request. Drop your knife, and I'll spare you."

Nitaan's eyes widened. A wild light flashed in them. "If I can't fulfill my duty—"

"No, Nitaan, wait!" Teyed darted forward.

Talanee reached the girl before Nitaan could plunge the knife in her own chest. Knocking the blade aside, Talanee slammed her fist into Nitaan's cheek. The girl stumbled back, hair flying free from her hood. She cradled her cheek.

Talanee kicked the blade away. "You don't get to run. You have to face this new future alongside the rest of us, whether we care for it or not."

Nitaan stared at her, tears brimming in her Kel eyes as a bruise formed on her olive-complected cheek. As she blinked, a single tear escaped to roll down her face.

Teyed crept forward and caught his sister's arm. "This is better, Nitaan. We can't defeat gods."

CHAPTER 25

Huddled in the gloom of the king's large antechamber, Lor made himself useful by stoking the fire in the hearth each time it weakened. Evening stretched into night, and the world beyond the palace room fell silent. If guards still stood outside the door, Lor couldn't hear them.

What's happening out there?

Keo hadn't returned. Ademas and his team of rescuers had gone off to find Lekore. The Lord Captain hadn't been seen in hours. Even Lekore's servants had run off somewhere and never returned.

Lor's stomach rumbled. He patted it. "I know, I know." He scanned the room but not a crumb from breakfast remained. No one had served dinner or supper.

What should I do? Stay here and starve, for how long? He rubbed his face and groaned. *They'll be back. They'll bring a feast for their king, and maybe you can beg a bite.*

Sobs broke the stillness. Lor froze, then dragged his eyes from the dancing flames to the closed doors adjacent to the large chamber. Bedrooms, if he rightly guessed.

Someone is still here?

He licked his dry lips and strained his ears.

The sobs continued.

Hadn't Lekore mentioned someone rested within one of the adjoining rooms?

Lor rose from his crouch, fingers twitching for a knife he didn't possess. He steeled himself, plucked up a solid gold candlestick from the nearest stand, and crept toward the noise. The sobs drifted through the crack under the door, wretched, heavy.

How well he knew that pain. Lor eased the door open, grateful the hinges were oiled and silent. The faint fire glow paved a path through the chamber's gloom, revealing a large bed and a weeping figure upon it.

Lor lowered his candlestick and padded into the room, drawn by the heartrending noise. He reached the bed, undetected by the young Kel woman crying into a pillow.

"Why do you cry?" His voice startled him. He hadn't meant to speak.

With a yelp, the young woman jerked upright and flung the pillow. He batted it aside then buckled beneath the woman's weight as she threw herself at him, clawing for his eyes. Lor struck the floor as he captured her wrists and held them away from his face.

Her red eyes, burning in the faint glow, held the wild wrath of an injured emockye. She snarled, long dark blue hair netting her face.

Lor tightened his grip on her wrists. "Stop. I will not harm you."

She writhed against him. "Liar! Scum!"

He adjusted his weight and threw her to one side, then climbed atop her and pressed her to the floor. "I am not an enemy."

She screamed as she tried to wriggle free. "Let. Me. Go!"

"No!" His voice cracked. Rarely had he yelled before.

She shrank and whimpered, falling still.

Lor sighed. "Listen, I am not an enemy. I am Lor. See? I have a name."

She rolled her head to one side and stared into the darkness. "You're Tawloomez."

He sighed. "And you are Kel. Yet we cry the same way."

She blinked, tears slipping down her face to drip on the floor. "You killed my family."

"No. *I* didn't."

Her eyes narrowed. "Liar."

Lor resisted a strong urge to shake the foolish Kel. He gritted his teeth and let the anger roll through him, then he released a breath. "Listen to me, *Kel.* I was banished by my own people because I would not cater to the Teokaka's wishes. I would not agree to send armies to your kingdom. I am tired of war. Tired of hatred. I am so tired."

His vision blurred, and he chewed on his lip. *Do not cry. Not here, not now. She'll only mock you.*

A tear dripped from his eye. He blinked his vision clear and found the Kel staring up at him, his tear running down her cheek.

"Liar." Her voice croaked.

He shook his head. "I am not a liar. I try always to tell the truth. You are Kel—I could blame you for enslaving my mother when I was small, for dragging her to these lands. But you didn't do that. Nor have I slain your family. That was a different Tawloomez."

She held his gaze, probing. "I hate you."

"Me, or my people?"

Her head rolled to the side. "Why aren't you killing me?"

"I am not your enemy." He sighed and let his head hang, his long hair curtaining them. "I told you, I'm weary of all this fighting. I want it to end. I want my people to thrive, not die in an endless cycle of animosity. When is it enough?"

Her body shuddered. Lor lifted his gaze to find her face. Tears flowed from her gleaming eyes, face scrunched in grief. "I want my family b-back."

Her pain washed through him, so familiar. "So do I." He

whispered the words. "But we never will. And if we keep fighting, others will suffer the same loss."

Her limbs slackened, and she lay beneath him, weeping. Lor slowly, carefully uncurled his fingers and released her. She didn't move. With great care, he took the Kel's arms and lifted her until she sat upright. She leaned into him and buried her face in his shoulder. Lor wrapped his arms around her and let her cry.

Weep for us both and all we might have kept, had hatred not possessed our peoples.

"What is your name?" he asked after a while.

Silence. Then, "Mayrilana." A breath. "Irothé."

"You are the Lord Captain's kin?"

She nodded against him.

"Mayrilana." He whispered the name, testing the strange order of syllables on his tongue. "Mayrilana, let us begin it."

She sniffed. "Begin what, Lor?"

"A new cycle. Let us bury hate, right here."

"I don't know...if I can."

He smiled. "Do you want to?"

"Y-yes. It's so heavy. It hurts so much." She clutched at her chest.

Lor stared at the open doorway and the flames painting shadow and light against the wood. "Breathe it out. Let us both breathe it out." He stroked her blue hair. "I don't want to hate anymore."

She drew a low breath and released it. "Neither do I."

CHAPTER 26

Clods of dirt hammered the ground as the tunnel collapsed behind Ademas and Farr Veon. They raced against the earthquake, the ground rumbling under their feet, dust coiling over the air to blind them.

Farr Veon tripped over debris and hurdled forward, dropping his torch. The flame guttered, then died before Ademas could snatch it. Plunged into darkness, he scrabbled instead for the Dark Hakija.

"Where are you, Holiness?"

Farr Veon coughed. "Here. Keep going."

Dirt poured down near Ademas's shoulder. "Right." He felt for the earthen wall and ran his fingers along its rough surface as he staggered ahead. *We won't make it.*

The booms and crashes drew closer. At the same moment, fresh air tickled Ademas's nose. He squinted, seeking a pinprick of light. Nothing.

"Do you smell that?" asked Farr Veon.

"Think so." Ademas stumbled over a cluster of rocks and soil. Straightened. Plunged onward.

There. A slivering crack of light in the ceiling yards ahead. He charged toward it, lurching over mounds of rock, steadying himself against the wall. He reached the pool of light seconds ahead of Farr Veon, and they stared up at a cracked slope leading to a sagging door swathed in cobwebs.

Farr Veon gripped Ademas's arm and shoved him ahead. "Go. Go!"

Ademas raced up the shuddering incline as the crack widened. The door moaned on its hinges, then burst apart as the walls collapsed.

He bounded forward and plunged through the gaping portal as dirt and splinters rained down on his legs. He rolled onto a derelict street, then lay flat, gasping. Sweat poured down his face, hair clung to his skin, and his limbs shook. Wincing, he lifted his head as the crash and thunder of the tunnel filled the air with noise and dust. At his feet, hunched over, arms shaking, Farr Veon stared at the ground as the quake ceased. The rumble quieted.

"Too...close..." the Dark Hakija gasped.

Ademas grunted his agreement and ran over a mental checklist of his body's condition. Minor scrapes and bruises to add to those the Tawloomez taskmasters had gifted him. No broken bones. Far too much dirt. He shook his head, and a cloud of dust scattered on the night's breeze.

After shifting to sit upright, Ademas probed the star-littered sky for the Temple of the Moon or the city wall to orient himself. There. The wall loomed on his right, lit up by the night watch whose prowling silhouettes stretched larger than life on the battlements. The gates stood farther east, just visible beyond the sagging buildings of the west slums. Ademas dragged his gaze along the south line of hulking shadows. The temple should be just—

Farr Veon shot to his feet. "Where is it?"

Ademas straightened at a more languid pace. "Must've collapsed."

"Impossible."

"Not with all those webbed tunnels, it's not. The foundation couldn't be very strong. I've seen rodent holes undermine the root structure of an old tree, if there's enough of them. That earthquake could've been half as strong and still buried these slums. We're lucky to be alive, Your Holiness."

Farr Veon's jaw set, brows knitted. His frame shook. "Yes. You're right, I know you're right." He angled to face Ademas. "You don't really believe the earthquake was natural, do you?"

The ground rumbled as an aftershock rocked the tunnels, then stilled.

Ademas's lips twitched up. "No, Holiness. I've seen Lekore draw on the might of Fire Mountain, taming it to his will. He definitely did this."

The Dark Hakija narrowed his eyes. "He's more powerful than I'd thought. No wonder the gods demand him for their own." He turned his back to Ademas. "To call on his powers, he must've passed the boundary of the temple grounds. We'll have no luck finding him in the dark. We should return to the temple and assess the damage there."

"Right." Ademas followed the young man as he drew his cowl over his head.

They moved along the shadows, keeping their steps quiet. Soon, the clamor of swords rang out a few streets westward, and Farr Veon glanced over his shoulder.

"We should investigate that."

"Agreed." Ademas lengthened his strides to keep the Hakija's pace.

Farr Veon darted into the nearest alley, swallowed by the blackened street. Ademas plunged into the darkness and willed his eyes to adjust to the gloom as the clatter grew louder the deeper into the slums they padded.

Footsteps tramped close and Farr Veon pressed against the building at the alley's mouth. Ademas followed suit, then stiffened as three figures emerged from the alley directly across the street. Moonlight pooled down on them, revealing their faces: Tora, Lekore, and Dakeer Vasar.

Farr Veon chuckled under his breath. "The Star Gods favor us this night."

Ademas arched an eyebrow but didn't mention the earthquake. *Let the lunatic think what he likes.* Only someone utterly deranged would defy the Sun Gods to their faces.

More importantly, Ademas had a choice to make.

It wasn't hard.

Grasping his hilt, he crept up behind the Dark Hakija, whipped his sword loose, and slammed the pommel into Farr Veon's skull. The man crumpled with a grunt.

Ademas sheathed his sword, flung back his cowl, and sprinted into the open. The party of three stumbled to a halt.

"Ademas," cried Lekore.

Dakeer stared at the starburst pendant on Ademas's chest, then the black cloak around his shoulders, eyes narrowed.

"Just moving discreetly in the night, Holiness," Ademas said, grinning. "Here in the slums, *you* stick out."

Lekore jogged to Ademas's side, face pale in the moonlight, eyes red-rimmed. "Are you hurt?"

Ademas cocked his head. "Me? You're the one we're all worried about. But it seems you're capable of getting yourself out of the very scrapes you step willingly into."

"Only sometimes." Lekore dipped his head as his shoulders shook. "Ank is—*Netye* is dead."

Ademas fell still. His mind curled over the words, weighing them. "I'm sorry for your sake, but that's all. He deserved to die."

Lekore's head flew up. Pain flashed in his red eyes, and his chin quivered. "Did he?"

"He committed treason, murdered our father, and left you for dead. Not to mention his mad choices as king. Perhaps you can forgive him. I won't fault you for that. It's your nature. But justice is *mine*. Netye deserved execution." He sighed and scratched his head. "This is no place to debate all this. The Hakija of the Night is slumped over in that alley." He pointed. "I'll bring him along. Let's get *you* back to the palace."

Tora stepped close, slitted eyes vivid beneath the moon. "I wholeheartedly concur. Let's be swift and silent."

No one argued. They moved into the alleyway, and Dakeer helped support Farr Veon. He and Ademas dragged the unconscious man along the filthy byroads, their progress slow.

"No offence intended, Holy Light," Ademas said as he shifted the Dark Hakija's arm over his shoulder, "but wouldn't it be faster to transport us like you did from the Firelands?"

"Yes, if I could." Tora rubbed his smooth chin. "That ability is best used over long distances. To use it within the confines of your city would tire me quickly, and my precision would be inhibited by the propinquity of my target location."

Lekore's footsteps slowed. "Pro...pin...quity? You use strange words."

Tora glanced behind him. "Sorry. Sometimes I can't suppress the scholar in me." He swiveled his wrist. "It's another word for proximity or nearness."

"Ah." Lekore quickened his steps.

Ademas smiled. His long-lost brother: the gentle savage.

"What about your wind, Lekore?" Ademas asked. "Can't it carry us to the palace?"

"Yes...it could. Normally. But it's preoccupied."

Ademas didn't press him. *What do I know about magic and miracles?*

"Will Nerenoth be all right?" asked Lekore as they turned onto a street outside the slums. Lanterns flickered along the thoroughfare, and candlelight snaked down through the curtained windows of a well-tended townhouse.

"Where is he?" Ademas asked.

"Fighting Teon Keela." Dakeer's voice lowered into a growl. "I knew that brute for a worm, but I didn't recognize the heretic beneath."

Ademas tried a shrug despite his burden. "Hard to tell different types of worm apart."

"True." Tora scanned the road. "Keep going."

They made their way south by the straightest course possible. Once, Farr Veon moaned but remained unconscious.

The march of two dozen or more boots brought the company up short, and Tora raced ahead, sword glistening in the lantern glow. He reached the end of the street as the troop of garrison soldiers rounded the corner. They faltered, and their captain stammered out a hasty apology.

Feet slapped the cobblestones behind them. Lekore whirled, and Ademas craned his neck to spot the newcomers. From a close alley, Mother appeared, followed by Rez, Carak, and the Irothé twins, all clad in men's clothes and black cloaks. Relief shot through Ademas's limbs.

"We finally caught you," Mother said, a hand pressed to her chest. "So much for all our schemes." Her eyes narrowed on Farr Veon's slouched frame.

"Excellent timing," Tora said. "Captain?"

The officer stepped forward. "Yes, my Holy God?"

"Please escort this man," he gestured at Farr Veon, "to the palace and keep him under careful watch. We'll follow closely."

"Yes, Holy God." The captain motioned, and two soldiers marched up to claim the Dark Hakija from Ademas and Dakeer.

As the soldiers trooped off to the palace, Ademas rolled his shoulders to loosen his muscles. His gaze settled on Mother. "So long as all is well, our schemes don't matter. There's more than one road to the same destination, after all."

Lekore faced the northwestern slums. "Someone shot Ank. The wind still has him in its grasp. What shall I do with the assassin?"

Ademas marched to his side. "Someone *shot* him, and you caught them? And you're just now mentioning this?" He caught Lekore's shoulder and turned him around. "Can you have the wind bring him here?"

Lekore nodded. "Yes. The wind spirits grow restless. Best to relieve them of their burden." He lifted a hand. "Bring your captive to me."

He flung up his hand like he released a bird onto the breeze, then watched it fly away.

Ademas tugged on his arm. "We should keep moving. The wind will find you, right?"

"Yes."

Lekore let Ademas lead him around the corner and along a narrow street lined by flowers, their petals closed for the night. The fragrance coiled around the company, Tora in the front, the twins in the rear. Insects danced in the light of a hanging lantern. The distant march of the troop ahead thudded in Ademas's ears. He glanced at Lekore from the corner of his eye, bewildered by his brother.

I better understand Talanee's concerns about him, but I'll not try to change who he is. He's chosen by the Sun Gods. I'm likely wrong to feel as I do, not him.

Ademas's gaze shifted to Tora. The youthful Sun God glided along the street, lithe and slender, otherworldly as a god ought to be. Ademas yearned to discuss theology long and hard with Tora. To clarify and amend the points of doctrine so long ingrained into the Kel. Slavery, bloodshed, sacrifice. What of these was acceptable and when?

Surely, he'll correct us.

And Lekore, raised by the Sun Gods, would help as well.

But if he wants me to forgive Netye, that's impossible. I can't and I won't.

Sun Gods or no Sun Gods, some feelings couldn't be buried, alive or dead.

CHAPTER 27

"Are we close enough?"

Tahomin checked the planet's proximity. "A few more minutes ought to do it."

"Good. I've had enough of living in this tin."

Tahomin shrugged. "You could always stop traveling."

Vay-Dinn sighed and plucked at the hem of his gold-and-silver lined jacket. He stood up from his wingback chair and trotted to Tahomin's side at the console. "Right. Because that's so much more appealing." The prince's pout vanished as he read the stats scrawling down the console's holoscreen. A gleam brightened his blue eyes, and he leaned closer. "Wait for me, little Seer. I'm almost there."

Tahomin wore a flat smile. "No doubt, they're eager to meet you."

Vay-Dinn chuckled. "You never know. We did rearrange their theological system, didn't we? Or am I thinking of some other world?"

"You set yourself up as a god, but that was with the nomadic people. Taw...something. Can't remember." Tahomin pressed a few keys. "That Ahvenian armada is still on course for the border."

"All the more reason to grab the Seer and get out." Vay-Dinn tapped his finger on the sleek black surface of the console. "What's got Majentay's notice? If we run into him, we don't have the support we need. Close enough?"

Tahomin checked the proximity report. "Yeah. We're good to go."

"Excellent." Vay-Dinn rubbed his gloved hands together. "Shall we?"

"Where do we want to appear?"

"How about outside that southern complex? We should announce ourselves properly, right at the front doors."

Tahomin nodded and pushed a button. "We're going ahead, captain. We'll be back soon."

"Yes, my lord," answered the voice through the speakers.

Tahomin closed his eyes and imagined the walls of the Ahvenian complex, with its ornate gates and white stone battlements. The floor tilted, and its texture softened as wind swept through his dark purple hair, snatching at his high ponytail. He opened his eyes to find the white stone wall sparkling under a full moon. The fragrance of the young world danced around him, crisp, hinting of blood.

Two hundred yards off, in the grasslands, camped a large army with blazing fires. Tahomin caught the whiff of smoking meat and leather. Perhaps that primitive race, the one that worshipped the active volcano?

Must be in the middle of a skirmish.

"Ahhh, how it's aged." Vay-Dinn paced to the gate at an easy saunter, shoulder-length A-line hair swaying. He pressed his hand against the carved wood. "Shall we?"

Tahomin let himself smile. "As you please."

Vay-Dinn grinned, eyes sparkling. "Knock, knock." Violet light snapped out from his fingertips to crawl up the gates like lightning, and the massive doors burst from their hinges with a roar to land inside the complex, cracking cobblestones. Dust plumed into the air like a pale cloud.

The night watch shouted, and torches bobbed against the sky

as figures darted down the wall's steps and poured from the guardhouses. Kel. Tahomin snorted. Figured. They'd turned the laboratory complex into a city. And why not? The Ahvenians had all been killed.

"Hello there," said Vay-Dinn and dodged right as a Kel soldier charged him, sword swinging. "Rude." Vay-Dinn shot a spray of violet magic at the soldier, who screamed as it struck him, then slumped over and sprawled across the ground. The Kiisuld prince turned to face the clump of soldiers hanging back. "Take us to your leader, hm?"

Tahomin suppressed an eyeroll.

"You're them: The Star Gods," stammered a youthful soldier.

Vay-Dinn lifted one brow. "Ah. If you recognize us, this should be easy. As your gods, you're wisest to do what we want, hm?"

The man swallowed. "I serve the Sun Gods alone."

Vay-Dinn's eye twitched. His lips quivered, and he coughed out a laugh. "Ah ha. Yes. I remember now. Indeed, and your loyalty is a credit to you. But you can better serve your shiny gods alive, right? So, bring us to your leader, and I'll spare you. Otherwise, you'll not enjoy the form I choose to send you in to meet your *gods*."

The man's red eyes widened, then he gripped his sword tighter and shook his head. "I'll not risk my soul."

Vay-Dinn shrugged and unleashed violet threads to wrap around the man, squeezing until the soldier cried out. "Loyalty is commendable, little Kel. So is wisdom. Anyone else care to escort us, or do you all prefer to die a martyr's death?"

No one moved.

Tahomin scanned the complex-turned-city and considered the distant structures blazing brightest. "I think that's their palace." He pointed to the middlemost edifice.

Vay-Dinn followed his gaze, as his power continued to squeeze the life out of the soldier. "Could be. I'd still appreciate an escort. Nobody?"

Footsteps crunched broken stone. A black-cloaked figure padded toward them, a starburst pendant winking against its chest.

A few feet away, the figure bowed low. "Welcome to Erokel, my glorious dark gods." The voice was a low, hungry whisper.

"Ah, a devotee." Vay-Dinn's expression hardened as the soldier's bones cracked and the man let out a harrowing scream. The violet light vanished. The man crashed to the ground, body broken. Vay-Dinn angled to face the cloaked figure. "Will *you* bring us to your leader?"

The figure didn't straighten. "As you wish, I shall obey. Do you desire to meet with our king or your mouthpiece?"

"I imagine my mouthpiece has what I came here for."

The figure hesitated. "He did, my god—but the world has been plunged into chaos this night. I'm not certain where your prize is."

Vay-Dinn sighed and ran a hand along his forehead. "Why doesn't that surprise me? Very well. Your king then. Let him explain."

The figure straightened, and red eyes glimmered beneath the shadowed cowl. "This way, my dark gods."

The clatter of armor sounded behind Vay-Dinn and Tahomin.

"Personally, I'd not bother," Vay-Dinn said without glancing back. "You know better than to squander your lives—but I leave the final choice up to you."

A handful of armored soldiers charged them, swords raised.

One shouted, "For the glory of the Sun Throne." He dropped dead with a gurgle as Tahomin struck him with a web of violet light.

Hollow lightning struck down the remaining four contenders as they came within yards of Vay-Dinn. The rest of the watch held back, eyes wide, fingers tracing a symbol over the open air.

The Kiisuld strode from the walls, southward, toward the distant lab-turned-palace. Tahomin studied the far-off second building rising over the rooftops: a cathedral, judging by the bells and the feeling of faith exuding from its façade.

"Fascinating." Vay-Dinn glanced at the structures lining the tidy street. "They've turned the storage buildings into townhouses and copied the Ahvenian architecture with surprising quality, for a medieval civilization. I bet they're more innovative than most."

"Likely," Tahomin said. "But still burning candles." He eyed a carriage parked on the side of the street, a wingless pythe harnessed to its front. *That's right, the Ahvenians tried to breed flight out of them.* "Their conveyance is still primitive as well."

Vay-Dinn shrugged. "Still, our influence and those of the *Sun Gods* have done something remarkable. I wonder if other civilizations we've left standing have similar societies or not."

"Depends on how we left them, I suspect." Tahomin glanced back and found a cluster of the city watch following at a safe distance, while the remaining guards returned to their walls.

"I suppose so." Vay-Dinn sighed. "This is going to take an age. You, disciple."

The cloaked figure turned. "Yes, my god?"

Vay-Dinn waggled his fingers at the carriage. "Let's take this. I don't want to walk across your little city."

"As you wish, my glorious god." The figure checked the harness. "It's prepared."

Vay-Dinn stepped into the carriage, and Tahomin slipped in after him as the cloaked figure took the driver's seat. The pythe let out a snort then wheeled the vehicle around to lope toward the palace.

Despite the cobblestones, the carriage glided with relative smoothness down the road. The Kel had created decent suspension for their bygone methods. The Kiisuld partners sat in silence, neither much bothered by the rumble of the wheels and the hush inside the vehicle. Tahomin often preferred these fleeting moments of stillness. He'd long grown bored of world dominance and mass destruction.

At least this is something different. Maybe we can try cultivating and manipulating more cultures instead of using them up.

Ultimately, that was up to Vay-Dinn. The prince called the shots; a fact that didn't trouble Tahomin. He preferred not to overthink things. When he tried, his frustrations only grew.

Vay-Dinn sat with an elbow braced against the window, chin propped on his palm. His gaze absorbed the outside world. "I wonder what plunged the masses into chaos. It better not spoil our plans."

"I doubt it's anything we can't handle."

"Hope not. I'd rather not become irritated."

Tahomin smiled in the seat across from him. "You've been leaning toward irritability for days."

"I can't help it." Vay-Dinn sighed and leaned back against the leather cushions. "It's your fault, you know. Every time you visit that blasted old man, you sulk, and it puts me in a foul mood."

That's probably true. Tahomin sighed. "I'll try harder not to sulk in the future."

Vay-Dinn grimaced. "No, don't do that either. A happy Tahomin scares me more than a sulky one. I just don't like it, that's all." He leaned out the window again. "Hopefully, this Seer will help."

Tahomin's hands curled into fists. *I'm counting on it.* Aloud, he said nothing.

The rock and clatter of the carriage filled Tahomin's mind. Five hundred years since last they'd visited this world. How slowly these primitive cultures advanced, even helped along by Kiisuld and Ahvenian influences.

Are we any different? Kiisuld haven't advanced in millennia. We're too arrogant to think we can improve and so our progression's halted entirely. Maybe we're worse than the societies creeping toward our past achievements.

Ahvenians were different. They advanced magically, scientifically, even philosophically, at a steady clip.

"You're treading a dangerous internal path again, aren't you?"

Tahomin blinked at his prince. A faint smile caught his lips. "Maybe."

"Definitely. I can tell. Stop sulking. We're almost there. We've almost got him—or her. Whichever." The man shrugged.

"Everything will change." His eyes danced with hunger. "Let my father try to stop me *now*."

Tahomin shifted in his seat. "Careful, Your Highness. We've snared Seers before. We've got to be more careful this time."

"Yes, yes. I know. Nothing hasty. We take our time."

Tahomin glanced outside at the passing city. "Yeah, but not until after we grab the Seer. I don't relish meeting that armada."

Vay-Dinn grunted. "Yes, that. I really would like to know what caught that man's attention so close to the border. It could raise my father's notice as well. We can't have that."

"It should be fine, if we're fast."

Vay-Dinn thumped the carriage ceiling. "Faster. C'mon. We don't have all night."

The carriage lurched as a whip cracked.

CHAPTER 28

Nerenoth slammed against the crumbling wall of a burned-out townhouse, teeth ground together, the taste of copper in his mouth. Teon leered as he pressed his sword against Nerenoth's, metal grinding.

Brute strength aside, Teon had more skill than he'd ever let on in festival tourneys.

Even so.

Nerenoth rammed his foot against Teon's kneecap, and the man howled and staggered back. The Lord Captain knocked Teon's sword away, sidestepped, and set his blade against the traitor's throat. "Any last words, Keela?"

Teon spat at the ground. "Star Gods rot you, vile sun-lover."

Nerenoth slid the blade along the man's flesh in a swift, smooth motion. Gurgling, Teon slumped forward and thrashed before he fell still. Blood pooled around his head.

Nerenoth wiped his weapon clean on Teon's white and gold tunic, then straightened and slipped the sword into its sheath. Silence hummed in his ears until an emockye howled beyond the city wall. Nerenoth wiped his lips and studied the blood smeared across his knuckles, then squared his armored shoulders and paced to Netye's corpse, ignoring a twinge in his ankle. Blood soaked his padded sleeve where Teon had nicked him. He felt no pain; he didn't have time.

He must reach his king.

He stared down at Netye. "You brought this upon yourself. I'd leave you here to rot, had I the choice." Nerenoth stooped. He shifted his long hair over one shoulder, and hefted the heavy body over his other shoulder, armor pinching under the corpse's weight.

Grimacing, he tramped toward the palace.

As the company, headed by Tora, neared the palace walls, the Ahvenian slowed to match Lekore's pace, regarding him with a searching look.

Lekore met his gaze with some reluctance. His heart hung low in his chest, grief settling in like a cloak to cover his soul.

"He meant a great deal to you," Tora whispered.

Lekore's breath caught in his throat. He swallowed. "Yes. He is all I remembered beyond my life in the Vale That Shines Gold. He was my hope."

The Ahvenian nodded, brows pinched as he stared ahead. "It isn't much of a consolation, I know, but in death he no longer suffers from his madness."

"Yes." Lekore sighed. "Yet I longed to help him, if I could." He stared at the twinkling heavens, for the first time finding them aloof. "Now I shall never know if I could have."

"He loved you, that you can keep close and cherish."

Lekore nodded. "Yet I feel that I cannot stay here now. The grief is too great, and the world too small."

"You could come with me, if you wanted." Tora gestured upward. "Raal Corenic is a training ground for the magical. I'd like you to see it."

A pinprick of hope jolted Lekore's heart, enlivening feelings beyond grief. "Perhaps...perhaps I—"

Tora's step faltered as he reached the gates. His eyes widened as terror poured off his soul like a flood.

Lekore eyed him, puzzled, then his flesh crawled. He whirled to face north and the thoroughfare leading to the Sun Courtyard.

"What is that?"

Skye appeared at his side. "Lekore, they've come. They jumped ship, using the Hollow to arrive faster."

Tora shuddered. "The Kiisuld are here. In the city. We're too late." His stricken expression sent chills marching up Lekore's spine.

"Where?" Lekore looked at Skye.

"At the gates."

Wind spirits fluted. Lekore looked up as the spirits lowered a man, bound and gagged by the wispy elementals, to the courtyard stones as Mother, the Irothé twins, and the single soldier shifted aside.

Ademas gasped. "Uncle Elekel?"

The man, clad in muted clothes, eyes wide, tried to speak through his sealed lips. Lekore gestured, and the spirits flitted away from his mouth.

"Nephew!" The man's eyes swiveled to latch onto Lekore. "You can release me, Your Highness. I intended to strike down Netye and that big brute alone. You were never in danger."

"*You* shot Netye?" Ademas asked.

The twins exchanged grins.

Mother strode through the cluster of onlookers. "I didn't think you had the fortitude to kill your brother. Certainly, you took your time about it." Her eyes slid to Lekore. "Adenye, this is your uncle, Elekel Getaal, youngest of the three brothers." Her face strained. "Last to survive."

Elekel wrestled against his invisible bonds. "First to lose his limbs if I'm not freed. Not that I don't value your *gifts*, dear nephew. But I find this experience extremely unnerving."

Lekore caught the man's gaze and locked onto it. "You intended to kill Ank?" He cringed. "Netye, as you call him."

Elekel sighed. "I realize he mattered to you, but I've no regrets. He was a maddened, weak, foolish creature. Adelair was my role model, my friend, as well as brother. Most lamentable of all is that you seem to remember your treacherous uncle rather than your noble father."

Ademas laid a hand on Lekore's shoulder. "Release him. He'll do no further harm."

Lekore's hand trembled as he motioned again. "Please unbind him."

The wind spirits retreated and sprang up into the cool night air. Lekore traced their movements until the chills plaguing his frame sharpened. His eyes dropped to the northern road. "We should enter the palace and plan a defense."

"Yes." Tora spoke, voice tense, blue eyes bright and wide, terror beating like a raging tide against his soul. He shook himself, and his eyes cleared. "We should do whatever we can against them."

The company swept through the palace gates, Elekel trotting beside Ademas, massaging his wrists. The twins and the soldier murmured amongst themselves. Lekore studied his uncle's face in glimpses over his shoulders as he limped toward the palace steps.

Talanee marched out between the opened doors, soldiers at her back. She twisted her pale purple skirts in her hands and started down the steps until Ademas raced ahead to stop her.

"Back inside," he muttered. "The Star Gods are here."

Talanee stared, then whirled and traipsed inside ahead of those climbing the steps. Lekore entered the palace, and his muscles eased at once. He grimaced. Walls wouldn't matter when the Kiisuld reached the palace.

Don't let your guard down even for a moment. His fingers pricked as *Calir* answered his silent inquiry. The sword would be ready when he needed it.

Will I be ready?

Skye glided beside him, silent, brows drawn. The apparition looked as though he'd aged, though that wasn't possible. His shoulders hunched together, and his fingers played at the air, perhaps itching for his ethereal sword.

Lekore reached for him, as he had a thousand times before. Skye was family; all he knew and remembered beyond the bittersweet memory of Ank until recent days. Yet he couldn't touch his ancestor. Couldn't feel his embrace. When Lekore had lain in fevered torment, Skye had looked on, words soothing, touch absent. When he'd fallen into a pit and injured his leg, Skye had stayed with him, unable to help him climb out. Instead, Lekore had learned how to call upon the earth spirits to help him.

Skye had always been close but never quite real.

Lekore's fingers closed over air where Skye's arm ought to be. The ghost met his gaze, sorrow etched into his red irises. The world rested on his shoulders, crushing his bright, translucent soul.

"I'm all right," Skye said, smiling.

Lekore shook his head but didn't argue. They both knew the ghost couldn't be well, not with his brother's mentors so near, closing in.

Tora had joined Talanee and Ademas at the head of the procession, and they raced toward the throne room, footsteps hammering the marble floor. Lekore turned his focus ahead, heart in his throat, limbs weary.

How do we defeat immortal beings?

He'd crushed Susunee under rubble and dirt but had that truly killed her or merely slowed her down?

Tora slowed as guards in gold and green pushed the throne room doors aside to admit him. Talanee and Ademas swept into the massive chamber after the Ahvenian, and Lekore followed, Skye still at his side. The rest hurried in and fanned out as Tora pulled the console from the floor and ran his fingers along the keys as before.

Lekore's arm throbbed. His ribs pounded in time to his headache. His side oozed blood.

Nearby, Talanee inquired in low tones after Nerenoth's whereabouts, and Ademas answered concisely. When he'd finished, she revealed that Lekore's would-be roof assassin had tried to kill the other Ahvenians in their beds. Lekore's muscles loosened as she explained how the situation had ended without anyone harmed.

"Though I'd like to have strung the foolish girl up and beaten her with a stick," Talanee growled.

Ademas chuckled. "You may still get the chance."

Tora turned from his work. "We have two options. I can either activate the shield around the palace to keep them out, or I can shield the other cities from the Kiisuld, leaving us exposed. The former is simple at the shield's present power levels, and it'll last for days at the high cost of your people. The latter is far more taxing on the kingdom's generators and might not hold up long. It could buy enough time for the emperor's armada to arrive—but we'll have to face the Kiisuld now. Most of us won't survive."

Lekore trotted forward. "Protect the other cities. We'll do all we can to defend ourselves."

Tora's brows drew together. "The shields won't do much if the Kiisuld decide to eliminate the world. That would be drastic and draw the notice and criticism of other galactic empires, but I still wouldn't put it past them."

Lekore rested a hand on the console. "Even so, we must do all in our power to protect Erokel. Let them come here. It will spare the Kel and assuage the Kiisuld better than locking them out."

Tora nodded, face a mask of calm as terror spilled off his bones. "I must agree." He pressed a single button and foreign words scrawled across the hovering window. "Done. The other Sun Cities and most of the surrounding land will be spared. We...likely won't be."

A clear, sinister voice drifted into the chamber. "Well now, I wouldn't say *that*, Your Imperial Highness. Not *all* of you will die."

CHAPTER 29

Lekore whirled to face the new voice.

A lean man stood in the open doorway, clad in a long black jacket and pants hemmed with gold and silver swirls. His hair, cut longer in front and shorter at the base of his neck, hung straight and blue; framing a thick, sharp circlet, half-gold and half-silver. His eyes, a paler shade of blue, twinkled in the throne room's dazzling light. A greedy smile hung on his lips as the same emotion poured off his frame, blended with pride and seasoned with curiosity.

Behind him, an inch taller, a margin more muscular, stood a second man: clad in gray trimmed with embroidered black swirls; hair a deep, poison purple caught atop his head and tumbling down his back; eyes a pale lavender. He wore a faint, mocking sort of smile, like the world existed for his private amusement, but under that smile teemed a well of disinterest and acrimony.

Both Kiisuld were beautiful, like the flowers of the Wildwood, deadly at a touch. Their high cheekbones and slanted eyes suggested a similar, ethereal quality as Tora and his companions, but the Ahvenians held none of the malice beneath a veneer of delicacy.

Tora summoned *Calisay*, and the blade chimed a dark note.

Calir called out to join its twin, and Lekore complied. Its weight lent comfort to his growing apprehension.

The Kiisuld both blinked, then their eyes narrowed. A cloaked figure peered around the purple-haired man, then shrank back.

"What's this; twin blades?" The closer Kiisuld took a step forward, blue eyes darting between Tora and Lekore.

"Be careful," Skye murmured. "That one is Vay-Dinn Fyce, prince of the Kiisuld Empire."

Lekore nodded slightly.

Vay-Dinn stopped when he'd conquered half the space between the door and the two swords. His gaze settled on Tora. "I'd no idea you'd be here. Is that why an Ahvenian armada hurries this way?"

Tora lifted his chin and met those eyes, cold expression chiseled like stone. "We've taken this planet into our empire, Prince Vay-Dinn. You've done enough to them already. Don't interfere."

The Kiisuld chuckled. "That's hilarious, Your Highness. *We've* done enough to them. Us. What about your people? These fascinating facilities? That impressive jungle?"

"We intend to make reparations."

"Oh, yes. No doubt your monetary efforts will compensate for the untold losses through experimentation and—dare I mention—mass genocide."

Tora's eyes narrowed into ice shards. "You can't possibly judge us after all you and your partner have done."

Vay-Dinn shrugged; a light, graceful motion. "We aren't trying to be anything else. I just find your claim on Erokel amusing, that's all. But that's fine. Claim this little mudball. Add the world to your imperial registry. We just want *you* and" —his eyes settled on Lekore— "I'm guessing somewhere under all that dirt, you're my little Seer."

The cloaked figure scampered forward. "So he is, my dark god! That is Lekore Star-Touched."

"Wow." The second Kiisuld strode into the throne room,

scanning Lekore. "He really does resemble the last Seer. The same smudged face and pale hair."

Vay-Dinn's smile crooked. "So he does. Uncanny."

Lekore shrank under their ravening gazes. "We'll not go with you quietly."

"Oh, that hardly matters." The Kiisuld prince wiped a hand over the air. "We don't mind a little noise, do we, Tahomin?"

"Not occasionally," the one called Tahomin said. He pinned his gaze on Lekore, and a strange emotion bubbled up. Guilt? No, not that.

A sword sang free of its sheath, and Ademas stepped between the Kiisuld and their targets. Talanee and Rez Kuaan joined him a heartbeat later. The twins inched nearer.

Lekore tensed. "Do not waste your lives."

"We'll do what we must to protect our god and our king," Ademas said, keeping his focus on the enemy. "If that means our lives are forfeit, so be it."

A hand lighted on Lekore's shoulder. He started and found Mother looking up at him, her own blade unsheathed.

"Let us do what we can, my dear Adenye."

The Kiisuld exchanged amused looks, mockery rolling over their frames.

"But it's pointless," Lekore said. "They can kill you with a glance."

"How about this?" Vay-Dinn spread his arms out at his sides, palms up. "Come quietly and we'll spare your loved ones. It's a generous deal. I'm not accustomed to holding back, but you're far more important to me than your darling family."

Lekore frowned as he tried to read the man. *Is he lying?*

"We can't trust you to keep your word," Tora said.

Vay-Dinn's shrug stretched wider. "No, you can't. But you can attempt to spare them, or I can kill them all outright, here and now, and take you just the same. We don't intend to wait around for your father's armada." The prince's eyes lost their light. "Pick fast or I'll make your choice for you."

Tora pursed his lips and turned to Lekore. "I'm afraid it's your call. I'll not risk your people to protect myself."

Lekore stared at the silver veins in the marble floor. "Nor will I."

Skye leaned close. "I'll try to get word to Majentay. Maybe he can hurry a little faster."

Inhaling, Lekore nodded and looked up. In his periphery, Skye vanished. "I will come with you, Kiisuld—but if you destroy my world, you will wish you had never laid eyes upon my flesh."

The Kiisuld's grin turned wicked. "The last Seer was equally feisty. I suppose it's a racial trait."

"He is my ancestor."

Vay-Dinn chuckled. "I suspected as much. Nothing like heredity to carry on a rare gift and a penchant for trouble." He held out his hand. "Come along. We'll go at once, keep things simple. No fuss."

Ademas whirled around, his cloak wafting up dirt. "You can't. Lekore, no."

"If this is what I can do for Erokel, I must." Lekore released his grip on *Calir*, and the sword vanished.

Mother squeezed his shoulder until he looked at her. She shook her head. "Don't, my son. I won't lose you again."

He gently pried her fingers loose. "If I can avoid the death of my people, I must." He wrapped his arms around her and drew her close. "Goodbye, Mother." He pulled back and turned. "Would you reconsider taking Tora. Might he be left behind? The armada would be less likely to chase you down."

Vay-Dinn snorted. "Out of the question. The crown prince of Ahvenia is too great a prize—too dear a temptation—to leave here. Sorry, that's too much to ask." His smile turned wicked. "Toranskay Ahrutahn and I have a special connection, after all."

Tora shuddered. "Special isn't the word for it."

"You… You're the crown prince of the Sun Throne, Holy One?" Dakeer gasped.

Tora winced. "Yes, I am. Tell my father what's happened once he arrives, Hakija. He'll come after us."

"That he will," Vay-Dinn said. "So, time's a-ticking. Let's go."

Tahomin strode past his prince. "Come on." He reached Lekore, set a hand on his filthy shoulder, and eyed Tora. "You too, Your Highness."

Tora drew near.

"Not happening!" Talanee cried out and plunged her sword through Tahomin's ribs. The man stiffened, eyes dimming. He slumped, then fell as Talanee wrenched her blade free. She spun toward Vay-Dinn. "We'll not let you take them without a fight."

"Talanee, no." Lekore darted to her side and caught her wrist. "Enough. All will be well."

"Is that a prophecy, O Seer?" asked Vay-Dinn, tones dripping with mockery, not moving from his spot. "You okay, Tahomin?"

"Sure." The Kiisuld's body twitched, then he dragged himself to his knees and tipped his head from side to side. He climbed to his full height. "Should I refrain from punishing the stupid little vixen?" He turned to eye Talanee.

Lekore slipped in front of her, and Ademas joined him.

"Leave her be," Lekore said. "You have my oath I'll come. Do not break our agreement."

"He's right, Tahomin. Let's just go," said Vay-Dinn.

"*Lekore*." Ademas's tone was a low growl.

"I will be well." Lekore smiled at him. "Tell the Lord Captain not to worry. And please send someone to look in on Lios. He'll be lonely in my absence."

Ademas searched his eyes and nodded. "Yes, brother. As you wish." He stepped back to stand beside Talanee and tucked his arm through hers to hold her still.

"You can't be serious." Talanee struck her blade against the marble.

"Relax, cousin." Ademas smiled. "Trust him, hm?"

Vay-Dinn chuckled. "Oh yes, trust the little Seer to return. It won't be that simple, but if it helps you sleep at night. Bring them, Tahomin." He vanished on the spot.

Tahomin gripped Tora's arm and gestured to Lekore, who crossed to join him. The Kiisuld touched his shoulder, and the world tilted. The bright candles vanished, and Lekore found himself standing on a polished black floor in a dark room lit by a single orb-like light hanging from the ceiling. A bed hunched against one wall. One window revealed an ocean of starlight.

"Welcome to your room," Tahomin said. "Stay here."

Lekore turned to face him. "What about Tora?"

Tahomin tightened his hold on the Ahvenian. "*Tora* is to be kept in a special room made for Ahvenian guests."

"Will you hurt him?" asked Lekore.

Tahomin's brows drew together. "Are you serious?" He scoffed. "You really don't know much about Kiisuld, do you? *I* won't hurt him. He's not mine to hurt. The Ahvenian imperial family is solely the property of Kiisuld royalty in the event any are captured. That's the law. I wouldn't dream of breaking it and risking Vay-Dinn's fury."

"Property." Lekore rolled his hands into fists. "You see them as slaves?"

Tahomin's brow shot up, and he blinked. "Definitely not. They're our enemy. We don't enslave them, we destroy them. Stay here, and I'll return shortly to make sure you're comfortable." He turned Tora around and led him toward a door that slid aside like those in the Wildwood facility.

Tora glanced over his shoulder and met Lekore's gaze. "Be brave." The door whisked shut.

Lekore stared at the metal barrier, unease growing into a hum between his ears. "What now, Skye?" He crouched down to his heels and leaned forward to hug his knees.

No answer came. Silence stretched into a deafening howl as moments slipped away.

The door hissed open, and Vay-Dinn stepped inside, boots

clicking on the smooth floor. "Ah, welcome, little Seer. Tahomin met me in the hall and said he left you here."

Lekore straightened to his feet and glared at the Kiisuld. "If you harm Tora, I won't cooperate."

"And if I *don't* harm him, will you do whatever I ask? No matter what?"

Lekore recoiled. "What do you want with me?"

"Your vision. I should think that would be obvious." Vay-Dinn strode to the window and stared out into space. "Do you understand the abilities of a Kiisuld?"

Lekore scowled as hot anger shot through his limbs. "I understand you siphon out the life of others to extend your own."

The prince chuckled. "Oh, that's only a small bit of it." He turned to face Lekore, eyes twinkling. "We siphon more than their remaining years. We also glean their natural abilities. If a man can magically heal people, I take that power when I kill him. If a woman can read minds, I inherit that gift upon her untimely death."

He shrugged. "There are a few exceptions to this rule, and among those rare few, stands you: A Seer. I've killed your kind before. Wiped out a world's population, in fact, trying to absorb their race's unique gift for myself. Sadly, I can't seem to harness it. I don't know why. No one seems to know. They merely hypothesize: 'Only the pure can see the future.' Ridiculous. The Star Seers were as imperfect as anyone else."

Vay-Dinn ambled toward Lekore and stopped before him, staring down into his eyes. He leaned close. "Do you fancy yourself a pure person, little Seer?"

Lekore shook his head. "I am mortal, prone to err."

Vay-Dinn caught Lekore's chin and held it still. "And yet..." He straightened and shrugged. "I want you to serve me, uh..." He laughed. "I'm not sure I caught your name. Either way, I don't know it."

"Lekore."

"Ah, Lekore. Easy enough. Serve me, Lekore. I want to see into the future, to predict the actions of my enemies. I'll make certain your life is comfortable. You'll lack nothing."

"Except my freedom."

Vay-Dinn snorted. "Obviously not that. But I can sweeten the deal even more, and mark you, I'm not usually so generous. Agree to stay with me, aid me, and I'll let the Ahvenians absorb your world into their empire without a fuss. Your people will remain protected from my people henceforth."

Lekore gripped his own fingers. "How can I believe you?"

The prince shrugged. "Look into the future. See if I'm lying. You're worth more than your tiny world and its primitive people. *Much more*."

Lekore staggered back as the full weight of Vay-Dinn's inborn malice slammed into his aura. "Yet what terrible things might I help you to accomplish in return?"

"Many, I'd wager. S'up to you. I'll persuade you in other ways, if necessary, but I prefer a straightforward agreement." The gleam in Vay-Dinn's eyes brightened. "I'm not big on making a fuss."

The door hissed open as he finished his sentence, and Tahomin strode inside, one eyebrow arched. "That's news to me, Your Highness."

"Hush." Vay-Dinn's smile turned into a grin. "What I do around you is altogether different. You're my subordinate; you have to put up with it. To everyone else, I must show some level of decorum."

"Right. Decorum." Tahomin approached and held up a metal collar. "Put this on, Seer."

Lekore eyed the cold ring. "What does it do?"

"Keeps you tied to the ship. No transporting out, no melding into the walls, nothing magical." Tahomin took a step nearer. "We can't have you slip away at the first opportunity, in the event you change your mind."

Lekore's skin prickled. He backed up, shaking his head. "I do not like it."

Tahomin sighed. "It's just until we reach Vakari. That's our homeworld."

Swallowing a lump, Lekore stared at the device. "I've agreed to come with you. Let that be enough."

Vay-Dinn sighed and plucked up the collar. "I'd love to trust you, Lekore, but we barely know each other." He crossed to Lekore in three swift strides and snapped the collar on his neck in a blink.

Lekore's vision dimmed. The sound of air in the vents muted. The flow of life faded. He bent under the weight of a colorless world and trembled. "Please take it off."

"Sorry, no." Vay-Dinn patted his head. "It's only temporary." He angled away. "Did you place one on Toranskay's neck?"

"Yeah, first thing," Tahomin said. "I'm not keen on troublemakers disrupting our voyage."

"Good, excellent."

Lekore looked up and found two sets of eyes on him. Both held no kindness, no pity, no remorse. They stared like he might be a rare gem or uncommon blade they'd discovered, hunger licking at their souls.

"You know," Vay-Dinn cupped his hands behind his back, "this has been an uncommonly good day. Two age-long goals tumble into my lap without any real fuss and bother on our part—and they willingly surrender to save others. I've always had a great fondness for the heroic type, you know that?"

Tahomin snorted. "I've noticed."

Chuckling, Vay-Dinn strode toward the door. "Let's leave him be for now. He's got a lot to assimilate, and I want to enjoy my other prize."

Tahomin's gaze lingered on Lekore a moment longer, then he turned and followed his prince out, and the door slid shut behind them.

Lekore backed up until he struck the wall, then he slid to the floor and hugged his legs to his chest. "Breathe. Panicking will avail you nothing, Lekore. You must be calm and think."

Aches wailed over his body. He bent and pulled up his filthy, blood-stained tunic to examine the wound Ank had given him. A shallow slice, already crusted over with dry blood, soon healed. More painful were his ribs. The skin had discolored to an ugly purple, and the slightest touch sent racking pain crawling over his flesh.

Lekore bit back tears, afraid to let them fall. Afraid he'd cry for Ank as well as for himself. If he released his pent-up grief, he might unleash his anger, too. The tears might never stop flowing.

"Skye." He drew his tunic over his abdomen and leaned his head against the wall. "Skye, help me. I do not know what to do."

CHAPTER 30

Nerenoth reached the palace to discover a throng of Kel standing at the open gates. He plowed his way through them until the crowd recognized their Lord Captain carrying the body of the dead king and parted.

He reached the palace steps and spotted Rez atop the landing.

The Lord Lieutenant met his gaze and tensed. "Sir!"

The man ran down the stairs, and Nerenoth handed over Netye's body. "What's happened? Everyone looks grim." He started up the steps, stifling a flinch as his ankle panged.

"The Star Gods, sir. They came early. Two of them." Rez shifted Netye's weight on his shoulder. "King Lekore—Adenye. Um. He agreed to go with them, as did Holy Tora, to spare the rest of us."

Nerenoth's head grew light as his stomach wrenched. "Are they gone?"

"Yes, sir. Vanished."

I'm too late. I've failed them. Nerenoth reached the landing and turned to face the multitude. "Return to your homes. Come back on the morrow for an official statement from the church." His voice rang out above the murmurs and silence fell.

The crowd broke up, torches bobbing in the night as Kel left the palace grounds.

Nerenoth turned and marched inside, Rez on his heels.

"Sir, what now?"

"I presume Dakeer is here."

"Yes, sir. In the throne room."

"He and I must confer about our next course of action. Lord Tora said the Sun Throne has sent an armada. They'll arrive within a few days."

"Yes, sir. Uh, sir?"

"What is it, lieutenant?"

"Holy Tora—he was called a prince. He's the crown prince of the Sun Throne. Sir."

"Yes, Rez. I know."

Rez's step floundered but he caught himself. "He told you, sir?"

"He did." Nerenoth didn't glance at his lieutenant. "Keep walking, Rez."

"Yes, sir."

"Give me every detail."

The Lord Lieutenant spoke until they reached the throne room. Kel nobles and priests had stuffed the chamber, some clad in festive clothes, others gowned in nightrobes, hair disheveled but eyes bright and aware. Heated debates echoed off the walls as hands gestured in anger.

Dakeer stood across the chamber near the empty throne, a thumb pressed to his lips as he stared into some other sphere, oblivious to the din around him. Nerenoth plowed through the pack of nobility and allowed himself a faint prick of pleasure as voices died and hands recoiled to let him through. Perhaps they read his face or saw the large red stain on his white cape, or perhaps Netye dangling over Rez's shoulder silenced them.

The Hakija blinked, stirred by the growing hush. He searched and caught Nerenoth's eye as the Lord Captain pressed through the parting crowd. A faint, sad smile brushed Dakeer's lips.

"Welcome back, Lord Captain. I gather your lieutenant updated you."

Nerenoth halted at the fringe of the masses. "He did. We've work to do."

The man's eyes dimmed. "Have we?" His voice strained.

Nerenoth marched up to the Hakija and caught his shoulders, smearing blood on the white robes. "The Emperor of the Sun Throne is descending with an army of Sun Gods in a matter of days, Dakeer. He will want to know what happened to his son and heir. We must be prepared for his arrival. We must likewise prepare the people for that event. Shall we fail the gods now in this hour, Hakija?"

Something like pain stormed in Dakeer's eyes, then he squared his shoulders and shook Nerenoth's hands off. "No, Lord Captain. We are chosen by the Sun Throne. Yet we failed to protect its holy prince. We may be struck down in the Sun Emperor's wrath."

"If that happens," said Nerenoth, "so be it. But before we make assumptions, perhaps we should consult with those Sun Gods remaining. Lord Raren must be made aware of the circumstances."

"Yes, of course." Dakeer shook his head. "I hadn't thought."

"Time to think, Your Holiness."

Ademas's voice sounded behind Nerenoth. "Lord Captain."

Nerenoth turned. "Prince Ademas, what is it?"

"We've got another matter to address, after we inform the Sun Gods. The Dark Hakija has been captured."

Nerenoth narrowed his eyes. "Has he? Who is it?"

"Lord Farr of House Veon," Dakeer answered.

"Truly?" Nerenoth frowned. So young a leader, yet should that surprise him? He and Dakeer had gained their illustrious titles younger than any other Kel. Of course, the Star Worshipers would seek out a candidate of their own to answer the new precedent. The Lord Captain let his hand fall to his sheathed blade. "Yes, Dakeer. We'll be quite busy in the coming days."

"So it seems." Dakeer turned to Ademas. "Where is Farr Veon now?"

"Under guard in the east chapel. I thought it a fitting location for a heretic leader to contemplate his sins."

Nerenoth quelled a smile. "You're much like your father, my prince."

A spark caught in Ademas's eyes. "I hope so, Lord Captain."

Nerenoth studied the crowd in his periphery. "Dakeer, we need to send them home."

The Hakija sighed. "Yes, I'll see to them. Head for the wing where Holy Raren and the others are resting. I will join you soon."

Nerenoth nodded and strode toward the side door. "Lieutenant, bring the body."

Rez followed, as did Ademas. The faint patter of slippers brought Nerenoth's gaze around to find Talanee trotting toward them. Her eyes met his, and the fire of her gaze dared him to refuse her. He had no such intention.

Talanee's step faltered as she spotted Netye's limp body. The muscles in her face tightened, and water gathered in her eyes, then she bowed her head. A heartbeat passed. Two. She lifted her head, eyes sharp as frost, jaw tight.

Ademas moved to her side but said nothing.

The company left the throne room, shoes clacking marble. Candles guttered in their wake as they conquered the corridors. Talanee slipped up next to Nerenoth to describe an event with the half-Tawloomez prisoners. He listened with churning regret. Two good soldiers killed, because Nerenoth had underestimated the misguided girl's resolve and skill.

"They're better guarded now," Talanee finished. "I ordered a new detail to detain them and added my bodyguards to their number."

"That was well done, Your Highness," Nerenoth said.

"Thank you, Lord Captain." Her voice held a frigid tone.

"What will you do with the girl?" Ademas asked.

"I would prefer the Sun Gods to pronounce judgment," Nerenoth said. "If they aren't inclined, I'll see to her fate."

Talanee sighed. "Holy Raren seemed disposed to spare her."

Nerenoth nodded. "Our gods appear more merciful than we had believed."

Rez cleared his windpipe. "Sir, should we bring the king's body to the gods' room?"

Nerenoth halted. "No, Rez. Take him to his personal chambers and order his servants to prepare his body for burial. King Lekore desired him to be properly tended to in death."

"Yes, sir." At the next crossing, Rez turned off to carry the king's corpse to his former chambers.

Nerenoth didn't miss a step. "You may go with him, if you choose, Princess."

Talanee shook her head. "He's dead. What can I do about it?"

Nerenoth's brow drew. "Mourn. You loved him."

She scoffed. "I *wished* to love him, which is an altogether different emotion."

"Perhaps." He said no more on the subject. Princess Talanee must sort out her feelings on her own. She might choose to love her father despite his actions, as Lekore did, or perhaps she would choose to detest his memory instead. Both would be easy to accept; the mind could delude itself into any sort of viewpoint it found most comfortable.

Upon reaching the proper wing, Nerenoth motioned the guards aside and entered the chamber where Toranskay's shipmates rested. The god called Rarenday stood at the window, dressed in borrowed Kel apparel, propped against his naked blade like it was a cane. Rarenday angled himself to eye them without abandoning his view of Inpizal, the golden threads of his otherwise white tunic glistening in the light.

"They captured him, didn't they?" The Sun God's voice cradled a feral growl, and his orange eyes blazed like a wildfire on the grasslands.

Nerenoth exhaled. "Yes. We have failed you and your prince, Holy Light." He clapped a fist to his chest and bowed his head.

Silence. A soft sigh. "Then you know who he is. That makes this a little easier. Please don't blame yourselves for something far beyond your power to prevent. Prince Toranskay informed me of their coming, but I didn't expect them to arrive so soon. I sensed them but couldn't move fast enough to rescue my prince."

Nerenoth straightened and lowered his arm. "Your holy prince said your divine emperor will arrive within the week."

The god faced the door. "Sooner, if I know Emperor Majentay at all."

Chills ran down Nerenoth's arms. *Majentay. Remember the name.*

Dakeer pushed his way into the room and strode up next to Nerenoth. "How might we best prepare for the Sun Emperor's arrival, Holy Light?"

A crooked smile stretched over Rarenday's lips. "That's a difficult question to answer. The most important thing is to keep your plains clear for his flagship in case he chooses to land. He may not. I'll try contacting him as soon as he's in range and we might forgo his arrival altogether, if I can be taken onboard. You understand, we must chase down the Kiisuld ship before it reaches the heart of its empire. We can't lose any time."

Nerenoth gripped his sword hilt. "I would like to request permission to join your mission. The Star Gods also took my king."

Rarenday's eyes narrowed to slits. "Did they? To what end?"

"They called him a *seer*."

The Sun God's head lurched back. "Really?" He pressed a hand to his lips and considered the floor. "That's problematic. Intel's long suspected he's been hunting for one. If your king is the genuine article, that opens up a whole new jar of troubles." He dropped his hand. "Thank you for telling me. Yes, if my emperor agrees, you can come along, and *should*."

Nerenoth inclined his head as relief flooded his limbs. "Thank you, Holy One."

"Another thing. Please call me Rarenday. I've never liked titles much."

Dakeer fell still as noises around the company ceased.

Nerenoth inclined his head again. "As you please, Rarenday. I am Nerenoth, this is Dakeer, Ademas, Talanee" —he glimpsed the twins peeking into the room from the open door— "and my brothers, Jesh and Jeth."

Rarenday nodded at each person in turn, following Nerenoth's gestures. "I'm grateful for your care of my prince and my people. The emperor will be equally appreciative, of that I'm confident." He pinched his tiny hoop earring and tugged. "Could I bother you to show me the console Prince Toranskay used to repair the shield?" He tapped the tip of his sword against the floor. "I'd need some support to walk there."

"Anything you wish," Dakeer said and moved forward. "I will support you, Hol— Ah, Rarenday."

Rarenday wrapped his arm around Dakeer's shoulders. "Thank you."

Again, the company moved to the throne room, pace slower with the injured god hobbling along. Talanee broke off from the rest as they neared the throne room.

Ademas watched her move north, then glanced at Nerenoth with a smile. "We'll catch up." He took off after her.

Nerenoth maintained his stride and entered the throne room several moments later. The twins stayed near him as Dakeer guided Rarenday to the middle of the sunburst motif where the console remained visible.

"He drew it up from the floor," Dakeer said.

Rarenday nodded and plucked away at the buttons, eyes darting between the hovering window of light and the panel beneath it. "This could take some time, depending on what my prince was able to repair. Could I bother you for a chair?"

A servant scurried off before Nerenoth knew to find her. Moments later, the liveried servant returned, a smile on her face, a chair hefted between her and a second servant she'd collared somewhere. They placed the chair behind Rarenday, who murmured a soft thanks as his fingers never faltered. He paused long enough to sink into the wingback chair and then lowered the console to match his new height.

Dakeer backed up to stand beside Nerenoth. "I think I'll slip away to clean myself up and see my physician. I feel wholly unsuited to stand in the presence of the divine as I look and feel."

Nerenoth's ankle twinged. "I'm in accord with that. Go, and I'll take my turn after you've come back."

Dakeer's eyes hovered on Nerenoth's face for a long moment, but the Lord Captain kept his attention on the Sun God.

"I've been sorely wrong about you, Lord Captain."

Nerenoth glanced at the Hakija. "Yes, you have."

Dakeer sighed and ran a hand over his head, as though to sweep off a miter he wasn't wearing. His fingers caught in the tangles of his long, matted hair. "Apologies won't suffice, I realize that. Even so, my past actions are highly regrettable. I will find some way to make amends, both to you and to our young king." His brow wrinkled. "I intend to start by stepping down as the Hakija when the moment is right."

"That could prove unwise," Nerenoth said. "To abdicate as soon as the Sun Gods appear, and on the heels of everything Netye and Farr Veon have done, may unsettle our politics too much. Best wait until all else feels stable first."

"Yes, likely that's so. Yet my heart rests uneasy to know I wear my mantle unworthily."

"Let the Sun Gods decide your worth and mine." Nerenoth nodded at Rarenday. "He and Lord Toranskay appear unruffled by your past treachery."

Dakeer's lips twitched upward. "They are more peculiar than I'd envisioned. So much like Adenye..." He sighed. "I'll return soon." He walked away, steps slow, shoulders weighed down so that he appeared twice his age beneath the burden of his guilt.

Nerenoth watched him until Dakeer stepped from the room, satisfaction tainted with pity. *He begins to understand his sins. Will he truly repent of them or will prejudice cloud his eyes again before the end of everything?*

The Lord Captain turned around and soaked in the sight of

Rarenday again. *Blessed Sun Throne, protect Lekore. Give me the strength to rescue him.*

Rarenday looked up from the console and met Nerenoth's eyes for a single moment before he returned to his work. Had the Sun God heard the captain's prayer?

CHAPTER 31

Talanee retreated into her well-lit private garden and sat at the fountain, her blade resting near her slippers. Torchlight flickered off the scales of darting fish as the princess swirled her fingers through the cool liquid, tears sliding down her cheeks.

Back to this again. What a pathetic wretch you are, Talanee.

She couldn't bring herself to stop. The image of Father slung over the Lord Lieutenant's shoulder like a pythe's tack had been seared into her mind forever. Dead. She hadn't been able to ask how. She couldn't bear the idea that the Lord Captain might've ended Father's life.

Did he even hesitate or is his precious new king the only one that matters now?

After everything she'd learned about Nerenoth's secret faith, did she know the man at all?

"I should be happy," she whispered. "He always believed."

"He didn't do it."

Talanee yelped and shot to her feet, skirts rustling. She glowered at Ademas. "Is this going to be a habit?"

He stood where the garden path ended at the flat stones circling the fountain, fully visible in the path of torches. His customary smirk had vanished, replaced with an infuriating sort of pity.

Talanee's cheeks burned as she spun around to face the fountain. "Go away. I despise you."

"I doubt that's who you despise."

She squeezed her eyes shut. "I can't do this right now. Please go away."

"No." Footsteps scuffed stone, then a hand caught her wrist. "He didn't kill your father."

She flinched. "You did it, didn't you? That's what you're saying."

"No. I would've to protect my brother—but I didn't have to. Elekel killed him."

Fresh tears pricked her eyes. "Oh." Her hands trembled. "Has he been planning to all these years?"

"No, I don't believe so. But he wanted to protect his nephew and avenge my father when the opportunity presented itself."

Talanee sniffed as her nose started to run. She dug into a hidden pocket within her dress and drew out a handkerchief. "Why tell me this?"

"Because you should know." Ademas tugged on her arm until she turned to meet his gaze. His smile was as soft as velvet. "I'm sorry you're in pain. You've had enough of that."

She rolled her eyes and looked away. "Don't pity me."

"This isn't pity."

She snorted.

"Talanee."

Her eyes collided with his.

"This isn't pity." He caught a strand of her long hair and looped it behind her ear. "I'm genuinely sorry you're hurting, and I wish I could take it away. If Lekore has suffered because of Netye's poor choices, so have you. Perhaps as much, perhaps more. I can't judge that. What I know is you're a victim too. Your father should've loved you, but he abandoned you as surely as he did my brother. You deserved better. Every child does."

Talanee's throat ached. She swallowed and dug her nails into her palms, but the tears fell anyway, obscuring the world. "Stop it, please stop it." Her words burned her throat and tongue.

"I'll stop." His arms encircled her, drew her close. She couldn't see him through her tears, but his warmth enveloped her. "I'll stop when *you* stop pretending. When you let go of the pain you've caged all your life. But until then, Talanee Getaal, I'll keep telling you that you deserve better."

She stood as stiff as a pillar in his arms, resisting her throbbing heart's desire; wrestling against the welcoming warmth of his arms; his scent, cinnamon and sweat, mingled with the fragrances of her moonlit garden.

"Talanee." His tones were tender, not mocking at all. "It's all right. I *see* you."

Like a key in a lock, his words opened a secret door in her heart. She slumped against him, all strength fled, sobs racking her frame. He held her, just that. No words, no soothing noises.

Time disappeared. She wept until her tears ran out, and then, blessed Sun Gods be praised, she slipped into warm, painless oblivion.

THE TRILL OF A NIGHTBIRD WOKE HER. TALANEE'S HEAD SWAM, and her eyes felt puffy and hot. She lay upon the ground, cradled in Ademas's arms, her hair a tangle around her face and shoulders.

"Awake?"

Her cousin's voice caressed her ears, soft, kind. Talanee nodded.

Ademas drew her back. She dragged her hair over one shoulder as he studied her eyes. "Must've been tired." His mocking smile was back.

Talanee flushed. "And what if I was?"

"I'm glad you slept. Somebody needs to. Things are a muddle, aren't they?"

Talanee twisted the fabric of her lavender gown. "What

happens now? I mean, what if the Star Gods keep Lord Tora and Lekore? My father is dead." She held Ademas's gaze. "That would make you king after all."

Ademas nodded. "I've thought of that, and I'm prepared, but the idea is more bittersweet than once I found it. Mother will be crushed. And I don't think I can rule the way the gods might want, if Lekore is their preference." He sighed. "I hate to think what they're going to do to both of them."

Talanee scowled. "They didn't even put up a fight."

Ademas huffed a laugh. "They did that for us, you know."

"Yes, but even so..." A rustle in the nearby grove of trees brought Talanee up short. Ademas tensed at the same moment.

A bird fluttered from the branches with a cheery song.

Chuckling, Talanee smoothed hair from her face. "My nerves are overwrought."

"Mine too." Ademas climbed to his feet. "We'd better return to the throne room, or we'll miss everything going on."

Talanee sighed. "I think I'd rather take a bath first. I'm useless right now, and..." She couldn't bring herself to say aloud the feeling throbbing in her heart: She was in mourning.

Ademas offered his hand and hoisted her to her feet. "Take your time. I'll see you in the throne room later."

He disappeared inside the palace and Talanee shifted to study the cascading fountain. "Gods forgive me. I feel so lost."

CHAPTER 32

Ademas entered the throne room moments after Dakeer returned—freshly bathed, groomed, and patched up. Nerenoth nodded to them in turn and waited as they crossed to join him.

"Apologies, Lord Captain," Dakeer whispered. "My physician put me to sleep for a bit. Where is Lord Rarenday?" He eyed the empty chair at the console as he adjusted the sword strapped to his belt. He had discarded his usual vestments for more casual Kel raiment, though still in the white and gold accents of a priest.

"Jesh and Jeth escorted him to a room nearby," Nerenoth said. "The Sun God explained that something called 'long range' communication had been damaged and he must repair it. I decided to wait here for your return."

Dakeer nodded.

Nerenoth eyed Ademas. "Where is Princess Talanee?"

"Bathing. I think she needed time alone to grieve."

A new, seductive voice spoke. "My, my. So many important men all in one place."

Spinning toward the high-rising windows, Nerenoth spotted a lithe figure dark against the glowing light of dawn. He didn't need to see the features of her face to know her identity.

"Impossible," Dakeer said. "Lekore crushed you. You're dead."

"So I was," said the Teokaka, voice smiling. "But it did not suit me."

"You vile little..." Ademas started forward, sword half-drawn from his sheath.

Nerenoth reached out and caught his arm, shaking his head once. "Contain your anger. Do not risk your life on an impulse."

Ademas scowled and slid the sword back in place with a soft click.

The Teokaka moved away from the dawn glow, revealing a dark, angular face and bloodred lips parted to show white teeth. All signs of her demise in the tunnels had been washed away. "That's right. I can come back again and again. Do not try to fight me, child. I am stronger than all of you."

"You cannot fight the Sun Gods," said Dakeer, lifting his chin. "They will destroy you once and for all."

"I think not," said the woman, smile stretching until her eyes glowed. "I am half a goddess myself, holy man. The blessed Teokaka. Divinity courses through my veins." She raised her hand to study her palm, then lifted her pointer finger and flicked it.

A ring of violet flame sprang up around the four men, cold and leeching. Fire licked at Nerenoth's boots. He backed up a step, but the bitter flames reached out to touch him, causing his bones to ache.

Gripping his hilt, he set his jaw and stared at the Tawloomez woman. "What now?"

"Lord Captain." Her smile weakened. "You have been a plague to me these nineteen years. Ever since you were called to lead the military, my campaign has suffered. You refuse to raid my lands, refuse to take more slaves, refuse to answer my taunts. Your beloved Hakija has always been so easy to manipulate, but you? You stubbornly stayed inside your city walls and answered with silence. Men such as you are rare. Have you no pride? No thirst for glory?" She sneered. "How very un-Kel-like."

Nerenoth said nothing, though satisfaction throbbed through his veins.

She chuckled. "Come here, Lord Captain. The rest of you, stay where you are." With a wave of her hand, the flames parted, providing Nerenoth a path toward the woman. He took it, still gripping his blade. The flames shot up behind him, confining the others again.

He approached, shoulders squared, heart steady.

"Remove your sword," she said. "Or the young man might meet a premature end."

He unbelted his sheath and dropped the sword to the floor. She beckoned with a finger, and he strode the last few paces until he stood before her. She was a small woman, graceful, even lovely. He towered over her, but she showed no fear. She reached up and cupped her hand over his cheeks, then slid her fingers down his neck, stopping over his plated chest.

"Such an exquisite man," she whispered. "Would you like to be my lover?"

He arched an eyebrow. "I would sooner kiss dung."

She tittered. "That could be arranged, dear captain, but my plans call for a different course of action. Kneel, or the Getaal boy dies."

Nerenoth set his jaw and knelt, ignoring the armor digging into his skin. He looked up at the woman. "Now what?"

"You truly have no pride, do you?" She dug her fingers into the dark hair at his scalp, bent down, and pressed her lips to his.

He remained still, giving nothing. Her lips lingered, probing, but he pinned his gaze beyond her ear and would not yield. Cold pricked his lips and trickled into his mouth, down his throat, constricting his lungs. He flinched and tried to draw back, but she dug her nails into his scalp and held him still.

The cold reached his stomach and spread out into his arms. His head spun. His bones throbbed. The only warmth he found was in the Teokaka's kiss. He struggled against the urge to draw her close.

So cold. His body shivered. His mind grew numb. The woman's nearness hummed in his ears, beckoning.

And he understood. *She's poisoning me.*

A surge of anger swelled in his chest. He reached up and caught the woman's wrist, twisted it, and shoved her backward. Staggering to his feet, he retreated from the snake.

"I will not be yours," he gasped, wiping at his mouth.

She straightened, brown eyes wide. Blinked, then chortled without humor. "No man defies me."

His legs trembled. Squaring his shoulders, he stared down at her. "*I* defy you, viper, and all that you are."

She screamed as her eyes shone with hatred. Balling her hand, she pounded the marble at her feet. A thread of lightning shot up from the floor and bolted toward Nerenoth. He threw himself to one side, but the bolt struck his chest, and he staggered back against the console. Something crashed to the ground as he slumped down and lost his sight.

Ice rattled in his lungs. His body burned with cold.

NERENOTH LAY UNMOVING BEFORE THE CONSOLE, FACE HIDDEN by his midnight blue hair. If his chest rose and fell, Ademas couldn't tell. Chest tight, the young man lifted his eyes to the Teokaka grinning at the fallen captain.

Ademas gripped his sword hilt tight, anger licking at his insides. First Lekore. Now Nerenoth. *The Star Gods won't win!*

Susunee hefted her chin. "Defiance of my will ends in death, Lord Captain. So much for your prowess. What are you to one chosen of the true gods?" She pushed locks of brown hair from her face. Turning to the two men standing in the purple flames, her eyes danced. "I will give one of you the great blessing of joining me in my domination of the Kel. Who will it be?"

"Do not tempt us, spawn of darkness," Dakeer said, red eyes

blazing. "We will never bow before the Night, but thou shalt be swallowed by it in the end."

She laughed. "Listen to the dithering old man preach. Let us not debate the final rest of our souls, Hakija, for we shall never see eye to eye. The question here is whether or not you wish to join the triumphant side."

Dakeer scoffed. "None of us will. You're wasting your breath."

Her eyes slid to Ademas, and she licked her lips. "What of the young Kel? He seems fit and skillful, with plenty of fight in his eyes. Perhaps I'll take him."

"You can try," Ademas said, gripping his sword tighter. "But you'll fail just as you did with the Lord Captain."

"Fail?" She chuckled. "It is a wonder the Kel have stood so long, with such a twisted notion of the word *failure*. Or do I understand it incorrectly? I had thought my lessons in your language proficient." She rested a finger on her lips. "No matter. I have always preferred words like *conquer* and *victory* anyway." A wave of her hand parted the purple flames. "Come forward, boy. What was your name—Ademas, right?"

He stalked from the circling prison. "Ademas Getaal."

Her eyes sparkled. "Not only the Lord Captain and the Hakija, but a lord of House Getaal—and next in line to the throne, if I heard you rightly in the princess's garden."

Ademas clenched his free fist. "Eavesdropping, eh? And then you used me as a shield against Nerenoth. I won't forgive you those offenses."

"And how will you exact your revenge? Run me through?" She stretched her arms wide. "Go ahead. Pierce my heart. I cannot die. I have lived for five hundred years, and nothing you do now will keep me dead. I am immortal. A goddess, born of my father, who reigns on high. I'm destined to rule the world and enslave its people, Kel and Tawloomez alike. Bow now, or fall with the others, boy."

He smirked. "You really believe yourself. Amazing." He held her gaze. "I won't bow to you, now or ever. I'd rather die."

She dropped her hands. "That, too, is acceptable. But first I have need of you. I have just two questions." She raised a hand and twitched her fingers. The door swung open of its own accord. Beyond stood Talanee still gowned in lavender, unbathed, a Tawloomez warrior at her back, a knife against her throat. Ademas stiffened but stifled any expression.

"Does this girl matter to you?" asked the Teokaka. She licked her lips again. "Comply with my wishes and she won't be killed."

Ademas gritted his teeth, weighing his options. There weren't many. "Do you swear it?"

"By my father's blood if that will suffice. The pretty princess goes free when I get what I want. After all, what is a royal hostage compared to the world?"

Using that logic, he knew he should sacrifice Talanee to protect the masses, but he couldn't act rashly. Other leverage could be found to bully him into submission and, besides, he shouldn't doubt the possibility of rescue. Rarenday was nearby. If Ademas could purchase a little time, there might be no reason to choose between the two sides of his heart.

He met Talanee's eyes. She glowered at him, the defiance in her stance urging him to make the better choice: Let her die.

He grinned. "I'm sorry, Talanee. I'm going to be selfish and keep you alive, even if you hate me for it."

Her eyes widened. "You stupid—" She cut off as the knife's point pressed against her skin. A bead of blood rolled down her neck.

"Hush, Princess," said the Teokaka. "Your hero is only thinking of your safety." She turned her smile to Ademas. "So, then, you agree to aid me?"

"First I want to know what's expected of me. What part of your plan am I to aid?" He flopped to the floor and folded his legs before him, propping his hands on his knees.

She raised an eyebrow, then gracefully sat on the floor facing him, her snakeskin gown crackling as it pooled around her limbs. "It is quite simple. My Seenth" —she gestured to the man with the shaved head and snakeskin robes, who clutched Talanee to his chest— "has explained that your young king was taken from this world by my godly father, and *that* means you are the next king. I wish to control the Kel. You will be my puppet."

Ademas snorted. "Is that all?"

"Once you've secured the throne, you will convert to the Tawloomez faith—and you will worship me. All Kel shall. Obey me, and your Kel cities will thrive. Fail me, and I will carve out your lovely cousin's heart, then I'll hunt you down and break your mind until you think yourself a beast."

"You know just how to motivate a man." Ademas looked between Talanee and the Teokaka. "But you'll probably do that to me either way."

"Not necessarily. Prove yourself resourceful and perhaps I will find a better use for you than madness or death." Her tongue darted across her lips again.

Ademas fought back a shudder. "All right, if Talanee and I are spared, I'll help you take over the world."

She grinned. "Excellent." Rising, she crossed to where he sat, and crouched down beside him. She leaned in and Ademas clamped down hard on an urge to shove her away as her earthen scent wafted over his face. He sat still, exuding calm, even as Talanee gasped. The Teokaka's lips found his. His mind railed against her forwardness, even as he understood this was far worse than a simple kiss.

Frost crept into his mouth. Had he made the right choice? Was he about to die, as Nerenoth had, or worse?

Clutching his sword hard until he couldn't feel his fingers, he tried to draw strength from it. *Resist what she's doing. Retain your sense of self. Be stronger than she is.* But his mind slipped, drawn into her warmth. *This is what Nerenoth fought.* But if Ademas pulled away, Talanee would die. There was no right choice, and it was too late.

He wrapped his arms around the Teokaka's slim figure. Pulled close. Welcomed the warmth as cold enveloped his heart. His last conscious thought was of his brother, of how much he'd wanted to protect Lekore. Wanted to see him on the throne. Then he saw only the Teokaka in his vision as she pulled away, bloodred lips stretching in a wicked smile. She was exquisite. Utterly wonderful.

"My dear Ademas Getaal, prove to me your devotion."

He rose to his feet with relish, ignoring his shivering frame and the cold lancing through his fingers. "What is my lady's command?"

"Kill Princess Talanee."

He turned to the captive girl and advanced, hungry to obey, blood pumping through his ears.

"Ademas, please." Talanee's eyes were wide. "Fight her. Don't let her win!"

The Teokaka laughed. "Too late, little girl. Your lover is mine now. He will obey only my wishes."

Ademas drew his sword.

"Hold!"

A powerful force slammed into Ademas, knocking him to the floor. Dakeer Vasar pinned him, glittering frost etched into the Hakija's cheeks. His sleeves were crusted in ice. He'd braved the tainted fire to stop Ademas.

"Release me, Hakija."

"I will not."

"Get up, Ademas," came the command of his mistress. "Kill the Hakija if you must."

Ademas tried to wrench his arm free, but Dakeer's grip was like iron. "I can't move, my lady."

She hissed and strode forward, caught Dakeer's long hair, and yanked him back. Dakeer folded to the floor, body shivering.

The Teokaka sneered. "What did you think would happen, running through my flames that way? Were you so eager to join the Lord Captain in death? You had but to speak your desire, Vasar."

Ademas climbed to his feet.

The Teokaka whirled on him. "Now, complete your task, my puppet. End the princess's life."

“As you please.” Ademas flexed his sword hand, his blade glinting in the mounting morning light.

Wrestling against the Seenth, Talanee growled as Ademas approached.

A figure darted through the nearest doorway and leapt onto Susunee, a candlestick glinting in his hands.

CHAPTER 33

The ship door slid open.

Lekore contemplated the black corridor beyond. It was lit up by faint orbs of violet light casting black-on-black shadows over the pitch-colored floors. No guard stood at the door, but with the collar around Lekore's neck, perhaps the Kiisuld found no reason to pretend he posed a risk.

He didn't intend to, not yet. His worry lay with Tora and the profound fear pouring off him as they'd confronted the Kiisuld in the throne room. It ran deeper than Lekore's fear of Farr Veon or his followers; more of a paralyzing, irrational terror Lekore couldn't comprehend.

He padded into the corridor barefoot, his boots abandoned in a corner of the guest chamber. He'd also tied his hair back in a tight braid, as the wind spirits weren't nearby to keep him from tripping over his long tresses. The braid's weight shifted like a snake down his spine, but he ignored it as best he could and tiptoed down the quiet passageway, drawing on his senses to seek out Tora.

The collar suppressed some gifts, not others.

Tora's aura pulsed like a white light in a bank of smoke and bloodlust, a beacon in the night. He followed the feeling down empty corridors, unhindered by Kiisuld or any other living soul.

THE HISS OF THE DOOR SLIDING OPEN BROUGHT TORANSKAY'S head up. He climbed from the floor to his feet and waited, hands manacled together behind his back. The purple-tinged forcefield boxing him inside a cramped space within the bare room hummed, and nausea washed over him, but he swallowed and willed himself to stand tall.

Vay-Dinn Fyce and Tahomin Harrulay entered the chamber, their coloring distorted through the faint sheen of the forcefield.

"Look at him, Tahomin," said Vay-Dinn. "His perfect composure, his unreadable face. Witness the infinite control of the Ahvenian prince. Toranskay is predicted to become the greatest of the Ahvenian emperors. Beautiful and intelligent, like some ancient goddess."

Toranskay kept his face still, not reacting, though his heartbeat ratcheted up.

Tahomin scoffed. "Goddess? Really, Your Highness?"

The Kiisuld prince chuckled. "The fine Ahvenian features certainly add a grace most men lack. There's also the rumor that the empress isn't fully Ahvenian, but half something else. What was it again, Your Highness? Nijaal? That makes you quarter-Nijaal, with all the gifts, physical and magical, that entails. Exquisite, isn't he?"

"Divine," answered Tahomin flatly.

"You know, Tahomin, you've really got to start livening up your life. It's passing you by."

Tahomin snorted. "Right, and I won't live many thousands of years more to enjoy it."

"But you never enjoy it. That's my point."

Toranskay studied Tahomin's wry face. Despite the man's apparent disinterest, he was still Kiisuld, and by all accounts he was as ruthless and cruel as Vay-Dinn when he wanted to be. The difference was, as far as Toranskay's family spies had determined, Vay-Dinn liked to play around and try new things. Tahomin stuck with what he excelled at: killing people. Small comfort.

The snap of a finger startled Toranskay.

"I've got it," said Vay-Dinn. "You always beat me in games of strategy, but let's see how you fare against the brilliant mind of Prince Toranskay Ahrutahn."

"You want me to play chess?" asked Tahomin, eyebrow arching.

"To start things off. I think Toranskay feels uncomfortable, and I'd like to put him at his ease. We've plenty of time between here and home. Let's build up the anticipation of," Vay-Dinn's lips lifted in a wicked smile, "*other* sport."

Tahomin sighed. "Fine. I'll prepare the game room."

Toranskay frowned at the Kiisuld prince. Was he really inclined to watch a game of chess, nothing more?

Vay-Dinn's smile deepened. "The loser plays a penalty game. I suggest you don't let that be you, little prince."

THE DOOR OPENED WITHOUT PRESSING A BUTTON, AND LEKORE spotted Toranskay seated at a polished table carved from wood, his chair a massive wingback of soft velvet. Across from him sat Tahomin Harrulay, studying a square tray set with tiny pieces for a game Lekore didn't recognize. Near the table, Vay-Dinn Fyce lounged on a settee drowning in pillows. He held a goblet in one hand, though his eyes were pinned on Lekore.

Their gazes met, and Lekore straightened up, leveling his chin.

"Welcome, Lekore," said Vay-Dinn, gesturing with his goblet to the posh dark chamber lined with chests and oddly shaped satchels. Red liquid sloshed against the side of the goblet. "I wondered if you'd join us. You're just in time for a fascinating game." He rose from his settee and, rounding the table, approached. His eyes glinted like a hungry emockye's.

Lekore backed up, mind latching onto thoughts of *Calir*. His back collided with the closed door behind him, and it didn't slide aside as he pressed against its cold surface.

"Why are you running?" asked Vay-Dinn.

"I am not running," said Lekore.

Vay-Dinn chuckled. "Really? Well, my mistake, I suppose." He caught Lekore's chin and lifted it. "Everything about you intrigues me. I crave your gift as I crave few things. I don't mind using you, but I'd prefer if you *gave* your sight to me, Lekore. Offer it willingly and perhaps I can keep it. If it works, I'll let you go back home. That's a good deal."

Lekore trembled under his hungry gaze. "I...do not think I can."

Vay-Dinn clicked his tongue. "Don't make me persuade you, Lekore. You won't enjoy that."

"I doubt I will enjoy anything you do, with or without my cooperation."

Vay-Dinn started to smile, but his lips curled down as he drew closer to Lekore's face. "There's something strange in your eyes."

Lekore flinched, but Vay-Dinn kept hold of his chin.

"I can't quite..." The Kiisuld blinked. "Ah, I know this. I've seen it before. Grief, that fascinating human emotion. Tahomin, come see. It's like a cloud over his heart."

The other Kiisuld snorted. "I have no interest in grief."

"Me neither, usually." Vay-Dinn tilted Lekore's head one way, then the other. "But in his eyes, it's almost—I don't know—sad."

"Isn't that what grief *is*?" asked his partner.

"I suppose, but now I find myself almost sad to see it. How odd. What happened, boy? Did your mommy die? I understand that makes most people sad."

A game piece clattered to the floor as Toranskay stood. "Vay-Dinn, leave him alone." His voice scraped over his throat, pinched and low.

Vay-Dinn glanced at the Ahvenian, and his smile appeared again. "Stay out of this, my dear prince. I want to know."

Toranskay's slitted eyes narrowed. "You have no soul."

Vay-Dinn chuckled. "As if we all didn't know that." His eyes speared Lekore again. "Tell me, what grief did you suffer? What's covered the sun in your countenance?"

"I said to leave him alone," snapped Toranskay.

Lekore dropped his eyes. "My uncle died. He was shot."

Vay-Dinn released his chin and rested a hand on his shoulder. "Ah, the loss of dear kin. I've seen this grief more times than I can count, so what about yours nearly moves me? Is it your powers, enhancing your emotions?" His fingers dug into Lekore's shoulder, bruising skin. "I must have them."

Lekore swallowed, then set his jaw and looked up. "You cannot. Though I've agreed to come with you, I will not let you use me or my gifts."

"You refuse me?" Vay-Dinn sneered. "Doesn't matter. Whatever it takes, Lekore, you'll obey my will."

Lekore trembled under the ravenous glint in Vay-Dinn's eyes. He wanted to devour Lekore, body and soul. The Kiisuld blinked, and the glint vanished. He angled toward Toranskay still standing at the table, blue eyes bright with a warning.

"Still, there's time. No rush now," Vay-Dinn said. "I might as well enjoy the process. We're honored today by such esteemed guests. We should welcome them aboard properly. More wine, hm? I feel like celebrating." He clapped his hands, and a panel in the wall across the room slid aside. A young woman entered, dressed in a simple black and silver jacket and pants, bearing a tray with several decanters of bloodred liquid and two new goblets.

Vay-Dinn poured wine into his goblet from one decanter, then filled Tahomin's goblet. He poured a third and offered it to Toranskay, who sat down and shook his head.

"Ah yes. You abstain, don't you, Your Imperial Highness? I'd heard that." Vay-Dinn turned to Lekore, proffering the goblet. "But you'll have some to toast the future, won't you, Seer?"

Lekore shook his head. "I do not desire to partake of intoxicating beverages."

Vay-Dinn regarded him blankly, then laughed. "We're in the presence of holy men, Tahomin. See how they disdain our worldly manners?"

Tahomin sipped his drink and shrugged. "A clear mind isn't something to scoff, Vay-Dinn. If I were a prisoner, I'd be just as stubborn."

"If it were just about imprisonment, I wouldn't scoff," said Vay-Dinn. "But to deny the pleasure of drink always, that I must mock."

Tahomin plucked the game piece off the floor and set it on the board as he batted his long purple ponytail aside. "But they don't live for ages like we do. Strong drink destroys the liver, I understand."

"Only in excessive quantities." Vay-Dinn caught Lekore's arm and drew him toward the settee. "Our friends were in the middle of a rather intense game. Let's watch." He pushed Lekore against the pillows and sat beside him, then pressed the goblet into Lekore's hands. "If you get thirsty, you might try it once. It's a good vintage from a world long extinct." Vay-Dinn flashed a wicked grin and turned to the game.

As Lekore observed, he came to understand that each distinctive piece could only move by certain rules, and some had more power than others. Each move was a careful calculation, and if he understood enough, Toranskay and Tahomin were well matched.

As Tahomin moved a piece that resembled a crenelated parapet, Vay-Dinn poured himself more wine. "How do you think I could best break down Lekore's mind, Tahomin? Torture? Brainwashing? Chemicals?"

"Whatever you'd best enjoy," answered Tahomin, his eyes riveted on Toranskay's cross-shaped piece.

"Don't be so patronizing." Vay-Dinn glanced at Lekore's untouched goblet. "What do you suppose he would do if he *were* intoxicated?"

"Speak too much," said his partner.

Vay-Dinn chuckled. "Would he assault us with sermons or reveal our darkest secrets?"

"Check."

The room fell silent as Tahomin regarded the piece Toranskay had just moved. The Kiisuld smiled and moved his own cross-shaped piece away from the threat of Toranskay's crowned piece. Based on the lay of the board and the actions of the players, Lekore surmised the object of the game was to capture the cross-shaped piece.

"Maybe both," Tahomin said. "Though I'm not too concerned with the latter. Do you *have* any dark secrets I don't know about, Vay-Dinn?"

Vay-Dinn tapped a finger against his lips. "None come to mind. You?"

"Same here. But I doubt you'd find him any more willing to give up his powers. Don't try wine."

"No?" Vay-Dinn looked at Lekore. "How best to break your will, hm?"

Lekore kept his gaze steady. "You cannot."

The Kiisuld smiled like the high frosts of Nakoth. "I've broken a million minds, a million wills, a million worlds. Why are you different?"

"I will not let you."

"You won't have a choice, Seer." Vay-Dinn caught Lekore's braid and tugged it. "You're my property now. The sooner you accept that, the less likely you'll go mad."

Drawing a deep breath, Lekore shut his eyes. "There is little you can do to me which would be harder to bear than the grief I feel already."

Vay-Dinn's breath tickled his cheek. "I can't replicate your grief, certainly—but I can add to its weight." Fingers gripped Lekore's arm, plucked away his goblet, and hauled him to his feet. The man's smile bore the weight of crushing earth. "I've thought of just the way to break you down, I think. Come with me."

He set the goblet aside and dragged Lekore across the room.

Toranskay rose. "Don't hurt him!"

"Should we pause our game?" asked Tahomin over the Ahvenian.

"Continue. Just let me know who wins." The door slid aside and Vay-Dinn pulled Lekore into the corridor. The Kiisuld prince glanced over his shoulder. "Don't fret, Toranskay. I'll be back for you soon." The door shut.

"Where are we going?" asked Lekore, instincts screaming. *Flee. Flee!*

But he couldn't run.

"The problem with people like you, rare though they are, is you care more about right than you care about yourself." Vay-Dinn pulled him down the corridor, strange potted plants and dark vases the only décor. "Any pain, any at all, I might inflict on you will only strengthen your resolve to defy me. It will justify your stance. People like you live for righteousness—that bizarre mindset which works so hard to ennoble the races of every world.

"The problem is, your powers respond to your desire to protect your truth. Where I might otherwise blackmail you, you'd gain the strength to resist. It leaves me in a quandary, but it's one I think I can solve." He reached a set of defined doors which slid to either side.

Lekore gasped as he stepped into the chamber beyond. He floated in a sea of stars. At least it felt that way, though his feet touched an invisible floor.

"Behold, Lekore: The Universe." Vay-Dinn gestured grandly. "This is my observatory, designed to reflect the stars uninhibited by walls or floor. That" —he pointed— "is your planet." His fingers tightened around Lekore's forearm. "You see truth as you see the sun, don't you? Clear like a cloudless day."

"Often, yes."

"Then look into my eyes now, Lekore, and see truth. If you won't give me your power, I'll destroy one of these worlds. I don't care which. And if you continue to resist me, I'll destroy Erokel and all your people with it. Do you believe me?"

Lekore bit his lip and nodded. "I believe you would, but I still cannot give you what you seek. Though a hundred worlds perish in your efforts to secure my Sight, I will defy you even still."

Vay-Dinn stared. "You can't be serious. You'd sentence countless lives to death for your sake?"

"I would keep you from using my gift to hurt countless more."

"The sin will be on your head either way," said Vay-Dinn.

"No." Lekore bowed his head. "In this I am innocent. You will slay others with or without my help, but I can choose whether to aid or thwart your efforts, even if only in small ways."

"Such noble sentiments. I think I might be sick." The Kiisuld turned his back. "Very well, Lekore. You've proved your stubborn ideology is fully ingrained. But I'm resolved to demonstrate my own obstinacy. We'll start with the enemy of your people. It's a small step, but one you might appreciate, despite yourself." He whirled, caught Lekore's throat, and snapped the collar loose.

Cold embraced Lekore's body as the world tilted. He stood upon solid ground. The rising sun glowered at him, and he shielded his eyes as familiar scents struck him. Warm wind blew across his face, but the cold chill of his bones choked the sensation.

Vay-Dinn gestured grandly. "Welcome back to Erokel."

Lekore's heart leapt.

"Try to escape, little Seer, and I'll make Toranskay suffer. Remember, he's still on my ship." Vay-Dinn jabbed the air with a finger. "That's the Tawloomez capital, isn't it? It's grown quite a bit since I was last here."

Lekore turned to study the landscape. Before him stretched the Tawloomez city built from the red rocks surrounding it. Above the rest of the structures towered the red-stone palace he'd threatened to destroy mere days ago. Fire Mountain seethed behind the palace, smoke pluming like a black scar against the bright sky.

Vay-Dinn studied him, smile faint, pale eyes still hungry. "What thoughts run through your mind as you view the enemy of your people, Lekore? The Tawloomez are responsible for welcoming

Tahomin and me to your world. They started the slave trade, they taught the Kel to hate. Your ancestor, the Seer called Skye Getaal, is dead because these savages embraced what Tahomin and I taught them.

"Let's destroy them, Lekore, together. Avenge your fallen people. It's only fair. It's only right."

The words, spoken so softly, caressed Lekore's senses. The Tawloomez were a blight on Erokel. They had killed hundreds of thousands. He'd stopped their tirades again and again, but they'd still destroyed Erokes. Attempted to kill Talanee. Murdered Nerenoth's family, leaving the Lord Captain's cousin Mayrilana broken.

He dug his nails into his palms, shuddering against his feelings. *These are not mine, they are his poisonous words.*

Lekore didn't choose justice; he never had. He bowed his head, letting prejudice roll away like beads of rain on the wild grasses.

"I choose mercy, Vay-Dinn," he whispered, then lifted his chin. "I choose to forgive the Tawloomez for any wrongs they have done me. Hatred will not cure the disease of murder; it will only perpetuate the sin."

The Kiisuld stared at him, lips parted. "You can't be serious. Strike down your enemy, Seer. They're a vile, savage race. If you don't destroy them, they'll destroy you."

Lekore shook his head. "I cannot choose hatred, or my sin will be greater than my enemy's." He shut his eyes and smiled. "I will have no enemies. I will find a way to love, even those with whom I cannot agree."

Laughter brought Lekore's head up. Vay-Dinn pressed a hand to his brow, head tipped back as he howled with mirth. "Never, never, never have I seen the like! You're the purest, most revolting example of goodness I've ever encountered. What makes you so special that you can elevate yourself to such a height? You think you can maintain that philosophy: loving all people no matter what they do?"

He scoffed and straightened his head, blue hair shifting around his thick circlet. "You can't remain unspotted, Lekore. You can't waltz through life without getting your hands dirty. Without encountering people you dislike. People worth despising. What about me? Can you honestly say I'm not your enemy?"

Lekore searched the man's blue eyes. "I do not wish you to be my enemy."

Vay-Dinn snorted. "And *I* wish for you to give me your power. We can't have it all, Lekore—though I've come closer than most, and I assure you it wasn't by honest work and loving my fellows." He shook his head, chuckling. "Let's put your new resolve to the test, shall we? You do your utmost best to love me, while I slaughter your not-enemies, hm?"

He lifted his hand and shot a stream of violet light toward the Tawloomez city.

Lekore reached out as though he could stop the bolt of magic, calling on wind spirits for help, even as he braced for impact. The stream of color arced upward and descended toward the palace, but then struck a flash of violet light and fizzled out.

Vay-Dinn whirled on him. "You little—" He broke off as his gaze settled on a point behind Lekore. His eyes narrowed. "Impossible."

Lekore turned to find Keo sitting on a jutting red rock, one hand raised in greeting, a crooked smile on his lips.

"Hello, Your Highness," Keo said, green eyes bright in the sunlight.

Vay-Dinn stared, lips parted. "You thwarted me, Kiisuld. Why?"

"Simple. To thwart you."

"*Why?*"

Keo hefted his shoulders. "Because I like these people, foolish though they are. And because I promised someone I'd protect them."

Vay-Dinn blinked. "My hearing must be off today. For a second, I thought I heard a Kiisuld use the word 'protect' in a positive context."

Keo's smile widened, though his eyes remained cool. "Forebears forbid."

"You must be crazy," said Vay-Dinn.

"Possibly. Probably. But I'm still going to thwart you if it kills me."

"Oh, you can count on the last, at least." Vay-Dinn caught Lekore's arm and drew him close. "Now what, traitor?"

Keo shrugged. "Now you hand over Lekore and go home like a good little boy. Leave Erokel alone and we'll have no cause to fight."

"That's what this is really about. You want the Seer for yourself, but I'm your prince and liege. *I* will triumph, and you'll suffer severely when I deliver you into the care of my personal guard on Vakari."

"They won't want me. They didn't before." Keo slid from the rock and started forward, his long black and green tunic fluttering around his legs in the rising breeze. "That's assuming you can actually manage to beat me in battle."

Vay-Dinn's grin returned. "It's been a while since I've fought a Kiisuld. He died, by the way."

"Impressive," said Keo. "How long did it take to drain him of his life reservoir?"

"Not as long as you might think." Vay-Dinn lifted his free hand. "Should I demonstrate?"

Lekore glanced between them, mind racing. If he tried to escape, he would not be able to return to Vay-Dinn's ship to rescue Tora, but if he went back with Vay-Dinn, he would be in no better a position to help his friend than here and now.

I gave my oath. I must remain with Vay-Dinn.

"If we're showing each other magic tricks," said Keo, halting in his tracks and folding his arms, "I'll start, shall I? Abracadabra." He waved his hand as if batting away an insect. A tingle crawled up Lekore's spine, and the scenery tipped, then changed.

He stood in the Kel throne room.

CHAPTER 34

Lor'Toreth of the Flame knew the moment Susunee entered the Kel palace.

He'd never been a strong hunter or scout, but his sense of self-preservation had taught him to feel Susunee's presence a mile off. It might be his one talent.

He stood up from the floor.

Mayrilana watched him from her place beside him. "Where are you going?"

"The Teokaka is here. I must do *something* to stop her."

The Kel shook her head. "You can't. We're powerless."

"Even so." He claimed the candlestick. "I'll not say I didn't try."

She eyed him, then stood, the white of her nightgown stark in the darkness. "I'll come."

"You don't have to."

She shrugged. "Who knows that better than I?"

They left Lekore's suite and paced down the corridors on bare feet, heading toward the throne room, Mayrilana leading the way.

Every step rattled Lor's bones. All his life, he'd run from what frightened him. Susunee, most of all, had plagued his days and nights.

Why am I seeking her? I can't do anything.

Mayrilana walked beside him, a stranger, a Kel, but not an enemy. He'd always thought Kel were evil, but Lekore had done all he could to rescue Lor's retainers, and the Lord Captain had protected Lor from the trapped souls in the Wildwood. He'd been allowed to remain with the Kel during their councils, and he'd found a shattered soul in Mayrilana, not unlike his own.

Our blood is the same.

It was just like the Golden One, Tora, had declared.

They reached the throne room. Lor halted, pulse racing, blood churning. His breath rasped in his throat.

Mayrilana took his hand. "Be brave."

Her red eyes gave him strength.

Lor peeked into the throne room and found Susunee, so near, commanding Ademas to kill his cousin.

She's controlling him.

That wasn't a skill Susunee could often employ. It taxed her too much, and her own people were immune to her control.

Lor drew a shuddering breath. Adjusted his sweaty grip on the candlestick. Burst into the room, charging his enemy. He leapt onto Susunee and slammed the candlestick into her skull, a sickening crack sounding in his ears. The woman collapsed under his weight, eyes rolling back in her head.

He panted for breath, hands quaking. The Seenth threw the Kel princess hard against the door frame and charged him, as Ademas did likewise. Lor sprang up, brandishing his candlestick, blood glistening on burnished gold.

Mayrilana darted past Talanee and rammed into Mahaka, the Teokkaka's Seenth, a curtain rope in her hands. Mahaka staggered forward as Mayrilana scrambled onto his back. She wrapped the coil of rope around his neck and wrenched as hard as she could, eyes wild and burning.

Lor dodged Ademas's sword thrust. Parried another with his candlestick and recoiled as the thrum of metal shuddered through his frame.

Movement caught his eye. Despite a bleeding head, Talanee crawled across the chamber toward the Hakija and Lord Captain. Lor couldn't tell if Nerenoth lived or not.

Ademas's blade swung close, and Lor danced back, glad he'd always been fleet of foot. *This may be my death.*

Why am I grinning?

TALANEE REACHED NERENOTH AND PULLED HIS MIDNIGHT BLUE hair aside to stare at his bloodless face. Touching his cheek, his flesh was cold as ice. No breath escaped his parted lips, or it was too faint to feel. She rolled him from his side onto his back and pressed an ear to his heart. Listening, praying, waiting.

Nothing. No, wait. There. A faint, weak thump. Another. She drew back, gasping. In the sudden silence of the room, the sound was deafening. The hair on her neck stuck on end as a presence loomed behind her.

"Does he still live, Princess?" asked a honey-sweet voice.

Talanee worked her expression into something like grief and twisted around to face the Susunee. "He's dead, you monster."

The Teokaka clicked her tongue. "Such a tragedy. His was a beautiful face." She reached down and seized Talanee by her hair, dragging her to her feet. "What a troublesome child you are, Princess. If you just cowered before me, I might spare you—but then, perhaps not. You are lovely, for a Kel. Such fine features. A tempting morsel for any man. We cannot have you using that, can we? Before I kill you, allow me to disfigure your beauty. I am really doing you a favor."

She took a knife from an intricate sheath at her waist and squeezed the handle to reveal three blades. Her tongue touched the corner of her lips, and she set one of the dagger-points to Talanee's face. "Shall I cut up or to the side?"

Talanee glowered, ignoring the roots of her hair screaming with pain. She refused to show fear. Let the Teokaka try to maim her; a face was nothing, *nothing* to her spirit. The three points of the knife bit flesh and Talanee steeled her mind. She wouldn't scream. She wouldn't flinch.

The knife pressed in, searing.

Talanee squeezed her eyes shut until the Teokaka gasped and stumbled backward, releasing the princess's hair. Talanee fell to her knees and threw a hand to her face as her scalp burned. Barely a cut on her cheek. Wrenching her gaze up, Talanee found Nerenoth standing above her, daggers in hand, one dripping with blood.

The Teokaka clutched her side, eyes scorching. "You were dead."

"Only half," Nerenoth said in a hoarse whisper. His legs shook, and his breaths came in ragged gasps, cold breath puffing in the throne room's warm air. His face held no color. The Lord Captain slumped to one knee, shoulders trembling.

The Teokaka laughed. "I am moved and sickened in the same moment. Please finish dying, Lord Captain, while I carry on what I began." She swaggered forward, eyes pinned on Talanee, but Nerenoth sprang to his feet again, agile despite his pain. He lashed out with one dagger, forcing the Teokaka backward again.

"Until I am truly dead," said Nerenoth, "you will not touch the princess."

The woman scowled. "Even dying, you continue to frustrate my efforts, Lord Captain. There are few men who anger me as you do."

Nerenoth smiled. The expression was so strange on his face, Talanee started.

Drawing his shoulders erect, Nerenoth softly said, "Even should I die, I will continue to frustrate your efforts, Susunee. I will haunt you until the day you join me after death."

"That will never happen," snapped the Teokaka, cheeks reddening. "And my powers will never let your spirit near me."

"But you're haunted already," said Nerenoth. "I see the ghosts of your many victims. They stand beside you, mocking you, taunting you. Can you not hear them?"

A flicker of fear caught in the Teokaka's dark eyes, but she scoffed. "Ridiculous. You're bluffing."

Nerenoth's smile remained. "You may have the power to defy Death, but you cannot banish him." He wavered and sank to one knee again.

The Teokaka's shoulders squared, and she approached. "The great Lord Captain falls once more. Shall I slit your throat and end your suffering?" As she reached for his throat, he rose, eyes flashing as he whipped his dagger out, forcing Susunee to dance back.

She clenched her teeth. "Stop getting up!" Launching herself at Nerenoth, she caught his arm as he sliced her throat. She gurgled blood and slumped to the floor. Nerenoth turned his attention toward Ademas and Lor locked in combat, the former drawing the latter toward a pillar, sword flashing in the glow of dawn.

Talanee pushed herself to her feet and caught Nerenoth's arm as he wavered again. Her head pounded, but she held steady, refusing to be a burden. She must help Nerenoth and Dakeer.

A thud sounded nearby. Talanee whisked around and found Mayrilana Irothé, draped in a simple white nightgown, standing over the Seenth's corpse, a rope in her delicate hands.

"Your Holiness, can you stand?" asked Nerenoth.

The Hakija hoisted his head and nodded. Talanee stared at the crystalline swirls of frost lacing his cheeks, then gasped as she met his eyes. They were a pale blue approaching white. As Nerenoth helped him to stand, Dakeer let out a breath that clouded before his lips.

She turned back to Nerenoth. He watched her, his own eyes a glowing red so vibrant her breath caught. Whatever the Teokaka had poured into them, it had altered their appearance.

"We need to get you to Holy Rarenday," Talanee whispered.

Nerenoth nodded. "We're running short on time. Her poison has tainted nearly all of me."

Talanee wrapped his arm around her. "Lean on me."

"No, Your Highness." Nerenoth pulled back. "Find him. He

went into the east wing with the twins. We'll remain here and keep Susunee dead." Nerenoth drew Dakeer's sword and rammed it through the Teokaka's heart. "Please hurry."

Talanee nodded. "Very well." She hiked up her skirts and sprinted east across the throne room. At the door, she glanced back. Dakeer and Nerenoth eyed one another, faint smiles flitting across their lips. Did they find their condition amusing?

Ademas chased Lor around the pillar, but the Tawloomez prince avoided a deadly strike, deftly slamming his candlestick against the blade.

Talanee darted from the room, heart lodged in her throat.

CHAPTER 35

An equal measure of satisfaction and befuddlement churned in Tahomin's chest as he contemplated the chessboard, where a single pawn and two kings stood in fixed positions, unable to advance. A stalemate. He supposed it was an achievement, in its way, pitted against an Ahvenian prodigy as he was. Still, Tahomin thought as he sat back in his chair, he would have preferred a loss to a draw.

He looked up and found Toranskay Ahrutahn eyeing the board with a thoughtful frown.

"Determining where you went wrong?" asked Tahomin.

Toranskay shook his head. "Calculating how to quicken the stalemate in the future."

Tahomin blinked. "Were you going for a stalemate?"

"Of course." Toranskay looked up, blue eyes earnest. "Anything else would require one of us to submit to a penalty game. This was the best way out of that scenario."

A smile twitched at the corners of Tahomin's mouth despite himself. He'd heard of Toranskay's brilliant mind, but to be at the receiving end of his strategies was something else. He'd *intentionally* led the game this way, playing Tahomin without him even knowing it? If that was so, Toranskay could've won, but instead he chose a diplomatic draw. It made sense, Tahomin supposed, since the Ahvenian prince was a prisoner and had no idea of Tahomin's temperament. If he won to avoid Vay-Dinn's penalty game, he risked Tahomin's wrath. This was the only acceptable alternative.

Tahomin could still easily feel insulted, led along to believe the game was evenly matched, but Toranskay had taken that chance.

"It's possible." Tahomin lifted his goblet. "Vay-Dinn will consider this a loss on both our parts." He took a sip.

"In which case he might not make the penalty game quite so severe."

Tahomin shrugged. "Probably true. Thirsty?"

"No, thank you."

"I can have some water brought."

Toranskay hesitated, eyes calculating again, lips curling down.

"If we wanted to drug you, there wouldn't be any way for you to stop us."

The prince nodded. "I am thirsty, thank you."

Tahomin clapped his hands, and the panel to the servant corridor slid aside to admit one of its denizens. "Bring water." As the servant disappeared behind the wall to obey, he idly scanned the game room, with its chests full of sporting accoutrements, and silent consoles awaiting a holographic command, before he finally turned back to Toranskay. "I understand you were once held captive by another Kiisuld."

Blood drained from Toranskay's face. His eyes lost their focus, and his shoulders tensed.

"Then it's true." Tahomin sighed. "The braggart went around telling everyone about his success and subsequent narrow escape when your father caught up with him. Vay-Dinn wasn't happy. Orders are to deliver Ahvenian royalty to the House of Fyce unharmed and at once. Your former captor is dead."

A bead of sweat ran down Toranskay's face as he blinked and looked up. "Dead?"

"Vay-Dinn made him suffer first, but yes, he died."

A light caught in Toranskay's eye.

Tahomin smiled. "You can consider all the possible ways to destroy a Kiisuld, but you won't find the right answer." He sipped his wine. "Millenia have come and gone since the Kiisuld Empire rose, and no one outside our race has discovered the secret to killing those of elevated rank if we wish to stay alive."

"But," Toranskay said, "don't most of your kind choose to die eventually? I understand they just stop collecting lives and ultimately run out of their store. Is it because they get bored of depravity and self-indulgence?"

Tahomin chuckled. "Possibly. I suspect each have their own reasons for quitting this life."

"Most Kiisuld don't believe in an afterlife, right? I've always found that odd, as your people often torture souls." He shifted, his brow creasing.

Tahomin shrugged. "We believe in an afterlife, just not your concept of it. You believe in salvation and damnation, but I don't personally feel anyone in this life deserves salvation. So, does that make us all damned? So motivating." He stared hard at his red wine. "You know your fate in Vay-Dinn's clutches, don't you?" He glanced up to find Toranskay's face strained, eyes haunted. "I thought so." He swirled his goblet. "Your friend's fate will be little different."

Toranskay's gaze flitted to the door. "I can't fight you outright, but you know both Lekore and I will resist you with everything we have."

Tahomin shrugged again. "I think Vay-Dinn would be disappointed if you didn't. But it won't change anything. Even if you're eventually rescued, you'll never be the same. Either of you. Your friend will probably suffer most, so Vay-Dinn can extract his Sight."

"From what I've observed, Lekore is stronger than any of us."

"No one's infallible."

Toranskay's silence was somehow satisfying. Tahomin rose as the servant panel opened, and he took the crystal pitcher and glass from the proffered tray when the servant approached. He poured water into the glass and handed it to Toranskay, then dismissed the servant with a wave of his hand. The servant weaved around a Ping-Pong table and passed under the goal posts of a violent Kiisuld sport, then slipped from the room.

Tahomin moved from the table and paced the chamber's edge, pausing to straighten a vase or toe at a wrinkle in the rug.

"How's your father?" he asked.

There was a heartbeat's silence. "Healthy as ever, thank you."

Tahomin nodded. "He's always been the picture of health. Always the energetic, eccentric sort. But I guess that's what comes when you're crowned so young. He's done wonderful things for your people."

"He's a great man," said Toranskay, tone wary.

Tahomin turned to the young prince. "Relax. I'm not trying to trick you."

"You would be hard-pressed."

"I know it." He smiled. "I was simply curious. I met him once when he was small."

Toranskay's eyes narrowed as his brows drew together. So, he didn't know the details. Tahomin turned away, exhaling a soft breath as his muscles relaxed. Scowling at himself, he considered what to do now. Vay-Dinn was obviously occupied, but Tahomin didn't relish entertaining the Ahvenian until the man's return. He just wanted to get back home.

Was Vay-Dinn having any luck?

"Shayra." The holographic AI appeared, clad now in a slimming black gown, revealing nothing of her skin below her collar bone. "What's Vay-Dinn's present location?"

"He returned to the surface of Erokel, along with the prisoner Lekore," Shayla answered.

Tahomin blinked. It wasn't the answer he'd expected. *I wonder what he's up to.*

Tahomin turned back to Toranskay. "Seems we're on our own for a while. You might as well rest. I've got better things to do with my time than babysit."

Toranskay nodded. "Fascinating. So do I."

Tahomin sighed and returned to his chair at the table. He flopped down and leaned back. "But you're too clever to be left unattended, aren't you? Vay-Dinn would kill me if you escaped on my watch."

"Literally?"

"He might."

"You've been partners for a long, long time," Toranskay said, brushing back locks of pale hair. "You're quite a bit older than my father, right? There are stories of your exploits dating back several thousand years."

Tahomin smiled wryly. "Yes, we're rather old by normal standards. Still in our prime, though. We've gleaned enough life to ensure that." He considered the chessboard. "But I'm only safe so long as I continue to fulfill my prince's every whim. He's the senior partner as well as my liege lord. I must serve him dutifully."

"Would you consider yourselves friends, or do Kiisuld value friendships?"

Tahomin smiled. "The scholar in you can't resist a private interview, huh? Vay-Dinn's above friendships. He lives for himself. Most Kiisuld do."

"Do you?"

Tahomin quirked an eyebrow. "Of course."

"And does that satisfy you?"

"Are we about to embark on the subject of morality, prince? Is this a lesson or a lecture in the making?"

"Neither. I'm merely curious."

Tahomin reached for his wine. "I'm rarely satisfied. It's not in my nature."

"You appear bored."

"I feel bored."

"It's not just a show?"

Tahomin smiled. "I believe in being myself. I'm not trying to impress anyone."

"You do show your partner a shocking lack of respect."

"Which he enjoys."

"So, it's a show, or isn't it?"

"Both," said Tahomin. "I'm easily bored and often indifferent, which amuses Vay-Dinn. Thus, he's entertained, and I'm not put out trying to act outside of character."

"But you're not friends."

Tahomin chuckled. "He's my prince, nothing less, though you seem dead-set on forging a friendship for us."

"You consider friendship a lowly pursuit?"

"I consider it a waste of time and effort."

"You don't enjoy effort?"

"Not a waste of it. I prefer to pursue the obtainable and worthwhile."

Toranskay's mouth strained. "Like murdering the innocent?"

"You must concur it's obtainable. And as it sustains my life, it's also worthwhile to me. If you look at it objectively, you'll agree with that as well."

"I can't look at the taking of innocent life objectively."

"Not even with your logical mind?"

"To do so would rob me of my human quality."

"Interesting. But you've killed before in the defense of your empire. You're a warrior, aren't you?"

Toranskay nodded and sipped his water. "And there, least of all, can I look from a neutral point of view. I must be aware of the blood on my hands, the taking of a life perhaps no better or worse than mine, the reason I raise my sword. Knowing it's in *defense* and not to reign supreme."

Tahomin snorted. "You claim not to reign supreme, but you're the heir of an empire most civilizations couldn't dream of. You claim unsuspecting planets as your own to expand your territory. Can't you grasp your own hypocrisy?"

"We don't annex a world unless its people desire it themselves. We place them under our protection to keep them out of *your* reach. To accuse us of being tyrants when you destroy worlds is hypocritical."

Tahomin nodded. "Very well. You're the hero and we're the villains."

"Do you pretend any differently?"

"I suppose not." Tahomin propped his head against the wingback and gazed at the ceiling. "It turned into a conversation of morality after all, but I owe you an apology. It seems I was the instigator, not you."

"Accepted. But I don't mind if you don't. I've always enjoyed debates."

Tahomin smiled. "I hate them. No one wins."

Toranskay laughed. "You need a victory?"

"Not necessarily. It just feels more conclusive, even if I lose."

"You want me to convince you I'm right?"

"It might be interesting. But then I'd have to stop killing and resign myself to death. Not exactly appealing."

"Death isn't so bad," said the prince.

"Wait until he comes for you. I understand he's terrifying."

Toranskay shifted. "Why should you be afraid to die if there's no damnation?"

"Because I have something to live for."

"Besides death and destruction?"

Tahomin lowered his eyes. "Believe it or not, yes."

The Ahvenian regarded him with keen interest. "Is it the comfort of your partner?"

"No, I've got that covered." Tahomin smiled. "You remind me of a cat. You know the saying about what happens to them when they're curious?"

"I'm not going to die from curiosity."

Tahomin's smile vanished. "No, I suppose not. You're going to die because Vay-Dinn will finally tire of you and decide to end you, a broken shell of all you now are. That's your fate. Curiosity, cleverness, skill—none will avail you here."

"You give me little credit."

"I give you considerable credit, but it won't help you now."

"I'm not helpless."

Tahomin scoffed. “But you’re young, for all your accomplishments. And you’ve got scars from your last captivity. You didn’t escape him on your own, but you expect to escape us?”

The strain returned to Toranskay’s face. He looked down, his golden-yellow hair slipping down to veil his face. “About him. That Kiisuld. He was alone, he didn’t have a partner. Don’t most Kiisuld travel in twos?”

“Most, but sometimes when a Kiisuld chooses to die, the living partner goes on alone rather than try to find another compatible colleague. We do have to get along with each other, cooped up long-term in our ships. And our objectives must be generally the same. Your former captor was a particularly loathsome man, considered so even among the Kiisuld. Some say his partner chose to die merely to escape the odious creep.”

Toranskay shuddered. “I can believe it.”

“How long were you with him?”

“Only a few days, I’m told.”

“You’re told?”

“It felt much longer than that.”

Tahomin noted the almost-imperceptible droop of Toranskay’s shoulders. He frowned. “I never cared for Meer-L Shimm. I thought the day he died should be declared a festival forever afterward.”

“I thought he was a Shimm,” whispered Toranskay, fingering the rim of his glass, lashes hiding his eyes as he stared into the water.

Tahomin grimaced. “The House of Shimm is full of loathsome creatures.”

“They must be very depraved to warrant the disapproval of their own kind.” Toranskay pulled his eyes from his glass and forced a tremulous smile. “I hope they aren’t a large force.”

“Not terribly. One of them travels with my father, but he’s the junior partner, so he can’t cause too much trouble on his own.” Tahomin scowled at the thought of Ashiin Shimm. “Snake,” he muttered.

"So, even among Kiisuld there are levels of morality." Toranskay set his glass on the table. "In a way, it's heartening to learn. Do you know any who become relative saints? Those not inclined to kill or maim?"

Tahomin started to shake his head, but a memory of a young man swam into his mind. "It's extremely rare, but I suppose we do have a few rebels. I met one once. He was different from any Kiisuld I've ever known."

"What happened to him?"

"He was killed, so the old man said."

"Old man?"

Tahomin grimaced. "Another time, Your Highness." He didn't feel up to expounding on that aspect of Kiisuld custom.

"Was the young man executed?"

"No idea. Probably. He was a little unstable."

"Born that way?"

"Don't know. He just didn't seem inclined to kill, tended not to regenerate from injuries, liked to stick to himself."

"Oh, the horror."

Tahomin chuckled. "He would've made a very nice Ahvenian, but for his sarcasm. I hear Ahvenians aren't sarcastic."

Toranskay kept a straight face. "Not in the least."

"I thought not." He gestured to the board. "Care to play again? We'll keep this one to ourselves. Don't hold back."

Toranskay's eyes glittered. "You'll lose."

"I welcome it."

CHAPTER 36

Standing in the throne room, marble cold under his bare feet, Lekore's eyes fell on Ademas fighting off Lor. Startled, he glanced right and found the girl Mayrilana standing over the corpse of a Tawloomez man in leather armor. Swiveling left, Nerenoth and Dakeer stood over Susunee dead at their feet, a sword stuck in her chest.

Nerenoth looked up and blinked. "Lekore?"

Dakeer inhaled a sharp breath. "What miracle is this?"

Lekore trotted toward them as the Teokaka let out a scream.

"Ademas, defend me!" she cried.

Quick as lightning, Ademas dashed across the chamber, sword singing as he slashed at Lekore, who backed away.

On instinct, Lekore summoned *Calir*. "Ademas, what is wrong?"

"He is under her power," Dakeer said.

Lekore met the Hakija's eyes and started. They had changed into a pale shade of blue. Lekore's gaze wheeled back to Ademas as the young man charged Nerenoth and drove the Lord Captain away from Susunee. She leapt to her feet as the sword crashed to the floor. The wound in her heart closed, exposing a patch of skin, and her tongue darted over her lips.

A smile spread over those bloodred lips as she found Lekore. "You've returned, *Akuu-Ry*. Did my father release you?"

"Your father is occupied." Lekore took a step forward. "Release your grip on my brother's mind and leave forever, or I will hold you accountable for your crimes this moment."

The woman laughed. "I won't release him, now or ever. He will be my Seenth, and I will enjoy making him grovel."

Fury shot up Lekore's limbs. His voice hung low as he spoke. "You have murdered Kel and Tawloomez alike for your selfish gain. You will never do so again."

"Ah, but that's not true. With your brother as my puppet, I will destroy your kith and kin." She licked her lips. "I will feast on their souls, one by one. And, after I've robbed you of all your loved ones, I shall return you to my father and take my rightful place in his pantheon."

"You will take nothing from me." Lekore raised his hand. *Spirit of Spirit, please come.* A silver-white flame flickered above his palm. "I do not know how to stop you, Teokaka, but I will do all I can to try."

She chortled. "You can't do anything to harm me, fool. I am the daughter of a god! You are just a mortal king, born to die."

Lekore took a step, heat surging through his limbs, fingers trembling.

Violet flames burst from Susunee's body. Lekore shielded his face as his white flame died in the wake of her power.

"You will never touch me, mortal!" She lurched forward and snatched Lekore's hair at his scalp. His grip on *Calir* loosened and the sword vanished. "Bow to me, little king! Bow and beg for your people. I will hear your pleas before I take your head!"

"My Teokaka," cried a voice.

Susunee turned, allowing Lekore to spot Ademas struggling against Dakeer's grasp.

"Come, my Seenth," said Susunee. "I will let you slay your kin."

Ademas rammed his elbow into Dakeer's stomach. The Hakija staggered back and bowed against the console.

The Teokaka regarded Nerenoth beyond the console, smile dripping with pleasure, a challenge dancing in her eyes. "Will you try to save him, Captain?"

Nerenoth's gaze dropped to Lekore's. The young man studied him, noting the trust in the Lord Captain's ashen face.

"Wind," Lekore whispered. The stained-glass windows shattered as the roaring wind swept inside. It descended, tossing hair, tearing at clothes, carrying the fragrance of the ocean and the plains in its torrential center. The vortex came at Susunee, visible by the stray leaves caught in its grasp. Her eyes widened, and she pulled against Lekore's throat.

"Stand down or he dies with me, and I will still return!" screamed Susunee.

The howling wind gave her no heed, but Lekore lifted his eyes and smiled. "Stay. Wait."

The wind stilled at once, leaves scattering across the marble floor. Susunee yanked Lekore's hair tighter and hissed in his ear. "You cannot win, but every effort to defy me will be held against your people. Die knowing that."

THE TEMPERATURE WAS PLUMMETING. NERENOTH'S BONES ACHED like frost clawed at them. He set his jaw, annoyed by his growing weakness. He mustn't let it impair him. He must find a way to turn the tables again.

Ademas advanced, and Nerenoth retrieved Dakeer's sword from the floor to meet him. The prince snared his gaze, and Nerenoth understood. He lunged, allowed himself to be parried, and slumped to his knees, feinting weakness greater than he felt. Ademas wasn't under Susunee's control. He was going to save Lekore.

Or so Nerenoth fervently prayed. Either way, the Lord Captain had no strength to stop him.

The young man passed him and approached the Teokaka, steps confident, sword lowered. "Do you want his head, my lady?"

The Teokaka's lips stretched in an inhuman smile. "Make it a clean cut, my Seenth."

"Stay your hand!" cried Dakeer Vasar. "You must not slay your king and brother."

Ademas ignored him, hefted his blade, and slashed at Lekore's neck. Nerenoth's heart faltered, but he kept his gaze pinned on the sword. Lekore's eyes followed his brother's arm, his face a portrait of calm. The blow glanced off Lekore, as though the wind knocked it away. Perhaps it did.

Ademas stumbled. Dropped to his knees. Thrust his sword upward in the next second, piercing Susunee's side. She cried out, staggered backward, and released Lekore. Ademas sprang to his feet, catching Lekore before anyone could think to move.

Susunee screamed a series of curses in her native tongue and threw a stream of violet at Ademas and Lekore.

A figure jumped in the way, taking the brunt of the attack. Prince Lor was thrown several yards by the impact; he struck the floor hard and rolled twice before he lay unmoving.

"I'll destroy you all!" The Teokaka raised her hands into the sky. "I call upon the powers of my Father, Lord of Darkness! Help me to destroy my foes!" Her body was swallowed in violet light, and tendrils of darkness writhed in the dancing shadows around her.

Lekore pushed Ademas back and lifted his hand. Nerenoth started forward, unwilling to let his liege lord face death alone. The malignant force surrounding Susunee hummed as its influence stretched.

Someone pushed past Nerenoth, and the Lord Captain blinked as he recognized Dakeer Vasar limping toward the Teokaka, a phial of water in his hand, a prayer on his lips. He stepped beside Lekore and lifted the phial high, yelled a prayer of faith, and tossed the water at the enveloped figure.

A scream pierced the air. The dark light flickered, and Susunee slumped over, then straightened. "Your so-called holy water won't finish me, *Hakija*!" She tromped forward and everyone flinched back, but for Lekore, standing firm, his palm stretched out. A silver-white flame leapt to life above his palm, but it shrank before the growing taint.

Lekore frowned and shut his eyes. "Spirit of Spirit, please return as once you did. Bring hope to banish doubt. Give me strength to purge evil."

As he spoke, the flame sparked and grew, casting white light against the shadows. The Teokaka tried to approach him, but she couldn't step into the light. She conjured a stream of magic, but the flame's rays deflected it.

A sorrowful smile tugged at Lekore's lips. "Teokaka Susunee, you are a work of darkness in a world of light. You have no place here. Begone." He lifted the flame high overhead. It burst into blinding light, and Nerenoth shielded his eyes. A scream rose, higher and more harrowing than any death-cry Nerenoth had heard before.

All fell still as the light receded from his vision. Where the Teokaka had stood was now a black smear against the floor.

Ademas collapsed in a heap.

CHAPTER 37

The ground cracked beneath Vay-Dinn's feet as he fended off another magical assault. As the wisps of Hollow faded into the wind, he turned back to the enemy Kiisuld, scowling.

"I've got better things to do with my time than duel a rebel," Vay-Dinn said, tugging his jacket to smooth the wrinkles.

The Kiisuld shrugged. "I've got all day."

"I'm sure you do." Vay-Dinn considered contacting Tahomin and ordering him to get here *now* to help pound the useless piece of filth into the ground. But then, Tahomin was keeping a certain Ahvenian prince from employing his clever mind to escape. It was worth an extra minute or two to avoid losing his prize. Lekore had already slipped through his fingers, though only for the moment. "Is this some misplaced cry for attention? Are you hoping to elevate yourself in the ranks by proving to me how strong you are, or do you have a personal grudge against me?"

"Neither," came the answer.

"What's your name?"

"Keo. Why?"

"No reason," said Vay-Dinn. "Just curious if I should know you."

"And should you?"

Irritation stabbed at Vay-Dinn's chest. "Your name is familiar."

"Pity you can't place it." Keo's fingertips glowed, infused with Hollow.

Vay-Dinn shook his head. "Not a pity. You're not worth all that. But you didn't tell me your surname, and I'd like to visit your House when I return to Vakari."

Keo tossed a stream of violet light. It crawled across the air, weaving this way and that. Not a straight-on attack, but something else. Vay-Dinn eyed it warily, weighing its intent.

Keo wiggled his fingers. The stream of magic wavered, then broke into a million pieces and shot at Vay-Dinn fast as lightning. He dodged the first assault, but three tiny streams sliced his arm and leg, and he staggered back. The ground cracked beneath him again, brittle under the influence of tainted magic.

This is getting old.

Vay-Dinn snapped his wrist, and a portal swelled open behind Keo. He hurled a string of magic at the man, and the Kiisuld flung backward into the portal. It swallowed him.

Vay-Dinn opened a new portal and strode inside. The world tilted. He stepped out through a second opening and stood before the Kel's capital city. The army of Tawloomez warriors remained camped, watchful, fear taut on the wind.

He smiled and fixed his gaze on the city. Lekore must be here somewhere. Perhaps he hid, perhaps he sought a way to rescue Toranskay. Didn't matter. Vay-Dinn stepped up to the broken gates, studying the wall of Kel soldiers guarding the breach. He must retrieve Lekore and return to his own ship before the Ahvenian armada arrived. Bringing the boy here had been a mistake, but he refused to let that thwart him. He would never let the Seer out of his sight again, not until he got what he wanted.

"Miss me?"

Vay-Dinn halted and rolled his eyes. "Your persistence is starting to annoy." He turned to Keo, who shrugged, smiling.

"It's not the first time I've heard that."

"No doubt."

Keo glanced at the walls. "We should maybe take this further out in the grasslands. I don't want to hurt the natives." His eyes found the camped army. "Any of them."

"Oh, no. *Here* will be fine. I'm not sure what disease causes a Kiisuld to care about the natives, but I assure you I've not caught it."

Keo shrugged again. "Suit yourself, but here the remaining Ahvenians will notice, too. Toranskay didn't land on Erokel all alone, you know."

"Who cares? I won't leave until I reclaim my prize." Vay-Dinn lifted his hand. "And you will suffer for interfering."

Keo's smile faded.

They lunged at the same time, Hollow clashing against Hollow with a shiver of power. The ground rumbled. The world shook. As they staggered back, a scream rent the air, chilling Vay-Dinn. Someone, some*thing*, had died. A great power had vanished from the world in a single blip.

"Lekore." Had someone killed the Seer? Had Vay-Dinn lost his prize before he'd ever really obtained it?

Vay-Dinn's comm beeped. The Kiisuld prince fumbled and snatched it from his pocket. "This'd better be important."

Tahomin's voice was harried. "It is."

"Problems?" asked Vay-Dinn.

"Oh, just one Ahvenian protector causing a little trouble onboard."

Vay-Dinn's eyes narrowed. "How did Rarenday get there?"

"He followed your trail, I believe."

"But that's impossible. He can't use Hollow."

"No, but he could follow Lekore's signature." There was a sharp intake of breath and the crash of glass.

Vay-Dinn cursed. How could he overlook such a basic flaw? "Well, dispatch him quickly. I'm going after Lekore and then I'll return."

"Take your time." Tahomin sounded as though his teeth were clenched. "No hurry here." Something else shattered.

"Try to keep my ship in one piece, hm?" Vay-Dinn cut the connection and glowered. So much for a pleasant day.

He stepped into a Hollow portal and appeared within the throne room a few inches from where Lekore stood. Before he could take a step toward the young Seer, sharp pain lanced through his chest, and he looked down to find a sword blade sticking through his heart. He slumped, falling into blackness.

He'd always hated the feeling of death as it stole over him.

CHAPTER 38

"I see I'm too late to help." The man called Raren hobbled toward Lekore, using his sword like a cane, orange eyes bright in the morning glow burning through the broken windows.

Lekore wavered, weariness biting at his bones. "Barely, I am sorry to say."

Talanee and the twins trailed into the room on Raren's heels. Talanee gasped and ran to Ademas's side, as Mayrilana limped to Lor lying across the sunburst motif.

"How are they?" asked Nerenoth.

Talanee pressed her ear to Ademas's lips. "Breathing. Barely."

Mayrilana looked up. "Lor is also just scarcely alive."

"Where's my prince?" asked Raren.

"Still on Vay-Dinn's ship." Lekore offered up as succinct an explanation as he could.

Raren tugged on his earlobe just above a small, hooped earring. "This is excellent news, in a way. I can't follow a Kiisuld's path that far, but yours is altogether different—and still fresh." He smiled at Lekore. "I'm going, while Vay-Dinn's distracted. Don't follow, I don't want to risk any of you." His fingers caressed the air where Lekore had appeared, and he vanished on the spot.

Lekore glanced around the room as his vision quavered. "Any

word on the armada?"

"Nothing new," Nerenoth said. "I'm afraid Rarenday has been in the midst of—of connecting with it."

Lekore rubbed the bandages beneath his shirt sleeve. "I do not wish to stand here, waiting for others to do all the work. What might we accomplish?"

"We need healers," said Talanee. "*Now*."

The young woman, Mayrilana, limped toward the door as guards poured into the throne room, two dozen or more of them, capes of green rustling in their wake.

Mayrilana jabbed a finger at one of them. "You, bring healers. Please."

The soldier saluted and left, while others moved into the room, most streaming toward Nerenoth. They hesitated as they read his face, calm but frigid under glowing eyes.

"Secure the room," the Lord Captain commanded.

With echoing salutes, the palace guards set up a perimeter.

Lekore shivered, his instinct stirring.

A violet portal opened in the air and out stepped Vay-Dinn Fyce. Nerenoth sprang forward and rammed his blade through the Kiisuld's chest before anyone else could move. Vay-Dinn grunted, then hung limp in the Lord Captain's deadly grip.

Nerenoth twisted the blade. "If we leave the weapon in his corpse, can he still return?"

Lekore swallowed bile. "I do not know. We should—"

"The answer is yes," said the corpse, lifting its head to show a wicked grin. Vay-Dinn gripped the blade with his fingers and pushed it loose. Blood spilled down his front, his fingers slick with it. Nerenoth shoved the blade back into the Kiisuld's heart, but Vay-Dinn stepped back and yanked himself free. His wound knitted shut, though the bloodstain remained on his clothes.

"If we could be incapacitated so easily as that, we'd be no better off than one of you." Vay-Dinn massaged his chest. "But it still hurts to die. You'll pay for that, pretty soldier."

Lekore strode forward. "Vay-Dinn, please. Release Toranskay

and be on your way. You have power enough already; you do not need mine. You have influence, territory, pleasure, and wealth; you do not need Toranskay. Let us be."

Vay-Dinn smiled. "Enough is never enough for a Kiisuld. We crave more, always, *always*."

Lekore stared at him. He could not understand such want. What brought a man to this point? What made him so dissatisfied that nothing could satiate his desire for more? Lekore had always been content to live as he had, with food and shelter, laughter, and the spirits for companionship.

A dull ache answered. *That is a lie, Lekore.* He rested a hand over his heart and understood. He'd always anticipated Ank's return; the hope of it had filled his lonely days with warmth.

"I could resurrect him."

The voice was so soft, so tender, Lekore did not at first recognize its source. Meeting Vay-Dinn's gaze, he flinched back as he read gentleness in the Kiisuld's features.

"You miss him," said Vay-Dinn. "You want to see him again. I can show you how, just give me your power in return."

Lekore offered a broken smile. "No, Vay-Dinn. You would capture his soul, binding him to the life he has quitted. I cannot ask him to remain as a spirit—nor do I want to. He was mad. He is now at peace."

"But his spirit wouldn't be mad. He'd be well, and capable of loving you as he should've."

Skye flickered into Lekore's mind. The ghost was his friend, his confidant and ally, his guide and mentor. But Skye wasn't content; he desired to move on to an existence more suited to his soul. Besides, if Lekore gave Vay-Dinn his power, he would lose the Sight to see spirits. He shook his head again. "I will not sell the worth of my own soul to retain that of another."

Vay-Dinn chuckled. "Will nothing tempt you, Seer, material or immaterial?"

"Nothing you can offer."

"What about an exchange? Toranskay's freedom for your

capture."

Lekore's eyes narrowed. "I would not give you my power."

"I'd still have the chance to convince you otherwise, but your conscience could rest easy knowing there's a chance I'll fail, and Prince Toranskay Ahrutahn goes free. I think it's more than reasonable."

"You want him as badly as you want me."

"True, but for different reasons. And in many ways, you're harder to obtain. So, I'll take one prize now and try for the other one after I've taken from you what I want."

Lekore weighed the truth, sensing twists in the man's words. He sighed. "Toranskay would never forgive me such a trade."

"Sure, he would. He's Ahvenian. Forgiveness is part of their religion or something."

Lekore shook his head. "I cannot trust your word, nor dare I risk his confidence in me. I will rescue him without the aid of his enemy."

Vay-Dinn's lips quivered with a smile. "But I'm not *your* enemy, even after all this?"

"No, you are not my enemy."

Vay-Dinn shrugged. "You realize that means I'll take you by force and keep both you and your friend."

"And neither of us will be alone," said Lekore.

"Oh, I wouldn't be too sure about that."

At the corner of Lekore's eye a faint glow appeared. Angling a little, he found Skye standing by the throne, red cape vivid against the gold and white of the chamber. Lekore's heart leapt.

Skye pointed upward. "I've been for a stroll through the heavens and return with glad tidings. Several dozen Ahvenian cruisers are approaching the planet, engines taxed and anxiety high."

Lekore closed his eyes and let his smile stretch wider. "I do not feel alone, even when I am kept apart."

The Kiisuld snorted. "Maybe we'll see how you fare in extended isolation." He raised his hand, but a dull beep gave him pause. He pulled a small black device from his pocket and pressed a button. "Yes?"

"We've got company," crackled a voice on the air. "You need to get out of there. *Right. Now.*"

Vay-Dinn scowled. "I'm busy just now. Did you get the Ahvenian protector out of the way?"

"Not exactly."

Vay-Dinn's face darkened further. "What do you mean?"

"Relax, I still have Toranskay. Just, that won't help us if you don't get away now. The Ahvenian Imperial Flagship is within minutes of orbiting Erokel."

Vay-Dinn's eyes widened. "Impossible. How? He couldn't get here that fast."

"I don't know," said Tahomin's voice, "but he's there. Get out, Vay-Dinn. We'll come up with another strategy and come back for Lekore later. You've got the Ahvenian heir. Let that be enough."

"Tell me you're well within Kiisuld space," Vay-Dinn said, glancing at the Kel around him with knitted brows.

"Getting deeper by the second. Hurry or you'll be out of range to—"

A faint click sounded from the device and Vay-Dinn blinked at it. "Tahomin?"

A new voice sounded from the black object. "This is Captain Dawris of the Flagship *Daybreak*, hailing Crown Prince Vay-Dinn Fyce of the Kiisuld Empire. We send greetings from His Imperial Majesty, Majentay Ahrutahn. He desires to know if you would prefer to surrender peacefully or in pieces?"

Color rose in Vay-Dinn's cheeks, and fire burned in his eyes. "Tell his Imperial Majesty I've got as much right to be here as he does. This is neutral ground."

The device crackled, and the taunting voice returned. "Not according to the natives. They appear to deem Ahvenians their allies. In fact, diplomatic relations are in process to formally induct Erokel into the Ahvenian Empire. Would you like to dispute the claim?"

Vay-Dinn's eyes settled on Lekore. "Very well, you've won this planet, but don't think we won't get it back."

The disembodied voice spoke. "Your threat has been logged, Your Highness."

Vay-Dinn sucked in a breath and threw the device to the floor. He moved forward to stomp on it, but Lekore gestured, and the wind spirits whisked it up and dropped it into his outstretched palm.

Lekore lifted the device to his lips, then hesitated. "This is King Lekore Adenye Getaal of the Kingdom of Erokel. Are you still there?"

"This is Captain Dawris. Go ahead, Your Majesty."

The title set Lekore's nerves on edge, but authority meant results. "Vay-Dinn Fyce has taken Prince Toranskay hostage aboard their starship. His partner, Tahomin, is steering the vessel deeper into Kiisuld Space."

There was a brief pause. "Copy that. Stand by."

Lekore looked up into Vay-Dinn's face.

The Kiisuld smiled cruelly. "We'll meet again, Lekore. This, I promise you."

Lekore recognized truth before the Kiisuld disappeared.

"King Lekore?" asked the device.

"Yes," said Lekore.

"Is Vay-Dinn Fyce close by?"

"He just vanished."

Another pause. "His Imperial Majesty would like an audience with you, if you're amenable to the idea."

"If it will not delay Toranskay's rescue too long," answered Lekore.

"It's in relation to that rescue. Emperor Majentay will be on his way to your coordinates in a few moments."

"I will gladly meet your emperor as soon as he arrives."

The device crackled again. "Thank you, King Lekore. Please stand by."

CHAPTER 39

Rarenday was a skilled warrior; trained on Raal Corenic, seasoned by battles, and groomed at the Ahvenian Imperial Sun Court. He knew well the taste of victory and bitter defeat. But lately his luck had turned entirely bad. Once, several years ago, he'd failed to protect Prince Toranskay, and the young man was taken hostage by a Kiisuld for several days. That event jarred Rarenday to his center, and he swore never to let history repeat itself.

But now it had.

He followed Lekore's fresh trail from the Kel palace, into a desert scape near a city carved from the red cliffs around it. The ground lay scorched and cracked, reeking of taint. Nauseated, Rarenday trudged through the taint, seeking Lekore's aura. He found it and, latching onto its warmth, pulled himself through the Void and onto the Kiisuld yacht. His broken leg spasmed. He gritted his teeth and endured it, grateful for the sturdy splint.

He appeared in a room filled with stars. The stain of Hollow clung to everything, rank and sickening. He squared his shoulders, moved to the door, peeked into the corridor beyond. Where might two Kiisuld hold their high-profile prisoners? Certainly, within reach, somewhere plush.

Evil often hid itself in luxury.

Shutting his eyes, Rarenday tried to reach past the taint around him, searching for Toranskay's signature in a sea of malignancy. There, a faint light answered his soul's request. He opened his eyes and started down the corridor, leaning heavily on his sword, steps quiet, nonetheless. He didn't know how many Kiisuld were aboard, and he didn't want to find out.

The hardest part would be leaving once he rescued Toranskay. Already Lekore's presence was fading, and Rarenday's would fade even faster, his Void signature negated by so much of its opposite. With a shudder, he pressed on.

The silence around him strummed an eerie note. Servants kept to hidden passages, according to several spies, and the few dozen courtiers who sometimes attended Vay-Dinn aboard his star yacht probably kept to the more lavish chambers, filling their hours with every perverse pleasure, content to avoid walking from place to place. Not to say Kiisuld were lazy; they kept fit and healthy, but such was achieved through genocide rather than exercise and abstinence.

Toranskay's presence grew stronger as Rarenday hobbled along the elegant corridor. He quickened his step, heart hammering. *Please let him be unscathed.*

If something happened to his lord and prince, Rarenday would never forgive himself. Toranskay's first ordeal with the Kiisuld had changed him. Only through years of reflection and healing had his eyes regained their fearless spark, and even still, there were moments Toranskay's sight dimmed, and his shoulders hunched as dark memories wrapped coils around his spirit. In those moments he became a captive of his past, chained to horrors he never confided to Rarenday. Only Emperor Majentay, one healer, and Ter N'Avea knew the details.

Rarenday only guessed them.

As he passed a chamber door, a laugh jolted him from his thoughts: a boisterous sound, full of malice and delight. Not there.

Rarenday shuddered and hurried on. Toranskay's presence drew near. He could almost reach out and touch it.

There, that must be the door. Rarenday halted before the barrier, gritted his teeth, pulled his sword free of its sheath, and waved his hand before the motion sensor. The door slid aside.

Beyond sprawled a lavish chamber of red and gray, dotted by several gaming tables, a goal post, settees and sofas, vases, throw pillows—and there. Toranskay sat at the table, studying a chessboard set before him, fingers drumming his chin. He looked a little pale, no doubt from the taint, but otherwise he appeared whole and well. Opposite sat Tahomin Harrulay, his face drawn in a grimace.

They were playing chess? Rarenday almost laughed, though his mind reeled. Such a harmless pastime—but had they laid stakes? Surely Tahomin had heard of Toranskay's reputation: His strategies had proved to be on genius level. It would be a risk to wager anything against him.

"So, you won," Tahomin said, then pried his eyes from the board to glance at the door. He blinked at Rarenday. "Your rescue is here."

Toranskay looked up and started. "Rarenday? How did you get here?"

"I followed Lekore's aura."

Comprehension dawned on the faces of the Kiisuld and Ahvenian.

"Clever," Tahomin said. "And effective. Vay-Dinn should've been more careful."

Rarenday approached the table. "I've come to claim my prince."

Tahomin shrugged. "I'm afraid I can't let you take him. Vay-Dinn wouldn't be happy, and when he's not happy, I suffer."

Toranskay chuckled. "Well, you've mastered the art of self-preservation."

"We Kiisuld excel at it."

"So I'd understood."

Rarenday glanced between them. Their camaraderie unsettled his nerves. "Will we have to fight, Kiisuld?"

"Seems so." Tahomin rose and brushed back his long purple ponytail. "But you'll not fare well on a ship teeming with Hollow and that busted leg."

"Admittedly, we're at a disadvantage," said Toranskay. "But you must understand we'll fight just the same."

"By all means. I'm bored of chess anyway." The Kiisuld flexed his shoulders. "Swords?"

Rarenday shifted his sword grip and tested the splint on his leg. "If you don't mind."

"Not really." The Kiisuld raised his hand, and a blade materialized in his grip.

Toranskay unsheathed *Calisay* from the air and slipped into an offensive stance. He and Rarenday lunged at the same time, but Tahomin deflected one blade and dodged the other, springing back. As Rarenday limped to one side, he brought his sword in at an angle, but Tahomin again pulled back, not showing the aggression the Ahvenian anticipated.

Tahomin jumped back and fished a palm-sized comm from his pocket. He pressed the button.

A voice sounded through the comm. "This had better be important."

"It is."

"Problems?" asked a voice on the other end. Vay-Dinn Fyce.

Rarenday started forward, sword raised.

Tahomin glanced at him with a wink. "Oh, just one Ahvenian protector causing a little trouble onboard."

"How did Rarenday get there?"

"He followed your trail, I believe."

"But that's impossible. He can't use Hollow."

"No, but he could follow Lekore's signature."

Rarenday swung his sword, and Tahomin danced back,

bumping the table. A glass of water hit the floor and shattered as a curse came over the comm.

"Well, dispatch him quickly," said Vay-Dinn. "I'm going after Lekore, and then I'll return."

Tahomin rounded the table and caught a pitcher of water. "Take your time." He heaved it at Rarenday, his teeth clenched. "No hurry here."

Rarenday dodged aside and glass shattered.

"Try to keep my ship in one piece, hm?" said the voice from the comm. There was a faint beep, and the comm went dead.

"Nice display, gentlemen," said Tahomin. "You've spared me having to follow after Vay-Dinn and clean up his messes." He raised his blade and saluted. "Shall we resume?"

"By all means." Rarenday wiped stray droplets from his face.

They connected, drew back, parried. Toranskay joined in, sending Tahomin back a few yards before he threw himself into the fight.

A panel in the wall slid aside, and a half dozen men clad in dark colors poured into the room.

"Not now," said Tahomin. "I'm fine on my own. Go away."

The bodyguards, apparently accustomed to this, stepped back into the hidden corridor, and closed the door behind them.

Rarenday tipped his head in the panel's direction. "They're well trained."

Tahomin shrugged. "The stupid ones don't last long."

Toranskay caught Tahomin's arm with his sword-tip, drawing blood. The Kiisuld flinched and glanced down, then chuckled.

"Well done, prince. I'll return the favor. In this sport, we're better matched than in chess."

"We'll see."

The pace increased. Rarenday felt like a part of some intricate, wild dance, where three bodies moved in perfect synchronization, forward, aside, back, parry, thrust, swing. His leg protested, and the splint weakened.

I'll not be able to keep up much longer.

Seconds later, Tahomin nicked Toranskay's arm in almost the same place his own had bled, though his wound had already healed. Rarenday admired the man's skill despite himself, but then, Tahomin Harrulay was much older. The Kiisuld's combat experience was on a separate level.

Toranskay recognized it too. His movements were swift, his muscles loose and agile, but he held back a little, likely formulating a strategy. Meanwhile, Tahomin didn't tire. His exertions were few, though he danced around the room. He was playing, entertained by his new toys.

Well, let him feel triumphant now. They'd find a way to turn the tables.

Tahomin circled a vase, smile crooked. "You're doing well, despite the taint. Do you need a break?"

Rarenday bristled, but Toranskay nodded.

"Yes, if that's all right," the prince said. "I could use another glass of water." He motioned to Rarenday, then the settee, and crossed to take a seat.

Rarenday hobbled to his side, wondering how stalling would help. Every moment aboard ship poisoned their souls more.

Tahomin clapped his hands, and a female servant appeared. "Bring water and three glasses."

She eyed the broken pitcher, expression never changing, then bowed and departed.

"I understand House Harrulay is the second most powerful of the Kiisuld Houses," said Toranskay as he folded his hands in his lap, sword propped against his leg.

"That's true," Tahomin said. "House Fyce aside, my House is considered the strongest in terms of magic, combat prowess, and intellect. We're often selected to become partners with royals as a result."

Toranskay nodded. "It's obvious why you were chosen to accompany Prince Vay-Dinn. You weren't jesting about your combat skills surpassing your chess moves, and even those are worthy."

A smile played at Tahomin's lips. "You flatter me, Your Highness."

"You've earned my praise. It's a pity we're mortal enemies." Toranskay twisted the signet ring on his finger. "I'd like to duel with you again."

"You may yet. Vay-Dinn won't throw you away any time soon."

"No, he won't have the chance," said Rarenday with heat, skin prickling. "We're not planning to stick around."

Tahomin cast him a patient smile. "Of course not, Lord Ahrutahn. But you and your princely cousin will remain here just the same."

The panel slid aside, and the servant entered with a tray and glasses.

Tahomin motioned to the water. "Drink and rest. We'll return to our duel when you've recovered."

A rapid knock on the door brought all three heads up. A Kiisuld with orange hair and eyes stepped into the room, his face pale. "My lord, can we speak for a moment?"

Tahomin rose and turned to his guests. "I'll be right back. Try not to escape while I'm gone, okay?" He slipped from the room after his subordinate.

Rarenday turned to Toranskay. "We might try the servant corridors."

Toranskay shook his head. "We'd have worse luck getting out that way than any other. It's crawling with people."

Rarenday glanced around. The vents were too small to slip into, and Tahomin was probably just outside the door.

"Are you hurt?" he asked.

Toranskay shook his head again. "No, somehow I've remained untouched. Vay-Dinn seems more preoccupied with Lekore. I'm worried about what he might employ to break him down."

"He'll have trouble with that. The Kel are surprisingly formidable, particularly their young king."

Toranskay smiled. "He is at that. He merely lacks experience and honing. I want to take him to Raal Corenic to receive both."

The prince rose and crossed the room to a console. “I wonder if I can hack into the system to deal a little damage.”

“Worth a try,” said Rarenday. “Maybe discover what had that Kiisuld so nervous.”

Toranskay’s lips crept into a smile. “I have a few theories.”

CHAPTER 40

No one dared to leave the throne room, all eyes darting toward Lekore in intervals. Talanee's slippered feet ached as she paced near Ademas, but she refused to leave even for a moment to find a chair or cushion. The temptation grew as time hammered fatigue into her bones, but Talanee resisted. So many people suffered right now. She could handle a battered foot or two.

A disembodied voice crackled over the air. "King Lekore?"

Talanee started up from her reverie.

Lekore lifted the tiny device to his lips. "I am here."

"Prepare to receive His Imperial Majesty."

"Thank you, Captain Dawris," said Lekore. "I am prepared."

Several figures appeared before the cluster of Kel.

Talanee dropped to her knees as her skin pricked, heart slamming against her ribs.

The Sun Emperor was an imposing being, clad in a white surcoat embroidered with orange, red, and gold flames. An exquisite sword hung on his hip, its pommel a depiction of the sun. Yellow hair trailed down his back in a tight ponytail, held away from his face by an ornate gold circlet, a sun etched at its center. His eyes blazed a vibrant green, slitted like a feline just as his heir and holy son's blue gaze.

The Kel fell to their knees a single heartbeat after Talanee—all but Lekore.

Standing just behind the Sun Emperor, two fair-haired men in glistening black armor stood in perfect stoicism, eyes forward, impressive swords hanging from their hips.

The Sun Emperor scanned the haggard party, his gaze boring into every soul, awake and unconscious alike. "Lekore?" His voice was startlingly quiet, though clear. Talanee had expected the palace foundations to rumble, but they kept their peace.

Lekore inclined his head. "Your Majesty, I am he."

That gaze rested on Lekore. "You're acquainted with my son?"

"Yes, Your Majesty. I'd been captured and taken aboard the Kiisuld ship with him but escaped by chance a little while ago."

The Sun Emperor probed the chamber again. "He traveled with others. What happened to them and their ship? We scanned the surface of your world and found recent wreckage."

"Yes. That was their vessel. A strange..." He hesitated. "I think Tora called it a pulse, or something akin to that word. It caused their crash. Regretfully, only a handful survived. The one called Raren..." He faltered. "Rarenday, possibly?"

"That's correct," Nerenoth said, pushing to his feet. He approached the Sun Emperor and clapped a hand to his breastplate. "If I may speak freely, Your Holy Eminence?"

Faint lines appeared on the emperor's face, but he nodded. "You may. But please, Emperor Majentay will suffice."

Talanee shivered at the holy name, committing it to memory.

"Thank you." The Lord Captain paused. "Emperor Majentay." He cleared his throat. "While the remaining Sun Gods are recovering from injuries sustained in the crash, Lord Rarenday found a way to retrace Lekore's path from the Star Gods' ship to rescue his prince. However, he hasn't returned."

The Sun Emperor glanced between Lekore and Nerenoth. "Very well. We're going after them immediately." His green gaze speared Lekore. "Please come with me."

Lekore nodded. "Of course."

Nerenoth caught his sword hilt. "Lekore is also their target, Holy God."

The Sun Emperor regarded Nerenoth with a faint smile. "As I said, Emperor Majentay will suffice. And I'm aware of Lekore's predicament to some degree. That, too, is a good reason to have him aboard my ship. Nowhere will he be safer."

Nerenoth bowed his head. "I request the right to come with him, Emperor Majentay. I am his protector."

"Granted." The Sun Emperor spoke into a device like the one Lekore had taken from the Star God. "Captain Dawris, prepare a medical team and send them here to tend the injured. Looks like Hollow taint."

"Yes, Your Majesty," came the voice from the device.

The Sun Emperor smiled. "Help is on its way." He offered his gloved hand to Lekore. The Kel heir took it, then extended his free hand to Nerenoth. When the Lord Captain accepted it, the three of them vanished, along with the black-armored guards.

Talanee blinked, then pushed to her feet, knees trembling. She spotted Dakeer Vasar, who remained kneeling upon the floor, head bowed, lips moving in a silent prayer. His strange blue eyes stared at the marble. Talanee could guess how he felt. She'd hoped and prayed for the Sun Gods to return to Erokel, but never so long or hard as the Hakija. His whole life had been devoted to that purpose, and now he'd been rewarded for his dedication.

TAHOMIN ENTERED THE CHAMBER WHERE HE'D LEFT THE TWO Ahvenians and halted, startled to find them sitting as they had been. "You didn't try to hide in the servant corridors?"

Toranskay shook his head. "Would we have been successful?"

"Well, no, but that's never stopped a prisoner before." He coughed out a laugh. "You certainly make my job easier."

"Was there a problem?" asked the Ahvenian prince.

Tahomin's smile turned wry. "Yeah, but I'm not at liberty to explain it." He wasn't about to mention Majentay's proximity. Vay-Dinn knew, which was enough. He'd be on his way back, no doubt of that, after having their communication interrupted by the Ahvenian flagship.

At least Toranskay hadn't tried to disappear, or Vay-Dinn's mood might've boiled into something unmanageable.

Tahomin slumped into his chair, heaved a sigh, and tapped the sword he'd left next to the table. It vanished into the Hollow where he stored it.

"Are we not continuing our duel?" asked Rarenday.

"No point. Vay-Dinn is on his way back, so his forms of entertainment will take priority." He glanced at the chessboard. "Better set up our pieces for the stalemate match."

Toranskay stood, moved to the table, and removed several tokens from the board, leaving two kings and a single pawn behind. He returned to the settee, sat again, and retrieved his water to take a sip. "Has his mood changed to something dangerous?"

"Probably." Tahomin took up his goblet and gazed at the red wine, then set it aside, disinterested. The thought of Majentay in pursuit had spoiled his humor.

The door slid aside and Vay-Dinn entered, fury blazing in his eyes. He wore a crisp new jacket, this one charcoal gray with the usual metallic swirls along the hems, along with a fresh pair of polished boots and pressed pants. His glower settled on Toranskay and Rarenday seated near the table, and he blinked, then his shoulders relaxed. "Impressive. How'd you get them to stay still?"

"By command. Sit. Stay. Play dead." Tahomin took up his goblet again, proffering it to his prince. "We're still working on that last one."

Vay-Dinn snorted and sauntered forward to take the goblet. "Should I help?" He drained the wine and handed the goblet back.

"If you like. Want more?"

"I shouldn't." The Kiisuld prince turned his gaze on Toranskay.

"Your rescue's on its way, but they have to enter Kiisuld Space. That won't go over well for them."

Toranskay sat in repose, hands folded in his lap. "I suppose your border patrol won't take kindly to their entry."

"Not a bit. They won't reach us."

"And if you're wrong?"

Vay-Dinn shrugged. "If a miracle occurs, we'll still be ready for them."

"Of course you will."

Vay-Dinn's eyes narrowed. "You seem a bit too confident for my comfort. Are you concocting something, little prince?"

"No," said Toranskay. "Not a thing."

There was a long silence, then Vay-Dinn started to pace. "Tahomin, go see if the border patrol has reported anything. The Ahvenian armada must've reached them by now."

Tahomin climbed to his feet and left the room. As the door slid shut behind him, he leaned against the cool metal and closed his eyes, sighing. The silence of the corridor was bliss until his thoughts strayed to memories of Emperor Majentay.

The ruler had been a prince back then, three or four years old. Just a child. Tahomin had seen recent footage of the emperor now, five hundred years or so since that day. Fully grown, powerful, confident, the most influential man outside of Kiisuld Space, except perhaps Owenekiras Rokahn, Dragon King. Majentay Ahrutahn's will was law, his reach extensive.

Tahomin pushed away from the door and started down the hall, hands in his pockets, shoulders hunched. Must he face that man now? He'd rather let Toranskay go, but that was ridiculous. Majentay was just a man, no different from so many Ahvenians Tahomin had killed through the years. He wasn't a specter.

Why should Tahomin fear him? Majentay had merely been there, an observer to that momentous event, though he'd been Tahomin's intended target.

"Stop thinking about it," Tahomin muttered. He headed for the bridge, quickening his pace to defy his willful thoughts. When he entered the bridge, the female image of the yacht's AI stood near the console.

She turned to him and said in smooth, indifferent tones, "No reports from the patrol yet. I've run a scan to determine the location of the Ahvenian flagship. The *Daybreak* has passed the border and maintains a steady course. Its propulsion systems surpass ours. It will reach us in thirty minutes."

Tahomin frowned. "What of the patrol? Were they defeated?"

"Scanning." Shayra fell still, then stirred. "There is no patrol."

Tahomin stared at her. "Repeat that."

"There is no patrol. They received orders to withdraw from the border."

"Who ordered it?"

"Prince Vay-Dinn Fyce. The order came from this ship." A frown dusted her lips. "How odd. The prince was not here when the orders were sent."

Tahomin snorted and passed a hand over his face. "Right. Toranskay isn't concocting anything *now*. He already did."

"I don't understand," said the AI

Tahomin snorted. "You've been hacked, my lady. Toranskay got into your system without you even knowing it. How does that make you feel?"

"Feelings are irrelevant. If you're right, I've been compromised. It's a fact."

He rolled his eyes. Talking to computers was worse than speaking with humans. He started back for the chamber where Vay-Dinn awaited news. He wasn't going to like it, not one bit.

CHAPTER 41

The bridge, so Emperor Majentay called it, was vast and complex, with myriad stations occupied by yellow-haired Ahvenians performing countless tasks. Lekore's eyes widened as he gazed every which way, devouring every detail.

The room fell in tiers, and Lekore stood on the top level, looking down at the humming consoles and floating images. Voices and the faint creak of shifting leather chairs rose in a faint drone.

Emperor Majentay stood beside Lekore, uninterested in the sight of rich wood walls and golden sunbursts, pale gold fabrics, and gleaming crystal light fixtures. But then, he was accustomed to it all. Nerenoth remained still, taking everything in with the calm, steady expression he always wore, an undertone of awe coursing through him. Despite the magical poison in his veins, he held himself upright.

Despite his weariness, Lekore took a tentative step toward a nearby console, where a woman sat, fingers flying across a smooth panel, while images flickered and fled across a hovering window. When no one stopped him, Lekore inched nearer.

"What are you about?" he asked.

She glanced at him, smiled, and continued her work. "Ship

diagnostics. We're entering Kiisuld Space, where our controls could malfunction due to the high levels of Hollow taint."

"I understood space to be a vacuum. How does Hollow exist within it?"

"Hollow and Void aren't subject to the temporal constraints of science," she said. "They're the spiritual—or magical—fabric holding space and time together in equal measures. Unfortunately, Kiisuld Space is like the dark matter on one half of a scale, and our ship is infused with Void. The friction could be lethal and it's tipped against us."

He canted his head. "How do you prevent that imbalance from crushing you?"

Her fingers paused. "We maintain pockets of Void throughout the ship, reinforcing where necessary, using portals networked right into the light side of the fabric. The operation is complex and I'm not the best person to explain it." She winked. "Oration was never my strong point."

"Am I bothering you?" asked Lekore.

Her smile grew. "Not at all. I'm thrilled when someone shows an interest in my work. What's your name?"

"Lekore. And yours?"

"Relivay."

"It is a pleasure to meet you."

"And you, Lekore."

"I will let you return to your work."

She nodded and threw her fingers across the panel again, engrossed. Lekore returned to stand beside Majentay, eyes darting from console to console, wondering what special task each crewmember pursued. He itched to ask but refrained. Now wasn't the time.

He shifted to study Emperor Majentay as the man discussed the strategy of chasing down the Kiisuld ship with several Ahvenians in uniform.

Majentay was an impressive man, with the same fine features as his son, though his frame was larger, his expression more self-contained. The sword at his hip caught Lekore's eye, and he reached out as it hummed a story. His fingers halted as images flashed in his mind, and he dropped his arm. A terrible sorrow dwelt in that sword, and he had no desire to witness the cause.

Emperor Majentay sighed and traced his smooth jawline with one finger. "We don't want to provoke an all-out declaration of war by dragging the entire armada over the border. Advance this ship alone. Give the order, Captain."

"Yes, Your Majesty."

Not wanting to be in the way, Lekore moved to the Lord Captain's side. "Nerenoth, should you not be seen to?"

Nerenoth offered a faint smile. "A mild twist of my ankle, nothing more, Your Majesty."

"What of the taint?"

"Your Imperial Majesty?" The familiar voice brought Lekore around. The uniformed man, also yellow-haired, eyes a bright violet, bowed to his emperor. "There's no sign of a border patrol. We remain at full alert, but I thought you should know."

"Thank you, Captain. I trust you to stay on guard."

Lekore approached. "Captain Dawris?"

The captain turned and smiled. "King Lekore, I presume. Welcome aboard. Forgive me for not greeting you sooner, but there were certain precautions requiring my personal attention before we entered Kiisuld Space."

"I spoke with Relivay," Lekore glanced toward the woman. "She touched upon the complexities of your voyage."

The captain's eyes darted to the woman, and he smiled. "Inquisitive type, are you? Lieutenant Relivay's one of my best officers. Very good at keeping us alive. Would you like a tour of the bridge?"

Lekore's heart lightened. "Yes, please." He glanced at the emperor.

Majentay smiled. "By all means, look around. Ask questions."

Nerenoth remained still as Lekore followed Captain Dawris to meet the ship's personnel and ask all the questions on his mind. It was a whirlwind tour, each officer eager to expound upon their duties. Navigation, weaponry, communication, science; each was its own field, crewed by a dozen or more Ahvenians working in harmony to fulfill the goals of all. Each field contributed to the function of the whole ship overseen by Captain Dawris.

"You must know each duty well, captain," said Lekore as they strode back toward Emperor Majentay.

"Just enough to get by," Dawris said. "That's why I have a crew beneath me who understand more than the basics."

"What does the rest of your ship contain?"

Dawris stopped walking. "More people. Those beneath the officers you just met. Many attend to the hardware of the ship, keeping it in good repair. Here we run calculations and make plans which are, in turn, sent to others across the ship to be carried out. It's a well-oiled machine."

Lekore canted his head. "What is oil?"

Captain Dawris chuckled. "Still asking questions? Your mind must be full by now."

Lekore shook his head. "I hope it is never full, for there is always more to learn."

"Wise words."

"They are not entirely mine."

Dawris grinned. "Did Prince Toranskay share them with you, by chance?"

"Not he, but a mutual friend of us both."

The captain's eyes narrowed. "Could you mean—?"

"Hello, Lekore, hello!"

Lekore whirled to face the voice at the bridge's main doors. "Ter!"

The captain snorted. "How did I know?"

Bounding from the top tier, childlike Ter N'Avea—in all the greens and browns of a forest—sprinted to Lekore and embraced him.

Lekore's body warmed through upon seeing his friend and mentor. "It has been too long."

"Only a few months," said Ter, long pointed ear twitching as he pulled back to search Lekore's face with his sky-blue eyes. Soft yellow-gold hair curled around his face, enhancing the youthful features of the ancient Ephe'ahn. "But I dare say you've grown once again." Ter's ears drooped. "I shall never reach your height now, you great tree."

Lekore laughed. "It is wonderful to see you. Have you traveled to new places?"

"Oh yes, quite a few of them. Time has met itself in recent years, and I am gathering those chosen to repair it."

"Then what are you doing here?" asked Lekore.

Ter hoisted his shoulders. "Oh, well—"

"He's the author of my arrival," said Majentay as he approached, arms folded, eyes blazing. "I'd been searching for Toranskay's lost ship without much hope, so close to Kiisuld Space, until Ter tipped me off to a world that doesn't appear on any of our star charts. He always comes through in the eleventh hour."

Ter tilted his head, his smile slanted. "Don't praise me so, my dear emperor. My head might start to swell."

"On the contrary, I consider it my solemn duty to unswell your head, N'Avea."

The child-sized fae chuckled. "But it's the only way I can possibly grow taller." He glanced at Lekore. "You are a witness to the disrespect this man shows me, though I practically raised him from a cub."

Majentay's smile resembled an emockye's. "You did at that." His lips twitched wider, and his light green eyes twinkled. "Which is why they say I'm so twisted now."

As the captain, emperor, and Ephe'ahn laughed, Lekore's eyes strayed to the floor. His thoughts retreated from the lights and laughter as the hand of grief closed over his heart, squeezing, squeezing...

A hand clasped his wrist, ripping him from sorrow and into the present. Ter's large blue eyes peered up at him, reflecting Lekore's gaunt face.

"I heard from Skye of your loss. Despite your Ank's foolhardiness, I am truly sorry, my friend."

Lekore dropped his eyes. "I did not know loss until now."

"Alas, all who live must one day endure it."

"I would rather have died instead."

Ter's grip tightened a little. "And left others to suffer as you do? Nay, Lekore, say it not. Death is hardest on the living. Bear up under its weight and be comforted to know you brave it instead of those whom you love best."

A quivering smile touched Lekore's lips. "I will strive to remember your words, for they bring some measure of peace."

"Peace is bought at a heavy price, my lad, do not forget; else it is taken for granted and swiftly lost. Once, you knew no other way to live, and it was taken from you by your own choices. How much more do you now value the peace you once had?"

"A hundred-fold," Lekore answered. "I long for it."

"You know you cannot go back?"

"I know."

"Nor can you stand still for long."

Lekore nodded. "I do not wish to stand still in this pain."

"Then you know what you must do."

He nodded again. "Keep walking."

"Indeed. I knew you had the answers already." Ter released Lekore's wrist to pat his shoulder. "You'll be just fine by and by." His eyes slid past Lekore. "Greetings, good captain of the Kel. You have acted most admirably these eighteen years. I am glad of it."

Nerenoth bowed his head and clapped a fist to his chest. "I have been honored to serve thee, Holy One."

Lekore shot Ter a pointed look as the fae's smile crooked again.

"Yes," said the Ephe'ahn, with a faint chuckle. "Well done." He caught Lekore's look and winked. "Belief is a powerful thing, my student. One does not lightly choose to rattle it for one's own convenience. Already, so many meddle with faith."

He turned back to the emperor and captain. "I'm placing my student in your hands for a time, Majentay. Do not *mis*place him, hm?"

The emperor's smile returned. "And risk your wrath? Don't tempt me."

Ter huffed a laugh. "Wicked boy." One ear twitched. "But I suppose I must call you a man now, if only for your stature."

"Please," Majentay held up a hand, "I'm not ready to grow up just yet."

Ter clicked his tongue. "And you a father of two." He spun to face Lekore again. "I must take my leave for the present. Do keep Toranskay in as much mischief as possible once you rescue him. It will be good for you both." He doffed his feathered cap and curved into a sweeping bow. Upon rising, he vanished on the spot.

Majentay sighed. "With all his encouragement, it's a wonder my son is still alive." His eyes met Lekore. "How much are you like the fae devil, I wonder."

Lekore offered him a slanted smile and a faint shrug.

"I was afraid of that," said the emperor with a tight laugh. "One Ter was bad enough." His mirth faded as his attention drifted to the viewport at the head of the bridge. Stars streamed by like streaks of white in a sea of black. Lekore angled to stare at the sight, transfixed.

"Beautiful, isn't it?" Captain Dawris said. "I never tire of sailing the stars."

Lekore considered the view. "It is beautiful, though I prefer the green world and roaring winds. Space is magnificent but confining for all its vastness."

The ship captain nodded. "It's too big for us, like strangers in a strange land."

His words sent a chill through Lekore's spine, and a scene opened before his eyes. He stood upon a plateau overlooking a vast ocean. Stepping to the plateau's edge, he looked down the sheer drop to find spires of sharp rock jutting toward him. A cave near the breakers howled with the wind. Something dark called to him, and he felt compelled to answer. It was deep, ancient. Cold.

"A stranger in a strange land," he whispered.

The image faded, and he blinked at the streaking stars, trembling, arms prickling with cold.

"Are you all right, my king?" asked Nerenoth.

He nodded. "I…I will be fine." The significance of the vision had faded along with the scene, but he knew that dread place lay in his future.

The bridge doors opened, and two young women entered, one gowned in pale green, with soft, platinum curls cascading down her back. Her eyes, a bright, clear pink, held a warm light despite the crease in her brow. She glided into the room, followed by the second woman, clad in white robes lined with blue hems.

The second woman, yellow-haired with deep green eyes, slipped ahead and strode up to the Lord Captain. "I'm one of the ship's healers. My scanners indicate that you're dying of an overdose of Hollow taint. Please come with me."

Nerenoth hesitated and glanced at Lekore. "I would rather not leave my king alone."

Lekore caught his arm. "Please see to yourself. I will be safe enough."

Nerenoth nodded and quietly limped after the healer, as the first woman positioned herself behind the emperor, saying nothing. The doors hissed shut.

"Your Majesty, we're fast approaching the Kiisuld yacht *Dictator*," said Captain Dawris, arresting Lekore's attention.

Majentay narrowed his eyes. "How long before we have a visual?"

"Coming up now."

The stars slowed and fell into view, sparkling and winking. Amidst them floated a large ship, though smaller than Tora's wrecked vessel. It was sleek and polished like a black rock against the black of space.

"Transmit our desire to negotiate," said Majentay, voice like steel. "Let's see what Vay-Dinn's mood is now."

"Yes, sire." The captain motioned, and the communications officer Lekore had met pressed a few buttons.

"The *Dictator* is responding, sire," the officer said. "Shall I put it on screen?"

"Proceed," said Dawris after Majentay's nod.

The viewport flashed as a new image filled its surface.

The Kiisuld called Tahomin stood magnified, a smile touching his lips, though his lavender eyes glittered with frost. "Greetings, Emperor Majentay. You do realize you're breaking our treaty by engaging us in Kiisuld Space."

Majentay stepped forward, hand on his sword. "Return my son immediately or treaties won't be the only thing I break. If he's unharmed, I'll even ignore the fact that you broke faith first by capturing him."

The Kiisuld chuckled. "*Faith*, huh? An interesting word to define a cold war."

"Don't toy with me today, Kiisuld. My son. Now."

The young woman in pale green whisked past Lekore to stand beside the emperor. Her long curls bobbed against her back. "Please. Release my brother." Her voice held a melody, demure and sweet.

Tahomin turned a scornful smile on her, then froze. His eyes widened. There was a long silence, then he swallowed. "Your daughter, I presume, Your Majesty?"

Majentay rested a hand on her shoulder. "Please, Sajaray."

She slipped back to stand beside Lekore, but Tahomin's eyes followed her. The color had faded from his face. A heartbeat, then another, passed.

He pried his gaze away to return his attention to Majentay. "I'm afraid my prince refuses to return his spoils of war. You'll have to engage in battle if you dare to risk your son's life. Good day." His eyes strayed to Sajaray again before the screen reverted to a view of the stars and the looming black ship.

Majentay turned to Lekore. “Forgive me, but this is where I need your assistance.”

“Anything I can do, I will do gladly.”

Majentay nodded to one of the black-clad men flanking him. The man pulled a strand of amber gems from his pocket and proffered them to the emperor. Majentay, in turn, held them out to Lekore. “Put these around your neck, please.”

Lekore wrapped his fingers around the gems, appreciating their weight, then he slipped the strand over his head. The cold stones chilled his skin through his soiled tunic. “What is their purpose?”

“They’re warding gems, often used by dragons to keep robbers from pillaging their hoards. They’ll ward off most magic and, quite often, notice. Your presence will be virtually invisible until you’re in plain sight.”

Lekore fingered the gems. “You wish me to go aboard the *Dictator*.”

“Unless you refuse. I wouldn’t blame you. It’s dangerous.”

Lekore shook his head. “I will readily go to rescue Tora.”

Majentay exhaled. “I’d go myself if I could. Sadly, any of my people who went would sicken once they entered the enemy ship. The Hollow overpowers us.”

“I understand,” said Lekore. “But how will I enter their ship, and how shall I leave again once I find Tora?”

The emperor smiled. “With this.” He pulled a blue-stone pendant from his pocket. Its surface rippled like the waves of the sea as he handed it to Lekore. “Clutch it and picture your destination. It’ll take you there, as long as you’ve been to that place before. Another reason you alone can accomplish this task.”

“And I can return by the same method.” Lekore pulled the pendant over his head and let it thump against his chest. It hung lower than the warding gems. “From what is it made?”

“Void, but the warding gems will keep its power from winking out.” Majentay’s eyes darted to the bridge doors, then back. “Your protector won’t be happy.”

Lekore shook his head. “Not at all. Will he recover soon?”

"From his ordeal, it'll take a long time to be fully restored. Hollow is harmful to those who don't wield it, even deadly, unless the victim embraces its evil influence. Your Lord Captain is a strong-willed man to forfend its seduction."

Lekore fingered the pendant. "I should go now, while you can still delay without raising suspicion."

Majentay rested a hand on his shoulder and squeezed. "Be careful." He removed his hand.

Lekore smiled, pictured the interior of the *Dictator*, and vanished.

CHAPTER 42

Lekore stood within the chamber filled with stars, but the cold taint permeating the Kiisuld ship was absent now. He fingered the gems around his neck.

Would Tora still be in the same room as before? Had Rarenday found him? Lekore reached out with his senses, but the Ahvenians' presence had darkened into nothing. Lekore's heart clenched. *Are they still alive?* Perhaps the taint had weakened their auras too much to sense.

What can I do to track them?

On Erokel he might ask the wind to aid him, but here the air was dead, stale, and he felt no sign of wind spirits. Earth, too, would be useless, and the lights of the ship weren't made of fire.

But what of water? Surely even Kiisuld drank that. Would it be dead like the air? He might try Spirit of Spirit but using it against Susunee had taxed his soul, and he could barely keep his feet as it was. To wield it again so soon might weaken him too much.

Lekore crept to the door and rested his ear against the metal to listen. No sound came from beyond the chamber. He pressed the red light, as he had in the guest room before. It turned green, and the door slid aside, revealing the corridor beyond. It was empty, cold, and foreboding, despite the orbs of violet light and tasteful décor along its path.

He prowled along the corridor, pausing from time to time to listen for sounds other than the faint hum of technology inside the walls.

The ship was so much larger than he'd thought. If Toranskay had been moved from this level, would he ever find him?

A faint trickle of water halted Lekore. He moved to the wall, perplexed. Water ran along the inside, faint, but there. He placed his hands against the wall and inquired.

Water spirits answered, equally perplexed. Who was he? Why did he speak to them? What did he want?

Lekore explained he was a friend to the Spirits Elemental and had come aboard this dark vessel to save another friend. And, pray tell, what was the water doing in the wall?

The spirits described pipes used to bring water to numerous areas of the ship, but the life of water spirits aboard the *Dictator* was brief. Recently the ship had replenished its stores, but soon the water would be recycled so many times, its spirits would die.

'*We do not want to die.*'

"I wish I could help, but I do not know quite how," Lekore said.

'*We understand. Please do not forget us. That is enough.*'

'*Enough.*'

'*Enough.*'

The spirits echoed the word down the pipe.

"I promise to remember you. Can you help me?" Lekore described Toranskay.

The water spirits gurgled. '*We know where he is. We have seen him. Hurry, hurry, almost out of time. The taint makes him sick. Makes him very, very sick. Weakening. The master will hurt him soon.*'

"Show me, please," Lekore said, and followed the rushing water down the corridor.

As Tahomin slipped into the long chamber, the coppery odor of blood teased his nose. Pale light illuminated shapes in the gloom. He picked out the charcoal-clad shape of Vay-Dinn standing over the crumpled form of Rarenday Ahrutahn, the latter now too weak to fight as Hollow coursed through his veins. Blood spattered the floor around him. But as Tahomin watched, the man rose again, staggering, breaths thick.

"Rarenday," whispered a trembling voice further in the room. "Please, that's enough."

Vay-Dinn chuckled, brushing locks of blue hair from his face. "Come now, Toranskay, let the man die for his prince. It's how all protectors prefer to end, I understand."

Tahomin cleared his throat. "Vay-Dinn?"

"I'm a little busy. Be brief."

"The *Daybreak* refuses to leave, as we knew it would. Emperor Majentay requests to speak with you."

"Keep him busy a while longer," said Vay-Dinn. "Our backup will arrive shortly."

"Our backup isn't coming."

Vay-Dinn turned. "What do you mean?"

"I mean the same individual who ordered the border patrol away took steps to destroy our long-range communication. None of your forces are coming. We're on our own."

Vay-Dinn laughed. "Ingenious, Toranskay. But your father wouldn't dare fire on us while you're here."

"I wouldn't be so sure," said Tahomin. "Majentay might consider it a better course of action than letting his son suffer at your hands. That man can be ruthless."

Rarenday collapsed to his knees, arresting the eyes of both Kiisuld.

"This one's half dead." Vay-Dinn licked his lips. "Detain them just a little longer."

Tahomin hesitated, an image of the Ahvenian princess flashing across his mind. "I'm not sure what else to try."

"Squabble over the treaty. Make a claim for Erokel. I don't care, just *go*."

Tahomin turned to leave when he caught sight of Rarenday pushing to his feet again. He shook his head. The man was a fool. Better to stay down and remain alive than fight and fail. It was a waste.

"Tahomin, please." Toranskay's tone, faint but firm, brought him up short.

The Kiisuld turned back. "What is it, Prince?"

"Spare Rarenday. Send him back to my father at least."

Tahomin peered into the gloom, spotting the young man slumped against a black wall, his blood brimming with Hollow. His collar glinted in the scarce light. The cold taint was worse than most forms of torture to an Ahvenian, but he was concerned about his protector? So, Toranskay understood Vay-Dinn's intent. Rarenday wouldn't be killed, just incapacitated, his mind and body broken. A fate worse than death.

"Sorry, Your Highness. I don't interfere with Vay-Dinn's work."

The door slid open as he neared it. Stepping into the corridor, his ears rang with the climbing rush of water. The door closed behind him. Frowning, he turned right, and his eyes widened. A wave of water rolled toward him, filling the corridor. He staggered back, bewildered, and the wave threw itself against him, sweeping his feet into a tumble. The world spun and he with it.

As the water carried Tahomin away, Lekore raced to the door the Kiisuld had exited. The water had led him here. Tora must be within. As he reached for the light beside the door, nerves tied knots in his stomach.

Lekore clenched his fists. How could he face Vay-Dinn and win? How could he free Tora? He had no real plan beyond this moment.

I do not have the knowledge to sabotage the weapons here, nor do I have the power to stay the ship.

He had only himself with which to barter, but he could not betray Tora's trust by offering himself in exchange. *And my powers must not be used for Vay-Dinn's conquests.*

Pressing his palms together, he closed his eyes. What could he do to escape with Tora and Raren unharmed?

"That wasn't nice."

The voice startled him, and he whirled to face the Kiisuld. Tahomin stood near, dripping, hair free of its tail and flat against his face, trailing down his shoulders. His dark clothes clung to his body. He wore a frigid smile.

Lekore's heart hammered. He had delayed too long.

The Kiisuld's eyes fell to Lekore's chest, and his smile weakened. "Warding gems, huh? Clever. I wondered how I didn't sense you. I presume you've come to free Toranskay. A noble sentiment, but not very intelligent. You walked right back into the enemy camp. Vay-Dinn won't let you go again."

"Would you?"

Tahomin raised an eyebrow. "Would I what?"

"Would you let us go, if it were up to you?"

The Kiisuld scoffed. "No chance. We need your gift, and your friend is the heir to the Ahvenian throne. His capture will alter the course of the war. It'd be stupid not to keep him. Besides, Vay-Dinn wants him."

"But you do not wish to keep him for yourself?"

Tahomin shrugged. "I'm sure I'd have some fun."

Lekore shook his head. "You are lying. You consider the torture of Tora to be a chore and one you loathe."

The man's eyes narrowed. "Perceptive brat. Maybe I should do everyone a favor and silence you permanently." He started forward.

Lekore backed down the corridor. "Tahomin Harrulay, why do you war with yourself?"

"Shut up."

"Do you dislike your blood, your people?"

"Shut up."

Lekore stepped into a puddle, and a water spirit lifted its head to watch him. "What is it you seek?"

"Shut *up*." Tahomin lunged forward and grabbed Lekore's wrist. "You might see things, but you don't understand them."

"I do not pretend to."

The Kiisuld's damp glove wrapped around his throat, squeezing. "Stop lording yourself above others."

Lekore tried to swallow. "I...did not...mean—"

Tahomin squeezed harder, and Lekore's ears rang. His heart quickened, and panic clawed at his mind. He grasped Tahomin's wrist and tried to pry him away, but the man's grip was like iron.

"Please," Lekore gasped. "I—I do not wish to die."

The water spirit bolted up from the puddle. As Tahomin opened his mouth to reply, the spirit flung itself down his throat. The Kiisuld gagged, released Lekore, and stumbled back, pawing at his neck. Unthinking, Lekore waved his hand before the light of the door and rushed inside as it opened.

Vay-Dinn turned toward him as the door slid shut.

They stared at one another, neither moving, Lekore fighting to catch his breath as he rubbed his burning neck.

"What an unexpected pleasure," said Vay-Dinn, arching a brow. "Welcome back, little Seer."

On instinct, Lekore wrenched the blue pendant over his head and charged Vay-Dinn. He looped it around the Kiisuld's neck and staggered backward. "Where do you live, Vay-Dinn Fyce? In a palace?"

As the Kiisuld stared at him, the pendant activated. Vay-Dinn screamed as Void sucked him into its confines.

Trembling, Lekore stared into the chamber's gloom. "Tora?"

"I'm here," came a faint whisper. "Rarenday is, too, but he's not moving."

Lekore squinted, then raised his hand, hoping fire would come despite how weak he felt. A weak flame sprang up over his palm, casting fiery light across the chamber. Toranskay leaned against the far wall, his sword beside him. Closer, Rarenday lay in a pool of blood.

Lekore knelt before the man and sought his pulse. "He lives, for now, but the taint of this place cannot be helping, and I have used our only means of escape."

"Where's Tahomin?" asked Tora.

"I encountered him in the corridor. When he recovers, he will be very angry."

"We need to contact my father. He can think of another way to retrieve us. Do you see a console anywhere?"

Lekore started to look around, then laughed. "No need." He pulled the communication device from his pocket and pressed the button. "Captain Dawris?"

There was a moment's silence, then: "King Lekore, good to hear your voice. What's your status?"

"Weary," answered Lekore. "I have found Tora and his protector, both the worse for wear. I have also lost the pendant of Void. Might you be able to send another or devise a new means of escape?"

"Where are the Kiisuld?"

"Vay-Dinn is gone for now—I sent him through the Void—but Tahomin is close and likely to reach us soon."

Another pause. "Understood. Please stand by. We'll think of something."

Lekore let his flame float beside him as he turned the communication device over and over in his hands, fingering the shape. "Are you badly hurt, Tora?"

"Not as seriously as I might be. You arrived just in time." The prince smiled. "Did you meet my father?"

Lekore nodded. "He is a most impressive man."

Tora chuckled. "He frightens people at first, but he has a heart of gold."

"He cares about you very much."

The prince's smile waned a little. "I make him worry too often."

Lekore's heart thrummed as his chest tightened. "You are lucky to have people in your life who worry."

"I suppose that's true." He leaned his head against the wall. "Did Vay-Dinn hurt you, Lekore?"

"He did not."

"I'm glad of that."

A flash of blue light brought Lekore's head up. Lord Captain Nerenoth stood beside him, clutching a pendant in his fingers, a string of warding gems circling his neck. He met Lekore's eyes and frowned. "Your Majesty, I've come to bring you home."

Lekore blinked. "But how, Lord Captain? Majentay said you could use a pendant only to go where you had been before."

Nerenoth bowed his head. "So they told me when I volunteered. I informed them that I have been with *you* before and that would be enough."

The device beeped. "King Lekore, has help arrived?"

Lekore raised the comm to his lips with a smile. "It has indeed, Captain Dawris. Nerenoth reached us safely."

"Then please bring Prince Toranskay back right away. We eagerly await your return."

"That we shall." Lekore pushed himself to his feet, wavered, and caught Nerenoth's arm for balance. "We are all quite a mess, good captain."

Nerenoth nodded. "So we are."

Lekore released him, and the Lord Captain bent down to pull Rarenday up, supporting him with one arm.

Nerenoth glanced up. "Your Holiness?"

The Ahvenian prince shoved off his sword to reach his feet and limped to join the other three, then touched the collar around his neck. "I can't remove this without killing myself, but either of you can, since you're not Void users. Just touch the button here." He tapped the metal ring.

Nerenoth obeyed and tossed the collar on the floor with a clatter.

"Shall we?" asked the Ahvenian.

As they each touched Nerenoth, a weighty gaze settled on Lekore's back. He craned his neck and found Tahomin leaning against the open door frame, arms folded. He inclined his head and made no move to stop them.

Blue light swallowed the chamber, the floor tilted, then they stood on the Ahvenian bridge, wincing in the warm glow. Cheers broke out across the chamber.

Lekore leaned against Nerenoth, weariness bleeding deeper into his bones.

Majentay strode to his son's side, placed an arm around his shoulders, and held him upright. The young woman, Sajaray, clutched her brother's sleeve, tears bright in her pink eyes.

Barking orders, the woman who had taken Nerenoth away earlier rounded up several people to escort Rarenday to what she called the medical ward.

Meanwhile, Captain Dawris gave the command to leave Kiisuld Space at once. A string of reports filled the air. Shields up. Full speed. No pursuit.

Lekore frowned as his thoughts settled on Tahomin. Why hadn't the man stopped them? Why did he not follow them now? Despite his words, he did not battle to keep Tora, even for the sake of his prince and empire.

How many kinds of people existed in the vast regions of space?

CHAPTER 43

Light streamed in through the parted curtain as Ademas peeled his eyes open. He found the posters of his bed and realized he lay in his new bedchamber within the palace.

"Good morrow."

He stiffened and turned his head to find Lekore seated in a wingback chair close by, groomed, bandaged, and clad in Getaal green. The young man smiled gently, eyes bright in the morning sunlight.

"Lekore, are—are you all right?"

"I am well enough," said Lekore, turning to stare out the nearby window. "Ademas, you will be crowned king in the coming days."

Ademas studied his brother's serene face, and his heart constricted. "You're leaving."

"I cannot stay. My place is far from here now."

Ademas pushed himself to sit up. "But you're the rightful king."

"Birth alone is not enough to give a man the right to rule. You will make a far better king than I."

"Does that mean you have to leave?"

Lekore fastened his eyes on Ademas and bobbed a single nod. "I will return from time to time to see you, though I must go now to discover my role in the Universe. Ademas, Erokel is too small for me now. My power is too great for one world. If I remained, your problems would be too easy to solve. No one would learn anything they were meant to know. And the Kiisuld will surely come after me. I must leave your world to escape their reach and keep you from their shadow."

His eyes found the window again. "You were raised to be a king. I was raised for another purpose; one I do not presently understand. You fought to obtain your future. I must go now after mine."

Ademas studied the complexities of his brother's face, noting the hint of grief, but something far deeper than that. "You're right, Lekore. You can't stay here. It would smother your wonder of life. It would kill you. But I also know I'll miss you more than words can express. No matter where you go in the vast heavens, think of me from time to time."

Lekore met his gaze. "A piece of my heart will remain in Erokel far longer than time can run. You are my brother, my blood, and you will always be my king." His eyes drifted away, and he smiled. "There is someone whom I would like you to meet." He reached for Ademas's wrist and gripped it. "Look with me toward the window. Do you see the silhouette painted by the sunlight?"

Ademas inhaled as a figure, faint, translucent, formed between the drapes. Sunlight refracted off the figure's ancient armor. He was a slender man; with short, pale blue hair; and eyes of the same bright, inquisitive red as Lekore.

"Who is he?"

"Our ancestor, Skye Getaal," Lekore said. "In history, he is known as the heretical Voice of the Stars, but in truth he is a hero. Since I can remember, he has been near me, guiding me, teaching me. His dying words were a prayer and a prophecy of the Kel's redemption. Through you and me, both will be answered."

"Can he speak?"

The specter smiled. "I can." His voice was an echo; faint, fluid.

Ademas bowed his head. "My liege lord."

Skye Getaal inclined his head. "My descendant and king, it is an honor."

"Ademas," said Lekore, tightening his grip. "Please restore Skye's truth in recorded history. Do not let his name remain smeared. His blood was shed by his brother. For our people he has remained here, a mere shade, to see his prophecy fulfilled."

"*Is* the prophecy fulfilled?" asked Ademas. "Are you free to move beyond this world?"

Skye's smile grew. "The process has begun, and Lekore has foreseen a bright future for our people. That said, I'm not yet ready to say goodbye. My beloved wife, dear Naal, whom my brother stole from me has not yet passed on. She waits for me among the worlds beyond Erokel."

Ademas and Lekore started.

Ademas gripped the blankets. "But it's been five hundred years. How can she still be alive?"

"My old mentor, Ter N'Avea, took her from this place at my behest. She resides in a realm outside of time, not aging, where she awaits me. I will travel with Lekore until I reach that place, and from there, she and I will go to our final rest."

Ademas swallowed a lump in his throat. "Then you'll leave Erokel as well. I confess I'm feeling a little abandoned."

"Your days and years will be filled with joy and with many welcome challenges, King Ademas," said the ghost, "and while you will think of us with affection, you will not feel sorrow for long."

"I will feel longing," he replied.

"That is no sin," Lekore said, "if it does not consume you."

Ademas turned back to his brother. "When will you leave?"

"Soon, not straight away." Lekore stared at his palms. "I must renounce my birthright; you must be crowned. The Tawloomez slaves must be freed. The Ahvenians will remain for a time as well. They plan to claim our world as part of their empire to keep us safe and will also send scientists to uncover what Talajin intended to accomplish. They have also set a patrol at the border into

Kiisuld Space. It is a mighty force and Erokel will be protected for a long time."

Ademas's chest swelled. "Then we're truly worthy in their eyes."

A strained smile flickered across Lekore's lips. "They are our allies, yes." His gaze strayed to the door. "There are others waiting to speak with you." He started to rise, releasing Ademas's wrist.

"Lekore, wait. Did you really foresee the future? Am—am I going to be a good king?"

The young man smiled, eyes bright. "I do not need to look into the future to know that much. You will be as great as our father was—perhaps more so." He hesitated. "There is one final thing you should prepare yourself for, Ademas. Lord Captain Nerenoth has asked to accompany me among the stars if I will accept his service. Is that acceptable?"

Ademas closed his eyes. "I'm glad. My mind will rest easier knowing he can protect you, at least from everyday dangers."

"You are not sad?"

"I'm terribly sad, Lekore, but he's lived his whole life for your sake. I wouldn't deny him the chance to go with you anywhere. He was meant to be your shield."

"I have not yet given him an answer."

Ademas leaned toward his brother. "Accept his service, Lekore. Let him fulfill the wish of his heart."

"But his heart is promised to someone named Lady Lanasha."

Ademas snorted and blew hair from his eyes. "After how many years? Eighteen? If they haven't done something about it by now, it won't happen. If you ask me, the Lord Captain ceased to love her long ago, if he ever did at all, but he considered himself too honor-bound to release her."

"Does one cease to love another?"

Ademas's smile softened. "Perhaps *cease* is the wrong word. Their betrothal was a matter of alliances, not affection. He's a careful man, and while he's bound by honor, his moral code won't allow him to marry a woman unworthy of his absolute devotion. But that's just my guess."

Lekore tipped his head to the side. "If he's bound by his promise to her, how can he come with me?"

"Oh, he's probably already thought of something."

Lekore's lips twitched in a wry smile. "Then it seems he and I face much the same dilemma."

"Oh?"

"I must tell Mother of my decision to leave Erokel. I doubt it will be well received."

Ademas bowed his head to hide his smile. "I wish you the best of luck, brother. You'll need it."

As Lekore entered Mother's bedchamber, his eyes lingered for a long moment on her poised expression, fathomless eyes, and regal posture. Her hands were folded on her lap, while she sat on a settee near the open window, gowned in silver.

"My son, come," she said in a cool tone, raising her hand to him.

He sat beside her and took her slender fingers. "I have come to say goodbye, Mother, though I know it will hurt and disappoint you."

Her eyes narrowed. "Goodbye? You would run from your duties?"

"Being king of Erokel is not my duty. You raised your second-born to lead the Kel, and thus he is best suited to the task. I am a free and wandering spirit. Even the wilds of Erokel are not enough to contain me now. I must go to find my purpose. Please do not chain me down. I cannot, I shall not, stay."

She clenched her fists, gripping his hand tight. "I forbid you to forsake your heritage."

"I do not forsake, but rather fulfill it. Is it a wise man who rules over others against his will? Is it a foolish man who gives his throne to one more worthy and ready for the hardship? Please do not fight me now. I would have us part with mutual affection and warm wishes."

Her lips tightened. "Affection? What has that brought me but pain? You, heart of my soul, desire to escape from this place and leave me behind, just as your father did. You're a cruel child."

"Mother, please. Do not say what we will both regret."

She turned her head away, the comb in her hair glittering with the movement. "Do as you wish, but don't expect my blessing or love if you give up all I've fought to reclaim for you."

Lekore squeezed her hand. "Lady Zanah, how quickly you forget your second son. It was he who fought on your behalf, and he who earned the right to the prize. His hands were dirtied, his love for you was tested and proved true. *He* is the stuff kings are made of. Look at me."

She pursed her lips and turned until their eyes met.

"You have done all things in the name of your dead husband," said Lekore. "By him, for him, through him, you sent your living child into a den of emockye to rise or fail in service of the rightful crown. Now, by the name of Adelair Getaal, past king and my dead father, I rebuke you for your selfishness. Behold your second-born and see his worth for the first time. Do not doubt him. He will be your king, and he will make you proud. He is the child of your love."

Tears welled in her eyes, and she bit her lower lip. "But *you* were the child I loved best."

"Love me still, please, but search your heart for truth. You could love him no less than me then."

"Cruel child," she whispered, "to leave me so soon after I've found you again."

He caught her face in his hands. "Mother, do not feel betrayed. Give me your love, and I will carry it with me from star to star and sun to sun. You will be at the center of my soul, a boon in my need, and a beacon in moments most bleak. For my part, I will never forget you, and I now gladly give what there is of my heart to your keeping. Will you accept it?"

The tears brimmed over and spilled down her cheeks, warming his fingertips. "Oh, Adenye. Blessed of the Sun Gods, truest, brightest soul to walk this world. I couldn't deny you anything you asked for. Yes, I accept your love and give you mine. Be safe, little fool. May the gods keep and preserve you for ages to come, so you'll be a light to anyone in need of hope."

Lekore leaned close and kissed her brow. "Dearest Mother, I thank you."

CHAPTER 44

Lady Lanasha looked up from her needlework as Nerenoth entered her parlor, pale, but tall and powerful in his polished armor and pristine white cape. His eyes appeared to glow in the sunlight pouring through her westward windows.

She smiled sweetly and set her work aside. "My love, please have a seat."

Nerenoth shook his head. "Thank you, no. I've come for just a moment."

She hid a scowl. For years he had only given her spare moments, here or there, never his undivided attention. She did admire his dedication to serve the king; and, after learning the truth behind his disdain of the church and how he'd kept his silence regarding the true heir of Erokel, she had to forgive him his faults. He was truly a man of honor, and by that, he was bound to her forever.

She'd never forced their vows to be exchanged before, fearing he would end in disgrace, excommunicated from the church, and burned at the stake for heresy. After all, she didn't want to end in disgrace herself. Besides, a better offer might come along. Lord Lithel was a strong candidate to become Hakija upon Dakeer Vasar's death. But now she longed to marry Nerenoth—a devoted and faithful son of the church, favored of the future king. Everything she wanted in a husband.

"What have you come to say?" she asked, daring to hope.

His level expression didn't change. "Lady Lanasha, I'm leaving."

"Leaving? For how long?"

"Years."

She stared, her mind hitching on the single word.

"My king is going with the Sun Gods into the holy heavens, and I'm allowed to accompany him."

She held still, unable to breathe, her lungs pinched.

"I don't ask you to release me from our promise, my lady. Upon my eventual return, we could be wed, but I cannot now say when, if ever, that may be. If you would rather, I will quit you of your promise so you might marry another. For my part, if you wish us to remain bound, I will be ever faithful."

Lanasha's mind raced. He'd been chosen by the Sun Gods? It was the highest of honors! But years? She'd waited eighteen years already. Did he expect her to remain young and beautiful forever? And if he returned, how old would he be? Would he even age at all? The potential horrors bloomed like weeds in her mind's eye, and she flinched back before she could stop herself.

There was only one thing to do.

She dropped her head. "Please, sir, you must think me a selfish creature indeed to hold you bound to a promise, if your heart is elsewhere. Go with your king, but I release you from your oath. Just know that I do it out of the deepest affection for you."

The whisper of his cape brought her head up, and she stared into his face as he knelt before her settee.

"Lady Lanasha" —he took her hand and kissed the air above her knuckles— "your sacrifice won't be forgotten. Fare well and happy." He rose and started for the door, then hesitated. Turning back, his smile hung faint and sorrowful. "I pray you find the ambitious match you've long sought."

The smile died, and he strode from the room, leaving Lanasha behind.

"Holy Light?"

Toranskay turned from Rarenday's bed and smiled at Dakeer Vasar standing in the doorway, dressed in a surcoat and breeches rather than his vestments. "Come in, Hakija, please."

The man entered the bedchamber, ice blue eyes darting between the Ahvenian in the bed, the white-and-blue clad healer beside it, and Toranskay. "I do not wish to intrude, but I desired a word with you."

"Certainly." Toranskay offered the healer a smile. "If Rarenday wakes up, please assure him I'm perfectly safe."

"Yes, Your Highness," the healer said, inclining her head.

Toranskay followed Dakeer from the chamber out into the palace corridor. A breeze brushed by the nearest window, letting in a chill from a brief, unseasonable rainstorm. Toranskay approached the window and leaned out to study a courtyard three stories below. Birds hopped from puddle to puddle, searching for sustenance.

"How do you feel?" asked Toranskay, turning to the Kel priest.

"Much better. I thank you for the care and attention of your healers."

"I understand it was a near thing."

Dakeer nodded. "They said scars remain on my soul, but with time it will repair itself."

"That's fortunate. Scars like that don't always heal. Your eyes, though, appear permanently altered."

Dakeer raised a hand to one pale blue eye. "I will consider it a battle wound and value surviving it."

"That's wise. It's a mark of distinction." He smiled softly.

Dakeer dropped his eyes to the floor, then looked up. "Holy Light, I hear you will be leaving soon."

"Not for a few weeks yet. My father must go, but I'll remain with a full complement of ships while I work with Prince Ademas on treaties between your people and mine, as well as between

Erokel and the Firelands. Lekore's also overseeing his brother's coronation and his uncle's funeral."

The Hakija's smile faded. "To bury Netye in state unsettles my soul."

"But it will provide Lekore much needed closure." Toranskay leaned on the windowsill. "What's to be done about Farr Veon?"

"His trial is tomorrow. I think it's safe to say he'll be executed for heresy and treason, after all he's done."

Silence lapsed between them.

"Is there something you need, Hakija?"

The man sighed. "Forgive me if I am too presumptuous, but there are so many things I would like to speak to you about, and more still I wish to hear from you. I—I intend to step down as the Hakija, and Lord Lithel has agreed to take up the mantel in my stead. He's recovering well from his wound and is fit enough of mind to handle the tasks ahead as his body heals."

Dakeer cupped his hands behind his back. "I should..." He inhaled. "I would like to travel with you, to join you among the stars."

MOANING, LOR OPENED HIS EYES AND STARED INTO A FAMILIAR face. Green eyes blinked down at him.

"You look awful," said Keo.

Lor managed a smile. "I cannot believe I live. I thought Susunee's attack would be my final moment."

"It turns out you're a better fighter than you thought." The Kiisuld pulled back to let Lor take in his surroundings. He lay on a soft bed in some part of the Kel palace; sunbursts and white drapes attested to that.

"How many days has it been?"

"Four," said Keo, leaning back in his chair and smoothing down his customary tunic.

Lor pushed himself into a sitting position. He blinked at the Kiisuld. "What of my people?"

"Safe and sound, I assure you. None were hurt, though it was a hefty price for me." He massaged his stomach. "I took a few more blows than I initially anticipated." His smile stretched wider. "Doesn't matter. You've won, the Kel have won, the Ahvenians have won. And each of you sacrificed for each other. Well done, Lor. You did your part rather well."

Lor flushed. "I never thought I would protect Kel."

"Not just any Kel. Their future king and his brother."

"So," said Lor, studying the embroidery of his coverlet, "Susunee is dead?"

"Yes. She's gone for good, and you'll be crowned king of Tawloom soon. And that means it's time for me to go."

Lor's head jerked up. "You are leaving?"

Keo chuckled. "You don't want me to?"

"Well. I thought... Isn't this your home?"

"My home?"

Lor bobbed a nod.

"I have no home."

"So, you're not returning to your people, ever?"

"No, never there."

"Then where will you go?"

"I don't know. Somewhere."

"If you do not know where you will go, then stay, Keo. Your home is here."

Keo shook his head. "I'll just attract trouble."

Lor clutched his blankets. "Would you not attract trouble elsewhere? Stay and keep other lands from trouble."

The Kiisuld laughed. "You really want me to stay?"

He nodded. "You are my first true friend."

The Kiisuld snorted, then his mirth faded. "The truth is I can't leave this world for long periods of time. I'm its Keeper of Memory, its historian. But I intended to slip into the background and be forgotten. Most Keepers of Memory aren't known to their world's inhabitants. But you... Well, Lor'Toreth, it gets lonely being apart from it all. I suppose I'll have time to slip away after you're old and dead. Fine. I'll be your friend."

It was Lor's turn to laugh. "Do not make it sound as though I wrenched your arm."

Keo shrugged. "Maybe you did. I don't mind though. Not this once." He winked and tucked a piece of parchment into Lor's hands. The communication spell. "I didn't come here for myself, you know. There's a young lady waiting outside the door. She'd like to talk to you."

Lor's heart skipped. "Mayrilana?"

The young woman peeked in through the open door and smiled a beautiful, shy smile. "If it's not any trouble."

"None," Lor said at once. "Please. Come in. I...I enjoy the company of good friends."

Talanee sprinted after Keo as he slipped out of Lor's room and trudged up the palace corridor. "Please wait." Her slippers slapped the marble floor. Keerva wheezed to keep up.

Keo turned and eyed Talanee. "Your Highness. What's got you in such a hurry?"

Talanee reached him. "I need to ask you, I must know. What—what happened to Khyna?"

Keo blinked, then snorted. "Incredible. Years of animosity, and now *you* worry for a Tawloomez half-pint and Lor develops feelings for a Kel noble. Blast him, but Skye did it after all."

Talanee scowled to hide a shiver at the Heretic's name. "Will you stop musing and answer my question?"

The man with green hair shrugged. "She's back in the Firelands, well enough to carry on. Without her mother to order her around, she'll live a normal enough life. She didn't want to hurt you. She didn't have a choice."

"I know." Talanee wrung her skirts. "I want her to know that, too."

"I'll tell her if I see her again soon."

Talanee searched the man's strange eyes. "What *are* you?"

Keo smirked. "I'll tell you what I'm not. A *god*." He turned and strode away.

The princess watched him leave, then turned and marched down the hall toward Ademas's chamber. Keerva followed, puffing as she always did. Talanee ignored her. If anyone would be willing to discuss the mysteries of Keo, and all the strange beings beyond the stars—divine and otherwise—it was her cousin.

Talanee allowed herself a little smile. She wasn't alone.

She had family.

And that family cared.

CHAPTER 45

Word of Netye Getaal's sins spread faster than fire spirits scattering flames over the grasslands in the strong winds of the Sunny Season.

As Kel nobility arrived by carriage at the royal tombs outside the city proper, faces veiled in delicate gold, Lekore bowed his head beneath the silent weight of disdain and fury rolling over the crowd. Farr Veon's trial had commenced yesterday, inciting vocal cries for his execution. Despite many demanding the Sun Gods to determine his fate, Toranskay and his fellows remained reticent.

In the end, the Hakija of the Night had been examined by the Sun Tribunal and found guilty of heresy, treason, and other heinous acts against life. As the sun set, he'd been burned at the stake.

Somehow, Netye's burial elicited a different kind of wrath. No one spoke. Kel shuffled into clusters, leaning away from the tomb where Netye Getaal lay in state.

Lekore, Ademas, and Talanee stood apart, draped in funeral finery, close to the open maw of the stone vault where King Adelair's and other dead kings' bones gradually turned to dust.

Earth spirits congregated, lured by the finality of death.

The Ahvenians had chosen not to attend.

The Lord Captain and Dakeer Vasar remained on one side of the tomb, both veiled like the rest. Lekore alone had refused the covering. Tradition or not, he wanted to say goodbye to Ank without his vision impeded.

His heart alone wore a cloak, heavy, oppressive; a great weight that might never lift. The thought burned his eyes, and tears pooled to cloud his gaze.

He pursed his lips and squeezed his fingers, willing himself to remain composed.

Lithel Kuaan—now Hakija on the heels of Dakeer's formal confession and abdication—stepped up beside Lekore, leaning heavily on his acolyte. The new Hakija turned and faced the crowd.

"By the will of the Sun Gods," Lithel said, "Netye Getaal has died. We entomb him now, lifting our hearts to the Sun Throne and its glorious gods to accept their servant if they should find him worthy."

The crowd's emotions slammed into Lekore: Bitter scorn and burning disgust roiled up, tainting the air. Lekore hunched, squeezing his mind shut against the soundless barrage.

He clenched his fists. *Do not address them. Do not add to the unjust verdicts. They cannot help their feelings any more than you can.*

Lithel droned on, quoting vague scriptures. The moments passed like slack water, and wind spirits settled on Lekore's shoulders and head, dangling Kel-like feet, whispering reassurances.

He barely heard them.

Talanee's feelings reached him, softer, sadder than the rest. She stood in perfect stillness, hands clasped before her, veil hiding her shame and sorrow. At her side, Ademas emanated a calming sort of sympathy, none of his deeper emotions surfacing, as though he could naturally shield against Lekore's ability to feel them.

"No one is immune to flaws," Lithel said in his lofty voice. "We leave the soul of this man at the steps of the Sun Throne, for the blessed gods know best of all the heart of this troubled man. Amen."

A murmuring echo of the Hakija's last word rippled through the crowd, discordant, skeptical.

Lekore turned from them and stared into the tomb. Among the stone coffins within, the name *Adenye Getaal* was etched across a marble box containing the remains of some unknown child buried in Lekore's stead. He had rejected Mother's entreaty to remove the bones. Let the dead sleep.

The shuffle of feet crunched the crisp wild grass as Kel retreated, leaving the Getaals to grieve.

Mother moved away with the crowd, Uncle Elekel escorting her. Neither spoke, though their relief undulated across the air, remorseless. Could Lekore blame them? They had been Ank's victims, robbed of Adelair, robbed of little Adenye.

Lekore stepped closer to the tomb, heart throbbing. So many years, so many nights spent longing for Ank's return.

You never came. Did you ever mean to, even once? Did you ever wonder if I had survived?

Lekore choked down a sob as it scaled his throat. He dropped his gaze and let the tears shimmer before his vision, dazzling in the sunlight. "Goodbye, dear Ank. I will remember you better than you were..."

He turned from the tomb and met Nerenoth's steady stare. The Lord Captain inclined his head, feelings settling around Lekore like a comfortable fur on a chilly night. Whatever Nerenoth's opinion of Netye now, upon the man's death, the Lord Captain harbored only concern and fondness for Lekore in this moment.

We are leaving. That is best. I cannot remain in a world where I find myself seeking Ank even now.

Ank never existed.

He was a lie.

Lekore reached Nerenoth's side.

"Ready?" asked the Captain.

Lekore tried to smile. "Yes, let us return to Inpizal. I must pack my few belongings."

He left the tomb behind, where Adelair and Netye, two men he had barely known, slumbered side by side.

CHAPTER 46

Clouds hung like a pall over the palace gardens as evening dipped toward night.

Golden skirts clutched in her hands, veil discarded, Princess Talanee moved through the solemn courtiers gathered for the traditional funeral dinner and dance, none as grief-stricken as they pretended to be. She hardly cared. No one had understood Father's private demons.

No one but his daughter.

Perhaps Lekore does, too.

Several nobles still draped in funeral veils parted for her, and Talanee moved between them as her eyes scanned the lighted grounds, skimming over the fountains, assessing the crowded paths, as she sought her target. Keerva kept close, staying silent.

Lekore and Ademas stood apart from the crowds, conversing in soft tones. At the start of the earlier dinner, Lekore had publicly announced his decision not to take the throne, declaring Ademas the heir apparent. If the Kel nobility were shocked, they didn't show it. The veils helped with that. Now, attendees clustered in their usual groups to gossip about Ademas and all they knew. And what they didn't.

But Talanee didn't care about either of her cousins just now.

There. Dressed in his gleaming armor, the Lord Captain surveyed the post-dinner dance with his usual calm, standing away from the bustle, his lieutenant and twin brothers flanking him. Jeth—it was definitely Jeth—looked particularly pleased, and Talanee could guess why. Beside him, Jesh resembled a wilting flower. The princess could guess about that too.

She approached and dipped into a curtsey as the Lord Captain broke off conversation to meet her eyes. He nodded a greeting.

Talanee fanned herself against the muggy air. "My lord, might we speak for a moment?" Her eyes flicked to the nearby garden path lined by tall bushes.

"As you please, Your Highness," he said, and passed his untouched goblet to his lieutenant.

Talanee led the way into the quieter realm of the labyrinthine garden path, Keerva keeping at a discreet distance behind her princess and the Lord Captain. They walked along the stone path until the music from the dance faded into background noise.

Talanee halted and turned to face Nerenoth Irothé.

She drew a breath, the potent green of evergreen bushes tickling her nose. "Are the rumors true, my lord? Are you retiring?"

He offered her a slow blink, perhaps startled by her blunt words. "Yes, Princess. I am."

She stifled a dismayed outburst, but her heart panged. "Does that mean you're leaving with Lekore?"

He nodded. "It does."

Talanee pressed a fist against her breast. "A commendable sacrifice. It—it also makes other rumors more likely."

"Such as?"

She chewed the inside of her lip. "Such as, Jeth taking your place as Lord Captain. And Lady Lanasha releasing you from your betrothal."

"Yes," he said, his gaze drifting past her. "Both rumors are also true. Jeth proved his sword skill against the Lord Lieutenant this morning at dawn."

Hope hitched in Talanee's lungs, and she inhaled to dislodge it.

"Then—then you're free."

His glowing eyes returned to meet hers. He nodded.

Talanee took a step toward him. "Please don't go." The words escaped her lips unbidden. "Not—not until I tell you—" Her cheeks blazed with heat. "Captain, I love you. I've always—ever since you saved me—" She drew a long breath and tried again. "I realize your feelings may not be as deep, or even akin to mine, but I had to let you know my heart."

His expression softened and a faint smile brushed against his lips. Under the dark clouds, his eyes glowed more vividly, and the pallor of his ashen skin was almost ghostly in the gloom. "Your Highness, I thank you for the honor of your confession. I regret that I can reciprocate none of your feelings. For that, I am sincerely remorseful."

She'd expected these words, but they struck her with more force than she'd braced against. Bowing her head, the heat of her face bled into her neck and down her shoulders. "That—that's fine. I didn't think you could." She clenched her hands into fists and willed herself to meet his eyes, hoisting her chin. "Still, I had to tell you. G-goodbye, Captain. I wish you safe travels in the realm of the gods."

Tears brimming in her eyes, she whirled and trotted away, Keerva at her heels. The Lord Captain never followed, too discreet to cause her further embarrassment.

Entering the wide grounds where the Kel nobility mingled, Talanee let the music roll over her, softening the heat of her skin. She drew out a handkerchief and dabbed at the stray tears on her cheeks.

Across the somber dancers, Ademas caught her eye and waved her over. She let her feet carry her around the edges of the garden until she reached him. He stood alone.

"Where's Lekore?" she asked.

Ademas grinned and arced a hand over the air. "He flew away on the wind. He's probably had enough of people to last him years."

"Enough of Kel people, anyway," Talanee muttered.

Ademas tipped his head to eye her sidelong. "Not all of us. And he'll come back. Count on that."

She shrugged. "Whether he does or not hardly matters to me."

"Doesn't it?"

Talanee scowled. "Why should it?"

"You just seem upset. I wondered if you were beginning to fancy him."

"*Lekore*?" Talanee shook her golden skirts. "That's ridiculous."

"Not really. Royal cousins marry all the time."

A laugh cut across Talanee's tongue, sharp, bitter. "Lekore isn't nearly prepared for the institution of marriage. Nor do I find him within my tastes."

Ademas chuckled. "Not tall and dark enough for you?"

Talanee's heart squeezed. "Something like that. Not that it's any of your business, *Cousin*."

"As the king, I could make it my business." His grin sparkled under the nearby lantern light.

Talanee rolled her eyes. "*Don't*. I've had enough royal interference. My heart is my own—and I intend to keep it that way. Possibly forever."

"Don't lock it up too tightly, Cousin," Ademas said. "Someone might come along who considers that a challenge too tempting to ignore."

Talanee shook her head as she swallowed a lump. "I don't want to talk about this right now. I've just buried my father. That's where my thoughts should linger."

Ademas caught her fingers in his. "Then let's dance in his honor. Forget all the clutter in your head, and let's show these shallow fools that you're grace personified. Shall we?"

Talanee's spine loosened, and she let her cousin guide her to the middle of the garden as the first notes of a soft dirge struck the heavy air. Thank the Sun Throne for Ademas's discretion and for Nerenoth's gentleness.

If only more Kel were like them.

CHAPTER 47

It was the last fair day before the Rainy Season set in early that year, like the world wept when the Sun Gods departed. So the stories would say afterward.

King Ademas Getaal was crowned before his people gathered in the grasslands between Inpizal and the ruins of Halathe. Seer Lekore Adenye Getaal performed the rite, while a contingent of Tawloomez officials; their rather subdued army; and their new king, Lor'Toreth, looked on. A peace treaty was signed between both races on the heels of Ademas's coronation.

Afterward, the Ahvenian ships disappeared into the heavens to watch over Erokel, save for a single small craft and its complement of warriors awaiting its passengers.

Lekore and Toranskay crested Isiltik to overlook the Vale That Shines Gold as the sun sank in the west. Flashes of gold and gems faded into the shadows of night as they gazed upon the dead.

"There's so much I still don't know," said Toranskay. "So much that connects you and me remains shrouded in mystery."

"At least we know the dead slumber in peace," Lekore said. He reached down and plucked a blade of grass, the folds of his tattered black cloak brushing against his hand.

The ghosts in the vale were gone. All was still among the dead.

"I shall miss this place, for all its joys and sorrows. For all I have learned, good and ill."

"You will always be a child of this world. It remains your home." Toranskay glanced over his shoulder, golden hair fluttering in the breeze. "I'll head for the ship and wait with Dakeer and Nerenoth. You take whatever time you need to say goodbye. And remember, Lekore. You're free to return here as often as you like."

Lekore nodded and said nothing until the Ahvenian prince had descended the hill and disappeared in the growing darkness. He turned back to the bone-littered vale. "It will never be quite the same now."

The wind kissed his cheek, and he laughed. "How I shall miss you, dearest spirits. If only I knew whether I shall be friends with your kind on other worlds. Please, if you can, tell your fellows across the vast Universe that I am your friend and would like to be theirs."

The grass swayed, the wind whistled, a stray dewdrop fell from a blade of grass, and a single ember from a far-off fire danced around him.

Together, they sang the last verse of Lekore's lullaby, words they'd heard him sing a thousand times or more.

'Journey now to what's beyond.
And then return by starlet's bond.
Tell me all thou seest there,
With thy smile, sweet and fair.'

The music fell into silence, and Lekore wiped a tear from his eye.

'Farewell, dearest Lekki,' the Spirits Elemental intoned.

He smiled through his shimmering vision. "Fare thee well, wilds of Erokel. Remember with fondness the child of the west winds. I go now to dance among the stars. Come along, Lios."

Emockye pup on his heels, cloak fluttering, Lekore turned from the home of his youth, where for long, lonely years he'd waited for Ank's return and from where he'd traveled to save a Kel princess.

Goodbye to his cave. Goodbye to the Wildwood and the running streams and whispering grass. Goodbye to the grinning skulls and shining golden armor of a fallen people. Goodbye to Inpizal, lit like a jewel beneath the velvet skies.

Hello to his new journey, until he returned by starlet's bond to tell the wilds all he had seen beyond the world, his once and always home.

Lekore's story continues in...

BOOK THREE: SONG OF THE LOST

DEAREST READER

Thank you for picking up *Rule of the Night*!

I'm delighted that you've chosen to continue Lekore's story, and I hope this second book in the *Record of the Sentinel Seer* has lived up to your expectations.

The ending of this book may be a surprise, as Lekore leaves Erokel far behind him, but you're not saying goodbye to Ademas and Talanee forever, I promise.

If you've enjoyed this book, please consider leaving a review on Amazon, Goodreads, and anywhere else online you'd like. Reviews are my bread and butter, and I love hearing your thoughts as the series progresses!

See you again soon in *Song of the Lost*.

Stay magical!

– M. H. W.

GLOSSARY

Characters

Adelair Getaal {*odd-eh-lair get-TALL*} – Deceased king of Erokel and father of Lekore and Ademas.

Ademas Getaal {*odd-eh-moss get-TALL*} – Lekore's younger brother. He grew up secretly on the island of Ra Kye.

Adenye Getaal {*odd-en-ī get-TALL*} – Lekore's given name.

Benye {*ben-ī*} – A servant in the Kel palace.

Carak {*kair-ack*} – A soldier in the Royal Army of Erokel.

Dakeer Vasar {*duh-KEER vuh-SAHR*} – The Holy Hakija; head of the Sun Church. One of the Triad of Erokel.

Dawris {*DAW-riss*} – Captain of the Ahvenian flagship *Daybreak*.

Elekel Getaal {*ELL-eh-kel get-TALL*} – A prince and the youngest brother of Adenye and Netye Getaal.

Erodem {*eh-row-dem*} – A deceased king of Erokel. King Adelair's father.

Farelin {*FARR-eh-lin*} – A deceased emperor of Ahvenia. Emperor Majentay's father.

Ginn {*gin*} – A servant in the Kel palace.

Het {*het*} – A Sun Priest.

Jesh Irothé {*jesh ee-RAW-thay*} – Twin of Jeth Irothé and younger brother of Nerenoth Irothé.

Jeth Irothé {*jeth ee-RAW-thay*} – Twin of Jesh Irothé and younger brother of Nerenoth Irothé.

Kalith {*kal-ith*} – A Kel priest in Jadom.

Keerva {*keer-vuh*} – Princess Talanee's handmaid.

Keo {*KEE-oh*} – An outcast Kiisuld living in the Lands Beyond.

Khyna {*kī-nuh*} – A Tawloomez servant.

Lanasha Jahaan {*luh-NAW-shuh juh-HAWN*} – Nerenoth Irothé's betrothed and a nobleborn Kel.

Lekore {*leh-KOR*} – A Seer and Elementalist raised by his ghostly ancestor in the Charnel Valley (*Also called the Vale That Shines Gold*).

Lios {*lee-oh-ss*} – An emockye pup and Lekore's friend.

Lithel Kuaan {*Lith-ELL koo-awn*} – High Priest of the Sun Church and Dakeer Vasar's righthand man.

Lor'Toreth {*lor TOR-eth*} – The prince and heir of Tawloom.

Mahaka {*muh-HAWK-uh*} – Seenth of the Teokaka. A Tawloomez warrior.

Majentay Ahrutahn {*mah-JEN-tay aw-roo-tawn*} – Emperor of Ahvenia.

Mayrilana Irothé {*may-ree-lawn-uh ee-RAW-thay*} – Cousin of Nerenoth and the twins. She lived in Erokes before the city fell to the Tawloomez.

Naal Getaal {*nawl get-TALL*} – Skye's wife, stolen by his brother upon his untimely death.

Nerenoth Irothé {*NAIR-eh-noth ee-RAW-thay*} – Lord Captain and military leader of Erokel. One of the Triad of Erokel.

Netye Getaal {*net-ī get-TALL*} – Denounced king of Erokel. Formerly one of the Triad of Erokel. (*Also called Ank*.)

Nitaan {*nee-TAWN*} – A half-Kel/half-Tawloomez girl.

Orra {*or-uh*} – The Tawloomez servant of Zanah Getaal.

Rarenday {*rair-EN-day*} – Toranskay's protector. An Ahvenian.

Relivay {*rell-ih-vay*} – An officer aboard the Ahvenian flagship *Daybreak*.

Rez Kuaan {*rez koo-awn*} – Lord Lieutenant of Erokel. Nerenoth Irothé's righthand man.

Sajaray Ahrutahn [*SAW-juh-ray aw-roo-tawn*] – Princess of the Ahvenian Empire.

Shayra [*SHAY-ruh*] – The AI aboard the Kiisuld royal yacht, the *Dictator*.

Skye Getaal [*skī get-TALL*] – Lekore's mentor. Also called the Voice of the Stars or the Heretic.

Susunee [*soo-SOO-nee*] – The religious leader of the Tawloomez.

Tahomin Harrulay [*taw-HO-min harr-oo-lay*] – The traveling partner of Prince Vay-Dinn Fyce.

Talajin [*taw-luh-jin*] – An Ahvenian scientist. He was killed by Nerenoth after Lekore defeated him using Spirit of Spirit.

Talanee Getaal [*tuh-LAWN-ee get-TALL*] – Princess of Erokel and daughter of King Netye Getaal.

Teon Keela [*tee-awn kee-luh*] – A warden in the Sun Cathedral's dungeon. He secretly serves the Hakija of the Night.

Ter N'Avea [*tair NAW-vay*] – Lekore's mentor. An Ephe'ahn.

Teyed [*tay-edd*] – A half-Kel/half-Tawloomez boy.

Toranskay Ahrutahn [*tor-RAN-skay aw-roo-tawn*] – The Crown Prince of the Ahvenian Empire. (*Also called Tora.*)

Toreth [*TOR-eth*] – The deceased king of the Tawloomez and Lor'Toreth's father.

Vay-Dinn Fyce [*VAY-din fice*] – Prince of the Kiisuld.

Zanah Getaal {*zawn-uh get-TALL*} – Wife of King Adelair Getaal.

Zanarin {*zuh-NAW-rinn*} – A priest of the Sun Church.

Creatures

Cheos {*chee-oh-ss*} – A carnivorous bird native to Erokel and the Lands Beyond.

Emockye {*ee-mock-ī*} – A canine animal similar to coyotes, though larger, with venomous claws and teeth.

Minkee {*meen-kee*} – A lemur-like animal native to the Lands Beyond.

Pythe {*pīth*} – A reptilian/equine cross between a dragon and a Pegasus. The pythe of Erokel have lost their wings through scientific experimentation.

Rabbun {*rab-boon*} – A rabbit-like animal native to Erokel and the Firelands.

Places

Ahvenia {*Aw-VEN-ee-uh*} – The empire of Ahvenians encompassing an entire galaxy. Its denizens include more than the Ahvenian race.

Cathedral of the Sun – The cathedral of Inpizal in Erokel, where the Kel worship the Sun Gods.

Charnel Valley (Also called the *Vale That Shines Gold*, the *Valley of Bones*) – A valley filled with the bones of those who fell during the War of Brothers five hundred years ago.

Erokel {*air-oh-kel*} – The kingdom of the Kel.

Erokes {*air-oh-kess*} – A Sun City in Erokel. It fell to the Tawloomez recently.

Firelands – The northern nation where the Tawloomez live. It's proper name is Tawloom.

Halathe {*huh-LAYTH*} – The holy ruins where Kel perform the sacred Lighting ceremony.

Inpizal {*inn-piz-ALL*} – The Royal City of Erokel.

Isiltik {iss-ILL-tik} – A hill above the Charnel Valley.

Jadom {*jaw-dum*} – A Sun City in Erokel.

Kellar {*kel-arr*} – A Sun City in Erokel.

Lands Beyond (Also called the *Wildwood*, *Ava Vyy*) – A massive jungle filled with deadly plants and animals, the Kel and Tawloomez alike avoid passing its borders at all costs.

Nakoth Mountains [*nuh-KAWTH*] – The mountains between Erokel and the Charnel Valley.

Ra Kye [*raw kī*] – The southern islands in the Kingdom of Erokel.

Raal Corenic [*rawl kor-EN-ik*] – A training ground for the magically gifted of the Universe.

Tawloom [*taw-LOOM*] – The proper name for the Firelands where the Tawloomez live.

Vakari [*vuh-KAR-ee*] – The capital planet of the Kiisuld empire.

Wildwood (See *Lands Beyond*)

Races

Ahvenian {*ah-ven-ee-ehn*} – An alien race mistaken for Sun Gods. Enemies of the Kiisuld.

Ephe'ahn {*eh-FAY-on*} – A woodland race of childlike people.

Kel {*kell*} – The people who dwell in Erokel.

Kiisuld {*kee-sool-d*} – An alien race mistaken for Star Gods. Enemies of the Ahvenians.

Tawloomez – {*taw-loom-ehz*} – The people who dwell in Taloom (*more commonly called the Firelands*).

Objects

Calir {*cuh-LEER*} – Lekore's sword, inherited from Skye. It is the twin blade of *Calisay*.

Calisay {*cuh-LEE-say*} – Toranskay's sword, discovered in a secret room on Ahvora, his homeward. It is the twin blade of *Calir*.

Titles and Terms

Elementalist – A person gifted to see and control one or more of the Spirits Elemental.

Elementalist True – A rare person gifted to see and control all five Spirits Elemental.

Empathist – A rare person who can sense the emotions and feelings of others on a deeper level than a normal empath. A master Empathist can sometimes read thoughts.

Hakija [*huh-KEE-juh*] – The holy leader of Erokel's Sun Church and Voice of the Sun Throne.

Keeper of Memory – A special historian chosen by Ter N'Avea.

Lord Captain – The leader of military affairs in Erokel.

Moon Throne – The holy throne of the Star Gods.

Snake God(s) – Deities worshiped by the Tawloomez.

Spirits Elemental – The guardian elementals in charge of protecting and defending the Elements of the world: fire, wind, water, earth, and spirit.

Star God(s) – The alleged gods who rule the Night. Kel who worship these fallen gods are considered heretical by the rest of their race. (See *Kiisuld*)

Sun God(s) – The alleged gods who rule the majority of the Kel and their faith. (See *Ahvenian*)

Sunslayer(s) – Servants of the Star Worshipers. Most are half-Tawloomez/half-Kel who live in the slums of Inpizal.

Sun Throne – The holy throne of the Sun Gods, according to Kel doctrine.

Teokaka [*tee-oh-kaw-kaw*] – The holy leader of Tawloomez's church and Voice of the Snake Gods. Literally translated as *Holy Voice.*

ACKNOWLEDGMENTS

The first book in this series was dedicated to Heidi, my older sister, illustrator, confidante, and sounding-board. Hard to believe we despised each other growing up (until I learned not to be a snitch and a condescending goody-two-shoes, at which point we became fast friends). Thanks for not killing me all those years ago!

This book is dedicated to my younger sister, Tawnee, who is my biggest fan, always cheering me on, crushing on [the *oddest*] characters in my books, and letting me jabber endlessly on and on about story concepts.

Thank you, Heidi and Tawnee, for remaining my biggest supporters through all these years!

Also, a huge thanks to my wonderful parents for letting me pursue my dream. You're both amazing people!

Many thanks to the rest of my family for enduring my constant daydreaming.

Huge shoutout to Mandi Oyster, my consistent, honest, fast-reading beta reader! So glad we connected online. Your mastery over commas is my saving grace.

And to my other phenomenal alpha and beta readers, thank you a thousand times over. Some of you had to bow out of reading this book due to real life conflicts, but you deserve a shoutout along with the rest for being nothing less than AWESOME HUMANS. Laura A. Barton, Sonya Bramwell, Elvira Foster, and Heidi Wadsworth, your support, encouragement, and time mean so much!

I also want to thank my Instagram writing community for your amazing support, stellar kindness, and stunning books. You're an inspiration. I'm honored to know so many talented authors! In particular, thanks to Brigitte Cromey, who inspired this book's tagline.

And a colossal thank you to my magical editor, Sarah B., whose tireless efforts always help shape my random ideas into tangible matter. I'd be lost without you.

And, always, special thanks to my Father in Heaven for guiding my hand and giving me breath.

ABOUT THE AUTHOR

Writer of fantasy, magic weaver, dragon rider! Having spent the past 20 years devotedly writing fantasy, it's safe to say M. H. Woodscourt is now more fae than human. *Rule of the Night* is her seventh published novel.

All of her fantasy worlds connect with each other in a broad Universe, forged with great love and no small measure of blood, sweat, and tears. When she's not writing, she's napping or reading a book with a mug of hot cocoa close at hand, while her quirky cat Wynter nibbles her toes.

Learn more at www.mhwoodscourt.com

 facebook.com/mhwoodscourt

 twitter.com/woodscourtbooks

 instagram.com/woodscourtbooks

ALSO BY M. H. WOODSCOURT

RECORD OF THE SENTINEL SEER

Science-Fantasy/New Adult

Prince of the Fallen

Rule of the Night

Song of the Lost

WINTERVALE DUOLOGY

High Fantasy/Young Adult

The Crow King

The Winter King

PARADISE SERIES

Portal Fantasy/Humor/Young Adult

A Liar in Paradise

Key of Paradise

Paradise Lost

(coming soon)

WORLD OF NAKANIA

Crownless

A YA/High Fantasy Novel

Printed in Great Britain
by Amazon